DESIRE THE STAR

MIRANDA SILVER

FROM THE AUTHOR OF *PRICELESS*

Contents

Editing by Mackenzie at Nice Girl, Naughty Edits
Cover Design and Formatting by Mayhem Cover Creations

Manufactured in the United States of America

First Edition April 2022

Content Notes

This story contains explicit sexual content, profanity, and topics that may be sensitive to some readers. For a detailed list visit mirandasilver.com or scan the code below:

PLAYLIST

Thank you to all the musical artists who have inspired this book. Each chapter is named for a song title (or lyrics). The full playlist is available on Spotify as "Desire the Star Official Playlist."

Prologue: New York City - Punch Brothers
1. Slow Like Honey - Fiona Apple
2. Empty Heart - Grace Potter
3. Circus - Dirty Loops
4. Snakes - Pixies
5. Magnet - Punch Brothers
6. Reptilia - The Strokes
7. Too Repressed - Sometymes Why
8. Magic Man - Heart
9. Dani California - Red Hot Chili Peppers
10. Speak - Nickel Creek
11. Slow Down - Sometymes Why
12. Strange Brew - Cream
13. Fortune Teller - Robert Plant, Alison Krauss
14. Spooky - Dusty Springfield
15. My Oh My - Punch Brothers
16. Good Evening Mr. & Mrs. America & All the Ships - Tom Scott & The L.A. Express
17. The Book of Right-On - Sarah Jarosz
18. Faster - Samantha Fish
19. Hot Knife - Fiona Apple
20. Syrinx - Jasmine Choi
21. Reine de Bois (Queen of the Woods) - Banda Magda
22. Insomnie (Insomnia) - Les Nubians
23. Keep Diggin' - Larkin Poe
24. Use Me - Bill Withers
25. You Are - Punch Brothers

To my dear friend L,
for ten years of creative inspiration and love

Prologue

New York City

Daisy

Ice, in April.

That was what I would always remember: a sudden cold snap in a tender New York spring. It froze buds on trees, heaped snow in gutters, and layered sidewalks with a beautiful, treacherous glaze.

I was walking down the front steps of Siderio Conservatory of Music with my friend Darian, carrying my flute case in my right hand and looping my scarf around my neck with my left. We were almost done with our freshman year, but I was still grateful every day that I was attending Siderio; that I'd gotten a full scholarship. That twelve years of living and breathing music were paying off.

As the wind whipped our faces, we chattered excitedly about the competitions we'd audition for, our upcoming freshman recitals, the summer gigs we were already booking.

"Promise you'll be my accompanist all through college?" I begged.

"Oh, you'll get bored," Darian teased, snowflakes glistening in his dark curls. "You'll run around on me with other pianists."

"Never!" I laughed. "I'll be faithful."

One minute, we were joking around.

The next, my boots hit an icy patch.

My feet shot out from under me. I was skidding, falling down the steps. The world tilted in a way that was utterly wrong. I hung on to my flute case with a death grip, but my left hand met hard ice with a sickening crack.

Gasps came from the sidewalk.

"Daisy?" Darian's voice sounded far away. My shoulders were in his grasp. "Daisy, talk to me."

My breath shuddered in the wintry air. I tried to scream, but couldn't, like a bad dream.

My wrist — the pain — it was so sharp. A knife that stabbed like an icicle up my left arm.

"She's not responding." His voice rose.

"Should I call 911?" someone yelled.

"Too late," I murmured. My bones were fractured. My dreams — shattered.

Darian put his hands on my cheeks. His palms were warm against my frost-nipped skin.

Why the hell did it snow in April?

The next day, I lay in my dorm room, staring at the twinkle lights strung across the ceiling. They shone like a galaxy, each little point haloed against the posters of the musicians I loved. My left arm was encased in a cast.

Both the large bones in my forearm were broken, along with my wrist. My nerves and tendons were damaged. Even after I healed, I'd never regain my old flexibility and stamina.

"If you go through physical therapy, eventually you'll be able to play again," the doctors had said. "But only for short periods of time."

I was done at Siderio. My scholarship gone, my career over. Even though my room was filled with flowers, it felt more like a funeral than a set of get-well-soon wishes.

My friends had stopped by to say how sorry they were. They meant it, but I heard the words they weren't saying: *Thank God it wasn't me. Maybe I've got a shot at winning the Concerto Competition now.* They'd asked what my plans were. I didn't have any. Then they scurried off to their rehearsals and master classes and practice studios, until only Darian remained in my room.

Snatches of music filled the air. Down the hall, someone was playing a haunting oboe melody, and the sounds wavered as they reached my ears.

On the desk beside my flute, my phone buzzed.

My mother picked it up. She'd rushed over from the dance class she was teaching uptown when Darian called her from the hospital. "Daisy, you have a reminder for — oh."

"I know," I mumbled. "The gig I had this afternoon. I canceled it."

The pain meds made me float too high. After today, I wasn't going to take any more.

"Go to sleep, honey." My mother smoothed my hair. "Get some rest."

I looked up into her worried gray-blue eyes, so much like mine, and tried to smile.

Darian hunched over my desk, earbuds in, his eyes glued to his phone.

"What are you doing?" I demanded. My life was gone as I knew it, and he was playing on his phone?

"Nothing," he mumbled.

"You could at least show me what's so captivating."

Reluctantly, he held up the screen. It showed a guy in his early twenties sitting at a piano. Shaggy blond hair hung over his forehead, and his big hands were poised over the keys, ready to strike.

I felt a sinking sensation in my belly. "Never mind. No music."

"I'll listen with you," my mom assured him. "Daisy needs to rest."

They retreated to my desk, sharing the earbuds.

"He came out of nowhere," Darian told my mom in an undertone. "Amazing, right? This is my future husband right here."

"Oh wow," my mother cooed at the screen. "He's *good*."

Mom, I wanted to groan, but I was slipping under into sleep.

Fog curled, pulling me into a dreamscape. Far ahead, four male figures, cast in shadows, stood at the edge of a yawning abyss. As I moved closer, I could hear their whispers.

We want you, Daisy. We see you. You're a star.

One of the men materialized from the fog — Nathan Davis. Mist shrouded his lanky frame and messy brown hair, his honey-colored eyes and the quick, shy smile I loved.

Flames flickered between us.

When I followed him, he ran.

So did I, until I reached the chasm's edge.

Behind me, I heard my best friend Sasha's voice, distant and hollow. "Don't ever fall for my brother."

And with that, I leapt into the abyss. I fell willingly, with no end...

1

Slow Like Honey

Daisy

They surrounded me. There were four again — there always were. Nathan was one of them, and he was everywhere, his face and eyes and hands, all hot and restless. His companions closed in on me through the mist — one dark, one bright, one cold and hungry. Fingers and tongues flickered over me as they urged me toward the edge of the abyss.

A chorus of hisses filled the air: *Play, Daisy. Play.*

I woke up with a jerk, my sweaty cheek pressed against the pillow. My heart thudded as my body throbbed for more.

The four men were gone. I'd dreamed of them almost every night since my fall. Always, they made promises. Always, they held out an unknown offering that was snatched away when I broke out of the dream. And always, I woke too soon to an empty bed, before I could find out who these faceless men were and what they would do to me.

Sitting up, I blinked at my darkened surroundings, which were still unfamiliar after two months.

The air conditioner hummed, working overtime during a Los

Angeles August heatwave. Vintage movie posters stared down at me, lit by the streetlamps outside. The clock on the wall said it was three in the morning. I was alone in my dad's apartment, sleeping on the futon in his living room, while he spent the night at his girlfriend's.

On the coffee table lay a stack of materials for my new college. Tomorrow, I'd start at Pacific Crest State University. Located ninety miles from L.A., it was a world away from New York and my old life.

Fumbling for my phone on the coffee table, I found a video of Jasmine Choi, my idol. I forgot that I wasn't listening to flutists anymore. I started her iconic performance of *Syrinx* by Debussy and hugged my pillow to my chest.

Before the fall, I'd played along with this video countless times. I knew every note, every gesture. She breathed her soul into the music and made it her own.

Through it all, I heard that voice whispering, *Play*.

When Jasmine finished, she kept the flute at her lips for a long moment, as if she couldn't bear to part with it.

Padding barefoot to the hall closet, I took out my own flute for the first time since my accident. My hands shook as I undid the clasps of the case. Fitting the joints together, I tried a simple scale, then the opening notes of *Syrinx*.

My movements were thick, clumsy. I sounded like a beginner. Two minutes in, pain shot up my left wrist and stiffened my fingers. I put my flute back in its case, unable to look at it.

My dad had left his car, hoping I'd go out and have some fun. Dressed in the old tank top and shorts I'd slept in, I started the engine and drove over cracked asphalt to Sasha's house.

I didn't expect any of the Davises to be home. All summer, Sasha had visited me between shifts at the restaurant where she worked. She'd brought over recipes she was developing, gifted me with crystals for luck, and was the only person who could make me laugh.

But Sasha had just left for eight weeks in Morocco. Her parents were on a book tour, and Sasha had made a vague comment about Nathan staying at college for summer football training.

When I pushed open the gate, the Davises' familiar patio looked ghostly in the moonlight. Like many L.A. backyards, the space was low on grass and high on concrete, bordered by palm trees and potted succulents. An empty wooden porch swing sat motionless amid chirping crickets.

In high school, I'd slept over often at the Davises'. After Sasha fell asleep, I'd sneak outside and find Nathan waiting in this swing, adorable in his T-shirt and boxers. He always had a pint of ice cream and two spoons, the ice cream still frozen, as if he'd guessed to the minute when I'd appear.

Thinking of him, I remembered the quiet comfort of being listened to. The steadiness of his presence. His honey-brown eyes, crinkling at the corners with laughter. The soft hair on his legs that I tried not to stare at during stolen nights together.

We always talked. Never touched. Sometimes I hoped for a kiss, but he didn't make a single move. He was two years older, and I wondered if he considered me too young, or simply off-limits the way he was to me.

Yet those secret talks with Nathan got me so excited that I couldn't sleep afterwards. I'd hug my pillow, reliving every word.

Now, I curled up on the swing and cradled my knees. I felt hollow. Without music in common, I'd lost touch with my friends from Siderio. I'd lost touch with fucking everything. I was nineteen and alone, and I couldn't see a future. Couldn't see any dreams that would come true.

A shadow fell over the swing.

"Nathan!" My heart leapt into my throat. For once, this was real. Nathan Davis towered above me: larger, broader, unsmiling. "I haven't seen you in so long. Not since Sasha's graduation last year—"

His brown eyes were smoky as he glared down at me. The moonlight outlined his massive body, bare except for boxers, with a silvery sheen.

What had happened? The Nathan I'd loved in high school had

been lean and gangly with a sweet, furtive smile. When I saw him last June, he was bigger, more restless, but still himself.

But this man was huge. Ripped. He must have put on fifty pounds of muscle. In the dark, I barely recognized him.

"What are you doing here?" Even his voice was different, deep and gravelly.

"Sasha didn't tell you?"

He laughed humorlessly. "We don't talk."

"I fell, Nathan. I injured my wrist. I'm done with the flute. Done with New York. I couldn't stay."

His hands opened and closed into fists at his sides. "You shouldn't be here."

I stared up at him, confused by his demeanor. "Where else can I go? I'm — I'm starting at Pacific Crest tomorrow. I know you go there. I thought maybe we could meet up, talk..."

"No," he muttered, shaking his head. "No, no, no."

"No?" I asked, bewildered.

He loomed over me, his eyes darting back and forth. I couldn't reconcile his size with the Nathan I knew.

Instinctively, I reached out.

As soon as my fingertips brushed his arm, I was sweating, blood rushing to my head, feeling more sensation than I had in months.

"Get up." His voice roughened as he gripped the porch swing.

I stood.

Suddenly, his hands engulfed my shoulders, sliding to the back of my neck in a possessive hold. My breath caught in my throat, but I wrapped my arms around him, pulling him in.

He gripped my braid, making me gasp. Then, without a moment's hesitation, he leaned in and closed his mouth over mine.

At first, the kiss was as soft and gentle as I'd always dreamed our first kiss would be. His lips were sweet and a little sticky, coaxing me to come alive and open my mouth to his tongue.

Then the kiss hardened. It devoured. It took. It was voracious, sucking out my essence, and my whole body flamed in response.

Nathan pushed up my tank top, his hot palm swallowing my breast. He squeezed my ass, pulling me roughly against the bulge in his shorts, and I cried out.

Desperately excited, I ran my hands up his thighs, finally feeling the softness of his hair, the heat of his skin, the bulk of his muscles. As I bit down on his lower lip, my fingers brushed the ridge of his cock.

He broke the kiss. Panic flashed across his face.

Before I knew what was happening, he pushed me away and streaked across the yard. His body was a huge blur, crossing the patio in under a second. The back door slammed behind him.

"Nathan!"

I rubbed my swollen lips, then hugged myself, shivering without his fever-heat. I was alone in the backyard, with only the crickets and porch swing to bear witness. And when I finally knocked on the door, no one answered.

"Cursed," I whispered.

2

Empty Heart

Daisy

Golden light streamed through the windows of the Pacific Crest University student clinic. I looked out at red Spanish-tile roofs and white stucco buildings, arched doorways and swaying palms. The scene was bathed in California sunshine, so glittering that it promised paradise.

Dr. Greenberg turned my wrist to examine it. "So you got the injury four months ago?"

I nodded.

"I understand from your records that it wasn't a clean break. You had multiple fractures and some nerve damage, correct?"

"Mm-hm." I glanced out the window again at my new college. In the late August afternoon, everyone was gearing up for fall semester. Backpacks, laptops, coffee cups, shouted greetings to old friends.

Observing them was like watching a movie, alone in the audience.

"Does it still bother you?"

My gaze drifted around the sterile beige examination room, then

13

to my chipped purple nail polish. "I suppose. Oh — you mean, does it still hurt?"

"Well, yes." Her brow furrowed in polite confusion.

"Now and then."

She released my wrist. "I'll prescribe pain meds..." I shook my head, and she looked startled. "Daisy, there's no reason for you to be in pain."

I pressed my fingers to my lips, feeling the heat of Nathan's mouth two days ago.

"Advil won't help," I said quietly, picking up the brace for my wrist from the examination table.

Dr. Greenberg rustled a pad of paper and a pen. "I'm giving you a prescription just in case," she said briskly. "And here's a referral to the counseling office. If you ever want to talk, they can help you." She shook my right hand — the one without the injury. "Best of luck with your sophomore year."

Outside, I tore up the pain med prescription and put the counseling referral in my purse. The afternoon air was hot and California-dry, and the campus stretched out in every direction.

Siderio had been one dot on the grid of streets in Manhattan. Here, I'd gotten lost twice already. Pacific Crest University sprawled out in an enormous spiral, dominating the small college town that held it.

I'd been keeping an eye out for Nathan since I got here, but I hadn't seen any sign of him. I didn't have his number, and I wasn't about to ask Sasha for it.

Squinting, I searched my phone for the campus map.

"Looking for something?" A male voice startled me. It was low, friendly, and at close range.

I looked up into a stranger's bright blue eyes, the same shade as the cloudless sky. "Actually, yes. I have no idea where I am."

Lines creased the corners of those eyes as he laughed. "You do go to this school, right?"

I glanced around at the white stucco buildings and snaking paths, then back at his sun-kissed, handsome face. "I do now."

"Put that away." He shook a finger at the map on my phone. "I'll help you find what you need."

I doubt that, I thought. But I studied his curly golden-brown hair pulled back into a man-bun, and the short beard framing his dazzling smile. Lean and graceful, he sported silver hoops in his ears, and an intricate sleeve of tattoos swirled over his left arm.

"Have we met?" I asked. There was a familiarity to him that I couldn't place.

His gaze flicked over the braid hanging down my back, then to my embroidered sundress wilting in the heat, and the wood-soled clogs that pushed my height close to his.

"I don't think so." His smile widened. "Freshman?"

"Transfer. I'm a sophomore."

"Even better." He patted my shoulder. A bright pulse of energy startled me, warmer than the sun overhead. For the first time since I'd arrived at Pacific Crest yesterday, I felt *awake.* "Let's get you where you need to go."

"Home," I murmured. "I'm headed home."

"Which is where?"

"Good question."

New York came to mind, a thousand memories seeping into the cracks of the sidewalks. After my parents split up, my mom and I moved to the city for my senior year of high school. Once I enrolled at Siderio, we met for dinner and visited on the weekends.

But my mom jumped back into dating soon after the divorce, and with men sleeping over, our cozy apartment felt far less congenial.

Maybe my dad's place in Los Angeles? Once Mom and I moved out, he sold the house where I grew up and rented a smaller apartment. I'd worn a crease on his couch this summer while I numbed myself with TV.

"Lee Tower," I said. "On West Campus."

"Ah, the tower. Closest to Greer Hill." My rescuer winked at me. "You know there are stories about that, right?"

"What stories?"

"Come on, you must have heard them." He led me along a path that looked straight into the sunlight.

I shielded my eyes. "I haven't talked to people much since I got here."

"Oh?" He looked at me carefully.

"Blake! Hey, Blake!" Three beautiful girls, bronzed and summery, strolled up to us and stopped for hugs and cheek kisses without giving me a glance. It didn't feel like a snub so much as this guy — Blake — taking up all their attention. A sun that beamed so bright, they didn't notice what was in his orbit.

Blake rested a hand on my back like we were old friends. "This is..."

"Daisy," I filled in.

"Hiiiii," the girls chirped, then walked on, looking back to smile at Blake.

"Beautiful name, Daisy." The sun glinted off Blake's curly hair. "They say that Greer Hill is haunted. School lore."

"Oh, good. I like ghosts."

His eyebrows shot up. "Really?"

I laughed. "I don't scare easily."

More people passed us on the path. They greeted Blake as if he were the best thing to happen to them all day, but their gazes slipped over me.

It was a strange feeling, invisibility. I was used to having a place. Daisy Fisher, principal flutist in the orchestra, up-and-coming soloist, child prodigy blossoming into a promising adult.

Ego? Sure. I could admit it now. But more than that, I'd loved music. It was my heart's blood and the fabric of my soul. And I'd lost both.

Blake and I turned a corner.

"So you don't scare easily," he said. When his blue eyes looked into mine, I felt seen in a way I hadn't since leaving New York. "What would it take to scare you?"

I laughed incredulously. "Is that a challenge? *You* don't scare me."

He raised an eyebrow. "Spiders?"

"Spiders are nothing compared to cockroaches."

"Snakes, then. I bet you *hate* snakes," he said with a wink. He really was criminally attractive.

"Are you kidding? I love snakes."

"Do you, now?" The flash of intensity in his eyes startled me.

"I do. They're beautiful. All muscle, and so graceful..." My voice turned flirty and teasing as Blake moved closer. I'd known this man for all of five minutes, but his warmth was melting me.

A frisbee veered toward us as we walked through the quad. Blake caught it and tossed it back.

Quickly, I crossed my arms. Before the fall, I'd tended to come on too strong. Too eager to cut to the chase. Probably because spending six hours a day in a practice room, alone with my flute, hadn't left much time for developing romantic finesse.

Or because I'd spent so many years sitting on my feelings for Nathan Davis that I didn't have patience left over for anyone else.

Blake whistled as we exited the quad through a stucco archway and crossed a broad plaza. Tables with red umbrellas were scattered throughout, dotted with people in shorts and tank tops enjoying smoothies and iced coffees.

"Where are you coming from?" he asked. "We don't want you getting lost again."

"Doctor's appointment. I hurt my wrist a while back." I lifted my left hand and hurried to change the subject. "You look so familiar. I swear I've seen you before."

He smiled easily. "Maybe you have."

When he took my right elbow lightly to guide me around a spurting sprinkler, a tingle of anticipation shot up my arm. My reaction must have shown on my face, because instead of letting go, he slipped his arm through mine.

It was an intimate gesture for two people who'd just met. But Blake's arm against mine felt warm, exciting...and strangely comfortable.

I snapped my fingers as recognition dawned. "Food. Are you into food? You're a chef?"

His grin widened. "Yep."

"My best friend told me about you! She sent me an article about how you're all up-and-coming. You work at this fancy restaurant nearby, right? Étoile? And you had an appearance on some TV show... Somehow, you're balancing it all with school. And you're graduating this year?" He nodded. "She also wants to be a chef. Her comment on the article was basically, 'I want to be Blake Phillips in two years.'"

I was talking too fast, suddenly nervous at the pressure of Blake's skin against mine. My flirtations never ended well.

Blake just smiled and gave my arm a squeeze.

"Her name's Sasha. She's spending this semester in Morocco." It felt safer to focus on someone else, instead of the buzz spreading through my body.

"Morocco, huh? Lucky girl." His grin turned wistful. "I'd love to travel someday."

"Hopefully you can soon."

We stopped, and I realized we were in front of Lee Tower. Blake's sky-blue eyes studied me.

"Soon, yeah," he echoed, giving my arm a final squeeze and letting go. "Very soon."

My heart began to pound, and I knew I was blushing. "Thanks so much for helping me find my way."

"Happy to." He took his phone out of his pocket. "What's your number? I'll text you mine. If you get lost again, call me, okay, Daisy? It's a big campus. I know what a difference it makes to see a friendly face."

I blinked. His words were platonic, but his voice was low and intimate. I gave him my number and returned his hug. His tank top was warm from the sun, and his bare arms were even warmer.

As he walked away, tall and lithe, I noticed other people staring. They called out to him, and he took the greetings in stride.

It wasn't just the article Sasha had sent. I'd *seen* this guy before. In the flesh...or in a memory...

My phone rang. I snatched it from my purse, wondering if Blake had decided to call instead of text.

It was my mom.

"Hi, honey!" Her voice was bright and cheery. Since my fall, she'd been extra positive. "How are you settling in?"

I ducked into the shade of a eucalyptus tree. "A hot guy found me wandering around like a lost sheep and walked me to my dorm. He was very friendly."

Mom laughed. "Now *that's* what I like to hear. Did you get his number?"

"Absolutely," I tossed off, as if I weren't still pining for Nathan. "He asked for mine."

"Good for you!" She sounded delighted. "You're diving right in. I know you had concerns about your new school, but it's going to be fantastic."

The eucalyptus leaves rustled, sending out a whisper of medicinal scent. My mom wanted so badly for me to be not just okay, but great. *The world is your oyster.*

"I still have concerns, Mom. Hot men or no."

"Give it a chance. You'll find your place."

Leaning against the trunk of the eucalyptus, I stared at the sun-soaked buildings and feathery palm trees. For seventeen years, the southern California landscape had been home. But I'd taken to New York so quickly that coming back here felt like visiting another country.

"Listen, Daisy." Mom's voice lowered. "I'm not comparing our situations, but to a certain extent, I do understand how you feel."

I closed my eyes, feeling rough bark press through my dress.

Mom was a dancer. She'd met my filmmaker dad in college, and while they were pursuing their dreams, a surprise showed up — me.

Having a baby at twenty-one was the last thing Teresa DiCosmo had planned for her career. She still danced now; she choreographed, taught, and occasionally performed. She was also forty and feeling the changes in her body.

But I wondered about those early years. How much resentment, sadness, and frustration she might have felt. Her dreams just out of her grasp, because she decided to keep me.

"Daisy?"

"I know, Mom," I said gently. "You had a hard time."

"I'm sorry. I shouldn't have said anything. You're the best thing that's ever happened to me."

My dry eyes pricked in the August heat. I hadn't shed a tear since the fall.

"Love, I only bring this up because sometimes things happen that we don't choose, but they give us gifts. This change in your life is a golden opportunity. It can open up new horizons." Her voice brightened. "Carmen pivoted, remember? And she's *very* happy."

My dad's girlfriend. A chipper ex-actress who now taught middle school drama.

"She went back to school!" Mom exclaimed. "She broadened her education, pursued other avenues..."

"Because she was sick of scraping up bit parts on TV," I interrupted.

"Honey, your life is not over. You've always been so single-minded. So *focused*. Now you can have a real college experience. Try everything! Make crazy friends! Date around! You actually have time for a boyfriend now. Or do you like girls too? I heard you on the phone with that cutie last year. What's her name, Jessamyn..."

I groaned. Yes, that phone call had been flirty, and absolutely nothing had come of it beyond one epic failure of a kiss. As was the case with all my crushes.

"But don't tie yourself down," Mom hurried on. "Explore! Date two people at once."

"Only two?"

"Three...four..." She laughed. "Just follow your heart, love. I want you to be happy."

My mom had the best intentions in the world, and I loved her more than I could say. But the pressure to reassure her that I was okay would always exist. That I would live out big dreams, because hers had gotten smaller.

I sighed. "I'll try new things, I promise."

"That's all I ask. Have some fun! It's Friday — go to a party. But be safe. Be careful with my only daughter."

"I will, Mom. Love you a lot."

Lee Tower had nine stories. I lived on the eighth. In the elevator, my phone buzzed with a text.

Hey, Daisy. It's Blake. Remember the stories that say Greer Hill is haunted?
It's not ghosts exactly — sorry to disappoint you. More of a presence. People say they feel something on the hill. Watching... waiting...wanting...

Where did I know Blake from?
Quickly, I texted a response.

Wanting what?

Who knows? Strange things happen there. I can show you sometime. It's better at night. You take care, Daisy.

I wrinkled my nose. *Take care?* Not so sexy. But why would he bother to offer me a private tour of some spooky hill?

Holding off on a reply, I dropped my phone in my purse and exited the elevator to walk into my suite.

Three single bedrooms were connected to a common room furnished with a couch and coffee table. My roommates, Michelle and Amy, lounged on the couch in white tank tops and neon running shorts.

Classes didn't start until next week, but Amy's biology textbooks were stacked neatly on the coffee table, while highlighters from the pack Michelle had bought lay scattered everywhere.

Michelle and Amy were best friends who'd chosen to live together. I was the add-on, assigned to room with them. They both had their majors picked and their futures chosen — Amy was pre-med, Michelle was in the school of engineering. They liked to grumble about how much work they'd have this year, but I envied their security.

Michelle waved a bag of tortilla chips at me, her brown curls bouncing.

"Have you guys heard anything about Greer Hill?" I asked, taking a chip.

Amy laughed, raking her fingers through her short black hair. "Oh yeah, people talked about it last year. Spooky...ghosts... No one goes there after dark."

I shrugged. "Maybe I will."

My roommates exchanged uneasy glances. "Well, don't go tonight," Michelle said. "You don't want to miss The Crush."

I walked to the fan and flapped the embroidered neckline of my sundress against my chest, trying to let in a breeze.

"What exactly is that?"

Amy pulled a smoothie from the fridge and held it dramatically against her forehead. "It's the big kickoff to the year! The whole school's going to be there."

The whole school. I felt uncomfortably warm, and my stomach lurched.

Meeting Blake had distracted me. But Nathan was the crush I'd held onto for so long, the yardstick I compared all other people to.

Michelle crunched a handful of chips. "It's called The Crush because so many people are packed into the quad. Come with me and Amy! We'll be a threesome."

"Ooh, you're smiling," Amy teased. "Someone there who you want to run into?"

I should make more of an effort...try to make friends...at least give my new school a chance.

"Okay," I said, my heart beating faster. "Let's be a threesome. I'm in."

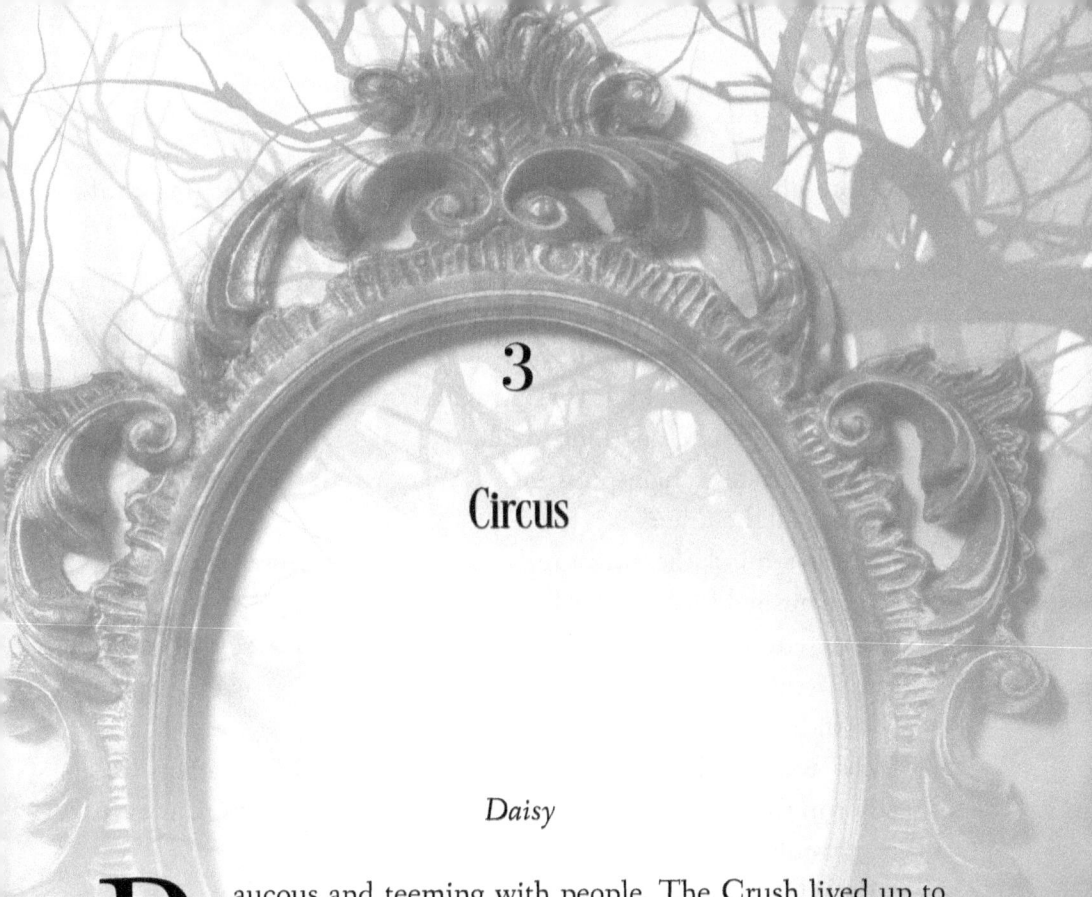

3

Circus

Daisy

Raucous and teeming with people, The Crush lived up to its name. Michelle, Amy, and I showed our student IDs at a turnstile and squeezed into the dark, crowded quad.

A sharp tug on my braid whipped my head around.

"Sorry!" a guy yelled drunkenly. "I just had to. It's so long...and blonde...like a furry fuckin' animal down your back..."

I shot him a look of death.

"Ugh." Amy shuddered. "Don't listen to him, Daisy. You're fire. If you want to impress anyone, tonight's your night."

I glanced down at my sleeveless black jumpsuit, which dipped low in the front and back. My blonde-streaked hair hung in its usual braid, heavy and thick. I'd gone the whole nine yards, even adding clinking earrings and red lipstick.

"I just want to impress you guys," I said. "If we're gonna have a threesome later..."

In the awkward pause that followed, I held my breath. Making new friends had its feeling-out phase, and with Michelle and Amy, who were already close, I walked the tightrope of being the third wheel. My deadpan sense of humor probably didn't help.

"Kidding," I clarified.

Amy snorted. "Thanks for that. "

Michelle patted my arm. "We get it. You probably had crazy times in New York, am I right? We want all the dirt."

I laughed. "There's nothing to tell."

"Was it really high-pressure?" Amy asked. "Practicing and performing all the time?"

"I didn't mind the pressure." I was grateful when the people behind us pushed forward, causing a distraction.

As we entered the quad, I looked around, my pulse quickening. I'd give anything for a glimpse of Nathan's honey-brown eyes.

I wouldn't mind seeing Blake, either.

Who was I kidding? My love life was a disaster. Nathan had already run from me once. If anything did happen with him, or even Blake, it would be over as soon as it started.

Michelle slipped her arms through both of ours. "Let's not get separated, ladies. Down to the front to dance?"

We threaded through the crowd. The air in the quad was heavy and hot. Michelle and Amy yelled to people they knew, introducing me as we passed. I tried to keep track of names and faces. But the DJ's bass was dialed all the way up, vibrating my body and making it impossible to hear.

As we climbed onto a platform, I tried not to fight the wall of sound. The past four months had been the most silent period of my life. I'd avoided concerts and clubs, even recordings. Getting reacquainted with music in this environment felt like a baptism by fire.

The platform was as packed as the grass, and bodies pressed in against mine. There wasn't much room to breathe, let alone dance. But the raised foundation — and my height at five-ten — gave me a vantage point to check out The Crush. I scanned the faces below, but there was no sign of Nathan.

"Do you guys know any seniors?" I shouted over the music.

"Like who?" Amy hollered.

"I have this sort-of friend. Like, not a good enough friend to actually have his number and call him, but—"

"Oooooh, Daisy's looking to hook up. I love it." Michelle gave me a sly grin. "He's the reason you're dressed up, right? And with that braid, you can rope him in."

I felt Nathan's grip on my braid. I'd dreamed about it since Wednesday.

"Nathan Davis," I said.

"What?" Amy screeched. Both girls stopped dancing. *"Nate Davis?"*

"Damn, girl," Michelle said reverently. "You don't aim low."

"Really?" I squinted in the bobbing lights.

"We're talking about Nate Davis, star football player. Right?"

I stared at them. "I mean, he played some football in high school. He's never been a star."

"Well, this Nate Davis is a monster. They say he walked on as a sophomore, and last year, he led us to victory after a long losing streak. He's unreal! He's a fucking celebrity on campus."

"Nathan?" I felt uneasy. "He's no monster."

Michelle and Amy peered at me. "How do you know him, exactly?"

"He's my best friend's older brother." My voice faltered, and I pressed my hands to my forehead. The Crush was making me dizzy.

"Have you walked by the main entrance?" Amy asked. "That's his face on the billboard. We're not kidding, Daisy. He's a star."

"Hey, look, there's your man." Michelle leaned across me, pointing to the center of the crowd. The guy she was indicating turned, and I saw his face.

It was Nathan. And yet, once again, it wasn't. Those honey-colored eyes, usually calm and patient, were stormy. I stared at his cut jaw, his thick neck. The shy smile I knew so well was nowhere to be seen.

He was a star?

That's what I'd always loved about him — that he wasn't one. And didn't want to be.

Restlessness pulsed from Nathan's body. He looked ready to burst through the white T-shirt and dark jeans that hugged his thick arms and legs. A mane of red curls brushed his shoulder, and when the seething mass of people parted, I saw a beautiful girl at his side. Her skin was pale, her body was voluptuous, and her hair flamed around her heart-shaped face.

I tensed, itching to get my phone out and text Blake so I could combat the sudden flare of jealousy. *Down, girl.*

The redhead was talking to Nathan, but he barely acknowledged her. As if he got this kind of attention all the time, and this particular girl meant nothing.

"Holy shit," I muttered. "He really is someone else."

"But it's the same guy?" Amy asked. "That *is* Nate Davis."

I nodded, unable to look away. *Nate? Since when does he go by Nate?*

Someone pushed in close to Nathan and the redhead, his curly hair hanging loose. The surrounding ring of people, which looked more like an entourage than a group of friends, made room. A tattooed arm reached around Nathan's shoulders, and neon lights flashed on silver hoops.

Blake.

They were friends?

Before I could say anything, the circle widened to include a husky blond guy. I stared at his shaggy hair, his rosy cheeks, and the polo shirt that hung untucked over khaki pants. Grinning, he grabbed Nathan and Blake in a drunken embrace.

The redhead reached out to greet Blondie. As he gave her an indulgent hug, I felt a shock of recognition. I *knew* him. At least, I knew his energy: hungry and surprisingly cold, though this man was flushed with alcohol.

And Blake? He burned as bright as a flame in the crowd.

A chill spattered my skin with goosebumps. Suddenly, I realized where I'd encountered Blake before. It wasn't just in an article that Sasha had sent.

Could it be...were they...were these the men who came to me during sleep? The men from my dreams after the fall?

But that was impossible. I'd never seen them before.

Yet I sensed the brightness from Blake, the cold hunger from the preppy blond, and Nathan's restless heat.

And the darkness from the fourth...

Right on cue, the crowd stepped back, buzzing with excitement. Someone was coming to join the group.

With a sense of inevitability, I took in the last member of this quartet.

His hair was dark as ink and well-cut, his skin a golden tan. His steps were measured. Unhurried. Dressed in a white open-collared shirt and black suit, he looked too wealthy to be here. He and I were the most overdressed people at this sweaty dance party, our black outfits signaling that we both expected something out of the evening.

Nodding to his friends, he scanned the crowd in a very specific way. Slowly, smoothly, his gaze laser-focused. Casual, but clearly looking for something — or someone.

His eyes swung across the dancers on the platform and stopped on me.

A bloom of heat spread over my chest. His stare was black and fathomless, sucking all the light from the scene. He was impossibly handsome. Carefully shaped stubble dusted his jaw, and his lips were full and sensual. They contrasted with the calm calculation in his eyes...which were lingering on mine.

I narrowed my gaze and crossed my arms over my breasts. At the movement, he glanced down my body, taking his sweet time. When his gaze met mine again, he smiled. A roguish dimple punctuated his beautiful mouth.

Flushing, I smiled back, then quickly turned away.

It happened in the space of a few seconds, but it felt like an hour. I blinked, emerging like I'd come up from a deep-sea dive.

"Who are those guys with Nathan?" I grabbed Amy and Michelle's arms.

Amy peered at me. "Daisy, you okay?"

"Just tell me. Do you know them?"

"Not personally," Michelle said. "But we know who they are. Everyone does."

"Evan Hayes, Blake Phillips, and Reeve McClellan," Amy filled in. "Evan's the blondie, Blake has the man-bun and tats, and Reeve..." She licked her lips, and I wondered if she knew she was doing it. "He's the one in the suit."

"Who wears a *suit* to The Crush?" I asked.

Michelle shrugged. "He's rich as hell. He does what he wants."

"Those four are *always* together," Amy added.

Based on appearances, they didn't look like they belonged together. Yet a current ran among them, sharp and electric.

Michelle elbowed me. "So are you going to say hi to Nate Davis? Introduce us?"

"Of course," I said airily. Straightening up, I pulled on a cloak of confidence, like I was about to go onstage. Sweat beaded on my skin as we fought our way forward.

But by the time we reached the edge of the platform, Nathan and his friends were walking away. The dark-haired guy — Reeve — led, the others followed, and people parted in waves to let them through. Hellos and high-fives showered them, girls and guys reaching out to squeeze their shoulders and hands, trying to rub off a little bit of magic by association.

A caravan followed in their wake. Apparently, it was a select group, judging by the envious looks from everyone they passed.

"Don't let him get away!" squealed Amy. "Once they're gone, they're gone."

"Where are they going?" I asked.

"To their house for an after-party," Michelle explained. "They made their appearance and collected their followers."

"*Followers?*" I stared at Michelle. "Please tell me you're joking."

"I'm dead serious."

"They share a house?"

"No," she said patiently, "they share a *House,* girl. Capital H."

"This is college! How capital can it be? You've been there?"

"Are you kidding? You need an invitation. You have to be on their radar."

"Well, we're going." I grabbed Michelle and Amy's hands. "I'm sorry, but this is fucking ridiculous. Nathan living in an exclusive house? I've watched him eat mac and cheese from the fridge in his sweatpants. I've seen him brush his teeth."

"Daisy..." Amy cautioned.

"Trust me, before the night is over, we will be on their radar."

"Let's do it!" Michelle whooped.

We pushed into a mass of swaying, drunken people. "Exit's over there," a guy yelled. I jerked away when he tried to pet my braid.

Once we made it out, Michelle took the lead, steering us away from the quad and toward the east side of campus. "Amy and I sneaked by the House last spring," she told me. "We didn't go onto the grounds."

"How much do you know about these guys?" I asked.

"Evan, the blondie, is a musician. Like you!"

"Not anymore," I started to say, cutting myself off.

"We heard him play piano last year, and he was unbelievable. People say he's even better now, like you can't talk to anyone or even think about anything else when he's playing. He's that talented."

"Good for him." I pushed down a surge of jealousy.

"Blake is a chef." Amy sighed happily. "What could be sexier? He works nights at some fancy restaurant downtown. I hear his food is out of this world."

"How about the last one?" I asked casually. "Reeve."

"Reeve is the one who owns the House." Michelle stretched her arms above her head. "And he is absolutely rolling in it."

"Excuse me. Did you say *owns?* Where'd he get the money?"

"There are rumors," Amy said reverently. "Apparently, he made his fortune on the stock market. He's ridiculously rich."

We followed a path that wound past the administrative buildings, the main entrance to campus, and the huge parking lot. The air was cooling down after the heat of the day. Branches curled against the purple-blue sky, and the full moon glowed through fuzzy stripes of clouds.

"Any idea how they became friends?" I asked.

"Nope." Amy's voice dropped to a whisper. "We found out about them as soon as we started here. Word is, they're super tight."

Twenty minutes later, we were lost in the web of streets around campus. Michelle scanned the road for landmarks while Amy peered unhappily at her phone.

"It's got to be coming up in a block or two," Michelle muttered.

I looked up and down the sidewalk. The street was lined with large, gracious homes, set back from the road by inviting lawns. Trees arched overhead, stirring in the night.

The neighborhood was deserted. You'd never guess there was a massive gathering happening on campus — or a wild college party in a House nearby. No horns honked, no tires crept across the asphalt. All I heard was the clicking of our shoes on concrete.

Closing my eyes, I tuned into my other senses.

Then I felt it — a crackle. A spark of electricity in the cool night air.

I opened my eyes and pointed. "That way."

"How do you know?" Amy frowned.

"Just a feeling."

We hurried down the sidewalk. When we reached the corner property, hidden by tall hedges, Michelle and Amy let out a whoop of victory.

A small brass sign marked *Private* stood beside a long driveway. As we shuffled down the path, points of light appeared — tiny lamps set along the pavement.

We rounded a corner, and a house came into view.

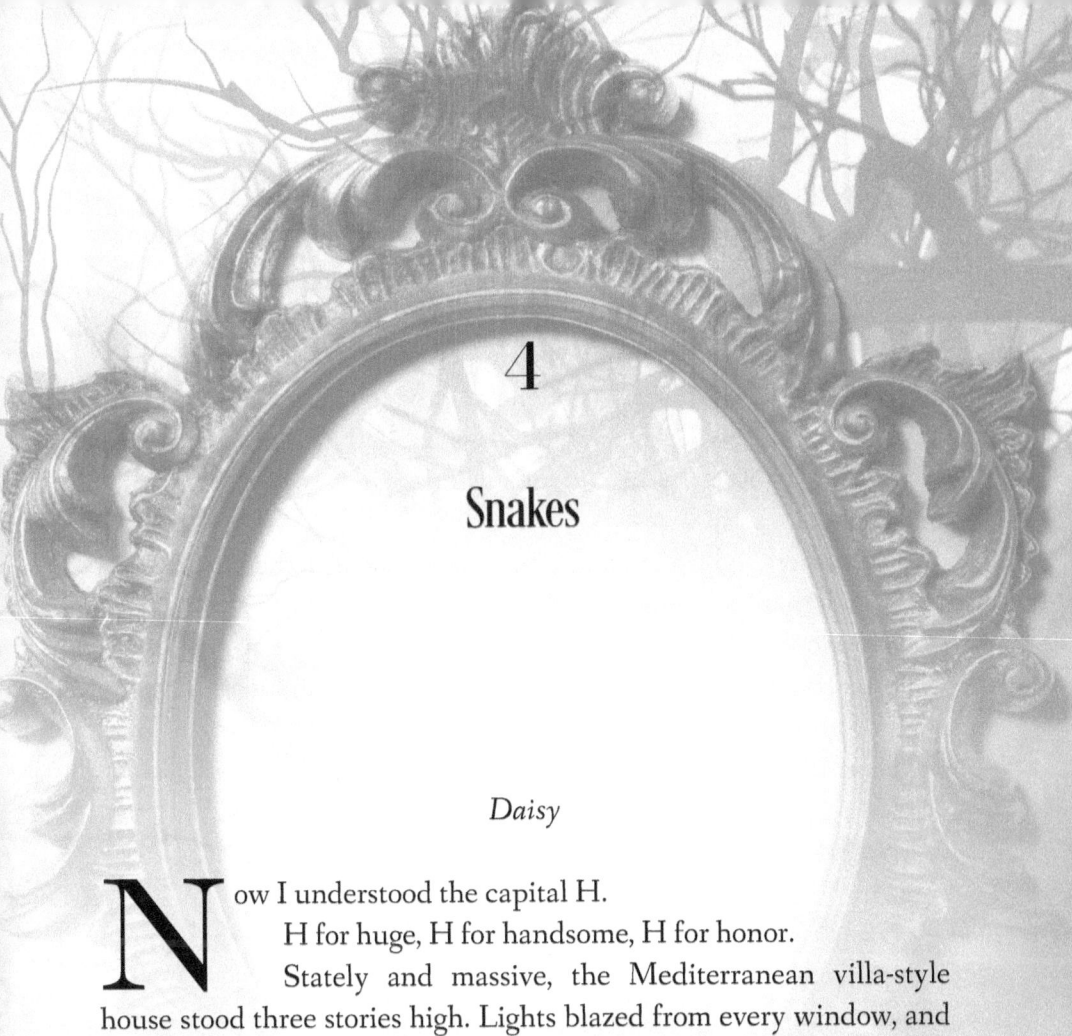

4

Snakes

Daisy

Now I understood the capital H.

H for huge, H for handsome, H for honor.

Stately and massive, the Mediterranean villa-style house stood three stories high. Lights blazed from every window, and a tower rose in the far corner.

Fig and jacaranda trees graced the walkway, whispering secrets in the dark. Here and there, statues surveyed the emerald lawn, each with its own spotlight. Bougainvillea vines dripped deep pink and purple flowers over veined marble columns.

I squinted at the grandeur, trying to picture Nathan living here after growing up in a modest home surrounded by concrete.

As we passed a fountain, someone opened the front door, and a sea of music and laughter spilled out. The sound cut off when the door closed.

"Soundproof," I murmured. "Impressive. That door must be incredibly thick. And the windows..." Michelle and Amy gave me a funny look. "I think a lot about acoustics," I explained.

Thought. Past tense, Daisy. Get used to it.

We approached the broad entryway, where arched windows showed an empty hall inside. There wasn't a soul in sight.

The dark wood front door was polished to a gleam. I lifted the knocker, a smooth brass spiral, and rapped three times.

"Hey, it's Daisy's hair." Michelle pointed to the knocker.

The complicated S-shape did have a braided look to it. But when I ran a finger over the heavy gold whorls, I felt scales. "No, it's a snake."

And where there'd been cool metal a second ago, the knocker was now so hot that I jerked my hand away.

The door swung open, and a man appeared. He wore a black uniform, had shoulders almost as wide as the door, and looked like he ate little girls for lunch.

Peering suspiciously at us, he tapped on a tablet. "Names?"

My eyes fell to the holstered gun at his waist. "Sorry?"

He cracked his huge neck. "If you're not on the list, you don't come in."

"*List?*" I demanded. "I'm a friend of Nathan Davis. I know Blake Phillips, too."

Glowering, the bouncer began to close the door.

I grabbed the doorknob and raised my voice. "Wait! I'm Nathan's sister's best friend. If you tell him Daisy Fisher is here, he'll let us in right away."

The bouncer sized us up. Michelle smiled at him innocently, and Amy made puppy-dog eyes.

"Wait here." He closed the door abruptly.

Amy took a step back. "Are we sure about this?"

"Ames! Don't tell us you're tapping out," Michelle groaned.

Amy eyed the serpent-shaped door knocker with a shudder and turned to me. "Do you really know Blake Phillips too, or were you bluffing?"

My cheeks went warm. "I met him today."

"You didn't tell us! Daisy, this is major! He's so hot, and I'm dying

36

to taste his food. You have to introduce us—"

The door swung open, blocked by the bouncer. He jerked a thumb to the right. "Get off the property."

"What?" I burst out. "Did you tell Nathan I'm here?"

His beady eyes flickered. "Yep. He said to make sure you leave and don't come back. Now, can you walk yourselves out of here, or do you need an escort?"

"We'll see ourselves out," I managed. The door slammed in our faces. "What the fuck?" I gasped.

"Daisy..." Michelle peered at me. "Is everything okay between you and Nate Davis?"

"*Yes.* This is absurd. Come on." I snatched Michelle and Amy's hands and pulled them into the shadowed bushes that surrounded the House.

Something rustled at our feet. My roommates jumped back when they saw vivid coils moving sinuously through the dirt, patterned with red, black, and yellow.

"It's just a California kingsnake," I whispered. "It won't hurt you; they're not venomous." I peeked through the bushes. The lawn was silent, with only the statues standing guard. "It's time for Plan B."

Michelle gave me an evil grin, her bravado returning. "Please tell me we're going to break in."

"Damn right we are."

Amy took a deep breath, then nodded.

Tiptoeing out of the bushes, we crept along the side of the House and stopped below an open window. The sound of rushing water came from above.

"Bathroom," Amy whispered, pointing.

"Perfect." I smoothed my sweaty palms on my thighs. The water shut off. We heard the creak of a door as it opened and banged shut. "I'll go first, then help you guys in."

Reaching up, I gripped the windowsill with both hands, braced my foot on the House, and pushed up.

As soon as I did, pain lanced through my wrist.

"Shit," I gasped, dropping to the ground.

"Jesus! You okay?" Amy and Michelle knelt beside me.

"I wasn't thinking," I gritted, cradling my wrist to my chest. Flames stabbed through my hand and arm. "I forgot."

"We don't have to do this," Michelle assured me. "Let's go home, all right? You can take it easy."

"Dammit." I stood up. "I just want to accomplish one thing. One! We are getting into this house, period."

Michelle and Amy exchanged a long look.

"All right." Michelle pushed up her sleeves. "I'll go first. Daisy, I'll help you from the top and Amy'll boost you up. Are we good?"

We nodded.

Somehow, we made it in. The bathroom was empty, cloaked in pink marble from floor to ceiling. We tiptoed into the hall.

Oil paintings hung on the walls, each illuminated by a small light. The carpet was soft and thick under our feet. Sounds of music, laughter, and tinkling glass rolled out from the end of the hall. The closer we got to the party, the more my heartbeat deafened me, blood singing in my ears.

We turned a final corner and walked into mayhem.

Chandeliers swung, glass smashed, and sparkling drops of champagne arced over the crowd. Everyone was beautiful, or at least they seemed that way. It was hard to pick out individual faces among the flash and glitter.

"*Yes,*" Michelle said triumphantly. A server stood nearby with a tray of delicate crystal flutes that fizzed with a berry-colored beverage. Michelle snatched three from the tray. "Drinks, ladies?"

I sipped. It was very, very good: complex, not too sweet, the alcohol an accent instead of the dominating note. Bubbles burst inside me until I felt as fizzy as the drink. Michelle and Amy finished theirs and reached for another.

As people wove around us, I scanned the seething room for Nathan. The space was like an atrium, with a high ceiling arching two stories above us. Couples and groups lay entwined on the velvet couches. Plush pillows were scattered about. The furniture was rich, soft, inviting.

In the center of the room stood a black marble table, loaded with platters of food and candelabras. With its raw edges, the gleaming slab reminded me of an altar.

I shivered.

Michelle and Amy both reached for their third drinks. Amy had found some powdered sugar cookies and was making ecstatic noises as she chewed.

A crash of dissonant notes made my head turn. A concert grand piano shone darkly from a corner, crawling with people in various stages of undress. One girl in a sheer red shirt stomped barefoot across the keys, making me wince in sympathy for the instrument.

"Evan!" some guy roared. "Play for us!"

A large figure loped through the crowd, weaving toward the piano. I recognized the broad shoulders and shaggy blond hair, the preppy clothes. He was one of the four. The cold, hungry one.

He staggered to the instrument, his guests fawning over him.

"Wait a minute..." I squinted, studying his sun-bleached hair, those big arms and hands.

It was *him*. The pianist from my friend Darian's video, the one he'd been watching the day after my accident. It was the same damn guy.

And he was even more sloshed than he'd been at The Crush.

"*That's* the uber-talented pianist?" I snapped to Amy and Michelle. "He's a drunken beast."

"C'mon, Evan, give us a piece of heaven," called the girl in red, still perched on the keyboard. "Save all our souls."

She pulled her shirt over her head. In one quick move, she unhooked her black bra and tossed it on the bench, shaking her breasts in Evan's direction.

Evan laughed, unfazed, and shooed the girl off the keys. Pulling out the piano bench, he swept away the bra, sat, and played a single chord.

One chord.

Just one.

And it slayed me.

It pierced my body like a honey-dipped arrow, lodging in my heart and sinking between my legs. Sleek, sensual, and barbed so it could never leave.

I squeezed my thighs together, stunned and throbbing. I felt the most intense, poignant, bittersweet sense of need and loss and the promise of dreams, dangling out of reach. If Evan played another chord... just one more...I could reach out and pluck that fruit. He could slake the desire that rippled through my body. God — I was wet, suddenly and shockingly.

I pressed my cold cocktail glass to my forehead.

His guests urged him to continue, but Evan abruptly stood up. He turned, and green eyes met mine.

Astonishment flashed over his face, sharpening his heavy features into handsomeness. My lips parted. I was panting, unable to tear my gaze away.

"Keep going, Evan!" someone yelled. "Don't leave us hanging."

Evan ignored the pleas. Shoving in the piano bench, he lurched straight toward me, pushing through the crowd.

"You." He loomed over me. I wasn't used to feeling small, but Evan took up all my vision. "*You.*"

Sweat beaded on his brow. His eyes were a pale jade hue, bloodshot yet hypnotizing. I tried to speak, but my throat was dry.

"I don't know you," I managed. A ring of curious faces hemmed us in. He was so close I could smell his smoky, woodsy scent, like a bonfire on an autumn night, overlaid with the tart-sweet drinks being served.

"You're here." He cupped my cheeks in his hands, and I gasped at the scalding heat of his skin, the nerve he had to touch me. "You found us." His voice dropped, too low to be overheard. "There's not much time. They don't know yet, but they'll learn."

My heartbeat accelerated. "I said I don't know you, okay? Leave me alone."

"Let's keep it our little secret for now. Yours and mine," he said huskily, running his thumbs over my cheeks, one huge hand sliding down my throat. "Not a word to the others, all right? I've dreamed about you, pet."

I snarled as he brushed the side of my breast, his fogged green eyes hungry and possessive. Shock, anger, and arousal bloomed over my body.

Panicking, I smacked his broad chest to push him away.

As soon as I touched him, sparks leapt up my arms — half pleasure, half pain. Pleasure, in the way they snaked through my veins like molten gold. Pain, in the swift lance through my left wrist.

I dropped my left hand. But my right hand, with a mind of its own, clutched his shirt.

"Shh — sshhhh," he murmured. "Come along now. Let's find a nice, private place."

I swore and stepped back forcefully, breaking Evan's hold, pushing through the knot of onlookers.

Nathan. I had to find Nathan in this crazy house.

5

Magnet

Reeve

The party was perfect, exactly the bacchanal I'd planned. All over the ground floor, indoors and out, people were acting out their desires.

And the four of us had a hand in making them happen.

We anchored the corners of the room: Blake by the kitchen, Evan near the grand piano, Nate at the door to the pool. I guarded the entrance to the front hall, overseeing the debauchery.

But somewhere, a note jangled out of tune. I sensed a disturbance outside: circling, stalking, gathering strength.

Tara caught my arm, her red curls brushing my shoulder. "Come on, Reeve, have a drink with us," she wheedled. "Everyone wants a toast."

Though I recoiled at her touch, I let her press a cocktail into my hand.

For years, I'd planned. I'd sacrificed. I'd put untold preparation into what would happen this fall, our crowning season at Pacific Crest. Nothing would interfere.

Tara leaned in, clinking crystal. "To senior year." Lifting her glass to the surrounding group, she flashed a radiant grin. "It's going to be unforgettable."

"I'm sure it will," I said calmly. Our eyes met, and she looked away.

"And to friendship," she toasted. Opening her ruby lips, she tipped back a swallow of Blake's creation. Everyone followed suit. "Oh... oh GOD," she gasped, her eyes sparkling. "Jesus, that's good."

I raised my glass. Blake's craftsmanship didn't flood me with pleasure as it did for the others. But like everything he turned out of our kitchen, it was masterful. I appreciated the artistry.

Before I could drink, fire lanced through my left arm.

Gritting my teeth, I bent over as the flames shot up, searing my elbow, my biceps, my shoulder. Beneath my jacket, my tattoo blazed an alarm.

It had been a long time since I felt pain.

"Reeve?" Faces hovered around me, curious and excited.

Straightening with an effort, I arranged my features into calmness. I clinked my glass against Tara's and held it high to the group. "To friendship. Enjoy the party."

I left the cocktail on a table and strode down the nearest hallway. Normally, I'd stop to study each painting that hung on the walls. Not now. The pain had abated, but energy buzzed angrily beneath my skin. The air crackled with an unfamiliar flavor: green melon, tart and unripe, with a hint of sweetness. I'd tasted it earlier today, when someone managed to fuck with the forces in the earth.

And I tasted it again when I locked eyes with that tall blonde woman at the Crush who stared at me with a mix of arrogance and fear, until her face turned pink and a smile sneaked across it.

I couldn't get her out of my head. She was a stranger, yet I *knew* her. She'd shone like a beacon amidst the seething bodies in the quad.

She tightened my balls and made my vision swim.

"Reeve! What's wrong?" Tara called. Catching up with me, she reached for my arm.

I held up a hand. "Don't touch."

Tara's large blue eyes widened, but when I looked at her, I didn't see her beauty — like a greenhouse flower coaxed to its maximum potential. I saw the other woman's face, the stranger's, and the glow that seemed to surround her.

Lust chased the fire in my arm as the serpent uncoiled, opening its jaws. I'd leashed it tight all year.

"Are you hurt?" Tara persisted.

I held her gaze until color rose in her cheeks. I was probably the last person on earth who could make Tara blush. "Go back to the party, Tara."

"But—"

"Do it."

"Fine." She flounced down the hall.

Hurrying in the other direction, I entered the last room on the right.

Two security guards manned a bank of TV screens, their faces bathed in a dim glow. Normally, I kept security light. But word circulated about the parties at Reeve McClellan's house, to the point where it had become a campus sport to try to break in. I enjoyed the notoriety, but no one had a chance of making it into this house uninvited.

The guards looked up, startled. "Is there a problem, sir?"

I inspected the screens. "Have you seen anything unusual tonight?"

"Nothing at all."

"No one's trying to break in?" I said flatly.

"Absolutely not. We'd see it."

A blur on one screen caught my eye. Heat scalded my upper arm, and I clapped a hand over it.

"Mr. McClellan?" One of the guards frowned, concerned.

"There we go," I said softly to the screen. "I found you."

A flaming arrow zoomed across the dark grass and resolved into a person.

45

A she.

The woman I'd seen at The Crush.

In the quad, she'd been a deer caught in the headlights. Now, she wore determination like a second skin. She was all long legs and long hair, tall and willowy, but she looked far from fragile.

She made straight for a bathroom window some idiot had left open. Her braid streamed behind her like a comet's tail. The serpent's coils tightened, and my cock instantly responded.

"We have a problem," I murmured.

She grabbed the ledge to swing herself up. As she did, she looked directly into the camera, pulling my gaze like a magnet. My tattoo flared, the fever-heat running straight to my groin.

On the black-and-white screen, her brows were straight and dark. Light, luminous eyes stared at me above high cheekbones. Her full mouth was emphasized with bold lipstick, and her jaw was strong and set.

Her pain and longing blazed through the screen, making her irresistible and dangerous. She didn't have the slick good looks of the people writhing in pleasure all over my house, but a thought intruded:

You're the most beautiful woman I've ever seen.

I brushed it away like an annoying fly.

"Don't worry," the security lead began. All he saw was an unarmed young woman with two other girls behind her. "We'll take care of—"

She lost her grip and fell to the grass, her face twisting in pain. Her friends flew to her side as she cradled her left hand.

"She's injured." The first guard frowned.

"You want us to escort them off the premises?" asked the second.

I studied her curled up on my lawn. A strange feeling tightened my chest.

"That won't be necessary," I said smoothly. "I'll see to her myself."

Unbelievably, she was back on her feet, trying again. I folded my arms and watched her break into my house. She couldn't have gotten in without her friends, but the sheer force of her will carried the action through.

"Sir?" the first guard asked.

"Let her be. I'll find her before she gets too far."

He glanced at his colleague. "And her friends?"

I tore my thoughts away to watch the last girl scrambling in the window. "They'll stick together, I'm sure. Don't let anyone else in. Are you hungry? I'll have food brought up."

The security lead grinned. "Appreciate it, Mr. McClellan."

Out in the hall, I unbuttoned my shirt and shoved it down to bare my left arm. The serpent writhed, inked in crimson, black, and gold. A thousand embers flared beneath the tattoo like pricks of a red-hot needle.

I'd kept desire at a constant simmer for almost a year. Now the snake was alive and hungry.

For her.

Her longing had burned white-hot, almost incinerating the screen. What did she want that I had?

The girl who'd fucked with the energy of the earth.

The girl, I realized with a flash of clarity, who'd haunted my dreams since last spring. I'd seen that tail of a braid, that powerful long-legged stride.

I needed to taste her.

I needed to neutralize her. She was a wild card and a threat to everything I'd worked for.

I touched the apex of the tattoo, where the serpent devoured its own tail. My cock jumped in response, rock-hard and aching. When I pressed down, I was flooded with images — all the lust I kept at bay.

My free hand clenched to wrap around that beckoning braid. I was shredding her clothes, devouring her sweet breasts, drinking in her innocent cries...

"Reeve?" Tara approached from the end of the hallway, carrying her high-heeled sandals. "Everyone's wondering where you are."

"I'm fine, Tara," I said shortly. "Go play. And don't come near me for the rest of the night."

She pushed her tousled red curls out of her face, trying to decide in slow motion how she felt about me talking to her that way. She'd had more than a few of Blake's cocktails.

Shouts suddenly came from the living room, accompanied by shattering crystal and Nate's angry voice. *Her* fault, I had no doubt.

I started toward the commotion. Tara threw me a glare and moved away, skirting the edge of the hall, but I barely paid attention.

This girl was here for a reason. Her purpose wasn't clear yet, but in the end, I'd win.

I'd come too far to lose it all.

6

Reptilia

Daisy

Rushing past the black marble table, trying to leave Evan behind, I stopped short at the sight of a familiar profile.

Nathan stood in the middle of a group, bulky and bristling with energy. Behind him, glass doors showed an emerald lawn and a pool that glowed aquamarine in the darkness.

When I saw him, my heart rose into my throat.

When he saw me, his drink fell from his hand.

I fought my way forward, the crowd thickening between us until it seemed like I wouldn't get through. Then the last few people melted away, and I was in front of him.

His normally tanned face looked sickly pale, and a vein throbbed in his forehead. "How did you get in?"

"To this school? I have a pulse."

A flash of anger twisted his features. I'd never seen Nathan lose his temper.

"I'm sorry," I said quickly. "That was rude—"

"To this *house*," he growled, cords standing out on his neck. "How. Did you get in. To this house."

"I have my ways." I gave him a tentative smile, which he didn't return.

"You need to leave. Get out. Now."

"What is going on?" I snapped. "You move into this fancy house and suddenly you're too good for me?"

To my shock, he turned me around by the shoulders, propelling me toward the door. Jerking free, I raised my voice so it carried over the din. "You can't just kick me out, Nathan. Not after what we did in your backyard."

Nathan stopped short, every muscle tensed and bulging. His honey-colored eyes burned into mine as he leaned in and said very quietly, "Don't make a scene, Daisy. One more word, and I swear you'll regret it."

My eyes stung. The rug — the expensive, beautiful rug — was being yanked from under my feet.

"Oh, really? That's how it is? I'm not afraid of you." I took two steps to the black marble table in the middle of the room. Grabbing the edge with my right hand, I clambered onto the stone surface.

"Get down from there," Nathan hissed.

Ignoring him, I strode along the table, weaving between the candelabras dripping wax and the gorgeous platters of food. I cupped my hands to be heard, because I had nothing left to lose.

"What's that you said? 'Don't make a scene?'" The music was loud, but heads began to turn to me. "Tell me again, Nathan. I can't hear you with all this noise."

"Jesus, Daisy," he gritted, edging toward the table. "What is wrong with you?"

"Why'd you kiss me?" I shouted. "Why'd you run away?"

He opened his mouth, but whatever he was about to say froze on his lips. As he turned toward the wide entrance, I followed his gaze.

Two sets of eyes were locked on me. With eerie synchronicity, Evan and Blake started toward us.

Nathan lunged to the table. Lightning-fast, he slung one arm under my knees, the other around my waist, and scooped me up.

"Oooh, now I've got your attention," I tried to joke.

Nathan didn't crack a smile. He stalked through the crowd, carrying me toward the door, his fingers splayed on my knee and my bare shoulder. His skin was hot, and his heart beat a rapid tattoo against me. Clenching my thighs, I had a crazy impulse to press my lips against his straining neck and taste the furious flutter of his pulse.

Amy and Michelle hurried toward us, alarmed. On the opposite side of the room, Blake and Evan loped in our direction.

Nathan kicked through a curtain that covered the entrance to the front hall, leaving the buzzing crowd behind. Ahead, across a broad, echoing foyer, stood the grand front door. The security guard was nowhere in sight.

"Nathan, you can't kick me out," I pleaded. "I need to talk to you."

He moved with unbelievable swiftness, even with me in his arms. We were at the door in two seconds.

Wordlessly, he let go of me with one hand to twist the doorknob. It stuck. As he rattled it, I kicked and wriggled free of his hold. Sliding to my feet, I backed up against the door and grabbed the knob.

"Please, let's talk," I repeated.

"No. Out." Urgency contorted his face.

"Give me five minutes. Outside — anywhere. I just want to understand."

"Don't go where you don't belong," Nathan growled. "That's what you need to understand."

I swallowed hard. "Right now, I don't belong anywhere."

He flinched, glancing back at the empty hall, then shook his head. "That's your problem, not mine."

I stared at his hard face, his muscled body. There wasn't a shred of sympathy or kindness to be seen.

It had all been in my head. All the longing of the past five years, the daydreams, the fucking idealization, the fantasies that had started out innocent and gotten explicit...

My first love, my sweet Nathan.

A knot of emotion clenched my body, and I turned away to hide it.

"Hello." A deep voice halted the storm.

My head jerked up. Reeve McClellan stood at the other end of the foyer, his dark hair hanging over his forehead, the velvet curtains forming a backdrop to his sleek, powerful body. A faint smile lifted his sculpted lips.

He started toward me, his stride cool and unfazed. Behind him, Michelle and Amy followed at a discreet distance, their eyes wide. He didn't stop until he was close.

Very close.

I smelled his crisp cologne, citrus and cedar. His eyes were so deep and dark that I felt like I was falling into the night sky. His hand came up to cup my chin, a touch much too intimate for a stranger, but I couldn't find it in me to pull away.

"Is there a problem?" he asked softly.

"Yes," Nathan snapped.

"I'm asking our guest, Nate." Reeve's voice was mild, but it made me shiver. I nodded. "Why don't you tell me what the problem is?" Gently, he stroked my chin. My glance slid to Amy and Michelle, who were gaping at us.

Finally, I found my voice. "You're touching my face before you even know my name."

He let go. A sudden smile showed his white teeth and solitary dimple.

"I'm sorry. Where are my manners? I'm Reeve McClellan." He held out his hand.

Nathan looked from me to Reeve with an urgency that I didn't understand. "She shouldn't be here."

"I'll be the judge of that." Reeve delivered his response quietly, with utter finality.

When I offered my hand, he took it in both of his. His skin burned like the desert sun.

"I'm Daisy." My stomach turned somersaults.

One dark eyebrow rose in surprise. "Last name?"

"I don't think we're on a last-name basis."

He grinned and released my hand. That dimple was going to be the death of me. "Then tell me what you and Nate were fighting about."

I flushed hot. "It's not important. I wanted to say hello. He wanted me to leave."

Nathan's fists clenched. "And now you're going to."

"Oh, no." Reeve shook his head. "What kind of a welcome is that? Please, Daisy, accept my apologies and come back to the party. As my guest."

I stared into his fathomless eyes.

Something was wrong with Nathan. His size, his attitude, his presence in this hedonistic house. Evan and Blake were involved, but I had no doubt that Reeve McClellan was the key. Whatever was happening to Nathan, the answers lay with Reeve.

And I was going to find them out, no matter what it took. Even if my stomach lurched at Reeve standing so close to me, his deep, confiding voice, his scent. Even if a treacherous part of me wanted him to touch my face again.

Wanted his hand to drift down...to stroke my neck, slide over my breasts...

"I'd love that," I said brightly. "My roommates can stay too, right?"

Reeve turned to take in Amy and Michelle, huddled by a cluster of potted palms.

"Well, that goes without saying." He shook their hands heartily and eyed Amy's plate of sweets. "You're enjoying the food?"

"God, yes," Amy gushed, as Michelle snagged a cookie from her plate.

"We can't get enough," Michelle put in. "Our compliments to the chef."

"Tell him yourself." Reeve smiled. "I'll introduce you to Blake. He'll take excellent care of you."

Nathan was giving Reeve a hard stare. But when Reeve turned to meet his eyes, Nathan bobbed his head curtly and pushed past Michelle and Amy, heading to the living room without a word.

Reeve put his palm near my back — not actually on it, but very close. "Ready?" he asked, his voice low and intimate. "I'll give you the grand tour."

7

Too Repressed

Daisy

Returning to the lavish living room with Reeve was very different from being carried out of it by Nathan.

When his hand came to rest on my back, the feel of him vibrated through me. My jumpsuit's neckline dipped down low, and his touch burned my bare skin. Cold radiated out from the heat, spirals of ice within fire.

I let him keep his hand there as he guided us across the sumptuous room. He was talking smoothly about the House, the party, the food. I fought not to be pulled in by the tide of his velvet voice. To pay attention to what he was actually saying, to take in every detail of the House.

The enormous black marble table in the center kept drawing my eye. What was it about that table? The square white platters, filled with finger foods that were miniature works of art? The stark, modern candelabras with their tall red tapers? The myriad points of light reflected on the polished slab, flickering...dancing...

"Daisy." Reeve's voice was soft. "Come along."

Dammit. The room was hypnotizing me. I had to keep my wits sharp.

"We throw these parties once a month," Reeve told Amy and Michelle. "The House needs time to recover in between."

They laughed, as if he'd made a hilarious joke. My gaze strayed to the full moon outside the tall windows.

"Why do you throw them?" I asked.

Those dark eyes turned to me. Hot male fingers spread out against my skin like the five points of a star. I was exquisitely aware of every part of his palm, his knuckles, his fingertips.

"I like to see people have a good time," he replied calmly.

"Well, you're getting your wish." My voice was hoarse. I tore my gaze away to study the chaos around us.

The people on the nearest couch had most of their clothes off. Even though there were cushions in the way, you could see enough flailing arms and legs to get an idea of what was going on.

Just beyond them, Blake stood at the center of a group, chatting and laughing...shirtless.

Ink swirled over his left arm and chest, and my breath caught at the intricate designs. Silver barbells winked from his nipples. Dressed, he was hot; half-naked, he was a serious snack. His golden-brown curls hung loose, shielding his high cheekbones, and his eyes sparked electric-blue in the candlelight.

Behind Blake was a state-of-the-art kitchen. Sasha would drool over the gleaming pans and knife blocks. Taking my phone from my purse, I held it up.

A firm hand dropped on my shoulder. "No pictures, Daisy."

My stomach lurched again at his touch, but I turned to face Reeve, trying to look innocent. Every time he said my name, his voice coiled around me.

"I just wanted to show my best friend. Nathan's sister Sasha — he's probably mentioned her? She'd adore this kitchen."

"Sorry."

Michelle and Amy were staring at Blake. Still holding my phone,

I put my hand on Reeve's upper arm and stepped closer. His eyes slitted, and I could swear he let out a faint hiss.

His woodsy scent made me lightheaded. "Why no pictures?" I asked, as sweetly as I could.

Reeve cupped my chin, and this time, I didn't snap at him.

"Because I say so, Daisy. This is my house. Nothing happens here that I don't want to happen."

He caressed my jaw with his thumb. I couldn't look away. I was clutching his arm, squeezing my phone against his suit jacket. Underneath the black fabric, his arm was solid and strong. Sleek muscles flexed in my grasp.

Abruptly, he let me go. When he clasped Blake's shoulder, a ripple ran around the group.

"Blake, we have some special guests. I'd like you to look after two of them, Amy and Michelle."

Blake's vivid blue eyes took in the three of us.

"Daisy!" He broke into a grin. It was impossible not to smile back. "What are you doing here?"

"You invited me, remember?" I teased. "You texted me an invitation."

He blinked. "No, I invited you to Greer Hill."

Almost imperceptibly, Reeve stiffened, his hand tightening on my back.

"Oops!" I shrugged, trying for cute and flirty. "I guess I got confused and wandered in here instead. But I'd love to see Greer Hill with you sometime. The spookier, the better."

Reeve tilted his head. "You know each other?"

"Old friends," Blake said lightly, but a crease furrowed his brow.

"We met this afternoon," I filled in. "Blake rescued me when I got lost. I just transferred here...I'm still finding my way around."

"I see." Reeve bestowed an intimate smile on me. "How fortunate that he found you."

He leaned in. As his scent wafted over me, my head went light

61

once again, and the room darkened around the edges. Pulling away, he clapped Blake on the back.

"Take care of Daisy's friends, all right? Make this a night that they'll always remember."

Blake wrapped his arms around Michelle's and Amy's shoulders. They both looked like they'd died and gone to heaven. "My pleasure. Great to see you again, Daisy."

I smiled at him before the press of Reeve's hand on my back made my breath quicken. I was being guided away from my roommates.

Feeling warm and dizzy, my gaze skittered to the piano. Evan was gone, but his fans swarmed over the instrument, sloshing champagne, stomping on the keys, and stubbing out cigarettes on the ebony gloss. Two girls straddled a laughing guy, pushing him down on the piano's lid.

I grabbed Reeve's arm. "Make them stop," I blurted.

His grin was too pleased, too hungry for my taste. "Orgies offend you?"

"Treating an instrument that way offends me."

He blinked in surprise. Thick lashes framed his dark eyes. "The piano always takes a beating at parties. I'll get it fixed up."

"But they're permanently damaging it. Liquid, burn marks — even if you get it revarnished, the sound will never be the same. Please, it's a beautiful piano. Just — do something."

Reeve studied me. Abruptly, he turned on his heel and strode to the piano. "Everybody off."

Like a switch had been flipped, a dozen people slithered away. The piano stood alone and abandoned.

"Better?" Reeve cocked his head, a tiny, triumphant smile tugging the corner of his mouth.

"Much." I returned his smile, trying to stay calm, as he took my arm.

The pressure made me lean into him without thought. As his suit fabric rasped my bare skin, his fingers suddenly laced through mine. "This way."

He steered me through a bewildering maze of rooms, filled with people drinking and laughing and dancing on every surface available. Reeve offered polite commentary on the House, its history, and its architecture, none of which shed any light on what Nathan was doing here. All I could focus on was the heat of his hand wrapped around mine and the seductive tide of his caramel voice.

As we approached yet another doorway, I tried to break the spell. "I like your name."

"Oh?" His brows lifted.

"*Reeve.* It's velvety and dark, like your voice. It fits you."

He gave me a sardonic smile. "It was my dad's. And my grand-dad's, and his dad's before him. My family tends to recycle names."

Caressing my palm with his thumb, he led me into a room that took my breath away.

A library.

Bookshelves filled the space and stretched up to the high arched ceiling, lined with richly colored spines. A stone fireplace graced the far wall. Flames crackled on the hearth, though it was late August, and deep leather armchairs formed a semicircle in front of the fire.

The room was blessedly empty of people. Between the forest-green carpet underfoot and the scent of old pages in the air, the hubbub of the party seemed to vanish.

"This is gorgeous." I gave Reeve's hand an impulsive squeeze. "Please tell me you actually read these books."

"As many as I can." His dimple winked at me. "But we were discussing names. What about you? Daisy's a pretty name."

My chest rose and fell under his dark gaze. "My parents liked the sound of it. But they also liked the connotations."

"They wanted a sweet little flower?"

I rolled my eyes. "Please. There's nothing little about me. Daisies belong to the Aster family."

"Oh?" Reeve raised his eyebrows.

"'Aster' comes from the Greek word for 'star.' You know, because the flowers look starry. My parents wanted me to be a star from birth,

I guess." I hugged my arms to my chest. "Too bad I disappointed them."

Reeve's eyes traveled the length of my body, making my skin prickle. "I have to disagree, Star. You're not at all disappointing."

Flushing hot at the nickname, I forced myself to hold his gaze.

When I finally turned away, I noticed a glass-covered bookcase in the far corner. Quickly, I crossed the room and knelt on the carpet for a better look.

Tomes bound in jewel-toned leather filled the shelves, bearing titles in at least a dozen languages. Some spines were blank or held only an image.

There was *Dream Magic. Summoning Circles.* And on one thick black spine, a figure-eight snake that made my breath catch.

Hissing filled the air, and swirling mists shrouded my vision as a chasm opened at my feet...

Blinking, I shook myself, focusing on the library around me. It was just my imagination acting up. But even as the air cleared, the rows of spines seemed to pulse on the shelves.

Beside the snake book, a title in gold caught my eye: *Healing Spells.*

My gulp echoed through the room. I held my left wrist to my chest as hope scrabbled inside me. Call me crazy, but those books radiated power.

If there was any chance of healing my hand...I had to take it.

"Everything all right?" Reeve asked smoothly. I realized I was on my knees in front of the bookshelves — in front of him.

"What's the story of those books?" My voice was an octave higher.

Reeve rested a hand on my head, sending tingles down my spine. "They're rare first editions. Beautiful, aren't they? I'm a collector of many things."

"Can I look at these rare first editions?"

"I don't trust people with my books until I know them very well.

We've just met, Daisy. I'd need to know you better to even consider giving you a look." He caressed my cheek.

"How much better?" I dared to ask. My heart was pounding.

Dark, lustrous eyes took me in as I knelt before him. Abruptly, he gave my braid a tug, making me lean into him.

Normally, I hated having my braid touched. But Reeve's pull echoed up my scalp, melting my thoughts. A puddle. I'd turn into a puddle at his feet, and he'd have to mop me up...

He let my hair go and adjusted his exquisitely tailored jacket. "I'd say we're off to a good start."

My mind and body reeled. But I sneaked another glance at the glassed-in bookcase. An ornate lock hung from the doors, meaning I couldn't slip back in later to "borrow" a book.

"So you like to see people have a good time," I said quickly, getting to my feet and doing my best to breathe. "What about you, Reeve? Do you have fun at your own parties?" I looked pointedly at his impeccable suit. "Because right now, you're the most covered-up person here."

"I prefer to watch, Daisy. That's my good time. Care to join me?"

He held out his hand.

Taking a deep breath, I put my hand in his. He led me out a tall back door to the emerald lawn.

Water-slicked bodies filled the pool, leaping and diving like dolphins. People clustered at patio tables under gorgeous trellises, heavy with flowers. Reeve's gaze, as he surveyed the scene, was analytical. Calculating.

But when he caught me watching him, he pulled me closer, playing with my fingers until it was hard to breathe.

As we passed the pool, lit with a thousand twinkling lights, he put his lips to my ear. "What are you doing at this school, Star?"

That nickname again. My stomach swooped at the sound of it.

"Me? Let's talk about you. You're filthy rich. You could go some-where elite, or just drop out. You don't need a degree. Are you even a student here? Because you don't seem like one."

He laughed at my eager questioning, and I pursed my lips in chagrin. "Of course I am," he said indulgently. "I'm studying history."

"Not finance?"

He shook his head. "I like a good story."

I could only blink as I digested that intriguing detail about him. With his love of books and stories, Reeve wasn't who I'd expected.

He smiled at me. "You know, that's a funny term, 'filthy rich,'" he said conversationally, steering me around a drunken group. "As if the rich are up to their elbows in muck. I made money with one goal: to get away from dirt. To rise." He looked me over, his dimple showing. "Maybe even to be a star."

"Don't make fun of me," I said sharply.

"Believe me, Daisy." His smile vanished. "I'm not making fun of you."

"Promise?" I looked straight at him, defiant and vulnerable. His eyes flared with sudden, recognizable hunger, and I felt it in my core.

He wanted me. *Me.* It felt so strange to be pursued.

"Promise." He brought my hand to his lips and kissed it.

I shivered. At the end of the patio, we approached a darkened pool house with a beautifully tiled entryway. The door was closed, and a flame flickered in the single window.

"What are you going to show me?" I whispered. "What do you like to watch?"

Reeve opened the pool house door.

"Desire." He pulled me inside, and all the air seemed to leave my lungs at the sight before me.

Candles ringed an entwined pair of bodies on the floor. In the changeable light and shadows, details came and went, but the couple was obviously naked. A man and a woman, surrounded by an audience that immediately made room for us, buzzing at the sight of Reeve.

I stared at the couple, captivated. He crouched over her, his face buried in her breasts. This wasn't the frenzied stripping and writhing that had been on display in the House. This was an intimate encounter, and there wasn't any question about how far it would go.

Quickly, I glanced at Reeve, who took my hand between his. "You look uncomfortable," he said softly. "Do you want to leave?"

I shook my head.

"If you do, then say so." His lips nestled against my ear. "You've never seen people have sex?"

"I mean, I've watched porn." My cheeks blazed, and I tried to keep my voice low. "God, you make it sound so normal."

He stroked a finger across my wrist. "There's nothing wrong with pursuing your desires. It pleases me that my guests feel comfortable doing exactly that, here in my House."

The girl moaned, clasping the guy's head in her hands. He dropped kisses between her breasts and down her smooth stomach. Her moans became louder as he spread her open, showing all her secrets to the room.

A wave of hunger ran through the humid pool house, sharp and palpable. As if everyone were about to fuck this girl with their eyes.

I couldn't look away from her lover's tongue, darting over the glistening pinkness between her legs. Her breasts were so beautiful, the nipples hard with excitement. She looked up to see who the newcomers were. When she saw us — saw Reeve — she cried out.

Reeve wrapped his arms around me from behind. Curious eyes ran over the two of us.

"Have you been pleasured like that before?" he murmured, his lips against my ear.

I shuddered in his embrace. "None of your business."

"You can tell me, Daisy." That was his tongue, stroking my earlobe. His teeth, scraping my neck. His voice, hypnotic. "You can tell me anything."

Blood rushed to every inch of my skin as Reeve's fingers swept upward to brush the sides of my breasts.

"No one has ever touched me there," I whispered.

"Just you?"

I nodded, my eyes glazed.

"How pure."

"I beg to differ." My voice was hoarse.

He grazed my breasts again, circling the small peaks, and I stifled a gasp. Very lightly, he caressed my nipples, coaxing them to points through my silky jumpsuit.

God, I was wet. I'd never felt so wanted, so desired. When I squirmed in his hold, he chuckled and lowered his mouth to mine.

Hastily, I turned away.

"You don't want me to kiss you?" He sounded surprised.

"No," I breathed. "Don't."

Reeve made a low noise behind me.

"Then watch," he whispered. "Watch him devour her pussy like he needs it to survive. She's going to come, Daisy. He's making her feel so good that she can't help but go over the edge in front of everyone. They want to see her climax, but me? This is the part I like best. Hovering on the precipice, charged with desire, unable to think about anything else. If it were you, I'd keep you on the edge for days."

"Reeve—"

"Sshhh. A pretty girl's going to come for us. Don't make a sound."

When her body bowed upward, frozen in ecstasy, I gasped and backed into Reeve. A heavy bulge thrust into my ass. His breath stuttered, and he gripped my arms.

Oh. Oh God, yes. I wanted him off-guard, revealing all his secrets. I wanted him undone and unbalanced. So I stayed where I was, my heart beating fast, every nerve ending alive to Reeve McClellan's cock against my ass.

"Guess you like the climax too," I breathed.

"Oh, that's not for her." Recovering, he wrapped a strong arm around my waist. "It's for you. My blushing company, so sweet and innocent."

"I'm not sweet," I whispered as the guy crouched over the girl, fisting his cock. "And I'm not that innocent."

My eyes widened when he covered her body with his, giving the lie to my words. Swiftly, Reeve pushed his finger into my mouth. He tasted metallic; gold on my tongue, old blood, like secrets buried in the dark. I sucked him, stunned and excited, until he pulled out and spun me around.

"Not so innocent?" he murmured. "Why don't you tell me all about it while I show you the upstairs."

As if we were in a dream, I followed him out of the candlelit room, past the gleaming pool, and up a back staircase in the House. My purse thumped against my hip. I'd forgotten I had it.

"The girl who came — she was just a prop for you, wasn't she?" I managed as we climbed the steps. "All the people at your party, they're just set pieces. Accessories. So you can have some kind of Great-Gatsby-on-steroids experience."

Reeve's dimple flickered. "I like you, Daisy. You're very insightful."

At the top of the stairs, I let him take my hand again.

He led me past a marble statue in an alcove, then pushed open a hidden door in the wall.

"No way," I said, giddy. "A hidden door?"

Reeve gestured toward a staircase that rose into the darkness. "Coming?"

The stairs were narrow, and the air smelled like sandalwood. When Reeve opened the door at the top, we stepped into a round, glassed-in tower.

Between the many windows, the walls were blue and gold, marked in swirling patterns. A brass telescope stood by one window. Other than a chair and a small table opposite the telescope, the tower was empty.

Stars perforated the sky, cool and brilliant through the glass ceiling. They seemed brighter, closer, than they did from the ground. The door swung shut behind us with a click of finality.

"It's so beautiful," I breathed.

"Take a look." Reeve swept a generous arm around the room. "This is my favorite spot in the House."

I dropped my purse on the soft chair and spun in a circle. Constellations whirled overhead. Dizzy and laughing, I turned to Reeve. "You like looking at the stars?"

"Love it. I had this tower built when I bought the House. Very few people have been up here."

"Who are the lucky few?"

"Blake...Evan...Nate...and now you."

I was supposed to be on my guard. Right? Figuring out what was going on with Nathan.

But my blood sang in my veins, drunk on desire from the scene in the pool house, and the tower was the most gorgeous space I'd ever seen.

When I looked into Reeve's eyes, the darkness shone like obsidian: beckoning, promising delights.

It had been so long since I *felt* anything.

I reached for him, my pulse pounding. As his woodsy scent enveloped me, he smiled like we were about to share the juiciest of secrets.

"Daisy," he murmured, tucking a wisp of hair behind my ear and stroking the nape of my neck. I rested my hands on his shoulders, my heart beating madly like a trapped bird.

His face came toward mine. He tilted his chin, leaning closer, until he stopped an inch from my lips.

"You're powerless here," he said calmly. "Now tell me, sweet flower. What are you doing in my house?"

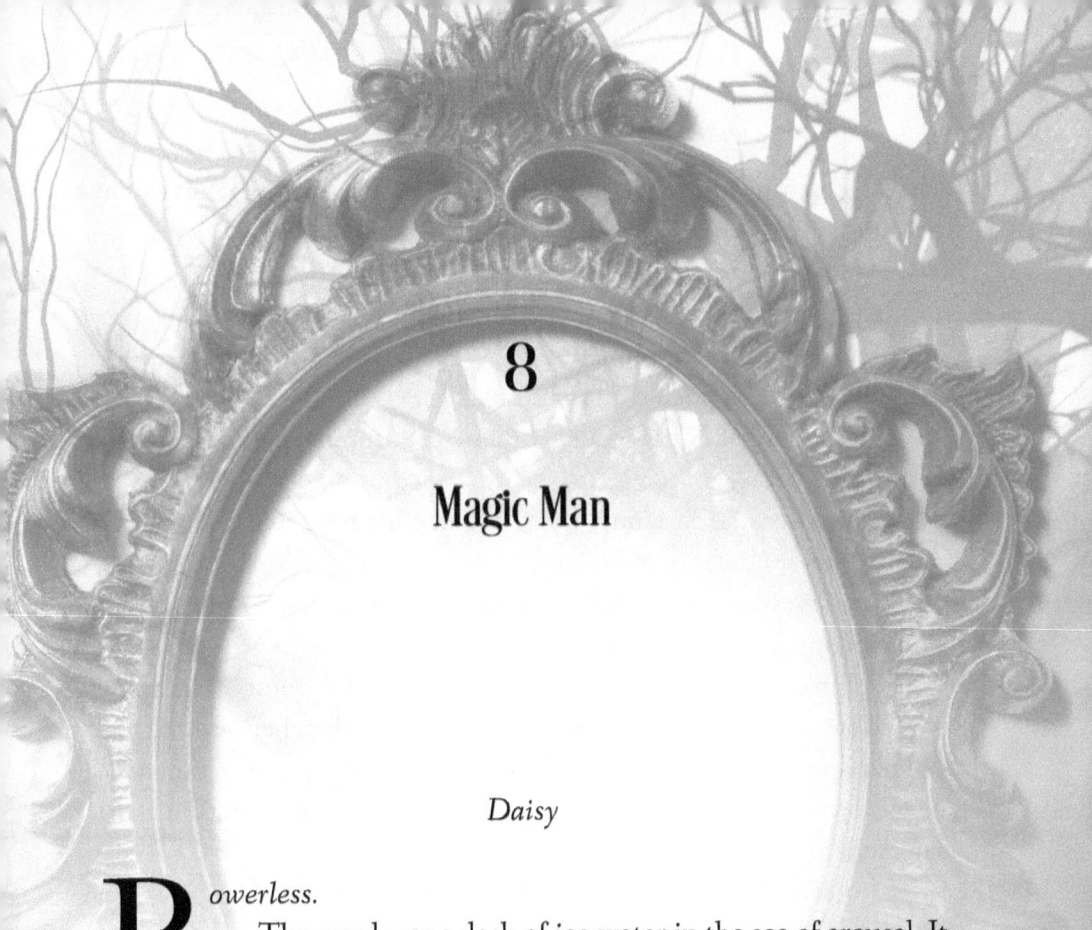

8

Magic Man

Daisy

Powerless.

The word was a dash of ice water in the sea of arousal. It slapped me in the face, pushed me back from Reeve, and sent me racing for my purse, which lay on a chair ten feet away.

Flooded with adrenaline, I pulled out a can of pepper spray and aimed it at him.

"Don't ever call me powerless."

Reeve blinked. For a moment, his beautiful mask cracked, and I didn't know what lay underneath. Then that devilish dimple peeked out.

"Is that *pepper spray?*" A smile hovered over his mouth. "That won't be necessary."

"Are you laughing?"

"Forgive me." He held up his hands, making no attempt to come closer. "I expected something more impressive."

"Sorry to disappoint you." My voice shook. "But if you think you can take me to your tower and — and have your *way* with me, you're wrong."

"And you're adorable."

"Keep going and I'll spray you," I growled.

"You don't like compliments?"

I flushed. "I'm not a stuffed bunny."

"How about 'gorgeous,' then? Stunning. Breathtaking. Beguiling."

"Points for the last one, but I'm not putting down the pepper spray."

He surveyed my hot face, the jumpsuit clinging to my sweaty skin, and my hand trembling on the canister.

"I think you misunderstand me, my beautiful guest." His voice was so warm, so reassuring. My fingers stayed clenched around the pepper spray, but I suddenly wanted very much to put it down. "I have no interest in hurting you. All I want is your honesty. Like I said, you can tell me everything."

I took a deep breath. "If I'm safe, why did you say I'm powerless?"

His eyes cut to the walls, embossed with golden swirls, then returned to me. "At the party, you were, shall we say, distracting. Here, we can talk."

"I don't get it. I'm just some girl."

"I think we both know you're not."

A current of darkness surged toward me. I'd felt it so often in sleep since my fall, pulling me deeper into my dreams.

"What do you want me to tell you?"

"Why you're here, Daisy." He smiled, but his gaze was calculating. "In my house. At Pacific Crest."

Nathan. Nathan Nathan Nathan.

"I dreamed about you," I blurted.

Surprise changed his face. He looked softer, more boyish, more imperfect and human. "When?"

"Since April. But in my dreams, you didn't have a face. And you

didn't scrutinize me like I'm a — a *thing*. A thing to study and manip-
ulate. You do a lot of that, don't you?"

Reeve grinned outright. "I don't need to. People are simple,
Daisy. They want. They want only a few things, no matter how they
dress them up. It's how badly they want them, and how hard they'll
work to get them, that interests me."

Keeping the pepper spray aimed at him, I stepped away until I
backed up against the telescope. He followed, his grin turning feral.

"I know you broke into my house," he said softly. "I allowed you
to. No one has ever made it in uninvited. You're going to tell me
exactly why you're here and what you're looking for. You're going to
be completely truthful with me, because deep down, I know you
want to." His stride was calm and deliberate as he came closer. I
stayed still, rooted to the soft carpet, the telescope pressing into my
back and the pepper spray pointed at him. "If you're a very good girl
and tell me everything, I might even give you a reward."

"Is that so?" Blood pulsed under my skin. When he cradled my
face, his handprints seeped into my cheeks. "What do you think I
want from you?"

"A kiss," he said softly. "In return for your answers." He was so
close, his scent of earth and moss causing me to swallow roughly.
"You're desperate for it, aren't you, Daisy? Even more than my hands
on you. You turned away from me downstairs, but you're dying for
me to give you a kiss. It's flashing from your body like a neon sign."

How did he *know?* I wanted to argue, but my willpower was
crumbling. I couldn't give him the satisfaction of leaning forward...
losing control... I couldn't risk the curse.

"Nathan," I breathed. "I want Nathan. That's why I'm in your
house. Forget about a kiss, just give me Nathan back."

Reeve cocked his head, his dark brows knitting together with
curiosity. "Is he yours, Daisy?"

"No," I whispered, staring down at the space between us.

"He's never taken you. Never said he wanted you for his very
own," Reeve murmured. Miserably, I shook my head, and Reeve

lifted my chin patiently with one finger. "Then how can I give him back?"

"You took him. I know you did."

"Nate's here because he wants to be, sweet. He's living the life he always dreamed of."

"He never told me that," I blurted. "And we had so many talks when we were in high school. I told you that I'm close to his sister, but when I slept over, I'd sneak out to the back patio in the middle of the night. Nathan would always be sitting on the porch swing. Sasha would have hated it if anything happened between us. But—" I stopped, self-conscious under his intent gaze.

"Go on."

My hands opened and closed, the pepper spray falling to the carpet with a faint thud.

"I wanted to give him all my firsts. It didn't work out that way." I blushed hot, and a faint smile flickered over Reeve's lips as I rushed on. "Nathan never told me that he wanted to be a star football player. He was the most down-to-earth, humble person I knew. He was never ambitious or trying to rise. And that's why—"

"That's why...?" Reeve prompted, stepping even closer. I could feel the heat of his body. I'd never shared my feelings for Nathan with anyone.

"That's why I loved him," I muttered.

Lightly, he kissed the nape of my neck. His lips were gentle, but hot as flame, promising fiery delights. "Is that all you want, Daisy? Your lost love?"

My hands came up against his hard chest, and I winced when I put too much weight on my left wrist. "I want what used to be mine."

"Your hand," he said softly. "I saw you favoring it when you climbed on the table."

I stared into those bottomless eyes. "I fell."

"A fallen star."

"Don't." I shook my head. "Don't make me into a thing again."

"But you're bright like a star. Glowing. Hot..." He flashed white teeth in the darkness.

I looked around the tower at the midnight blue carpeting, as if we were standing in the night sky. The telescope waited like a sentinel, angled toward the heavens. When I turned back to Reeve's gaze, it was darker and deeper than the earth.

"You're ambitious," I burst out. "It keeps you up at night, doesn't it? The dreams and the desires and the fucking *wanting*." I ran my finger along his cheek, up to the shadows under his eyes, and he flinched. "What would you do if you lost it all?"

"I won't." Harshness scraped his voice, claws catching on velvet.

"But if you did?"

His hands closed over my arms. "What do you know about loss?"

I swallowed. "I was studying at Siderio Conservatory in New York. I wanted to be a professional flutist."

"Keep talking."

My fingers clenched on his chest. "Music was my plan A. There was no plan B. I practiced six, seven hours a day. I competed, I traveled, I performed, but mostly, I just wanted to play, because when I did — I felt powerful. It wasn't just my identity; it was my fucking soul."

The stars gleamed coldly through the glass ceiling, deceptively close.

My voice faltered. "One day...I slipped on some ice. My hand... my arm...if I'd just paid attention..." I stared at my hands against Reeve's white shirt, ghostly in the night lights. "Now I'm just a shell without a soul."

He pulled me into a tight embrace. My arms came up around his neck, clinging to him.

"Don't say you're sorry," I whispered. "And don't tell me everything's going to be okay."

He roughly cupped my head. "You've given me what I asked for. Allow me to return the favor."

"I didn't say you could kiss me," I blurted.

"But you want me to."

"I can't," I said desperately, turning my face away. "I'm cursed."

"*Cursed?*" A lopsided smile hovered over his lips. "That's what you're so afraid of?"

"Go ahead and laugh. I've never gotten past one kiss with anyone. Believe me, I've tried."

"You're just full of surprises. How many people are we talking about, Daisy? Hundreds? Thousands?" His dimple mocked me.

"Enough to make a pattern. Every time I kiss someone, they run away. There's never a second kiss."

"Even Nate?" His fingers twisted in my braid.

"Especially him. He ran away just like the others. And I don't —" I stared into Reeve's dark eyes. This beautiful, wealthy, mysterious stranger I had no reason to trust. "I don't want you to run away."

He laughed softly. "I won't."

"You should be afraid. That I'll, I don't know, unleash some dark magic on you."

His eyes widened, flicking to the ceiling full of stars, the walls with their golden coils, and back to my face. "I'm not afraid of dark magic."

Taking a deep breath, I stretched up toward him, and our lips met.

God, Reeve's kiss. It seared me; it opened me. He was taking all the secrets I had, reading them, *knowing* them...

Suddenly, he went rigid in my arms. A guttural noise left his mouth. He grasped my waist to shove me away, and I braced myself for the moment to shatter.

For him to run, like everyone else had.

I pulled back, breathing hard as we locked eyes.

"*Fuck,*" he growled, and his lips crushed mine.

I clutched his sleek back, stunned at the sudden passion. He covered my mouth with his, swallowing my gasp, as if everything up until now had been child's play and this was deadly serious. Our lips met in a second kiss, a third, a fourth, until I lost count as the kisses strung together, burning and eager.

I'd never felt so *wanted*.

He pushed me against the wall. His mouth was all over mine, sucking my lips, his tongue plunging deep. His hands were every-where, squeezing and taking.

When I cried out, overwhelmed with excitement, he broke the kiss.

"*What — are — you?*" he hissed.

I put my fingers to his lips, my mouth throbbing. "I'm not a what, Reeve. I'm a who."

He gripped my wrist. Slowly, my fingers lifted from his lips. "Who are you, Daisy?"

I stared into his fathomless eyes. "I don't know."

This time, I was the one who leaned in.

When our lips met, Reeve growled, pinning me to the wall again, moving to suck on my neck until my head went light.

Lust overtook me as I ran my hands up his jaw, burying them in his hair. He slipped the straps of my jumpsuit over my shoulders and held them there.

"Don't stop," I begged. "Keep going, please keep going..."

Any minute, that fucking curse would take hold and he'd run. And I was desperate for this one chance to escape it. To escape the numbness that had frozen me since April.

The straps fell down my shoulders. Reeve stared at my bare breasts with such raw hunger that I clenched my thighs together.

"No bra," he muttered. "Such exquisite little tits."

"Reeve," I whispered, feeling eager and vulnerable all at once.

His eyes met mine, and his tone softened. "Sweet girl. You're beautiful. You're absolutely gorgeous."

"So are you."

"No, Daisy," he chided, his voice caressing me. "Say 'thank you.'"

"Thank you," I breathed.

His hands closed over my breasts. I whimpered when he cupped them fully, goosebumps tightening my skin. He praised me when my nipples hardened to puckered buds, flicking and pinching them.

As he stroked and squeezed, his mouth brushed my ear, telling me how delicious I was, how perfect, how innocent and needy and untouched, until I couldn't take it anymore.

I bit his lower lip as hard as I could and reveled in his groan. I sucked on his tongue and fumbled to undo the buttons on his shirt. I did things I'd only dreamed of doing with anyone.

But when I tried to tug off his jacket, Reeve caught my hands.

"Ow," I gasped when he grabbed my left wrist.

He let go, chagrined. "Are you all right?"

"Yeah. Just — don't touch me there."

"I won't forget that again, sweet. Don't try to take my clothes off." Surprised, I nodded. "But you need me to touch you in other places, don't you?"

My face flamed. "Yes, please, yes."

He pressed my shoulders against the wall. Ducking his head, he took my nipple into his mouth, sucking and biting until it throbbed. When he let it go, it was deep pink and swollen, standing out from his attention. He turned his head to my other nipple, sucking it roughly. My cries turned to sobs as I buried my fingers in his hair.

He lifted his sleek head, and his eyes gleamed pure black.

"You're wet," he hissed. "Hungry... needy... I can smell you."

I whimpered as he released my left shoulder, slowly dragging the waistband of my jumpsuit away from my stomach. I barely knew Reeve, but all I felt was want. My hips bucked toward his hand. When he halted, I moaned.

"Please," I breathed.

"Please what?" he taunted.

"Touch me." Heat stained my cheeks.

Slow and sure, his hand slid inside my panties.

I gasped when he brushed my lips. My thighs shook uncontrollably at the first touch of someone else's hand on my pussy.

Cupping my mound, he stroked me with hot fingers. Sparks shot through me, and the sensation was so intense that I jerked in his arms, closing my thighs around his hand and biting his shoulder through his jacket to quell my scream.

He murmured to me as though I were a skittish horse that needed calming. Gradually, I stilled in his arms, resting my head on his shoulder and letting him massage my pussy. When he spread me open, sliding over wet heat, I arched and moaned.

"Fuck, you're burning up," he rasped.

I buried my face in his neck, daring to lick the saltiness off his skin, making all kinds of noise as he explored my slickness. When he finally touched my clit, I shrieked.

He massaged the swollen bud, staring at me with glittering eyes as I trembled in his arms.

"What am I going to do with you? Hm?" He pinched my clit.

"Ah!" I cried out.

"Hush, Star. I need you to be quiet for me."

"Don't you want — to hear me moan?" I panted.

He teased my opening, pushing against the tightness, and I tensed. "No. You're going to be a good, quiet girl after causing a ruckus in my house tonight."

My pussy clenched at the command. "Please let me make noise," I whispered, scarcely believing I was asking for permission.

In response, he covered my mouth with his, swallowing my moans. Pushing his hand fully into my panties, he covered my pussy with his palm, holding me securely without any stimulation. I tried to rock against him, but he anchored my hip firmly to the wall.

"Now are you going to be good?" Lust contorted his voice.

It hit me: he was fighting something he could barely control, wrestling with his own desires. So he was trying to control me instead.

I was so curious. I was so fucking turned on. I was dying to see what he'd do next.

"I promise, Reeve," I whispered. "I'll be good."

He groaned softly. The tip of his finger nudged my tight

entrance. "Tell me again. This is your first time, isn't it? I'm the first one to touch you here."

I nodded, panting. "I don't —" My chest rose and fell. "I don't see why that matters. Being my first or not."

His voice was velvet. "I'm interested in firsts, Star. First times have power."

"Well, I'm much more interested in seconds. And thirds. And fourths."

"Why?" His lips brushed over my neck. If he hadn't been gripping me around the waist, I would have swayed.

"Because firsts are easy. But someone who sticks around for more? Hard to find. Plus—" I bit back a moan. "Practice makes perfect."

"I can't imagine anyone not staying for more of you. Curse or no curse."

He stroked me firmly, drawing circles over my clit and lips. Each time he grazed my entrance, he pressed in slightly, but he didn't penetrate me.

"Please," I gasped.

His bottomless gaze caught mine. "What do you want, Star?"

"Come inside, Reeve...I need you inside..."

Instead, he leaned in, his woodsy scent wafting over me. "Did you want it to be Nate?" He sucked my lower lip, and I drew a shuddering breath. "Did you want him to be the first to know your *hungry* little cunt, to learn how absolutely fucking soaked you get? Did you want him to teach you about pleasure?"

"Don't ask me that," I managed.

"Daze..." The brief, sweet nickname took me by surprise. "You promised to tell me your desires."

"Yes!" The confession leapt out of me in a shout. "I've thought about him touching me so many times."

"That's my good girl." His finger pushed into my pussy, big and sharply exciting.

"More...more..."

More was all I could think. *Yes* was all I could think. There was only Reeve, leaning over me, with his tousled hair and endless dark eyes.

"Oh, I'll give you more, sweet. As much as you can take."

Pleasure flared, edged with discomfort, when he worked two fingers inside me. I was slippery with arousal, but I'd never been opened like this. I squirmed, excited and overwhelmed, and he kissed me softly, speaking praises, ordering me to lift my leg against the wall. I obeyed, my moans rising as he fingered me more deeply.

"Reeve — oh God — you feel so big."

"Sshhh," he soothed.

But when he increased the pressure on my swollen clit, I began to beg.

Encouraged by his groan, I slid my palm quickly down his chest to cup the hard bulge bursting through his slacks.

"No." His hand locked on my right wrist, swift as the click of a cuff.

"But—"

"You promised you'd be good, Daisy." His voice was strained. "If you can't be a good girl, we're done."

"I don't want to be done," I pleaded.

"Then while we're in this tower, we respect each other. I leave your left hand alone; you leave my cock alone."

"Did I hurt you?" I whispered.

He sucked in a breath. "No questions, sweet." The iron grasp on my wrist sent my heartbeat skyrocketing.

I could *feel* the dark energy buzzing from Reeve. The same sparks I'd felt from Blake when he hugged me, from Evan when I pushed him, from Nathan when he carried me out.

Releasing my wrist, he dragged his lips down my neck, sucking until I moaned. His fingers never stopped moving. When I threw my head back, bucking my hips, his free hand wrapped around my throat.

"You're being such a good girl for me now," he crooned. "A *very* good girl." Gently, he squeezed my neck as he fingered me. I could breathe freely, but the pressure made me lightheaded. "You've missed this intensity. You need me to take your innocence, and I want it so fucking much."

"It's yours." Right now, I believed every word. "My innocence — you can have it. Anything that's left of it."

His smile was every promise that had ever been made. "Think about your dreams."

"Reeve, help me. I'm so turned on..." I made soft noises, humping his hand.

"Hush." He kissed me hotly, deeply. "Don't think about the having. Think about the wanting. Stay on the edge with me, Daze. Right here...on the edge...taken over with desire until you can't think about anything at all..."

Tears trickled from my eyes from the intensity. His scent was making me drunk, his grip on my throat had me breathless, his thumb circled my clit so lightly that it was sweet torture, and his fingers invaded me again and again. My moans flowed from me in a mix of "oh" and "God" and "yes."

"Don't stop." The wet trails on my cheeks stunned me. For months, my eyes had been dry. "Reeve, don't ever—"

He laughed, the sound raw with desire. "You want me to keep you here all night? On the brink, able to climax or not, according to my whim?"

"*Yes.*" All I cared about were the sensations spilling through me, the intensity I thought I'd never feel again.

He bit my lower lip, quick and hard. "I can taste your soul, Star. I promise you, it's not gone." Our lips met again — softly this time. "You're going to give it to me soon. Would you like that?"

My God, Reeve was crazy. Was he for real?

Was I actually into it?

My pussy throbbed, hugging his fingers, my clit so sensitive to his touch...

Bang! Bang!

Someone was pounding on the tower door.

Reeve froze. A faint grin twitched his mouth.

"Daisy?" came a girl's voice. It sounded like Michelle.

I gasped, seizing up with excitement at the possibility of being discovered.

"Keep going." I buried my face in Reeve's shoulder. "Just keep going. I don't care if anyone comes in..."

He kissed the top of my head and pulled his hand out of my panties.

"Wait." I reached for him.

Bang! Bang!

"Daisy!" Amy's voice, this time. "Are you in there?"

Reeve took my shoulders in his hands. "Do you like to touch yourself, Daze?" he asked, low and charged. "Do you like to play with your little clit?"

My face burned. "On occasion."

"Don't."

"What?"

"I want your next orgasm, sweet." His eyes caught mine. I was baited, hooked, wriggling at his whim. "Don't come or even think of touching yourself until I see you again. Wait for me and give me your pussy."

I stared at him.

More pounding on the door. "Daisy, there's a fire outside! Blake said you'd be in here. Say something."

"I'm here." I pulled away from Reeve, my heart hammering, and yanked the straps of my jumpsuit over my shoulders. "I'm coming."

Through the glass window, I saw smoke rising.

"There's a fire in your backyard," I called over my shoulder to Reeve, before I rushed through the door.

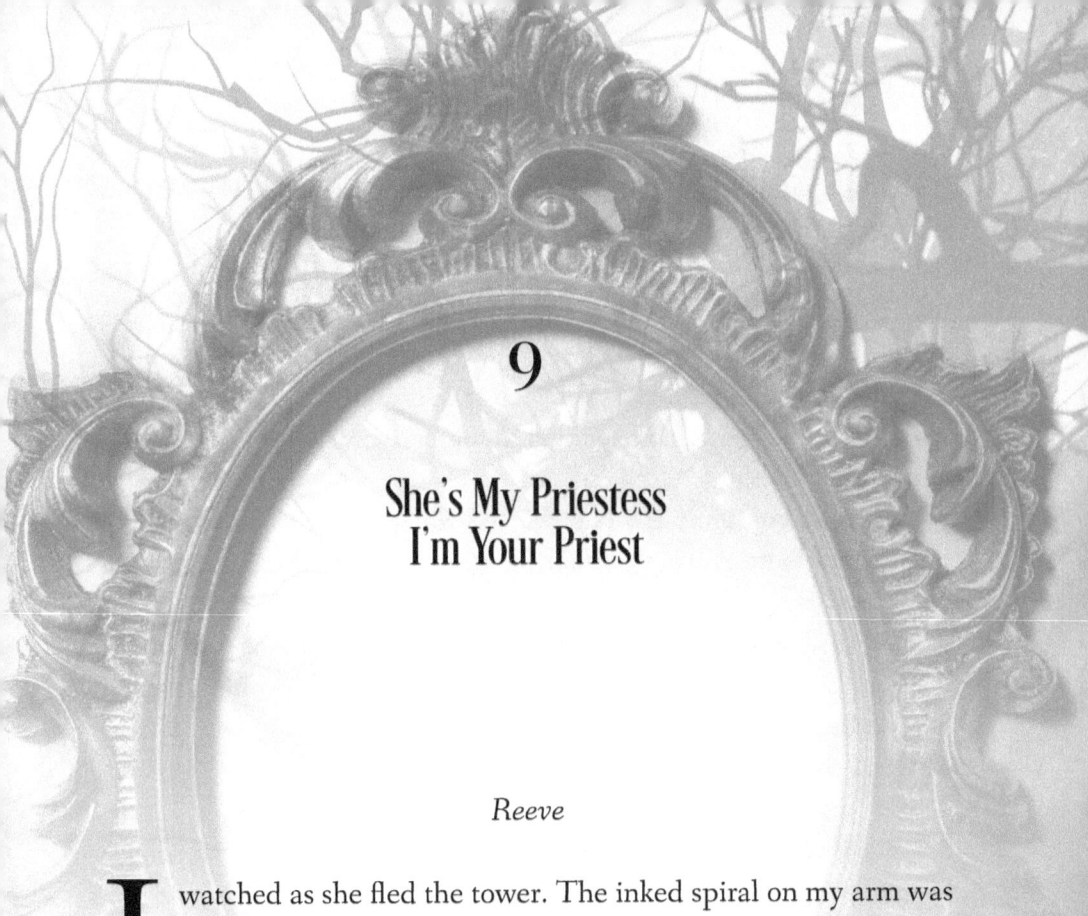

9

She's My Priestess
I'm Your Priest

Reeve

I watched as she fled the tower. The inked spiral on my arm was on fire.

My dick ached, and the desire to bury myself in her almost obliterated me. I knew better than to try for relief, though. There would be none.

Outside, the conflagration roared in the backyard. I barely paid attention. It bore all the hallmarks of Blake's work: showy, playful, a lot of flash and smoke, yet ultimately contained.

I paced the darkened room as flames flickered on the glass. While shut up in this room together, the serpent had blazed. I'd been in an agony of pain and pleasure, barely able to control myself. If she'd come— If I'd allowed her to keep her hand on my cock—

I stopped by the telescope and clenched my fists, exhaling. She hadn't touched my tattoo directly, but the guys would have felt the snake tug at its bonds. I'd warned Nate off, but Blake was smart enough to interpret it as a distress signal.

And Evan? He was too drunk tonight to notice. I'd have to talk to him about that.

The golden sigils on the walls danced in the play of flames. In a final flare, the brightness of the fire flooded the sky and began to die away.

This room should have protected me from anything Daisy threw my way. But it hadn't done a thing to mitigate my desire for her. And her kiss...

I rubbed my temples. The "curse." She'd expected me to laugh, but I knew better. Jokes, casual mentions of magic — I took those seriously.

Others had run from her, but that first kiss told me she was what I wanted. Desperately. Money and power, bonds and loyalties, and all the rest faded to black.

And that made her fucking dangerous.

Taking a deep breath, I opened the tower door.

Blake stood on the other side, alone. The windows no longer danced with flames; the tower was dark again, lit only by the stars.

"We need to talk," I said. When his eyes dropped to my unbuttoned shirt, I fastened it with quick jerks. "Where are the girls?"

He stretched his bare arms, displaying the swirling tattoos. We'd all made a home for the serpent, but Blake had inked it into an entire garden.

"You mean, our special guests? Gone. Daisy hustled them out. Of course, the fire in the backyard might have helped. A lot of pandemonium, people running around..."

"Your doing?"

He shrugged modestly, but a wicked grin lit his eyes. "No one was hurt. Only minor property damage — nothing we can't fix. You sent up a smoke signal, I responded."

"She's all right?"

"Daisy?" He squinted at me. "She's fine. I told you no one was harmed in the making of this fire."

That wasn't what I was interested in knowing. "Fine" wasn't good enough.

I wanted to see her across campus — safely. Walk her up to her room and tuck her into her goddamn dorm bed. Stroke that messy blonde hair off her neck as it unraveled from her braid and tell her she didn't need to worry about insomnia, because I had it too. I could stay awake for both of us while she dreamed her dreams.

Jesus, I wanted to protect her.

I wanted to fuck her senseless.

Her hunger pulled at me with a thousand tendrils.

What had she done to me?

I squeezed my upper arm. "Don't go to Greer Hill alone with her. She's dangerous."

Blake's eyebrows shot up, and he broke into a grin. "Daisy is?"

"Dangerous and powerful. Would I mislead you?"

His face sobered. "Does she know it?"

"I can't tell yet." I blew out a breath. "But it's no accident that you crossed paths. You found this lost flower, thought you'd flirt with her a little, see if you could scare her? Maybe she'd grab your arm in the dark, maybe you'd comfort her and hold her tight... Trust me, brother, you invited her for a reason. Consciously or unconsciously, she's pulling the strings. Nothing is coincidence."

"Tell me if you want me to take her to Greer Hill."

His eyes locked on mine: sincere, trusting. No one else got to see this Blake outside the House. The rest of the world saw the showy, easygoing flirt. The chef poised on the brink of stardom, whose food they could never forget.

I saw absolute devotion.

"You can take her up there, but don't touch her, and bring Evan for backup. I want to know everything that happens." I nodded toward the open door. "Is the House cleared?"

"Just about."

"Get rid of the stragglers. Have Nate help you. Evan's useless right now, so make something to sober him up."

89

Blake hesitated in the doorway. "What about Tara?"

"Send her out too."

"She's been on edge lately. We need to keep her happy."

"Believe me, she doesn't love our company any more than we love hers."

"She could cause trouble." He frowned. "The omens said—"

"Fuck the omens."

He leaned against the doorway. "That doesn't sound like you, Reeve. Not at all."

"No?"

"I've never known you to be hasty."

"I need to think."

Nodding, he clapped me on the shoulder, but his hand didn't linger.

Blake was the most affectionate of the four of us, always happy to offer a back rub or a neck massage. He was more reserved when he reached for me, though. He knew I could rarely handle being touched.

I'd let Daisy go much too far with me tonight. I felt the marks of her mouth and hands all over my face, my neck, my chest. She'd weakened my resolve, made me vulnerable.

"Go," I said sharply, and Blake held up his hands in apology.

"Who is she?" he asked in a low voice. "She feels so familiar. So damn good."

"Get the others and we'll talk."

He bobbed his head and left. After a few minutes, I went down the narrow stairs and stumbled into the first bathroom I found. Turning on the tap, I splashed cold water on my face until it plastered down my hair and ran onto my jacket and collar. Wet rivulets branched over my pure white shirt in a network of veins.

Daisy's eyes, her throaty voice, her long body beat in my blood. I could almost taste her ragged soul and the sweet shreds of her innocence among the wreckage of her dreams.

We could help her with those dreams. More than she knew.

Or did she?

When I looked in the mirror, four pairs of brilliant green eyes stared back at me. The whites were gone, the pupils narrow black slits, implacable and hungry.

Closing the tap, I turned to face my friends, who had joined me in silence.

"So," Blake said softly. "Let's discuss Daisy."

"Stay away from her," Nate growled. "She's not your plaything."

Blake squeezed his shoulder. "Far from it, Nate. Reeve took her very seriously."

Evan said nothing, but he watched me intently.

Finally, I spoke. "She's the Star."

Nate paled. "You have no way of knowing that. You're making a guess."

"True. But in the next three weeks, between now and the Joining, we're going to find out for certain."

"No," Nate bit out. "Forget her. Tara—"

"If we have the Star, we don't need Tara," Evan spoke up. He was stone-cold sober now, his eyes glowing with eerie intensity.

"How can we be sure?" Blake asked reasonably. "We can't speak the truth to her."

I held up a hand. "There are signs. Tests. For the Star, we'll find a way. Be cautious, my friends. If she's what we want, what we need, the one — then she has the power to destroy us all."

10

Speak

Daisy

Back in our suite in Lee Tower, Michelle and Amy plopped down on the couch, talking excitedly. "Did you see... They were all naked... God, that House... The food..."

Amy sat up straight. "Wait, did anyone call the fire department? That blaze in the backyard was huge."

"Blake said he was taking care of it," Michelle assured her.

"Ohhhh, Blake," Amy sighed. "I was too distracted by his nipple piercings to remember."

"Me too. Let's be sister-wives."

I stood by the door, my heart beating fast. Once I'd left the tower, I'd grabbed Michelle and Amy's hands, and we hadn't stopped running until we reached our dorm.

When I stepped forward, Michelle let out a whistle. "What happened to you?"

I caught sight of my reflection in the mirror by the mini fridge. Wisps of my hair stuck out like straw, messy and disheveled. My red

93

lipstick was smudged, mostly kissed off. And my eyes were as wide as if I'd seen a ghost.

"Reeve happened." My voice was hoarse.

"Holy shit!" Amy squealed. "You hooked up? Is he good?"

I pulled a tissue from my purse and scrubbed at my smeared lipstick. I was wide awake, electric and filled with him. I was never going to get to sleep tonight.

"Yeah," I whispered. "He's good."

"Get it, girl." Michelle reached for a plastic container that was nestled protectively in the couch cushions.

"Is that a *Tupperware?*" I asked.

Amy beamed. "Blake sent us home with some goodies he made. Like I wasn't in love already."

"Very generous of him to make you a care package while there was a raging fire." I eyed the container.

"It wasn't raging," Michelle protested. "There was just a lot of smoke. Too bad, the party was just getting good."

"How'd the fire start, anyway?" I asked.

"Maybe the backyard spontaneously combusted from all the people having sex out there," Amy giggled. She held out the container of sweets. "Want one? They're *orgasmic.*"

I peered inside. Truffles and petit fours, gorgeously decorated, were jumbled carelessly like jewels — pirate's treasure in a plastic chest.

"No, thanks. You enjoy."

"Let's do this again sometime," Michelle called after me.

In my room, I leaned against the closed door, my heart pounding.

Since getting my roommates out of that House, I'd been riding a tide of adrenaline. The blaze in the backyard was nothing compared to the inferno inside me. Reeve's kisses, his hands, his whispered words...his caresses on and in me...I could feel every one, imprinted on my skin and mingled with my breath.

What do you want, Star?

For a few minutes, I'd forgotten all about Nathan, in that tower with Reeve. I'd forgotten everything except the deepest longings that wrapped around my soul.

I needed to be very careful from now on.

The lights were out in my room, but the glow of a single candle bathed the walls and bed.

On my dresser, crystals surrounded a flickering pink votive. Ashes from the paper I'd burned tonight dusted the wooden surface. Rose petals circled the crystals, deep red against the pale quartz and amethyst. Curtains fluttered at the open window.

A love spell.

I'd cast it before The Crush. I'd been careful not to focus on Nathan, because it was wrong to compel someone to love. Instead, I spread a general net, hoping to open up possibilities. To attract the right person.

It just hadn't occurred to me that it might be someone else.

I started casting spells when I was fourteen. But in the five years since, I'd never dabbled in love intentions. Nathan was always at the back of my mind, and it would've felt disloyal to Sasha.

She was the reason I got into magic, starting with a viewing of *The Craft* at a sleepover and going down the rabbit hole of herbs and crystals.

At first, it was a joke. We made a solemn pact, stifling our giggles, sitting cross-legged on her bedroom floor with a candle between us, to be good witches. We vowed to use our powers with the purest of intentions.

But we quickly got serious. We cast spells for everything we could think of: success at tests, auditions, competitions, jobs.

Our casting started out sloppy. But we studied and gathered ingredients. Sasha became an expert in herbs. I never went anywhere without a pack of tarot cards in my purse, and I obsessed over learning incantations. As the months went by and our focus sharpened, the spells began to work.

"It's coincidence," Sasha would tease. "We're succeeding because we work our asses off. We're strivers with good looks and raw talent."

But the times I failed — a low grade, a less-than-stellar audition — always happened when no spell was cast.

I started getting superstitious. Relying on my crystals, cards, stars, and herbs at Siderio, even as I practiced flute for hours each day. Because I couldn't afford to fail.

Until I fell. No spell could have prepared me for that.

Monday dawned hot and expectant. Sun-warmed air poured through the open window.

I'd barely slept all weekend. When I did, my dreams shimmered with fire and chasms. The men surrounded me: Nathan's tight grip, Blake's smile, Evan looming over me with his pale jade eyes, hissing *You.*

And everywhere, Reeve's honeyed voice swirled in my blood. His seductive words pulled me close. His tongue on my nipples...

My hand slid between my thighs, and I jerked it away. Reeve's order not to touch myself was beyond presumptuous. But every time I felt horny, I held back. I wanted to find out what would happen if I played his game.

Springing out of bed, I got dressed and grabbed my tote bag. My first class wasn't until nine o'clock, but I was restless. I needed to pace, to think.

Michelle's and Amy's doors were closed. All was silent in our suite. In the small living room, Blake's container of sweets sat in a place of honor on the coffee table. Sliding my feet into flip-flops, I hurried out.

As I cut through the quad, washed with gold in the early morning sunlight, my phone buzzed. A vivid blue door filled my screen, bright against a turquoise-painted house. A caption accompanied it.

This is the gateway to your future. Doors everywhere will open for you...

Sasha.

I smiled, picturing my best friend. Her shag haircut was dyed black, with roots the same sandy brown as Nathan's. When she worked in a restaurant kitchen, she pulled it back in pigtails and tied a bandana over it. She almost always wore coveralls, and the purple pencil that lined her hazel eyes was the only makeup she usually bothered with.

At night, she took out her contacts and put on granny-style glasses with red frames. I would always associate Sasha in glasses with late-night cheesy movie fests, hatching our life's plans, messing around with witchcraft, and laughing hysterically.

We'd rarely kept our voices down, because her parents were rarely home.

Now, I imagined her racing around with her phone out to capture as much of Morocco as she could, because she grabbed what life had to offer.

Since landing in Marrakech last week, she'd texted me a picture every day. Richly textured rugs, spices heaped in stalls at the souk, steam rising from a cup of mint tea. I could practically smell and taste it all through the screen.

Quickly, I snapped a photo of the nearest building and texted it to her:

Yet another white stucco building

After I sent it, I felt bad. Sasha didn't deserve my snark. Taking out the pack of tarot cards that I always carried in my purse, I pulled one for her and smiled.

The World.

A garland surrounded a woman as she floated in the air. I sent a photo to Sasha.

This is YOUR future. You're going to run the world with harmony and love. And amazing food

You and me together, Daisy

I sent her a quick *xoxo*. Right now, Sasha had far more faith in me than I had in myself.

When I looked up, I couldn't find my bearings.

I checked the map, then the nearby buildings, confused. The campus was beautiful, despite my complaints to Sasha. But the buildings really did look the same.

Before I could put my phone away, it buzzed again. Sasha was calling.

I wasn't ready to tell her about Reeve. So when I picked up, I grabbed at the first word I could think of.

"Steroids."

"Hmm. Unexpected," said Sasha. Across thousands of miles, her voice was as bright, fast, and wide-awake as if she were beside me. It was late afternoon in Morocco. "Let's see, all the guys at your new school are taking them?"

When I moved to New York, we'd decided that answering the phone with *hello, hey,* or *what's up* was too boring. So we picked a different word each time, and the other person had to guess the significance.

"Nope," I said. "But your brother is."

Sasha burst out laughing. "Oh, that's beautiful. Nathan's the last person— Hold on."

I heard some muffled conversation, then a door closing. She sighed.

"Everything okay in Morocco?" I asked. "Have you learned all your host mom's cooking secrets yet?"

"Not even one. I asked if I could make a video of her cooking. Turns out, she guards her recipes and hates an audience. Now she won't let me in the kitchen. It physically hurts to eat her food, because it's utterly delicious and I can never recreate it from memory alone. The spice blends are so complex..."

"I feel your pain."

Throughout high school and our first year of college, Sasha and I had made so many plans. She'd become a world-famous chef and open her own restaurant. I'd dazzle audiences over the globe with my playing. We'd bring food and music to people everywhere, host free concerts and festivals, spread beauty and happiness.

She was still on track, at least.

"Are you doing anything with music at your new school?" Sasha's awareness of my thoughts was one level below mind-reader.

"Nope."

"What about vocals?" she pressed. "That doesn't require the use of your hands. Or composing. Be a film scorer! You could work in L.A. while I rise through the restaurant ranks."

"Hon, I don't have what it takes for singing, or a talent for composition."

My flute was sitting on the shelf in my dorm room closet. I couldn't bring myself to leave it at my dad's apartment in L.A., but I hadn't touched it since the night I kissed Nathan. I pictured the blue velvet interior of the case. The silver joints, bristling with keys, and the satisfaction of fitting them together into a long, slim instrument.

By the time I was in high school, I'd stopped seeing my flute as a separate entity. It was one of my limbs, an extension of my body, a partner and a lover.

"Daisy...it's not like you can't play for the rest of your life. Even if you're not making a career out of music, I remember what you told me. You said you didn't feel whole without your flute in your hands. You can still be whole."

"Can I?"

Palm fronds flapped in the breeze. I peered at the closest white stucco building, then stopped at a bench to pull out the campus map.

"There's something you're not telling me," Sasha prodded. "I hear it in your voice."

I peered at the map. As I did, a static-y buzz pricked my body. An image of the House floated across my mind, pulling at me.

Steeling myself against it, I followed the path in the opposite direction and took a deep breath.

"I met a guy this weekend. When I was with him, it felt like it did when I performed. Alive. Electric. In the now."

"What?!" Sasha whooped. "Did he break the curse?"

"Absolutely." My cheeks warmed, and my voice dropped to a whisper. "He's gorgeous and mysterious. Rich too," I added, after some hesitation. "We made out in a tower. And I swear if my room-mates hadn't knocked on the door, and there hadn't been a fire in the backyard, and he hadn't had some kind of no-touching rule, I would have fucked him. I was that caught up in the moment."

"Tower? *Fire?* Who are you hanging out with at college?"

Two joggers approached me on the path. I moved to the side and kept my voice low.

"Sasha, has Nathan said anything about his friends here? Have you met them?"

"Ugh. Why are we talking about my brother now? So boring." Disdain curled her voice.

"Nathan lives in the House with the tower," I whispered rapidly. "He has three friends — Blake, Evan, and Reeve. Reeve is the one I hooked up with. He owns the House. Do you know them?"

Sasha sighed elaborately. "Daisy, you know how our family is. I swear, your divorced parents talk more than my married ones. No, I don't know Nathan's friends. We haven't talked in months."

Sasha and Nathan's parents were writers with offices at opposite ends of their home. They had a tendency to disappear into their own worlds for days at a time or go out of town on signing tours, leaving their kids to fend for themselves.

Sasha had relished the freedom in high school. With a job in a restaurant from the time she was sixteen, she was busy and kept her own hours.

But for the first time, I wondered how friendly, sociable Nathan had felt, growing up with three people who basically ignored each other. And him.

"Did you know Nathan's this big football star now?"

Sasha snorted. "Football. Who cares?"

"He's huge. And muscular. Really moody, too — like he's gone through a personality change. I'm not kidding about the steroids."

"So you've been checking out his manly physique? Gross." She gagged.

"*Sasha.*"

"Okay, he must have been hitting the gym," she said dismissively. "And Nathan has had mood swings for years. It's nothing new."

"What? But he's so sweet."

I broke off. There was an awkward silence.

"He's never shown that side to people outside the family." Sasha sounded impatient. "But we saw his ups and downs. His last year at home before college, he started talking in his sleep. He'd call out, he'd sleepwalk — he'd *hiss*. It was quirky, but it wasn't a big deal."

"I had no idea," I said quietly.

"Why would you?"

When Sasha and I started getting close in high school, I found out that her former best friend, whom she'd known since kindergarten, had essentially dumped her to date Nathan. The relationship didn't last, but the friendship didn't survive either.

I get attached to people, okay? Sasha's eyes had flicked toward the empty living room. Both her parents were out of town again. *When someone's my person, I want them to stay that way. So I'm laying it out now: I don't want to lose you to Nathan. Whatever you do, don't fall for my brother.*

"So, Reeve," I blurted, trying to change the subject. "At least we know I can kiss someone now."

Sasha laughed, sounding relieved. "You just had bad luck. There was Darian on New Year's Eve..."

"Bi-curious on December thirty-first, gay on January first."

"Come on, you already guessed. Anyway, Darian was your conservatory husband. You wouldn't have wanted to *actually* get together — it would have ruined everything."

I felt a pang. I'd barely spoken to Darian since leaving Siderio.

"Then there was Jessamyn in the bathroom of the Kennedy Center on your orchestra tour..."

"Yep. She realized right away that she wasn't really interested in girls. She was just rebounding from her last boyfriend."

"And that boy, what's his name..."

"Sam. We went out to dinner, and when we kissed on the sidewalk afterwards—"

"Oh God, I remember," Sasha moaned.

"He realized he had to find his ex and patch things up *right now*. I've never seen a bassoon player sprint so fast."

"And his ex was..."

"Jessamyn," we chorused together.

"Daisy, can I be dead honest? I'm glad you're out of there. You've escaped that tiny, incestuous school that fed off your life and spirit like a vortex."

"Tell me how you really feel," I interrupted.

"That place put a girl in the psychiatric hospital! Half the kids there were taking beta blockers!"

"Okay, performing is high-pressure—"

"I intuitively believe your new situation is better for you." Sasha was in full unstoppable mode. "You're at a big school now and you have a whole playground to romp around in. A giant sandbox with two slides and a merry-go-round and LOTS of bouncy animals."

With one person off-limits.

Under the weight of my braid, my neck prickled. I could feel the House. It sent tingles up my spine, pulling at me.

"Do you like this guy?" Sasha asked. "This Reeve?"

I was at the edge of the quad now. My flip-flops slapped the stone path. "He makes me nervous."

"Then keep sowing your oats, 'kay? You've got a fucking dessert tray at this school. Go forth and sample! Card of the day?"

"The Lovers."

"Cheater," she teased. "I got Nine of Cups."

"Yes! Wishes granted. You'll be in your host mom's kitchen by tomorrow."

We both laughed. Pulling a tarot card for the day was a long-standing tradition. Even during the months after my fall, it was the one habit I kept up.

"You should make a charm," I said impulsively. "Cast a spell for success and I'll bolster you from here."

"Really? You haven't been witchy since April." Sasha sounded surprised, and I felt a pang about the love spell I'd cast. But what did it matter? Nathan would never want me anyway. "You're the best," she added, blowing a kiss into the phone. "Love you."

11

Slow Down

Daisy

I was going to be late. Shit — first day, first class — not how I
wanted to start this year.

I'd lost track of time, pacing around main campus after
saying goodbye to Sasha. What did Nathan's sleepwalking mean?
The calling out, the hissing?

My dreams of the men had been filled with hisses, too. And shim-
mers that looked like scales.

Racing inside the Earth Sciences building, I checked the
numbers on the classrooms. I had Geology of National Parks to look
forward to. I was taking this class to fulfill a core science requirement,
and I'd basically picked it at random.

At Siderio, I'd taken pride in arriving early to class. Now I was
rushing in, frazzled and sweaty, my mind whirling.

I opened the door to the darkened lecture hall, which had rows of
stadium seating. The professor stood in front of a projection screen.

How many people were here? Two hundred? Four hundred?

The crowd practically equaled the population of my last school. Every seat seemed to be taken, except for two in the top row.

As I mounted the stairs, a few necks craned to watch the late girl. Laptops sat open, but all the screens showed social media.

I took one of the empty seats, next to a guy who was settled in for a nap, then opened my laptop.

Closing my eyes, I let myself remember the stone steps at Siderio. The mix of brownstone and concrete buildings, the sculptures in the lobby. The marble eagles guarding the entrance and how unearthly they looked with a dusting of snow in the winter. The ice on the ground...

My eyes popped open. On the projector screen, craggy rock formations loomed.

Brown, I typed one-handed. *With bits of orange.*

Next to me, Nap Boy let out a snore, his head pillowed on his backpack.

Class sizes at Siderio had been small, and no one would dare sleep or goof off. God, I missed it, despite what Sasha had said. I missed the structure and expectations, even the intense pressure, with a sudden ache. Everyone who walked through the doors of my old school cared. Passionately.

Sighing, I opened a batch of browser windows on my screen and did what I hadn't allowed myself to do over the weekend: I googled the hell out of the four men.

First up: Reeve McClellan IV. Pages of search results came back, with his picture at the top: sleek, dark, impossibly handsome.

My roommates were right; Reeve didn't come from money.

I read about his hardscrabble childhood in a small California farming town, the eldest of five kids. The get-rich-quick schemes he'd tried since he was old enough to hand-letter a sign and hang it in his driveway. The jobs he'd worked in high school — concrete-pouring, landscaping, contracting — to help support his family.

I tried to picture Reeve sweaty and dirty with a saw in his hands. I couldn't.

Eventually, he'd saved up enough money for college. He was the first in his family to go.

I found this out from the "rags to riches" news stories that profiled Reeve McClellan IV, overnight king of the stock market. His freshman year in college, he began buying stocks. He bet against the market, and he was almost never wrong. He enjoyed modest successes that increased more and more steeply with each quarter that followed, until he was one of the biggest names on Wall Street.

The SEC investigated him twice. Both times, the investigation concluded quickly, and he came out clean. In the past year, he'd taken enormous risks and was almost never wrong. Seemingly out of nowhere, he made a fortune.

His photo stared up at me: implacable obsidian eyes, crisp white collar, sculpted lips framed with dark stubble.

Quickly, I moved to the next window to search for Evan. He made me the most nervous out of the four; hopefully, knowledge would mean power.

The results made me blink: Evan was the son of world-renowned conductor Rowan Hayes.

I *knew* Maestro Hayes. He'd guest-conducted the Siderio Orchestra last winter, and I was pretty sure most of the players were still traumatized from the experience.

From the moment he'd taken the podium, he'd upbraided us in rehearsal. He called us worthless slugs, undeserving of attending Siderio. We were pathetic, lazy, and a sign of the decline of modern civilization in general. By the time the first rehearsal was over, half the orchestra was speechless, and the other half was crying.

Why did we put up with the abuse? Why did any of his ensembles? Because on some level, that was what so many of us believed when we struggled in a practice room or prepared for an audition. Because we all had our moments of thinking we'd never live up to the great musicians who came before us. Because Rowan Hayes delivered the insults in his crisp British accent that made it seem like maybe, possibly, he was joking. Because he was the conductor, and eventually, under his baton, we sounded incredible.

I'd practiced our repertoire like crazy, especially the flute solo in Stravinsky's *Firebird,* praying I wouldn't earn a glare from Maestro Hayes like I had in the first rehearsal. It paid off when he pointed at me during the dress rehearsal and said, "Now *that* was a solo. Everyone take note." I wasn't sure it was a compliment until I saw the narrowed gazes of the players around me. Conservatory life was competitive, but we usually supported each other. Rowan Hayes had divided us.

And I didn't like the way his eyes were resting on me.

In short, Rowan Hayes was brilliant, terrifying, and caustic to any group that he directed. He was also in his seventies and on his third wife. I hadn't known he had a son close to my age.

I stared at a picture of him and Evan, both wearing suits, taken a few years ago at an event. Rowan's broad shoulders were stooped, his silvery mane brushing his collar, while Evan's face looked younger and softer than it did now. With his shaggy blond hair and golden tan, he reminded me of the surfers that Sasha had lured me away from practicing to ogle on Venice Beach in high school, stuffed into a navy-blue jacket and hoping to ditch his dad to take advantage of the open bar.

But there was a hard line to his jaw, a cold glint to his watchful green eyes. Both men had the same leonine grace, their smiles fixed in place.

Unlike Reeve, Evan had grown up surrounded by wealth and privilege in Hollywood Hills, only a few miles from my L.A. neighborhood. But I couldn't imagine being Rowan Hayes's offspring. If he treated his orchestras like shit, what would he do to his only son?

Even more interestingly, Evan hadn't started to show real promise at the piano until he began attending Pacific Crest.

Pushing away the memories of Rowan Hayes's reign of terror, and Evan's drunken, possessive hands on my face, I searched for Blake next. I hoped his dazzling smile hinted at a happier family history, but very little turned up about his background. There were articles reviewing Étoile, the restaurant where he worked in Pacific Crest, celebrating him as a brilliant emerging chef. But in interviews, he was masterfully vague. His place of origin was murky — somewhere in Northern California — and there was nothing about his education or family.

Finally, I searched for Nathan Davis.

He was a football star, all right. Dozens of articles turned up about his incredible plays, his speed and talent.

He's the most gifted player I've ever worked with, his coach was quoted as saying. *But when he arrived on this campus as a freshman, he didn't have these skills yet. He didn't have the confidence. Those talents were waiting to come out; they needed to be nurtured along.*

At the bottom of the lecture hall, the door banged open. Nap Boy startled awake, jostling me. When I looked up, every muscle in my body tensed.

Nathan filled the doorway, his tight red Pacific Crest T-shirt showing off his bulging pecs and delts. Barely giving him a glance, the professor clicked to the next image on the projector. "And these are the Grand Tetons..."

Like they were drawn by a magnet, Nathan's eyes raked the darkened hall until they landed on me, then the empty seat to my right.

His huge shoulders hunched, and his lips pressed together in a thin line. When he started up the steps, nearly every female in the hall turned to take in the back view. A few guys looked too.

Thumping into the empty seat, he glared at me as if he expected me to shrink to make room for him. When his arm brushed mine, it raised all the hairs on my skin.

"What are you doing here?" I hissed.

"I'm taking this class," he said in a low voice. "It fills a requirement. You?"

"I have a deep and abiding love of rocks."

Dammit, I finally had a chance to talk to him alone, and all I could do was snipe.

His eyes flicked to my bare legs in their denim cutoffs, then to my screen, with — oh shit — its side-by-side browser windows on the four men. Sliding a finger across my mouse pad, he closed the browser.

"Excuse me?" I whispered.

He got out his own laptop and shoved it open. "Don't get mixed up in things you know nothing about. And stay away from my friends."

My heart beat fast. "What's so bad about them? You're close, right?"

Honey-colored eyes met mine, and I didn't recognize what I saw in their depths. "We are. You shouldn't be." His fingers clattered on the keys.

"Sshhh," grumbled Nap Boy.

I began taking notes again, trying to ignore Nathan next to me, but his presence pressed on the air between us.

Hot.

Restless.

Hungry.

When I glanced at him, he was staring at me. Sunset-colored rock formations were being shown up front, and his face glowed pink, orange, and red in the light of the projector.

"Nathan..." Impulsively, I caught his arm, and the contact jolted my body.

"What?" he whispered brusquely.

"I know you're in there somewhere."

"What are you talking about?" His hand locked on mine. For a second, I couldn't breathe.

"You're not yourself. It's like — *something* — has taken you over. You're twice as big and about twelve times as moody. I want to help you."

His eyes narrowed. "You're wrong, Daisy. This. Is. Me. I'm not 'in here somewhere.' I'm more myself than I ever was when you were a kid hanging around my house. Just stay away from us. That's all."

A kid.

Deep down, I'd always hoped he felt something for me. All those nights we talked on his patio and I shared my hopes and ambitions...

My stomach twisted. I'd done most of the talking in those late-night porch swing sessions. The words had poured out of me, and Nathan seemed happy to listen. It was one of the things I'd loved about him.

But what if he'd had his own ambitions? And he'd never mentioned them because I was so busy talking about mine?

"You really thought I was a kid?" Damn my voice for sounding so small.

"You were too trusting. You were naïve. You still are." Though his words stung, he still gripped my right hand.

"*Me?*" I whispered. "I've had plenty of life experience. How much of the world have you seen, Nathan?"

He blinked a few times, and his mouth opened and closed. His gaze swung to the colorful rock formations.

"You know how to compete and practice and perform," he muttered. "You don't know shit about real life. You splashed our private business all over the House on Friday. Jumping on the table, yelling. Why'd you do that?"

My chest closed. He didn't care about our past, just that I'd made a scene. "Why'd you kiss me?" I shot back.

His lips twisted. "I felt sorry for you."

"Why'd you run away?"

He shut his eyes, and I stared down at his hand grasping mine. "I can't tell you that."

At the front of the room, the professor's voice rose, yanking my attention back to the lecture.

"...And right here on campus, we have our very own Greer Hill. It's geologically different from the surrounding area, almost like it's been transplanted here. Stories abound about the strange phenomena that occur on the hill. But scientifically, the strangest part of all is what's inside the earth."

"Is it haunted?" a girl yelled out.

"Yes," a guy replied.

Laughter bounced around the room. I realized Nathan and I were still touching, my hand sandwiched between his palm and his arm. Blood pulsed through my body like a drumbeat.

Abruptly, he released my hand, and I glanced at him sidelong.

"Have you been to Greer Hill?" I whispered.

Instead of answering, he looked at my brace. My left wrist prickled, and I curled my hand over it protectively.

"There are people who'll take notes for you," he said out of the side of his mouth. "You can request accommodations."

"Sweet of you to say so. Not necessary."

"You're going to go on like this all semester?"

I sniffed. "I can take care of myself."

He shook his head. "I just can't stomach seeing you pecking away with one hand. Little bird with a broken wing."

"Stop it." I glared at him. "What is wrong with you?"

The air crackled with electricity. I'd call it imagination, but Nathan recoiled. He rubbed his forehead and stared straight ahead.

Neither of us said a word for the rest of the lecture. On my other side, Nap Boy snored in peace.

When the professor concluded the final slide, Nathan turned to me.

"Daisy," he whispered with sudden urgency, "you have to promise me you won't try to hang around my friends. There's no place for you with us."

Hang around. Like a dog hoping for a bone, a few crumbs of affection.

"Is that so?" I snapped. "I'm really not into other people making decisions on my behalf."

His lips thinned. "You'll regret it."

"Is this a *threat?*"

"It's a warning."

"You don't scare me, Nathan."

He sighed and closed his laptop. "I sure as hell don't need your help, and I can't give you what you want. Neither can Blake or Evan. Or even Reeve, no matter how much he promises you."

"What exactly do you think I want?"

Pressing his lips together, he shook his head. The projector screen went blank, and fluorescent lights flooded the lecture hall. Class was over.

Nathan tried to leave quickly, but when he reached the aisle, he was mobbed. A thick stream of people clogged the staircase. Everyone seemed to want to say hello or just scope him out. For a split second, Nathan looked impatient, but he was considerably more gracious with his fans than he'd been with me.

Stuck in my row, I was trapped behind him. I could smell his wet hair — the same clean, breezy shampoo he'd used since high school. I stared at his smooth neck, his bulky shoulders and thick arms corded with veins. His fists curled as if he sensed my attention.

Beneath the sleeve of his red shirt, stretched tight over his biceps, a scribble of ink peeked out. He pushed up his sleeve to scratch, exposing it further.

It looked like a tail, alive and intent.

A tattoo.

My fingers tingled. As we descended the stairs, I squeezed onto the step beside him for a better view. He bent his arm forward, revealing the full design, and I froze.

On the inside of his left biceps writhed an exquisite serpent. Crimson, flecked with jet black and gold, it coiled in a complicated knot. At the apex, its mouth opened to devour its tail.

Seeing that snake up close, vivid and intricate, made my throat go dry. My left hand itched to touch it. Without thinking, my hand, wrapped in its brace, reached for Nathan's upper arm.

Before I could, Nathan moved forward. The crowd on the stairs cleared, and he was gone.

In the quad, I dropped onto a bench and searched for "snake eating its tail" on my phone. It turned out that it had a name.

An ouroboros.

It was a very old symbol. Typically, it appeared as a circle rather than a coiling knot. It represented infinity, renewal, sex.

Did Nathan choose it to broadcast his new identity? Sloughing off his old self, being born again as a star athlete?

Shaking my head, I read on. The symbol of a snake eating its tail showed up in many mythologies: Norse, for example, where the great serpent of Midgard, one of Loki's beastly children, was tossed to the bottom of the ocean and grew so large that it encircled the earth, biting its own tail.

The ouroboros was also used in alchemy, where it represented eternity and endless return.

Its first documented appearance was in a collection of spells called the Greek magical papyri. The papyrus fragments, discovered in Egypt, were believed to form only a fraction of the magical documents from that time.

I stopped on the phrase "One is All." Clicking on the article, I scrolled until I found a paragraph that made me pause.

"On the papyrus, in a double ring, appears the complete maxim, of which 'One is All' is only a part: 'One is All, and by it All, and for it All', it reads, 'and if it does not contain All, then All is Nothing.'"

"One is All" — those were powerful binding words.

The papyri had been translated to English and compiled in books. But no matter how much I searched, I couldn't find any images of the ouroboros in a contorted spiral shape like I'd seen on Nathan's arm. The only shapes that showed up were circles and, occasionally, figure eights.

Heat flashed down my body as I remembered the scarlet coils pierced with black and gold. The ache between my legs wasn't just because of Nathan. A beautiful snake, inked on those bulging biceps, was getting me wet.

I pressed my fingers to my forehead. I needed sources, research. I had to hunt down any texts that could illuminate that tattoo.

12

Strange Brew

Daisy

Like most buildings on campus, the Pacific Crest main library was a broad white stucco structure with arched doorways and a red Spanish-tile roof. Students streamed in and out, carrying coffee cups and chatting.

My ears perked up at the four names I kept hearing: Nate Davis, Evan Hayes, Blake Phillips, and Reeve McClellan.

They were everywhere.

There was talk about the football season starting and how amazing Nate would be; a concert Evan would play soon; how hard it was to get a table at Blake's restaurant; how filthy rich Reeve was and whether he'd made his money illegally. There were hushed whispers and bursts of laughter about the orgies at the House on Friday night.

As I paused outside the library, a colorful mosaic around the entrance caught my eye. The bright stones formed a spiraling geometric design, but when I looked closer, tiny snakes writhed along the tiles.

Quickly, I snapped a picture of the mosaic with my phone and hurried into the air-conditioned lobby.

Two students, a guy and a girl, sat behind the reference desk with identical surly expressions. They both looked like you'd ruin their day if you asked for help.

"I'm looking for a book," I said. The girl arched a penciled eyebrow and gestured at the shelves around us. "About magic." I pushed on. "Where can I find books on magic?"

"We have computers you can use," the guy piped up. "Search the catalog."

"I did. Nothing came up."

The girl twirled a lock of dark hair which had fallen down from her bun. "Then we've got nothing."

"Maren's right," the guy added, like a backup singer. "We've got nothing."

"What about alchemy? Ancient symbolism? Or—"

Maren, who'd been slouching and chewing on a pencil, straightened up and shoved the pencil through her bun. Her face brightened. "Oh, hi! Hi, Tara! Hiiiii!"

I turned to see the cause of the transformation. Standing with one hand on a library cart, tapping the metal frame with tapered, jeweled nails, was the redhead who'd danced with the four men at The Crush. She was stunning, no question, with thick coppery curls, creamy freckled skin, a heart-shaped face, and huge blue eyes. A white crop top and tight jeans hugged her curves.

She inclined her head graciously to Maren, like a queen acknowledging her devoted subject. But when she turned, she fixed me with a cool, assessing stare that made me flinch. She fingered a sparkling pendant at her throat, then sashayed off.

"Whoa," marveled the guy. "What'd *you* do to make Tara Heller give you the stink-eye?"

"Javier, did you see?" Maren squealed, grabbing the guy's arm. "She smiled! We made eye contact!"

"I don't know her," I began. "Is she dating Reeve McClellan, by any chance?"

That was the last thing I needed. To be the other woman without knowing it, embroiled in even more of a mess than I'd thought.

Maren frowned at me. "We don't speak of such things," she sniffed. "Are we done?"

"Actually, I'm looking for books on a particular symbol. A snake swallowing its tail? Often called an ouroboros?"

Maren and Javier shrugged simultaneously. She went back to her pencil-chewing, and he took out his phone and began jabbing at it.

Giving up on them, I searched the library shelves and settled into a third-floor study carrel with a stack of books that seemed promising. As I flipped through the pages, my hope dwindled. The little that I found about the ouroboros, or instances in mythology of snakes swallowing their tails, echoed what I'd read online. There was no new information to be found here.

I thought longingly of Reeve's vast book collection, the padlocked shelves in the back of his gorgeous library. How could he do such a thing? Hoard knowledge? Hide books away?

Unfortunately, thinking about Reeve's books made me think about Reeve. Not that I'd stopped. I hadn't forgotten Blake's bright blue eyes and pierced nipples either, or Evan's single chord at the piano and his hands cupping my cheeks.

I've dreamed about you, pet.

And Nathan. God, Nathan. The serpent tattoo writhing on his arm, his kiss still burning my lips.

Opening my purse, I pulled out the pack of tarot cards I always carried, like an amulet or a security blanket. I owned a variety of decks, switching them out depending on my mood. Today's deck was the classic Rider-Smith-Waite, the first tarot cards I'd bought when I was fourteen.

Quickly, I shuffled. I needed answers. And until my fall, the cards had never let me down.

Picturing Reeve's bottomless dark eyes, I laid out three cards on the wooden desk.

The Nine of Swords. The Devil. The Tower.

My hands twitched as I straightened the cards. A three-card spread could represent Reeve's past, present, and future — or mine, with him.

I drew one finger over his past. A ladder of nine swords hung ominously above a figure awake in the middle of the night, sitting in bed with their face in their hands. I knew that feeling, the burning ambition that kept you awake with hope or despair.

And his present, the Devil? No surprise there. Reeve was temptation itself. Yet every card could be interpreted as both positive and negative. The Devil didn't have to represent evil. He could mean freedom, playfulness, rebellion, pleasure...none of which I'd felt in months.

Until Reeve touched me.

But the Devil also implied addiction and an overwhelming appetite.

Quickly, I inspected the future — the Tower. Scary-looking card, with the top exploding off a stone tower that protruded into the heavens. Lightning burst from the broken roof, and two figures hurtled through the air.

My left wrist twinged, and I tensed as the image jogged a memory of my fall.

Don't forget the positives, I reminded myself. The destruction of the Tower could mean new beginnings, upheaval — or orgasm. The figures could be falling or flying.

Picturing Nathan's honey-colored eyes, I turned over a single card.

The Knight of Wands, upside down.

I could have interpreted that card a hundred ways, but what came to mind was that Nathan was trying to protect, to be chivalrous. But something was off. His attempts at honor were backfiring.

My mind jumped to Blake's dazzling smile, the piercings that winked in the lights of the party, as I turned over the Ace of Pentacles: the promise of talent, wealth, and the beginnings of success.

Fair enough; he was obviously making a name for himself in the restaurant world, and working with food tied him to the earthly sustenance that the Pentacles implied. Once he left Pacific Crest for a bigger city, he'd probably be a star.

Which made me wonder: what were these men doing here, ninety miles from L.A., at this undistinguished university, if they were all so good at what they did? They could be in New York — the best place on earth, not that I was biased — or anywhere they chose.

With a shiver, I remembered Evan's pale jade gaze, his grip on my arms, and turned over his card.

Strength.

A lion nuzzled a woman's lap while she cradled the beast's huge head.

Physically, it fit. Evan was a husky guy, crackling with energy. He was potent, powerful — a beast. I could see him as a lion.

But something about the woman and the beast, twined together, nagged at my attention.

I laid out the four cards in a rough square: the Knight, the Ace, the Beast, the Devil.

Choosing a final card for myself, I set it at the bottom of the group.

The Star.

A woman with long golden hair knelt naked on the grass. One foot rested on the surface of a pool. Jugs of water poured out from each hand, while a cluster of stars shone overhead.

She stood for hope. Inspiration. Vision, guidance, purpose.

Everything I'd missed since April.

In the months since my fall, I'd never picked her once.

"You're wrong, Nathan," I murmured. "I belong with you and your friends. There's a place for me — a purpose. I just don't know what it is yet."

Blood rose to my skin as I studied the five cards that formed the points of a star.

A cough broke my focus, and I turned. The beautiful redhead — Tara — stood behind me.

She smiled, and I blinked up at her. I waited for her to say something, since she'd obviously been trying to get my attention, but she simply went to a carrel across the aisle and a row past mine. She sat down and began paging calmly through a fashion magazine.

I stacked the books on my desk, sorting them to return to the shelves, but my neck prickled.

When I looked up, our eyes met, and she gave me another slow smile. Studying me from head to toe, she crossed her legs and toyed with the diamond pendant she wore. Then she raised the magazine to hide her face, like we were in a bad spy movie. It should have been funny, but a chill ran down my spine.

"Well, hello there."

The deep male voice startled me. I looked up into a pair of sky-blue eyes.

Blake leaned over the carrel, his tattooed arm draping along the top. He flashed me a dazzling grin, framed by his golden-brown beard.

"Hey, Blake." I smiled back, feeling warm and fluttery as he squeezed my right shoulder affectionately.

But my stomach tightened when Evan strolled up. Brushing blond hair off his forehead, he took me in with a lazy green gaze. Sober, he reminded me of a huge cat, still and watchful.

"You planning to introduce us, Blakey?" He thumped Blake's back. "Sharing is caring."

Blake rolled his eyes, inviting me to laugh with him, but I folded my arms. *"Introduce us?"*

Blake's brows drew together. "What's wrong?"

Evan said nothing, but an unreadable look crossed his face, and I got a flash of the cold hunger I'd felt from him in my dreams.

Something dark and needy in me answered to that flash.

I focused on his pale eyes. "Do we really need introductions, *Evan Hayes*? When you grabbed me at your party, you seemed to know who I was."

Blake looked genuinely surprised. "What's this all about, Ev?"

Evan's eyelids flickered. "Fuck. The party? I was wasted beyond recognition." He spread his hands apologetically. "I'm sorry. I have no idea what I said to you, but I'm sure it was incriminating. Blakey's cocktails were a little too good, and I guarantee I had too many." He tilted his head, offering a slight smile. He didn't have a megawatt grin like Blake; his smile was a suggestion that tugged you closer, so you'd work for more. "Will you forgive me? And tell me your name?"

I squinted at him. "You weren't blackout drunk. You said weird things like, 'It's our little secret.' What's the secret?"

Evan blinked. "No idea. You have to understand, I'm an idiot when I drink."

"And yet he still does it." Blake tousled Evan's hair.

"You told me you dreamed about me," I persisted, but my voice dropped.

"Well, seeing you now, I sure as hell wish I had." Evan gave me his slow smile as he looked me over. "But trust me, that was the alcohol talking."

Blake laughed. "Don't worry, Daisy. Ev doesn't have any secrets from us."

"*Daisy.*" Evan drew out the syllables so they lingered on his tongue like melting chocolate. "That's your name? Very pretty."

"I agree," Blake put in. "It's perfect for you."

There was something about the knowing glance they exchanged. Especially when Blake kneaded the back of Evan's neck, his thumb rubbing his collarbone. It could just be bro energy, but was it more than that? Did it include Reeve — and Nathan?

Evan patted the stacks of books on the desk. "Deep into studying already, Daisy? College isn't just about books. You should have fun."

His tone was joking, but his eyes flicked assessingly over the titles about alchemy and magic.

Soft blond hair glistened on his husky forearm. My eyes travelled upward until I stared at the short sleeve of his polo shirt. With a jolt, I saw a hint of crimson ink peeking below the hem on his biceps.

"I don't need fun. I'm doing research. If I get into something, I really get into it," I said shortly.

"These look heavy." Blake hefted a book and winked at me. "I have to say, school's never been my thing. Not like Reeve — he's the only one of us who actually enjoys it. I'll be glad to get my degree and get out of here. Kitchens are my happy place."

"Why get a degree at all?" I asked. "You don't need one to work with food."

Blake and Evan traded fleeting smiles. "It's better this way," was all Blake said.

"How?" I pushed. "I'm curious."

"About...?" Evan picked up the top book, on the history of alchemy, and began flipping through it.

Every time his big fingers stroked a page, I shuddered. I'd always had a thing for pianists' hands, and Evan's were enviable. He'd have a huge spread on the keys. It was undeniably sexy. When I realized Blake was watching, amusement crinkling his eyes, heat rushed through me.

"About the secrets of your success," I said, my heart pounding. The men laughed.

"So serious," Blake said.

"You should learn to have fun, Daisy," Evan drawled, that half-smile tugging at his lips. "We can teach you."

Whatever Evan's idea of fun was, I should keep a safe distance. But hadn't I given myself up to Reeve in the tower? I'd offered him my innocence — Jesus, anything he wanted.

Had he told them?

My eyes kept returning to the flick of scarlet ink below Evan's sleeve. He leaned close, sliding a finger underneath the hem.

"Is there something you want to see?" he whispered teasingly.

My lips parted. "Yes." I couldn't lie.

Slowly, Evan pushed up his sleeve, baring his arm, until I stared at the twin of Nathan's serpent tattoo.

Every detail, as far as I could tell, was identical. Up close, the serpent looked even more lusty, more insatiable, as it sank its fangs into its own tail. It seemed to writhe on Evan's skin. Or maybe that was just the pulse of his muscle.

"You like it?" Evan murmured.

I did and I didn't. It unnerved and attracted me in equal measure. A strange rush filled my ears, hisses and whispers.

"It's beautiful." I met his slight, knowing smile. "Did it hurt, getting it done?"

"Hurt like hell. But it felt so good." His brows lifted into his shaggy hair, mocking me, daring me to ask.

Blake casually leaned over the carrel, stretching his lean left arm to show off the inner expanse of skin. In the forest of ink, curling into his tank top, crimson coils glowed.

I swallowed hard. His serpent was almost hidden, surrounded by a thicket of thorny brambles. But seeing his tattoo beside Evan's made it clear that they were exact copies. Not one aspect differed.

"We didn't hear back from you about Greer Hill, Daisy," Blake said softly. "We think it would be just your kind of place, and we'd really like to show you. Will you let us do that?"

"Maybe." My voice was thick in my throat.

Evan bent toward me, his gaze more friendly, and patted the array of cards on the desk. "What's all this?"

"A tarot spread," I said briefly. He didn't seem aware that I had not, in fact, forgiven him. "I pulled cards for you and your friends, since everyone seems to be talking about you."

"So who's who?" Blake leaned over the carrel as I nudged the Ace of Pentacles. To my surprise, his lips parted, making my own breath come faster.

"Why don't you guys take a guess?"

Draping an arm around Blake, Evan jabbed the reversed Knight of Wands. "That's our Nate. And here's Blake in his glory," he added, tapping the Ace. "This one's me, obviously." He patted Strength, lingering on the beast. "Reeve — damn, you picked three for him. He must really be on your mind." Heat stained my cheeks as he flicked the Nine of Swords, the Devil, and the Tower. "And you, in the middle of us all — the Star." He stroked the woman's arm.

I jumped at a phantom caress on my own arm.

"Everything okay, Daisy?" Evan ran his fingers casually over the Star's fall of golden hair. I could practically feel his hand in my own hair, tugging the strands.

"Just fine," I managed.

"Was Ev right about the cards?" Blake's dimples showed.

"Every single one. He gets an A-plus."

"Then I want a better look." Evan picked up the Star, examining the kneeling nude as he stroked the card's surface.

I bit my lip at a sudden twinge in my nipples. There was pressure, teasing and possessive, on my breasts.

How could I feel every touch on my own body?

"Evan—" I breathed.

"Are you okay?" A little smile tugged his lips. His thumb coasted downward, and I gasped at the sensation of thick flesh pressing into my pussy. It split my lips, finding the source of sweet dampness and pushing against my clit.

He looked up at me with a wicked grin on his face, and I let out a strangled whimper as I gripped the carrel.

I was imagining things. I had to be.

"I'll take that." My voice was high and thin as I snatched the card from his hand.

Behind him, I saw that Tara had changed her seat, moved closer to us.

"Say our names, Daisy," Blake said softly, his voice too low to be overheard beyond our carrel. "Our true names."

What the fuck was going on? What had I walked into?

I licked my lips. The names itched to be spoken, waiting on my tongue.

"The Ace," I said, looking up into Blake's sky-blue eyes, which crinkled in a smile. "The Beast," I continued, and Evan's nostrils flared. "The Knight — Nathan. The Devil — Reeve."

"And you," Evan urged. "The Star."

My eyes dropped. "Not me."

"Never doubt it," Blake said softly. "We don't."

A beep from my phone made me jump. "I have to go to class," I said quickly, scooping up the cards and stuffing them in my purse.

"We were just leaving," Blake said, grinning broadly.

Evan leaned down, his lips close to my ear, and my skin tightened into goosebumps.

"I have a concert run this week," he said in a low voice. "It's sold out, but I can get you a ticket. You'll come, won't you, pet? Tomorrow night, eight pm?"

I pulled back, aching with need. "I'm not your pet."

He gave me that half-smile. "And you haven't forgiven me yet, I know. Let me make up for whatever I said to you when I was drunk. Crowne Hall, downtown. A free ticket to the best seat in the house. You want to know our secrets, Daisy? This is the first step."

I felt a surge of envy over his sold-out concert run. "I'll think about it."

"Good," Blake said with a wink. "You've got my number. Let us know."

He leaned in to kiss my cheek. His lips were soft, warm, and so close to the corner of my mouth.

Evan didn't try to touch me, but he gave me a long look, and I forced myself to hold his pale gaze.

Finally, I tore myself away. When I hurried between the rows of carrels, there was no sign of Tara. The fashion magazine lay face-down on her desk.

But as I headed down the stairs, a cloud of jasmine perfume enveloped me. A hand grabbed mine, pressing a folded paper into my palm. I stared at Tara's back, her swaying hips and long red curls, as she moved quickly ahead of me and left the building.

Just before I arrived at my next class, I unfolded the scrap of paper. In pretty, rounded handwriting, it said:

Don't trust them.

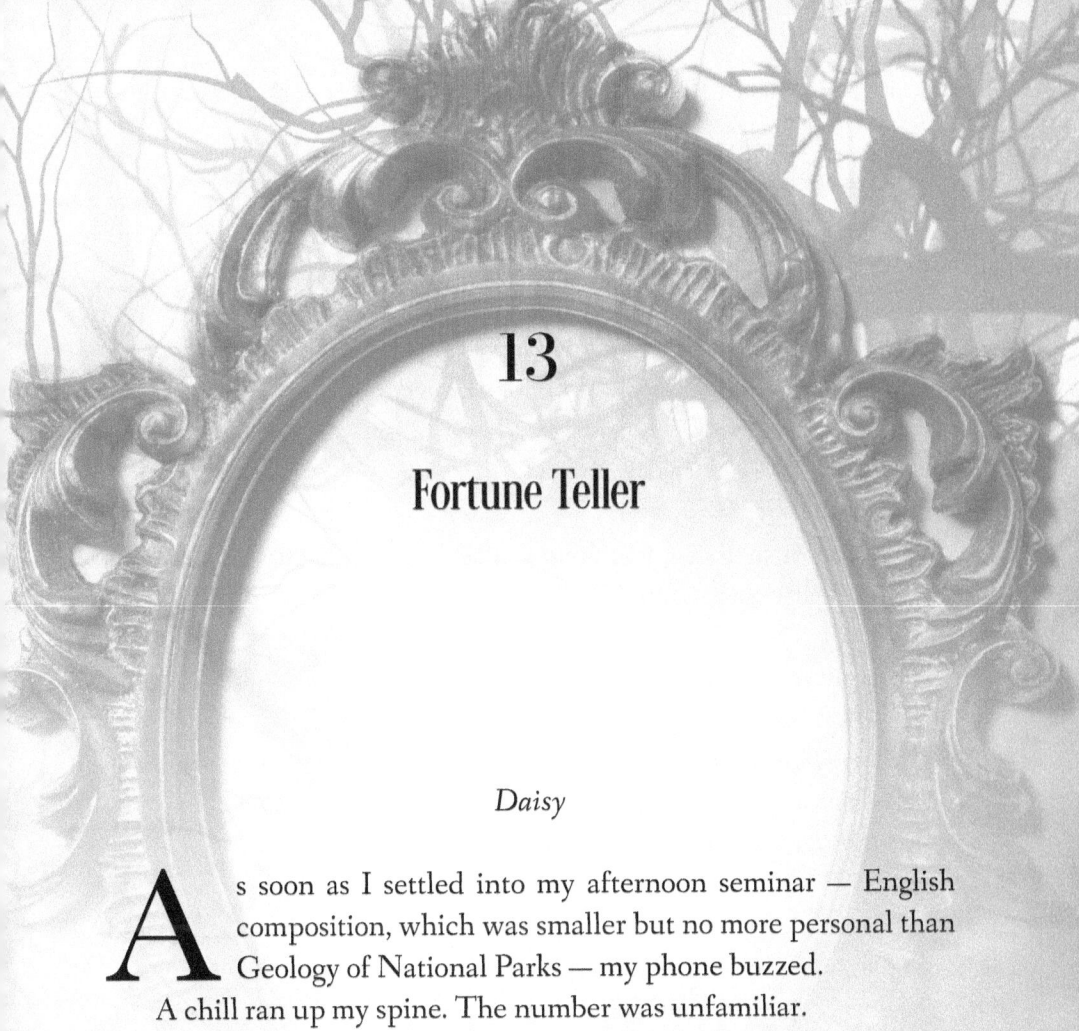

13

Fortune Teller

Daisy

As soon as I settled into my afternoon seminar — English composition, which was smaller but no more personal than Geology of National Parks — my phone buzzed.

A chill ran up my spine. The number was unfamiliar.

Come to Evan's concert with me.

Who is this?

This is Reeve.
I got your number from Blake.

I stared at my screen, my skin prickling all over. The professor saw my phone and gave me an irritated glance. I slid it under my book, but when it vibrated again, I couldn't help looking.

I'd like you to be my date.

The nerve. Did Reeve even consider that the answer might be no? Still, I added his name to my contacts. Cradling my phone in my lap, I typed one-handed.

How about starting with "Hi, Daisy. This is Reeve. Remember me? The guy who felt you up in front of a crowd and whisked you off to a tower? Did you get home okay after our very special evening together?"

No response. I kept checking while the class discussed judicious use of adjectives. Finally, I gave up and dropped the phone in my purse.

Ten minutes later, it buzzed. I jumped.

Hi, Daisy. This is Reeve. Remember me? The guy who felt you up in front of a crowd and whisked you off to a tower? Did you get home okay after our very special evening together?

I burst out laughing. The professor stopped mid-sentence and glared at me, while everyone turned to stare.

"Sorry." I waved my hands. "Just really taken by the humor in, uh, choosing the right adjectives."

The professor gave me a long-suffering look. I tried to focus on taking notes, but the next chance I had, I pulled my phone back out. I could picture Reeve's dimple as he sent my own words back to me.

Smart-ass. Did you copy and paste?

I believe in never working harder than necessary.

Oh, I think you're a hard worker. You must be very busy with your stocks
Too busy to bother finding me over the weekend

Find you? I had to recover first. You're exhausting, sweet flower.
I'm happy to talk about money, though.

Excuse me? We just met

And I just shorted silver to 20 dollars an ounce. Want to get in on it? I predict a huge turnaround.

I blinked. I wasn't sure what Reeve meant, but I understood the general idea. He was flexing the stock market, and the offer was surprisingly tempting. Now that my scholarship was gone, student loans hung over me like a dark cloud. I had savings from flute gigs and teaching music lessons, but they were bleeding away. Reeve obviously had a Midas touch when it came to money.

And King Midas's story did not go well.

I don't gamble

Neither do I.
Come to Evan's concert with me, Star.

Why should I?

Because I can't stop thinking about you.

Tell me more

There was no answer. Heat bloomed over my face. Feeling exposed and a little embarrassed, I shoved my phone in my purse and scribbled some notes. Skimming the chapter we were reading, I raised my hand to answer a question.

A series of buzzes from my purse, over and over, made me blush hotter. I forced myself to wait until the discussion shifted to take a peek at my phone.

I can't stop thinking about how brightly you glowed in my tower.
How soft your braid felt as I twisted it in my hand.
How hot and sweet you tasted.
How absolutely fucking soaked your cunt was, your cherry so tight as it met a man's fingers for the first time.
I've never felt anyone's heart beat so fast.

My head turned light. I bit my lip hard, catching the flesh between my teeth.

You're a star.
And I can't wait to see you go supernova.

The room went dim.

My hand was sweaty on the phone, my heart pounding. When my vision cleared and I could breathe again, I typed back.

How do you know that's going to happen?

Because I'm going to make it happen tomorrow night.
IF you've done what I said.
Have you, sweet girl? Have you kept your hands away from your hungry little pussy for me?

I couldn't breathe. Couldn't think.

Maybe. I'll let you wonder

If we play this game, Daze, understand that going against my wishes will cause you to be punished.

I dropped my phone in my lap. I was light-headed, dizzy, and hadn't heard a word of the lecture for the last five minutes. Finally, curiosity got the best of me.

PUNISHED??? How?

Denial. I'll make you plead for hours as I tease and torment your sweet body. You'll cling to the ghost of a chance that I might take pity and let you come. You'll beg for my kindness, my compassion, but you'll find they're in short supply.

Shit. My temperature soared sky-high. I tried not to rock in my seat.

That's all? Oh no, I'm so scared, Reeve

There was no reply. My face flamed as I tried to focus on the discussion. The girl next to me took pity when she saw me scrambling to find our place in the handout we were using, and silently showed me the page. She glanced at my phone with a knowing smile, and I wondered if it was obvious to the entire room that I was sexting.

When my phone finally buzzed, I felt the vibration between my legs. My whole body was tuned to the announcement of Reeve's thoughts.

*I might take a break from playing with your pussy to spank you.
You've never been spanked, have you, sweet girl? Maybe I'd tie you up
so you couldn't move...or display you in a window so all of Pacific
Crest could see you on the brink of orgasm. Your adorable pink nipples
pressed against the glass, your pussy so hot and juicy...Your gorgeous
face agonized as you beg for relief...*

*But I'm giving you the chance to be good.
Come to Evan's concert with me, Daze.
Good girls are rewarded, and I can be very nice when I want to be.*

I was wet, absolutely soaked, my panties clinging to my pussy. I crossed my legs for fear that a damp spot would show on my cutoffs.

I didn't have to agree to any of this. The concert, the deal, the threats of punishment, Reeve toying with me like a mouse in the jaws of a snake.

But I couldn't be scared forever. Couldn't hide from music all my life.

I couldn't walk away from the men and leave Nathan.

Staring at the dark pleasures Reeve described, I didn't want to.

Okay. I'll play. I'd love to go to Evan's concert with you

Excellent. I'll pick you up tomorrow at seven.
Afterward, I'll take you to the House. And you'll get exactly what you deserve.

When class ended, I stayed behind.

My thighs were shaking, my panties soaked. I couldn't go out into the hall like this. I needed time to recover.

At the back of the classroom, a door beckoned. Inside was a drab, beige utility closet housing a projector and a metal cart. I slipped into the closet and locked the door.

It wasn't just Reeve's words that had me keyed-up and ready to snap. I hadn't gone to a concert since my fall, and the invitation would have been stressful enough without Evan being involved.

I'd tried once before I left New York, slipping into a free noontime concert in a church. In the back pew, I ached all over as a string trio lost themselves to the beauty of Schubert. They swayed to the music, transported to a place I could only dream about now.

It was a gorgeous piece, but all I felt was bitter envy. It twisted and writhed in my stomach, replacing beauty with ugliness.

I'd ended up stumbling out to the street, where I emptied all my cash into the violin case of a busker on the corner and bawled at her to appreciate every moment of her music while she had it.

Not an experience I wanted to repeat.

I pressed the heels of my hands to my temples. Seeking guidance, I pulled the five tarot cards from my purse that I'd dealt earlier, shuffling so that the images flashed before my eyes.

The Knight, the Ace, the Beast, the Devil, the Star...

I stopped on the Devil.

The longer I looked at the card, the hotter I got. When I pictured Reeve shrugging off his elegant suit to reveal a ravenous demon underneath, I felt faint.

Desperately excited, I unbuttoned my cutoffs and slipped my hand inside.

"You want to play games?" I mocked. "You think you own me? You don't."

Fingers trapped in my panties, I stared at the naked couple in the Devil's thrall. Collars on chains circled their necks. When I thought of Reeve doing that — collaring me, leashing me for his whim — when I thought of Blake and Evan doing the same, then offering me to Nathan, who couldn't resist me chained for his pleasure — I almost came on the spot.

"Jesus," I groaned. "What are you all doing to me?"

I pressed the Devil card against the seam of my shorts, teasing my clit with the tip of one finger, until I couldn't stand it anymore.

Impulsively, I shoved the Devil in the waistband of my panties and reached for the other cards. Crouching on the linoleum, I placed the Beast before my face, the Ace below my breasts, and the Knight between my knees.

Unbidden, I felt a tongue flickering over my cunt, hot and thick and soft. When it flattened against my clit, my body tightened like an over-tuned string.

"Please," I whimpered. Feverishly, I worked my hand back into my shorts.

Knowing that I was going against Reeve's wishes, that I was

defying him — it heightened every stroke, magnified every moan. I circled my clit, sliding a finger into my pussy, and shivered at the delicious way it hugged the intruder. I could guess how snug I must have felt around Reeve as he curled two big fingers inside me.

"Can you feel this, Reeve?" I taunted. "Do you wish it were you?"

Hands caught my hips. Beneath me, the Devil was naked and sleek, his eyes a starless sky.

It felt so real when he pierced me, though I knew it was only my fantasy. I gasped when he drove his cock upward, looking into the Beast's arrogant smirk. He caught my braid as the hot, smooth head of his cock brushed my lips.

Beside me, the Ace offered soothing words, promising that I could handle everything the men gave me. His hands cupped my breasts, caressing them in sensual circles as I opened my mouth to taste the Beast's cock.

A slap on my ass shook my body. The Knight was behind me, spanking me while I rode the Devil. Shocked, I stifled a cry, craving his aggressive smacks as his friends stroked and fucked me.

"I'm sorry you weren't my first," I gasped to the Knight, pulling free of the Beast's cock. "But you can be my second, as soon as the Devil comes inside me—"

My pleas were cut short by a blunt, lubed head pressing against my sensitive back hole.

"Do you really want me to wait, little slut?" the Knight growled. "After waiting so many years for you?"

I gasped at the raw hunger in his voice. "Don't wait."

I threw my head back, sucking hard on the Beast, as the first man I'd ever loved began to slide his cock into my ass. He rubbed my clit firmly, and I was so close, about to come for all of them—

No, Star, said Reeve's dark, silky voice.

I whipped my hand away, empty and alone. My pussy ached for release. Just one more touch—

Don't you dare. His tone turned rough, making me moan. I collapsed on top of the tarot spread, hugging my knees to my chest.

"Please," I begged. My limbs felt like jelly, and my left hand ached. I'd used to it touch myself while I propped my weight on my right.

Oh, you'll be pleading a lot more than that tomorrow night. Dirty girls like you don't have a right to come.

I growled in protest. This was all my imagination, my fantasy. I was the one conjuring up Reeve's voice. I was in control...right?

So why couldn't I bring myself to finish?

My thighs quaked at his cruel words. I wanted to find out exactly what he'd do if he learned I'd disobeyed him.

A door banged in the outer classroom.

Scooping up the cards, I jumped to my feet, heart pounding in the safety of the utility closet. I zipped up my cutoffs and made sure the door was locked.

"Can you believe the plans for the new parking garage were canceled?" groused a male voice. He sounded middle-aged, probably a professor. "We don't have any space for the overflow. Parking's a mess here."

"I believe anything these days," replied a woman, her voice muffled. I pressed my ear to the door. "From what I hear, Weston was paid off by McClellan."

I tensed, straining to hear more. They had to be talking about Reeve. And Weston? That must be the school chancellor. He'd addressed the new students at orientation last week.

You've made an excellent choice in Pacific Crest, a school that owes its heritage to the very land it's built on.

"McClellan, our own golden boy," the man chortled. "He must value higher education — he's certainly donated enough. Obviously, he doesn't care about parking for the plebeians, though. You really think he bribed Weston to cancel the garage?"

"Oh, it'll be built." The woman crossed the classroom, high heels clicking. "Just not under Greer Hill."

I waited for more. Instead, the closet doorknob rattled, and I dropped the tarot cards in my purse. The utility closet smelled like... pussy. My pussy. My cheeks turned hot with embarrassment, and a trickle of sweat ran down my neck.

"Locked, for Chrissake," said the man. "Got a key?"

"Try these," said the woman. I stiffened as various keys scraped the doorknob.

In the distance, the classroom door creaked open. Laughter and conversation filled the room — students coming in.

"Forget it. I'll go hunt down my key ring." The man's voice faded as he walked away.

Warily, I cracked open the door. People milled around in pre-class chaos as I slipped out of the closet and down the aisle. To my relief, no one paid attention.

In the hall, I stopped a girl to ask, "How do you get to Greer Hill from here?"

Caution edged her voice as she gave me directions. "It's fine now, but don't go after dark."

"Why, is it haunted?" I laughed.

"There are stories. Just don't try." She hurried off before I could ask.

Outside, I slowed in the sunshine. The hill would still be there in a few hours. I had homework, and I wasn't used to a university curriculum. Give me a difficult orchestral excerpt to master, and I was golden — or had been; give me a paper to write, and I floundered. And I wanted to do more research on the ouroboros, maybe the history of Pacific Crest, before I made my way over there.

Plus, I urgently needed to shower.

Late in the afternoon, after my research had once again turned up nothing, I set out for Greer Hill.

I'd considered texting Blake, but decided against it. For now.

As I approached the edge of campus, where the road dead-ended into a grassy slope, the ground sent out a current of energy. I'd hoped for this, even expected it, with all the talk of the hill being haunted. Locations held sacred power; I'd always believed that. Certain areas were favorable for casting spells.

In New York, I'd had my places. A hidden nook in Central Park. The sixth practice room on the right, second floor, of the main music building at Sidero. The northwest corner of the rooftop of my mom's apartment building, where mint and geraniums grew.

In LA, I'd had them too.

Magic was all about favorable conditions, intentions, intuitions — clearing the way for what already existed and just needed to bubble to the surface. Finding a place with strong energy was key.

Rising above the curving road, Greer Hill was green and lush, its slopes cut through by hiking trails. Students dotted the hillside, studying and relaxing on colorful blankets. California poppies held up cups of gold to the sun, and a breeze set the leaves rustling in a grove of eucalyptus.

Nothing about the scene seemed spooky or haunted. Laughter, conversation, and the strums of a guitar filled the air.

Above the open slope, the hill was partially forested. The densely woven branches seemed to beckon: *Come closer.*

As I climbed the snaking path, gravel crunched under my soles. My tote bag swung from my shoulder, filled with supplies for shoring up Sasha's success spell. If there was a favorable spot on Greer Hill, I hoped to take advantage.

When I reached the forested area, the woods were very quiet. I breathed in the fresh, clean scent of leaves and dirt, alone among the lacy greenery. The noise and bustle of campus life was left behind.

As much as I missed the urban grit of Manhattan, this natural beauty was intoxicating.

I didn't see any signs of humans in these woods. Undergrowth quickly swallowed the path I'd followed, and overarching branches obscured the sky.

The quiet was absolute. I didn't even hear birdsong.

Walking deeper into the woods, I stepped into a clearing and gasped. It was perfect. There was just enough space to set up a circle, and everything about this enclosed, forested spot said *You belong here.*

Quickly, I knelt and took a votive candle in a glass jar from my bag. Striking a match, I lit the wick and set it in the center of the clearing.

As I placed sticks in a circle around the candle, I fixed my mind on success for Sasha. I visualized her host mom, Farida, welcoming her into the kitchen with open arms. Sasha had sent me a photo of her host family, so I could picture Farida's face. I imagined her taking Sasha under her wing, teaching her all the tricks and recipes in her repertoire.

The spell could only work if Farida was already inclined, even in the smallest way, to help Sasha. If she were adamant about barring Sasha from her kitchen, no spell could sway her.

Using sticks, I divided the circle into four quadrants. I placed a bundle of cinnamon sticks in the first quadrant for success, a bunch of thyme in the next for affection and reputation, dried chamomile in the third for luck, and peppermint leaves in the fourth for cleansing — a fresh start — and extra luck.

The candle burned bright in its jar, casting a glow over the circle and banishing the shadows.

I chanted the words of my favorite wish spell three times, gazing into the flickering flame. Holding a scrap of paper with my hope for Sasha written on it, I dropped it into the votive jar and let it burn.

She needs this, I thought, trying to reach Farida. *Cooking and food are everything to her. She acts bold and flippant, and I know she offended you, but she's sorry. And she needs the reassurance of being in a kitchen. It's warm, homey, reliable...nurturing...*

All qualities that Sasha and Nathan's parents could have provided a lot more of.

Suddenly I was angry at the Davises. They'd always prized independence, for themselves and their kids. On paper, it sounded great.

But they'd gone too far.

I forced my attention back to the spell. Muddy intentions didn't make good magic.

Help Sasha. Please.

The flame leapt up. The woods suddenly went still, without a stir or a crack. As if — something was listening.

Nothing moved, yet I felt surrounded.

Embraced.

Wanted.

The last word of the spell left my lips. The flame burned clear and steady.

Brushing dirt from my knees, I gathered up my supplies and blew out the candle. I offered a silent thanks to Reeve for preventing a parking garage under Greer Hill.

As I left the woods, a strange reluctance tightened my body. Branches seemed to reach for me. The leaves were like hands, refusing to let me go.

I turned to face the trees.

"I'll be back," I said. "I won't let anything happen to you."

And I swear, those branches relaxed. They *allowed* me to leave.

I hurried down the hill, kicking up gravel as the sky darkened.

14

Spooky Boys

Daisy

"Which one?" I held up a white chiffon blouse and a black corset-style top from the pile on my bed.

"Black. It's sexier," Michelle said.

Amy turned up the music on her phone. "I like the black too, but put something over it. Then you have options on dialing up the sexy."

I grabbed a black shawl from my closet, and Amy nodded her approval.

Combing out my wet hair, I twisted it into a complicated French braid that snaked sideways and hung over one shoulder. With each strand that I braided, I wove a black ribbon through it to signify protection, murmuring an intention under my breath to connect that protection to power.

I'd always been partial to hair magic, and tonight, I needed all the help I could get. Between making it through Evan's concert in one piece, investigating the men, and the "reward" that Reeve had promised me afterward, the evening was going to be a roller coaster.

I hooked up the corset, which lifted my breasts to provide a hint of actual cleavage, and stepped into a long, ruffled black skirt.

Michelle shook her head. "I can't believe you're going out with Reeve fucking McClellan."

I'd been nervous all day. Now my heartbeat rocketed. "That makes two of us."

"Three," Amy corrected.

"Thanks, Amy." Going to the mirror, I fumbled with the clasp of a black beaded choker. Taking a few deep breaths to calm down, I added dangly gold earrings and a layer of plum lipstick.

She spread her hands. "Hey, I'm just saying. He's rich as sin, doesn't date, and is always with his hot male friends. The only time I've seen him with a girl, it's been this redhead, and they don't even seem into each other."

"Good." That had to be the girl who'd slipped me the note — Tara. Why would she warn me off, and what was her connection to the men? "I'm heading down. Wish me luck."

In the elevator, I checked my messages. This morning, I'd woken up to a whole series of photos from Sasha: a tagine, gorgeous and earthy; a bright, fresh carrot salad; a bowl filled with glistening green herbal sauce.

Farida invited me into her kitchen! It's so damn good to get my hands in food again and she's a master. She's been so welcoming... Daisy, we fucking did it! You shored up my spell, didn't you? You're back in the game.

When I exited Lee Tower, a new text popped up from Reeve.

We're around in back, sweet flower.

We? My stomach fluttered. I had assumed he'd be alone.

Behind the tower, a beautiful car waited at the curb. Its dove-gray curves gleamed, as if no speck of dust would dare cloud them.

The two men leaning against it were even more beautiful. I paused to take in the sight of Blake and Reeve together. Their tuxes fitted their bodies like they were tailor-made — Blake, lean and angular, and Reeve, sleek and powerful. The slanting evening sunlight cast a California glow over Blake's golden-brown curls and Reeve's tousled hair, dark as a crow's wing.

They conversed in low tones, their body language showing an easy familiarity.

It gave me butterflies to see the two of them, but it also irritated me that Reeve hadn't bothered to mention Blake would be joining us.

I cleared my throat as I approached. "I hope I'm not interrupting anything."

"Not at all." Blake straightened up, his smile bright, and looked me over appreciatively. "You're the best thing that's happened to us all day. All year, in fact."

Reeve pulled me close with one casual arm, calm and in control. My body surged toward his like a magnet. "You look stunning, Daze."

His beautiful face leaned in, his gaze intent. When my lips parted, his mouth covered mine.

For a second, I was spinning, tasting him, his lips and tongue, his metallic heat. Then my gaze flicked to Blake. To be kissed in front of him, while he stood so close... As Reeve's hands slid over my cheeks to cradle my face, Blake flashed me a dazzling grin.

I shivered in the evening air. I couldn't believe that this was happening, that the party hadn't been a fluke, a dream.

Reeve deepened the kiss. I responded eagerly, my irritation forgotten, sharply aware of Blake watching us. But when I dared to stroke Reeve's chest, a firm grip on my right wrist stopped me.

"No touching, sweet girl."

The command excited me, but it also woke me up. Stepping back, I looked from Reeve to Blake as voices and laughter drifted around the corner.

"Shouldn't we get going?" I said quickly.

"There's no rush." Reeve smiled at me. "We have plenty of time. Unless you're eager to get there early?"

I bit my lip. "It's been a while since I went to a concert. It didn't go so well last time."

"You can tell us." Blake put a reassuring hand on my back.

"Go ahead," Reeve said calmly. "We're listening."

My eyes moved over Blake's loose curls and keen blue eyes, then Reeve's wavy black hair, his set jaw and sensuous lips. They were both standing close enough that their woodsy, mossy scent wafted over me, drugging my senses.

They smelled the same. I wondered if they shared cologne, or shampoo, or... Fuck, they smelled good.

Haltingly, I spilled the whole story of the church concert in New York, falling apart, dumping the contents of my wallet into a violinist's case while I ugly cried.

"I understand, Daze. It was too soon." Reeve's deep voice was surprisingly sympathetic as he cupped my shoulder.

God, his skin was hot. It sent a shudder through me and started my thighs shaking.

"So you see why I can't..." I trailed off.

"Are you going to hide from those feelings forever?" Reeve asked.

"Not forever, but — I don't know if I'm ready."

Reeve's thumb rubbed my shoulder, meeting the crease of my neck. When Blake stroked my cheek, I shivered.

"Evan's concert will be different," Reeve promised.

"How can you be so sure?"

"Because he's one-of-a-kind, and we'll be at your side."

"If you try to give Ev all your money or promise him your firstborn child," Blake added, "we'll hold you back."

"Very funny," I managed, but a smile broke through.

"I promise it'll be worth it, Daze," Reeve said. "You have our word."

"I'm nervous," I blurted. "He's intensely talented, and I'm jealous."

"We know." Blake traced the shell of my ear. "We can stay here as long as you need."

He inclined his head, his lips close to mine. When I glanced at Reeve, he just smiled.

I didn't know what to do with all this attention. They were both seducing me; on some level I knew that, but why?

My chest rose and fell as I panted for breath. "I — I think we should get in the car."

Reeve's lips brushed my ear. "As you wish...naughty girl."

Heat bloomed on my skin. Did he know I'd disobeyed the rules of our game?

Smoothly, he guided me to the passenger side and opened the door. An enormous bouquet of roses lay on the seat. The lush petals were a deep blackened red, the color of blood at midnight.

Reeve handed them to me. "For you."

For a minute, I couldn't speak. What finally came out of my mouth, absurdly, was "But I'm not performing tonight."

Blake laughed. "We don't expect you to. We already know how talented you are."

I blinked, cradling the roses.

Reeve's dimple flickered, and he rested a hand on my knee. "I did my homework, Daisy *DiCosmo*. You told me how much music meant to you, but we didn't know how much you meant to music."

I closed my eyes. So they'd looked me up — the competitions, awards, scholarships, and interviews. They'd probably watched videos of me playing.

"I shouldn't have expected anything less," he went on. "You're extraordinary."

Blake echoed his agreement from the backseat.

Why did they care? Why were they stirring up the past? Was there something wrong with me, that I suddenly wished I could play for them both?

I opened my eyes. "I'm impressed, but you didn't dig deep enough. You just found my stage name. Not that I ever needed one."

"Star of the cosmos." Reeve squeezed my knee. "How appropriate. Who chose it?"

"My mom." I smiled a little, thinking of her. "DiCosmo's her last name. She kept it when she married my dad, and she liked the idea of me using it. She's a dancer, but she put that on hold when I — never mind."

"Fair enough, Daisy Fisher. By the way, congratulations on your dad's latest release. *The Last Quake?* Looks gripping."

I groaned. "Fine. You really did find me. You win a prize; what do you want?"

Blake chuckled from the backseat. "I think we all know what Reeve wants."

I buried my face in the roses, inhaling their heady sweetness, to hide the sudden flash of fear. Was I making a mistake, sitting in this car with these men?

Cheeks burning, I tried to steer the subject away. "I went for a walk yesterday. It's fun to explore campus, wander around... Greer Hill is so pretty. Beautiful place for a picnic," I continued brightly. "Everyone seemed so happy in the sunshine."

The two men exchanged glances.

"It's a fantastic picnic spot," Blake assented. "Though, like I said, it's better at night. My offer still stands."

"Maybe I'll take you up on it," I said, hedging. "I'm just glad it won't be turned into a parking garage."

"Was it going to?" Reeve asked pleasantly. "That would have been a shame."

I eyed him. "I heard you had something to do with that."

Reeve just laughed. "People say all kinds of things, Star. My name's been linked to more projects and donations than I care to say."

Damn, he was slippery. "The strange thing was, no one was going past a certain point on the hill, so I had the woods all to myself. And now, since you may or may not have paid off Chancellor Weston—" I aimed a look at Reeve — "I can go back to those woods whenever I want."

Both men stiffened as if a shock ran through them.

"Funny, sweet flower," Reeve said coolly. "I like your sense of humor."

"Excuse me?"

"No one goes in the woods," Blake explained. "There are stories... rumors...it's just not done."

"I did," I chirped, pleased to see them squirm. "It's peaceful. There's a lovely clearing there surrounded by magical moss-covered logs. Five birches in a circle, a foxhole below... I almost expected to see Bambi prance by."

There was dead silence in the car. Reeve braked sharply as we approached a broad building that towered above us, all curving glass and concrete. People in suits and cocktail dresses milled on the steps, circling the fountain that splashed around an abstract metal sculpture.

Crowne Hall, announced the marquee. *Evan Hayes with the Pacific Crest Symphony.*

When Reeve spoke, his voice was very soft. "If you've been in those woods, Daze, I wouldn't advertise it. That information stays in this car."

I shuddered. "Are you *threatening* me?"

"We're advising you," Blake said reassuringly. "We care deeply about your well-being."

I flicked my braid over my shoulder. "So do I, which is why I plan to go back. Hanging out in the woods is healthy, right? Forest-bathing? And I'm especially curious about going at night. Blake, you were the one who said people feel a presence there. If you have any ghost stories, I'm all ears."

"Not alone," Reeve said swiftly. "Blake, take her to the hill some night this week if she's so curious. You should have a guide, Daze."

"My pleasure," Blake said. "Tomorrow at midnight? I'll be at the restaurant until eleven."

I stared from one to the other. Their faces were bland and

composed, giving nothing away. Were they looking out for me, keeping tabs on me...or something more sinister?

I smiled brightly. "I can't wait."

Pulling into a red-velvet-roped area, Reeve parked at the valet stand and escorted me out. I took his arm, then Blake's. Walking between the men, I turned to watch Reeve's sleek car as the valet drove it away, my roses still on the front seat.

15

My Oh My

Daisy

In the lobby of Crowne Hall, laughter and conversation came from every corner. College students were mixed in with the older patrons — a young crowd for a classical concert.

In my strappy black sandals, my height matched Reeve's and came close to Blake's. Heads turned as we crossed the crimson carpet.

"Everyone's looking at us," I said under my breath.

Blake grinned, his eyes traveling the length of my body. "That's because we look good together. Enjoy it."

For a moment, I saw us from the outside: Reeve's tousled dark hair, his perfectly trimmed stubble and sleek tux. My long blonde braid draped over my shoulder, my clothes and lipstick dark against my skin. Blake's loose curls, his pronounced cheekbones and easy stride in his formal clothes.

I laughed. "We look like a perfume ad."

"Is that a bad thing?" Reeve's lips quirked.

We reached the usher guarding the door to the auditorium, and Reeve held out three tickets for him to scan.

Through the doorway, the concert hall sloped downward. Red-and-gold carpeted aisles separated rows of plush seats. Orchestra members were taking their places on the brightly lit stage. Overhead, chandeliers sparkled against a field of constellations on heavenly blue.

As I stared up at the painted stars, I stopped short.

A sudden lump constricted my throat. My heart beat too fast. I couldn't breathe. My chest was tight, about to explode.

Panicked, I clutched Reeve's arm, unable to speak.

"Excuse us," Reeve said to Blake and the usher.

Swiftly, he led me around a corner and down a long hallway. Pulling me into a secluded area, he held my arms firmly. I stared into the lightless pools of his eyes.

"Be here with me," he said. "Breathe with me, Daisy."

I grasped his forearms and struggled to breathe.

"In...out." His jacket was so dark, swallowing light like his eyes. "In...and out." The fine fabric rumpled in my grasp. "In with me again...and out."

I gulped a shuddering breath. My voice came out ragged, barely audible. "I'm scared."

"I know."

"I'm ruining our date."

"How are you ruining it?" There was no sign of teasing on his face.

"I'm freaking out! I probably embarrassed you in front of everyone."

His voice rasped like claws on velvet. "Do you think I care about that bullshit? No, I do not."

"I'm just cursed, that's all. The tower was too good to be true."

A faint smile flickered across his face. "I tasted your soul, Star. *That* was too good to be true."

I stared at him. How could he say these things with a straight face? With so much conviction?

His thumb rubbed over my lips. "What are you afraid will happen if you go into the concert hall?"

"My own personal hell," I muttered. "I'll be consumed by envy. A beast, swallowing me whole."

"What if you swallow the beast instead?"

The Strength card flashed in front of my eyes, woman and beast twined together, and my hands tightened on Reeve's shoulders.

"Contain it," he murmured. "Master it. Let it live within you."

I looked away. "Envy's not meant to be tamed."

"I didn't say anything about taming it." His voice was the rich, dark velvet of the roses he'd given me. "And let's find a more appealing word than 'envy,' shall we? How about...desire."

Slowly, I met his eyes. "How about it?"

"Is desire so wrong? Would there be ambition without it? Achievement? Would anyone accomplish anything at all?"

"When you put it that way...no."

He stroked the outline of my jaw, trailing down my neck to caress my throat. "I'm going to bring you home tonight," he said softly. "And I'm going to lead you along the edge of desire until you can't remember your own name. I just need to know: Do you want to hear Evan play?"

"Reeve..." My hands moved to his shoulders.

"I didn't tell you just how beautiful you look tonight. I was remiss, Daze." He tugged lightly on my choker. One hand slid over my corset to squeeze my waist.

"Reeve, please." Instinctively, I leaned into his grasp.

"Tell me what you want."

I took a deep breath. "I want to go in."

Reeve swept me down the hall. "This way. It's less crowded."

We climbed a flight of carpeted stairs. At the balcony door, he showed our tickets to the upstairs usher.

"Ready?" His dimple showed, but his arm tightened protectively around me.

No one had ever been protective of me before.

"All right." I took a deep breath and accepted a program from the usher.

The brightly lit stage, the mingled scents of perfume and wood, the red velvet chairs, the sounds of the orchestra tuning — anxiety surged, but the scene also made me shiver with excitement.

We walked to the balcony's edge, and I ran my hand over the smooth, cool railing.

"So many memories." I bit my lip. "It's like an avalanche. I'm not ready for them to just be memories."

"What if I told you they don't have to be?" Coal-black eyes moved over my face. In their depths, there was the yawning abyss from my dream. And there was fire.

I shook myself. I was sleep-deprived; I must be seeing things.

Taking my arm, Reeve led me down a short flight of steps, out of the balcony seating, and through a set of heavy red curtains.

We entered a gilded box that overlooked the orchestra. We were sitting stage left, which meant we'd get to see Evan from above and behind — see his hands on the keys.

Blake lounged in one of the chairs, the house lights winking off the silver hoops in his ears. Nathan took up most of the remaining space, huge in his black tux, his hands resting on his spread knees. They were laughing and talking animatedly. It was the happiest I'd seen Nathan since he'd changed, and I felt a pang at his smile.

Before I could say anything, their heads turned. Blake grinned broadly at the sight of us, but Nathan's face darkened to a thundercloud.

He rose to his feet. "You can't be fucking serious. Bringing her here..."

"I came here myself," I snapped. "You can talk to me; I'm standing in front of you."

Nathan's eyes met mine, smoking with anger. "I warned you."

"But you never explained. Why should I listen?" I glanced from Blake to Reeve, who both looked unperturbed.

"Can you really handle being here, Daisy?" Nathan muttered. "Last week, you tried to touch your flute. You were a mess."

I stiffened. "I never told you that. How'd you know?"

Blake shifted uneasily, and Reeve folded his arms, his face implacable.

Nathan's eyes darted. He opened and closed his fists, a vein beating in his forehead. "What else could you possibly be upset over? What would you give a damn about, besides your music? You've never cared for anything else."

I swallowed hard. "Jesus, Nathan. You make me sound like I'm not human. Like I don't care about the people I love, or — or —" I turned away, my eyes stinging.

"That's enough, Nate." Reeve took my arm, his voice quiet and cold.

A dull red crept over Nathan's cheeks. "Don't say I didn't warn you."

He strode out of the box. I sank into the chair he'd just vacated, which was still warm.

Blake put his arm around me. "Trust me. Nate will come around."

"Will he?" I muttered.

"I guarantee it." He tickled my arm, trying to coax a smile to my face. "He's just moody right now. Don't take it personally."

I lifted my head as Blake walked his fingers up the inside of my arm. He stroked the crease of my elbow until I squirmed in my seat.

"Is it steroids?" I asked, determined to focus. "Has he been sleep-walking? Talking in his sleep, maybe?"

"No steroids, Daze," Reeve assured me. He didn't seem at all bothered by Blake's hand sliding around to rub my neck. "I wouldn't allow it."

I shuddered at Blake's touch. Reeve's obsidian eyes, moving over the two of us with a strange satisfaction, unsettled me even more.

But I didn't want it to stop. Any of it. When Blake gently squeezed the sides of my neck, my head went light.

"Are you in charge of everything that goes on in the House?" I asked Reeve.

"Absolutely."

"If I come home with you tonight, will you be in charge of me?"

"You bet he will." Blake chuckled, caressing my throat. It was such an intimate touch that my breath caught.

We were in public. Exposed in this box. When my head jerked toward the orchestra seating below, stares and whispers rippled through the crowd.

Reeve's lips brushed my right ear. "Does it excite you, Daze, to be the object of so much attention?"

It did. But I wasn't ready to say so. My eyes darted to the gilded rim of the box, where four champagne glasses sat, fizzing and sparkling.

"We can have those here?" I asked hastily. "In the concert hall?"

"In the nice seats, yes," Blake said matter-of-factly.

When I chose a glass, Reeve took it from my hand and put it to my lips.

"Allow me," he said softly. "Cheers."

My face burned. But I tipped my head back and let him feed me a sip of champagne.

The cold liquid fizzed on my tongue, and a drop ran down my chin. As Reeve and Blake hemmed me in, heat rushed over my body.

"You know what I'd do with a whole bottle of this?" Reeve asked. "And you?"

My chest rose and fell. "Why don't you show me?"

Reeve's smile gleamed. I glanced at Blake, and his bright blue eyes flickered over me.

"So impatient." Reeve angled my glass above my chest. The crystal hovered in midair, a single drop suspended on the rim. "I thought you knew how to wait."

"I've been very patient." I couldn't look away from that golden drop.

"Oh? You've done everything I said? You've been a good, obedient girl?"

He tipped the glass. The bead of champagne hung suspended from the edge, then fell.

Icy cold, it trickled between my breasts.

I swallowed. "I've tried."

"I hope so," Reeve murmured. "Because good things come to those who wait."

Another drop of champagne splashed my breast. My nipples tightened, and my eyes darted from Reeve to Blake and back.

"Tell me more about these good things."

I shuddered when a third drop of champagne hit my skin. Blake cocked his head as the chilled liquid left a trail. He glanced at Reeve, who gave him a slight nod.

"Patience is a virtue, Daisy." Crouching slightly, Blake kept his eyes on mine. I stared at him as his face came toward my chest in slow motion. He was giving me enough time to move away if I chose.

I didn't.

My chest rose and fell until his lips gently nuzzled the spot right above the hint of cleavage that my corset displayed. Instinctively, I arched toward him.

Reeve's hands tightened on my waist as Blake's tongue darted out. I gasped when wet heat grazed my skin. His mouth was practically on my breasts, and anyone could see us up here in the box, and — oh fuck, that was a tongue piercing, sexy as hell, the metal barbell teasing my chest as he licked up the sticky drops.

Blake pulled away and gave me a wink. "You're delicious. Much better than the champagne."

I didn't dare look beyond him to the concert hall below. My heart was about to thump through my chest. The thought of others watching us was both thrilling and terrifying.

Reeve lifted the champagne glass, his hand on my waist keeping me upright. "If you're virtuous, Star, you'll reap your reward."

He pressed the glass to my breast, and I gasped again. Like a butterfly wing, it brushed my nipple through the corset.

"What reward is that?" I breathed.

Reeve quirked a dark eyebrow. "You'll see."

I flushed hot, looking from him to Blake, who simply smiled.

The house lights dimmed, and the sound of the orchestra tuning distracted me. I'd always loved that sound, so full of expectation and promise. A hundred instruments, preparing to play as one.

I tensed. Instinctively, I reached for Reeve's knee.

His hand engulfed mine. "It's all right," he said quietly. "I'm here."

When the overture began, I gripped his hand and closed my eyes. Each note was like a knife dipped in honey — everything I'd had and lost.

I didn't realize I'd reached out to the left until a second hand covered mine — gently, without putting pressure on my wrist. Blake's skin was as hot as Reeve's, but his fingertips were calloused, and his thick silver ring pressed against my knuckles.

My eyes popped open, and I glanced at him sidelong. He flashed that smile at me, brilliant even in the dark, and rubbed his thumb over the back of my hand.

Crossing my legs, I tried to breathe as both my hands were clasped. When the music swelled, each note emphasized the distinctions between the two men's fingers, their palms, the way they held me.

The applause came before I was ready for the piece to be over. None of us spoke or moved. Blake and Reeve didn't free their hands to clap, and neither did I.

Normally, Evan would perform after the overture. That was standard concert order: an opening piece, a concerto with a soloist, and a symphony to end the program. But he must have been closing out the program, because the orchestra went straight into Tchaikovsky's Fifth Symphony. I'd played this piece with a youth symphony in high school, and the memories were sweet and stinging all at once.

At intermission, ushers hovered nervously in the aisles while the audience milled. The air hummed with anticipation. As I chatted with Reeve and Blake, without any idea of what we actually said, heads turned to check us out in the box.

Unconcerned, Reeve stroked my wrist with his thumb, while Blake drew slow circles on my palm. I was covered with goosebumps, aware of every brush of my shawl and the tight fit of my corset.

Freeing my hands from Blake's and Reeve's, I stood up.

"I'm going to the ladies' room," I said quickly. "Be back soon."

I hurried out of the box to the elegant restrooms on the upper floor. In the ladies' room, I splashed cold water on my face.

I was alone.

I was wet.

Not just the water dripping down my cheeks, but the hot, insistent throbbing between my legs.

I couldn't forget how Reeve and Blake had teased me, deliberate and purposeful. I was desperate for their touch. Horny as fuck. Even though a little voice reminded me I'd only known them a few days.

I ran my hands over my body and pinched my nipples through my corset, seeking relief. They were tight and needy, and when I thought about Reeve's mouth on them...or Blake's, or — oh God, both of them together...

What would that be like? I couldn't believe two men had held my hands at once, the touch simple yet charged with sex. Or that I'd allowed Blake to kiss my chest — in full view of a concert hall — while Reeve looked on with satisfaction.

How far would we go tonight? How far did I want to go?

The bathroom door flew open. I dropped my hands, reaching into my purse to squeeze the pack of tarot cards.

In stalked Tara, her high heels clicking.

Up close, she was even more striking. Coppery curls spilled over her freckled shoulders, framing her heart-shaped face and huge blue eyes, and her strapless white dress molded to her lush curves.

I tried not to be too obvious about checking her out. She leaned toward the mirror, displaying a deep valley of freckled cleavage, and made a show of touching up her foundation while we looked at each other sidelong.

"I saw you in the box with Reeve and Blake," she announced. "You looked really cute between them."

"Cute," I repeated, thrown off by her comment, considering the note she'd slipped me.

She sprayed her neck with perfume, filling the air with a cloud of jasmine scent. "Did I say cute? I meant scared."

I raised my eyebrows. "I'm not."

She offered me the bottle of perfume, and I shook my head. "I don't know what game they're playing," she said cheerily, "but you need to understand that I've known these boys since the beginning."

"Of what?"

"College." She rolled her eyes. "You're a little out of your depth, aren't you? I doubt they bothered to inform you that *I'm* the girl in their group. They have a way of not telling people things."

"Well, I know that you're Tara." She didn't need to know how I knew that already.

The curve of her lips was an invitation, a challenge. "And you're Daisy. I know. I've asked about you."

Jesus, was everyone here investigating me? I'd expected to be a nobody at Pacific Crest.

I took my lipstick out of my purse and removed the cap. "I'm sure there's room for more than one girl. I mean, there are four of them."

She gave me a pitying look. "You'd think. But it doesn't work that way. You show up out of nowhere, and suddenly they're all over you. Do you think it'll last? You think you're the first woman they've ever love-bombed?"

"Why don't you tell me?" I touched up my plum lipstick. Studying my reflection in the mirror, I pointedly adjusted my cleavage in my corset. It was kind of an evil thing to do, and there wasn't much to adjust. But hell, I'd never been seen as sexual competition before. A twisted part of me was enjoying it.

"You don't need to do that." A knowing smile, almost a sneer, bent Tara's mouth. "Your tits already look great in that top."

"You think?" I asked, trying to play it cool.

"All you need is a little help."

Stepping behind me, she untied the bow at the base of my corset and gave the laces a sharp tug. I sucked in a breath as the fabric tightened. She redid the bow more slowly, taking her time. When her soft hands slid under my shawl to brush my shoulders, I stared at our reflections in the mirror.

Her crystal-blue eyes moved deliberately over my body as she touched the black ribbon woven through my braid. With her white dress and fiery cloud of hair, she looked like a dazzling angel; in my draped black clothes, I looked like a bat out of hell.

I dropped my lipstick in my purse and moved away. "Are you coming on to me?"

She faced me, her smoldering expression lingering, then stepped closer. "Would that be so bad?"

I shrugged, trying to act like this was nothing, but my throat was feeling drier by the second.

"It wouldn't," I said lightly, controlling my rapid breaths. "If I weren't cursed. People run away when I kiss them. Except Reeve. He's the only one I haven't scared off."

"Liar," Tara scoffed. "Reeve hasn't kissed you."

"As a matter of fact, he has." I tried to stay calm, but my mind whirled.

"Then he's toying with you. But I bet he hasn't let you go below the waist."

"What do you know about these men?" I pushed.

"You'll just have to find out. In the meantime, my advice is, play them, but don't trust them. Don't trust them a fucking inch. And while you're at it? Milk Reeve for all he's worth. Get him to drop cash on you, because that's all he's good for — money."

I shook my head quickly. "I don't want his money."

Tara laughed at my expression. "I almost believe you. You know what, Daisy? You think you're so frightening, but me? I wouldn't run away from you."

She raised an eyebrow, curling one corner of her full lips. Something dark and teasing coiled inside me, urging me to close the gap between us and taste that cherry red mouth.

What was going on here?

Our eyes locked.

"You're so fucking innocent." Tara tapped my cheek. "I can feel it. You have no idea what you're in for with those boys. You're like a deer in the woods, and they're going to see how long they can chase you."

I reached out to cup her coppery curls, her seductive energy tugging me closer. "What if I'm chasing them?"

"That I'd like to see." One jeweled nail traced the outline of my lips. She leaned in, but I turned my head away, and she laughed softly. "Cursed, huh?" She smudged my lipstick with the tip of her finger. "Hold still, you missed a corner."

The door to the bathroom opened.

"What are you doing, Daisy?" came Reeve's calm voice.

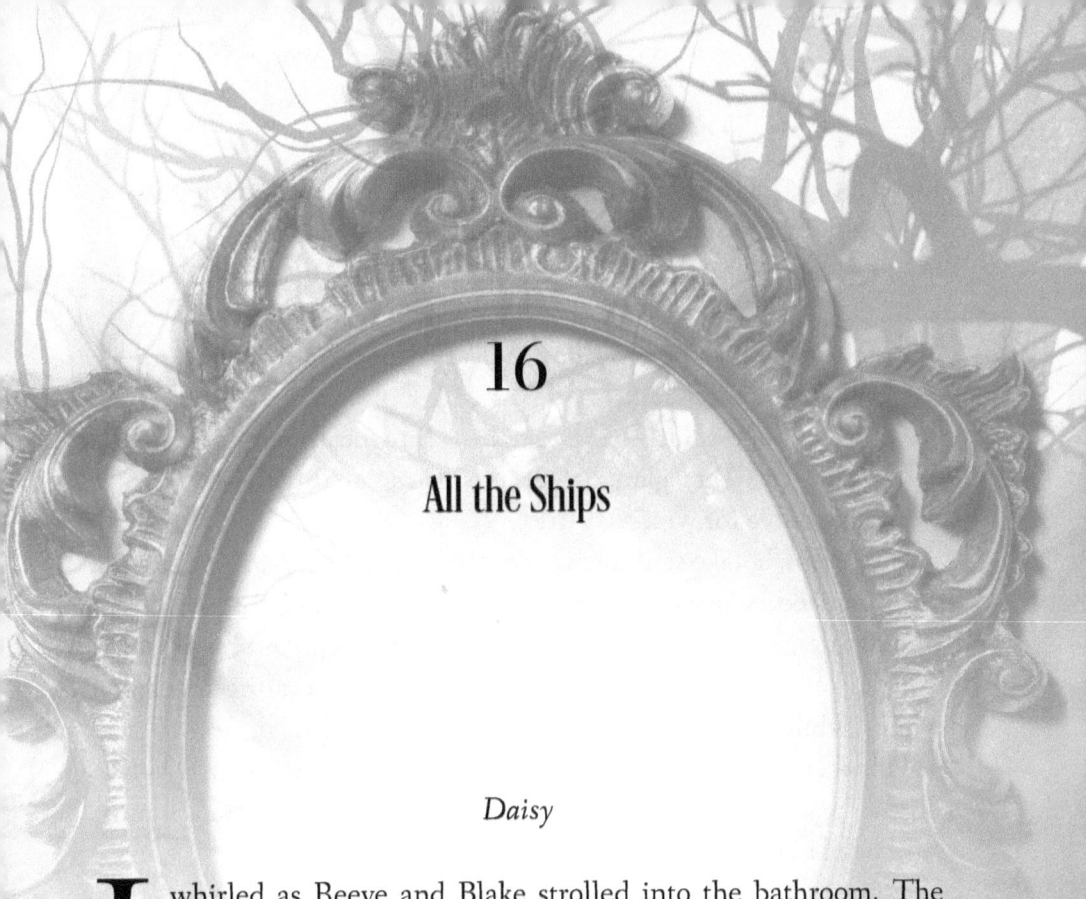

16

All the Ships

Daisy

I whirled as Reeve and Blake strolled into the bathroom. The door swung shut behind them.

"We're having a chat." My voice sounded strained.

Reeve moved between Tara and me, putting a possessive hand on my back. "I see I can't leave you alone for a second."

"Looks like our Star has a knack for trouble." Blake leaned against the sinks, whistling.

Tara stared at Reeve's arm around me in disbelief. "How far are you going to take this?"

Reeve finally turned his attention to her. "How nice that you two have met. You can go now, Tara."

"This is the girls' room," she sneered. "Get out of here."

"No one else will be coming in, because no one wants to leave the concert hall." Blake gave Tara a nod of dismissal.

"Right," she snapped. "No one can miss even one second of Evan's brilliant performance. What are you doing with this poor,

169

innocent girl? You should be ashamed of yourselves." Turning to me, she said, "They're only killing time with you."

"Leave Daisy alone," Reeve said quietly. "Don't lay a hand on her."

"So she's yours now? We have a deal." Tara looked furious.

"What deal?" I asked.

"It's not important," Reeve told me. "Tara means nothing."

"*Nothing?*" Tara glared. "Oh, you'll regret this. I can make a world of trouble for you."

"Careful," Blake said softly. "You really don't want to go there."

I blinked, wiping sweaty palms on my skirt, because Blake's friendly demeanor had turned quietly threatening. And his sky-blue eyes looked — different. Green sparks curled across the irises and whites, while the pupils narrowed and lengthened.

I looked quickly to Reeve, whose eyes were dark as always. When I turned back to Blake, his eyes were the pure blue I expected. It must have been a trick of the light.

"Get out." Reeve's voice was cold. "We're done here."

Tara stalked toward the door, her curls quivering. At the threshold, she turned on her heel.

"I'm giving you three days to take this back, because I'm a kind and forgiving person. Say the right things to me and we can forget this ever happened." She glared from Blake to Reeve, who both looked amused. To me, she suddenly smiled and blew a kiss. "Bye, Daisy. Don't let them get too fresh, now. Save second base for me, okay?"

She sashayed out of the bathroom, her hips swaying.

"What was that about?" I demanded. "Am I one of many?"

Both men looked confounded.

"Tara dropped hints," I explained shortly, though I realized she hadn't said anything definite. "She said, 'How many girls do you think they've love-bombed before this?'"

"*Love-bombed?*" Blake leaned his head against the wall, howling with laughter. "That's a good one."

Reeve chuckled, his dimple punctuating his cheek. "Zero, Daze. We have neither the time nor the inclination. You've got nothing to worry about."

"Look, I'm not saying that I — that we —" I shook my head, because there were no words to describe whatever it was that was happening with these men. No words to describe my dreams.

Reeve laid a finger on my lips. "To answer the questions you haven't asked, we've never touched Tara, and she has never been romantically entangled with any of us."

"Then how *is* she entangled? Because she obviously is. You have a deal together?"

Reeve's face shut down. The smile vanished, his eyes shuttered, and his beautiful features became a mask.

I glanced toward Blake, but he was equally silent, watching Reeve for cues.

"Never mind that," Reeve said, his expression smoothing out. "All you need to worry about right now is whether you've been a good girl for me. I believe those were the terms of this evening."

I breathed in sharply.

"I gave you one rule to follow," Reeve added. "Have you?"

These men clearly weren't going to say anything further about Tara. I'd have to track her down, ask more questions. I shuddered at what I might find out.

In the meantime, I'd learn what I could by playing along.

"I've been good, I promise." My voice dropped. A game, it was just a game.

Moving swiftly in front of me, Reeve cupped my face in his hands. "Really? Tara was about to kiss you when we came in. Would you have let her?"

"No." My hands came up to clutch his waist.

"I'm glad to hear it. You can have a lot more fun with us." His scent intoxicated me, calming my nerves, clouding my reason. He rubbed his thumb along my neck. "Blake, bring the champagne."

Blake's smile lit up the echoing bathroom as he carried the three champagne glasses to us.

"So we're going to make a toast in the ladies' room?" I breathed.

"You're the toast, Star." Reeve stroked my cheek, making my heart race. "This is for your future."

Heat stung my face. "I don't have one. Not the way I planned."

"Stick with us," Blake advised, setting the glasses down on the dryer beside us, "and you'll think differently."

"What are you talking about?"

"Do you want to be like us, Daisy? The Ace, the Beast, the Knight, the Devil — and the Star?" Blake was about to go on, but the words seemed to catch in his throat. Reeve gave him a slight shake of his head.

"What we're interested in finding out," Reeve said smoothly, "is how much of a star you are."

"None whatsoever," I began, but Reeve put his finger to my lips again.

"Never underestimate," he murmured. "Our first principle. Let's make you a toast, Star. Take your shawl off, because you might get wet."

My head swam. *Our first principle.* That meant they had others. Tenets that their brotherhood, or whatever they called it, was built upon.

Skin prickling, I slid off my black shawl and hung it over the door of a stall. "What's your second principle?"

Reeve's lips brushed my ear. "Forget your past."

Blake lifted a champagne glass over my chest, waiting.

"How about the third?"

"Embrace your present," Blake intoned. A cold drop fizzed between my breasts, and my thighs clenched.

"And the fourth?"

"Possess your future."

Touching the tip of his finger to the champagne trail, Reeve drew a wet line across the tops of my breasts. Goosebumps followed.

"You understand that, don't you, Daisy?" he asked, low and seductive. "You owned your future once. You can do that again."

"What are the other — principles?" I panted.

"Be a good girl for us and you might find out." Blake dipped his fingers in the champagne, flinging droplets over my neck and collarbone, spattering my corset. "You're coming back to the House afterward, aren't you? We'll make sure you feel welcome this time."

My mouth opened.

"For dessert, Daze." Reeve's dimple flashed. "Save your appetite."

I swallowed. "I don't want to wait."

Reeve's voice was hypnotic. "You're aching to come, aren't you?"

My cheeks went hot, and I glanced from Reeve to Blake. "Yes..."

"You've been on the edge since Friday night."

"God, yes." As I stared at Reeve, Blake cupped my cheek. "What are you going to do about it?"

Reeve chuckled. "Keep you there, for now."

Three chimes sounded, signaling that intermission was almost over. The noise made me startle.

"You guys..." I sputtered, coming back down to earth. "Look at me. I'm so wet. I'm covered in champagne, it's on my corset...I'm, oh God, I'm..." They both raised an eyebrow at me in eerie synchrony. "I'm so fucking wet."

To my surprise, we all burst out laughing.

Blake brought a handful of paper towels and began gallantly blotting at my corset. Reeve took off his sharply cut tux jacket and draped it over my shoulders. Folding my shawl neatly, he presented it to me like a trophy. We'd barely touched, but the ladies' room smelled like champagne and sex.

Shivering as the champagne dried on my skin, I tucked my arms through Reeve's and Blake's and let them sweep me back into the box.

How could I trust them so much? I'd been totally open to them in the bathroom, willing to allow them complete license. Not to mention that I couldn't think of anyone else who could drip alcohol on my favorite clothes and get away with it.

In our seats, I pulled Reeve's jacket close around me and leaned toward him. "Why me?" I asked. "Why us?"

He gave me a considering look. "These are good questions, Star."

The curtains rustled behind us. Nathan stalked in and headed brusquely to the empty seat.

I tried to catch his eye, but he thumped into his chair and stared at the stage, his jaw hard. His nostrils flared as though he scented me.

To my surprise, Blake put a hand on his shoulder. Nathan jumped like a live wire had touched him, shaking Blake off. The two men exchanged a brief, charged glance.

"What was that about?" I whispered to Reeve as Blake took his seat. "Are they — are you guys — are any of you together in any way?"

"Not sexually," Reeve said with a slight smile.

I wanted to trust that Reeve was telling me the truth. But there was a definite current between Nathan and Blake.

The house lights dimmed, and the stage lights brightened. The audience went dead silent. The orchestra stilled, like statues on the stage.

The conductor walked to the podium to polite applause. But when Evan appeared from the wings, the room went wild. Applause burst like thunderbolts. Excitement lanced the air like lightning.

My breath caught. Every clap jolted through my left wrist, which flared with pain.

I bit my lip until I tasted blood. The envy I'd dreaded spread outward from my core — a bottomless, light-swallowing abyss.

Reeve's low voice pierced my consciousness. "Daisy, stay with me."

I took his hand, struggling to breathe.

Evan bowed and sat at the piano. Big as he was, everything about his stance signaled humility. Almost too humble, like he'd been given a gift by the gods and it was his responsibility to carry it. Making eye contact with the conductor, he struck the keys.

A black ocean spread in front of me. It lapped and curled with green-tipped waves. The Pacific, under the night sky. I was parked a mile from the Santa Monica Pier at three in the morning. Sleepless, dreamless, right after Nathan kissed me and ran away. I was looking at my future: a roiling, implacable ocean with no promise.

"Daisy," came an urgent voice.

I was in Crowne Hall, thrust back into my body. Nathan knelt in front of me. I gripped Reeve's and Blake's hands, frozen in my seat, my eyes wide.

"You don't have to do this," Nathan hissed. "Come on, let's go. I'll take you out of here."

"She's fine," came Reeve's unperturbed whisper. "She can handle it."

"Let her talk." Nathan's fingers dug into my knees.

Evan's fingers flashed over the keys, striking ebony and ivory.

"This is where I need to be," I murmured. God, why? Why did I have to go through this? All I knew was that there was a reason.

Nathan squinted at me. Shaking his head, he returned to his seat.

Springtime in New York. After the fall. Lilacs in Central Park, dogwoods flowering along the streets. My mom was teaching a night-time dance class and Josh, her shitty boyfriend, had his bandmates over like it was high school and their parents were gone for the weekend. Pizza boxes and beer everywhere, my mom's favorite vase smashed.

I shut off the music and yelled at a group of stoned men twice my age to get out. Josh was in my face. Yelling back. I told him to get his things and leave, that he treated my mother like crap, that this was my house too.

"Spoiled brat. Think you're something special, but you're not."

He'd grabbed my left wrist. I don't know if he remembered the injury at first, but when he saw my face contort in pain, he twisted it.

I bolted awake in my seat as if from a dream. My left hand rested in Reeve's, and his hold was gentle.

"It's okay," he whispered. "It's all going to be okay, Daze."

My mom had come in. Jolted into fury, she called the police. Josh and his terrible friends left for good.

But without me there, would anything prevent her from making bad choices over and over again? What would it take to end the cycle?

Even with me there...

Was I any help?

Two nights before the fall. I was practicing in the music building. It was midnight, and I was in the zone. My muscle memory was clicking into place, and I was riding the high of practicing for hours, in a bubble, separated from the rest of the world.

My phone buzzed. It was my mom calling. I ignored it. She called again. And then a third time.

Dammit, Mom...

I turned the phone off, annoyed at the interruption. I stayed in the practice room for another two hours, driving myself.

It wasn't until I left the room that I turned my phone back on and got the message. My grandfather, my mom's dad, had passed away after a long illness. My mom was emotional, a mess. And I'd been selfish.

The music changed: softer, slower. The scene blew away. Evan was in front of me, around me, taking up every molecule of air with his presence and playing and intense green eyes.

Dimly, I was aware that he was playing the second movement.

Junior year in high school. My parents sat me down, but I already knew. I'd known for years.

There's something we need to tell you... We didn't mean for you to find out this way...

Then there was only the music again, swelling with promise. It buoyed me on the ocean, the waves ceaseless and sparkling with sunlight.

It was beautiful. Real. Raw. Evan was in front of me again, and I was riveted. He was brilliance. He was power. He was sex. I felt fuzzy, connected with everyone in the hall like I was on ecstasy.

This is why the hall is packed. Everybody wants a piece of this.

The thought was swept away, a wisp of cotton in a huge cathedral of sound. The high notes arched up to heaven. The low notes dug into the earth. The crescendos shook the walls, and the quiet passages were the smallest, most intimate moments, a secret that Evan's fingers whispered only to me.

The ocean waves bore me to the edge of the earth. Looking down, I saw the abyss from my dream, an endless black hole. Beckoning...winking.

Hovering over the chasm, I gazed up. A cluster of stars hung overhead, beaming a vision of hope. I stretched toward them, suspended above the abyss, adrenaline rushing through me at the question of whether I'd fall or rise.

It ended after a moment and an eternity.

"No," I breathed, reaching for the stage.

As Evan stood, a forest of arms stretched out to him.

When the applause finally came, it was deafening. Everyone rose to their feet in one motion. The room begged for an encore, and he obliged.

After the encore, I collapsed into my seat. A tear trickled down my cheek.

"Worth it?" Reeve asked.

I could only nod. There were no words.

17

Book of Right-On

Daisy

Reeve's car pulled noiselessly into the long, circular driveway. Above us rose the House, gleaming in the moonlight.

The windows were dark, but lanterns twinkled along the driveway and illuminated the marble statues that graced the courtyard. The grounds were even more beautiful than I'd remembered from racing across them breathlessly with Michelle and Amy.

The tower loomed against the starry sky. Evan's playing rang in my head like a bell that wouldn't cease.

After the concert, Reeve and Blake had flanked me as the audience surged in a near-riot for the doors. Nathan had pulled ahead, lost to the crowd. We'd found Evan outside the stage door, surrounded by people and flowers.

Forgetting all my reservations, I'd thrown my arms around his neck.

"I saw my life flash before my eyes," I gushed. "And you — you gave me hope when I thought there wasn't any."

Evan grinned. "Well, shit, Daisy. Don't make me blush."

Others had pressed forward, hoping for his attention. Ignoring them, he'd crushed me in a bear hug.

My breasts had pressed against his husky chest. My stomach dropped. Everything in me seemed to sink downward, and in a flash, I was wet. I clutched the front of Evan's tux to stay upright, but his grip was too firm to let me fall.

"Thank you," I whispered. "For the hope."

"No, Daisy." He gave me a peck on the cheek, sending an electric current through me. "Thank *you*."

Now, Reeve opened the passenger door, helped me out, and put his hand on the small of my back, leading me to the grand front door. I clutched the roses he'd given me, their sweet, heavy scent filling the air.

"This time, you can come in properly," he told me. "No bathrooms, no breaking in."

I touched the twining serpent knocker on the door. "What is this?"

"A door knocker." He grinned when I gave him a look. "Come inside."

The entry hall was quiet, lit only by a few wall sconces. In the high-ceilinged living room, rows of candles flickered, reflecting points of lights off the black marble table. Clinking sounds came from the kitchen.

Reeve led me to one of the sumptuous couches piled with pillows. Filling a crystal vase with water from the bar at the side of the room, he took the roses from me and placed them inside.

"It's hard for me to talk right now." Too excited to sit, I paced around the room. "Evan's concert was— it was—" I shook my head. "It was like I was absolved. I saw my darkest moments, but in the end, they made sense. It's like they happened for — I can't believe I'm saying this, but for some higher purpose."

"I'm so happy for you, Star." Reeve stood by the couch, a faint smile playing over his lips.

"I have to play again." I crossed to him, staring into those bottom-less, inscrutable eyes. "Whatever it takes, I'm getting back to it. I refuse to be limited by what the doctors said. Is that crazy?"

"No." He put his hand on the back of my neck, rubbing the nape with his thumb. It did something primal to me, like he was possessing me solely by finding the right spot to stake his claim. "Evan was that inspiring, hm?"

"You're *asking*? What about you? Didn't Evan's music just — sneak inside you and wrap around your soul?"

"I told you, Daze," he said, his voice patient. "My pleasure comes from watching. Seeing you during the concert was enough for me."

I opened my mouth to ask if he felt anything at all. If he trusted me enough now to let me see his locked-up books, so I could attempt to heal my hand.

Before I could speak, he inclined his head to kiss my cheek. The touch of his lips practically singed my skin. "Dessert should be ready now. Make yourself comfortable, sweet."

I took a seat in the center of the couch and smoothed down my long skirt, fighting the urge to sink into the soft pile of pillows and pull Reeve on top of me. As Reeve sat down on my right, his leg pressing against mine, Blake and Evan strolled out from the direction of the kitchen.

They'd shed their jackets. Evan's shirt was unbuttoned, his bowtie hanging loose around his neck. His shaggy hair was damp, the tips darkened.

Blake had lost the shirt altogether and was wearing a white cotton tank top that hugged his lithe chest and displayed his intricate sleeve of tattoos. His nipple piercings showed through the thin fabric, and his golden-brown curls hung loose to his shoulders.

"Voilà." Blake set a lacquered tray on the ottoman in front of us.

I stared.

Arranged on the tray were a classic New York cheesecake, a chocolate cake glittering with gold-leaf designs, and a stack of enor-mous cookies that reminded me of the ones Darian and I used to split from our favorite bakery across the street from Siderio. Plates and forks were piled next to the desserts.

"Those are so beautiful." Impulsively, I reached up to squeeze Blake's arm. Was it my imagination, or did his tattoos writhe under my touch? "I feel like I'm back in Manhattan."

Blake gave a nonchalant shrug, but he was beaming. "Thought you might like it."

My palm tingled from the contact with his skin, and I rubbed it on my skirt. Must have been his muscles flexing. His blood pumping. Any natural explanation that ruled out his ink actually moving.

"You whipped up these desserts, just because?"

"Ev likes cheesecake." Blake reached over to muss up Evan's hair. "But I was thinking of you, Daisy. Reeve told us you miss New York."

I looked sharply at Reeve. I'd never told him that. His beautiful lips curved into a smile, and my eyes dropped to his left arm, covered by his black jacket.

"Blake's a nice guy. He loves making people happy." Evan dropped onto the ottoman beside the tray, forked up a piece of cheesecake, and held it to my lips. "Want the first bite?"

I blinked. All three men were watching me closely. Blake settled onto the couch to my left, so I was sandwiched between him and Reeve.

Suddenly, I remembered Amy and Michelle, clutching the container of sweets from Blake like it was their most treasured possession.

Was Blake's food actually that fantastic? Or was there something in it? Something... addictive?

My gaze darted around. I let my shoulders rise and fall while I tried a cute giggle.

"Please, you guys first. I never eat on an empty stomach," I joked.

"Hilarious." Evan gave me a lazy smile and popped the bite of cheesecake into his mouth. "Mmmmm... oh yeah. *Fuck,* that's good, Blakey." He smacked his lips.

As the men sampled each of the sweets, my stomach, which had been knotted up, let out a rumble.

I was starving. The desserts seemed safe. And they looked absolutely incredible. I reached for the tray, but Blake was there first.

"Allow me." He swooped down, scooping up cheesecake. "Now open your mouth. Breathe in, inhale the aroma..."

Evan howled with laughter. "So pretentious," he crowed. "Just eat it, Daisy." Reeve chuckled, and I couldn't help giggling.

Blake rolled his eyes. "Humor me, okay? You'll get more out of it this way."

"Blake, our girl's hungry," Reeve said calmly. "Let her eat."

Our girl.

It could have been a slip of the tongue. Maybe he meant to say *the girl.* But the phrase sent a warm thrill down my back. Butterflies flapped in my stomach.

"It's okay." I smiled up at Blake. "I'll do it your way."

I let my lips part and inhaled the tangy sweetness of the cheesecake, the brown sugar of the graham cracker crust. A flood of memories pressed at the corners of my mind.

"That's it." Blake's voice was soft and crooning. "Good, Daisy."

"What do I do now?" I gazed into his bright blue eyes.

I was looking at the sun sparkling on the ocean, my vision from the concert. It was suddenly exciting, and a tremendous relief, to be waiting for instructions. To let go.

"Let it touch your tongue," Blake ordered. "Don't chew right away. Allow it to melt while you experience the taste."

I stuck out the tip of my tongue. Ever so briefly, Reeve's hand tightened on my thigh, and a smirk spread over Evan's face.

The creamy cheesecake touched my tongue. It was tart and sweet and lemony and the completely intense distilled essence of cheesecake. It was home — my adopted home. It was late nights on the Manhattan sidewalks after rehearsals and scraping together enough cash for desserts in our favorite restaurants and the excitement of concerts and shows and the whole world ahead of us.

My lips closed around the silver fork, and I shuddered as Blake pulled it out, leaving the morsel of cheesecake on my tongue. The graham cracker crust was everything it should be — thick, crunchy, caramel-sweet.

"Oh — oh God," I whispered. "Oh my God, that's so good."

Reeve stood and went to an elaborately inlaid cabinet. Opening it, he took out an exquisite crystal decanter and four small cups. "Time for a toast. Drink with us, Daze?"

I cleared my throat. "Do I actually get to drink this time, or are you just going to pour alcohol on me again?"

Evan leaned in, brushing a graham cracker crumb off the corner of my mouth. "Sounds like I missed all the fun."

Reeve laughed, holding up the decanter. "This, you'll get to drink."

I wasn't a big drinker, and I'd already had champagne tonight — inside as well as out. But the liquor in that decanter was so beautiful, a deep golden-ruby shade, like the embodiment of Reeve's voice when it poured over me.

"I'll try it."

Reeve deftly filled the tiny cups. Carrying two in each hand, he brought them back to the couch and offered them around.

"To friendship." He held his cup aloft, with a wry smile that softened when he looked at me. Blake and Evan grinned, clearly in on the joke.

We clinked glasses and sipped, and I gasped at the first drop on my tongue. It was liquid fire, sweet and scorching at the same time.

The liquor sparked as it went down. It snaked along my throat, dancing inside me.

As we sipped the amber drink, I felt included, welcomed. Part of an inner circle. I held out my empty cup to Reeve.

"Please, sir, may I have some more?" I teased, light-headed and giddy.

"Sir." His eyes moved over me smoothly. "I like the sound of that from you."

"It's only a quote. Don't get any ideas."

"You're giving me ideas." He took the cup from my hand. "Why don't you eat first? I'd rather you not drink too much on that empty stomach."

"Bossy," I giggled. "I already had cheesecake."

The drink curled and flowed inside me. I felt looser, more relaxed. It was delicious. Around me, I saw three empty cups.

"Oh yeah, Reeve's very bossy." Evan winked at me. "Better get used to it. We have."

Interesting. The thought formed, then flew away.

"Aw, Evan loves it." Blake waved a piece of chocolate chip cookie in front of my mouth, and I let him pop it in. A pleasant shiver ran through me when his thumb brushed my lower lip. "The boy needs a restraining influence. A strong figure to rein him in. A firm hand—"

Evan laughed. "Fuck you, Blakey."

I was too busy munching the cookie to pay much attention. It was crisp on the outside, buttery and chewy on the inside, with jagged chunks of rich dark chocolate that melted and burst on my tongue. It was so delicious, so perfect in its essential chocolate-chip-cookie-ness, that I tried to chew as slowly as possible to savor the experience. Reeve watched me, his nostrils flaring, his hand moving up my thigh.

"This is exactly like the cookies at my favorite bakery in Manhattan, except better," I said to Blake. "I didn't think that was possible. Have you been there?"

He sighed. "Sadly, no. I've never been to New York."

"But you guys have," I appealed to Reeve and Evan.

Reeve crossed his arms and shook his head.

Leaning back on his hands, Evan nodded toward his friends. "Not since meeting these fools."

"You must travel, though," I said to Reeve. "You could go anywhere. You've probably seen the most amazing things..."

"I haven't," he said quietly. "I've never been outside the state of California. So why don't you tell us where you've been?"

Reeve's expression made it clear he didn't want to discuss it further. Maybe he was an unadventurous hermit who couldn't stand to leave the comforts of the House.

So I did my best to share my experiences. It wasn't easy to talk between bites of Blake's desserts. I tried to focus as I described the competitions, festivals, and performances I'd done in the States and Europe, in Asia and Australia, glossing over the parts that actually involved music.

The three men drank in my words: Reeve to my right on the couch, Blake to my left, Evan in front of me on the ottoman.

"You're a lucky girl, Daisy," Evan teased. "You got to go where you chose. I traveled because my dad dragged me after him. We had the best accommodations, but I was bored senseless. I had nothing to do but get in trouble."

"My parents never had much money." I shifted on the couch as Reeve refilled everyone's cups. "Sometimes there's more, sometimes less. They sacrificed a lot for me. And I got scholarships." I bit my lip. "Creative work... it fluctuates."

Evan leaned forward. "Unless you're at the top." His knee, in black tuxedo pants, nudged between mine. I bit back a gasp.

Blake squeezed my left leg. "Everything all right, Daisy?"

"Everything's fine." I stared at Evan, who gave me his slight smile. Electricity zigzagged over my skin. All I could think about were my dreams.

Reeve handed the cups around. He seemed completely unfazed that his friends were touching me. That I liked it.

"Why don't you make the toast this time, Star?" He caressed my right thigh. Relaxing under his attention, I allowed Evan's knee to slip farther between mine.

"Okay." Giggles were rising like champagne bubbles. I held up my drink. "To snakes."

The men went still. Three gazes fixed on me with unnerving focus. Instinctively, my legs clamped on Evan's knee.

I widened my eyes. "Is there a problem?"

Finally, Blake broke the silence. "Snakes, huh? You told me how much you like them."

I laughed. "They're all over the House. On the tray..." I pointed to the lacquered gold coils on the dessert tray. "The candlesticks, even the wallpaper. They must be your favorite too."

Evan squeezed his upper left arm. The movement seemed unconscious.

"Careful, Daisy," Reeve said softly. "Snakes bite."

"Not here." Emboldened by the men's reactions, I trailed a finger down Reeve's left shoulder. He caught my hand and placed it firmly in my lap. "You've got California kings on your property. They eat the kind of snakes that bite. And they're not venomous — they're constrictors. They don't bite their prey, they squeeze it."

"You know so much." Reeve's caramel voice poured over me.

We clinked our glasses and sipped. The fiery drink slid down my throat, and once it was inside me, all I could think about were snakes. Coiling, squeezing, spiraling...

When my knees tightened around Evan's bulky leg, he leaned forward. "You've got a pretty strong grip yourself, pet. You don't let go of things easily, do you?"

"Damn right." My voice was raspy.

"Here, Daisy." Blake reached for the gold-leafed chocolate cake. "Have some more."

Breaking off a piece, he nudged my lips, which parted to let him feed me. When the cake slipped in, my mouth impulsively closed around his fingers.

"Mmm, that's nice." He laughed, but a vein stood out on his forehead, glistening with a faint sheen of sweat.

He was smiling that million-watt smile at me, the candlelight twinkling on the silver hoops in his ears, and the only thing that made sense was to swirl my tongue over his fingers.

Blake's blue eyes sparked, the pupils widening until the blackness swallowed me. I sucked him deeper into my mouth, quick and eager, tasting his salty skin.

"Well, fuck. Looks like someone really is hungry." Evan rubbed his knuckles over my cheek. My thighs clenched around his leg again.

"Did I say you could have Blake for dessert, Daze?" Reeve's deep voice was very soft, and I didn't know if it was a tease or a warning.

Blake pulled his fingers out of my mouth. Flushed and dizzy, I faced Reeve. "Sorry, I thought he went with the cheesecake."

"You're adorable." He lifted his cup. "Though I seem to recall, that word offends you."

Propelled by instinct, I turned on the couch, climbing over Evan's leg. I straddled Reeve, my knees planted on either side of his legs, my bare skin brushing his fine dark slacks.

"What offends me," I giggled, "is that we've been in your house all this time and we haven't kissed yet."

He raised one dark eyebrow. "What are you going to do about it?"

Running my hands over his chest, sinking into his endless eyes, I tasted his lips.

His mouth was sensual and demanding, his tongue hot and hungry. It tangled with mine, tasting and taking. He caught my lower lip between his teeth and wouldn't let it go until I moaned. When I returned the favor, he cursed softly.

On either side, Blake and Evan pressed in, watching everything.

I can't believe this is happening.

The thought echoed through my mind as the two of them encouraged me.

"So hot."

"Oh, yeah."

"Kiss him harder, baby girl."

"He doesn't know what hit him."

When strong hands squeezed my shoulders, I gasped. More hands ran up my legs, caressing them through my long skirt.

"Please touch me," I rasped to Reeve, as he spread his arms along the back of the couch.

"Why should I, when Evan and Blake are already doing such a good job?" he teased.

I sucked in a breath. On the right, Blake stroked my thighs. When I turned to the left, Evan's pale green gaze consumed me.

"You gave such an incredible concert tonight," I said to him. "You deserve..."

"What?" He gave me a heavy-lidded smile, rubbing my back. I was going to drown in those jade eyes. "What do I deserve?"

Everything. The thought flashed through my mind.

I plucked at my shirt, driven by desires too strong to deny. "It's so hot in here."

"Do it, Daisy," Evan purred.

Inch by inch, I pulled down the cups of my corset to show a peek of cleavage, feeling a rush of freedom.

Blake and Evan's eyes were glued to the small curves. When I dared to pull the cups down farther, my nipples sprang out: two pink points, tight and puckered in the heat of the room. Blake inhaled sharply, and Evan let out a low growl.

Giggling, I arched forward to kiss Reeve again, his stubble pricking my chin.

"Mmm." He pushed me firmly back. "On your knees, Daze."

I rose to crouch over him. A hot hand slipped underneath my skirt. When Reeve's fingers teased my panties, I gasped.

He gripped my thigh, refusing to move higher. With his other hand, he anchored my waist.

As I stared at Reeve, Blake cupped my cheek, his thumb brushing my lips again. Mesmerized, I opened my mouth to taste him. I wanted dessert.

"I hope you've been good, Daisy." Reeve's voice was low, steady, merciless. "I hope you've done everything I said. Do you want to see how nice it can be when you're good?"

I nodded, sucking feverishly on Blake's thumb. His free hand caressed my neck, and I moaned.

"She likes that," Reeve murmured to Blake. "Squeeze her throat; it makes our girl so happy."

Our girl. A warm flush ran over me. He really did mean it. I felt wanted, cared for. Like I belonged.

Blake's tattooed fingers covered my throat. He squeezed the sides gently, and my vision swam as I went lightheaded. My pulse pounded against his grip.

My breath went jagged. Too aroused to handle myself, I bit down on Blake's thumb. He chuckled, but his bright blue eyes were fogged with lust.

"Fuck." Evan stroked my back, tugging on the ribbons that laced my corset, pulling them tighter. I was being squeezed, embraced, caught in undulating coils. "That really turns you on, doesn't it, pet? You like being constrained ...filled..."

"So good for us, Star." Reeve rolled my nipple between his fingers. "You're glowing so bright, you're lighting up the whole room. How could we ever stop touching you?"

Don't, I tried to telegraph with my eyes, as — oh God — Blake began to move his thumb in and out of my mouth. *Don't stop.*

Reeve cupped my breast above the crumpled corset, leaning in to taste my nipple. I shuddered as his tongue swirled around it, shocked at the intimate touch in front of his friends.

"You want to be a good girl for us, don't you, Daze?" he coaxed.

I nodded frantically.

Beneath my skirt, he pulled at the waistband of my panties. When his knuckles dipped inside, I gasped.

"Shhh," Blake soothed, nipping my earlobe. "Doesn't that feel nice?"

As his beard brushed my cheek, Evan moved firmly down my waist and over my hips.

"That's it, baby girl." Huge hands gripped my ass with a promise of roughness. "Open up for Reeve."

Oh my God. I was living in a fantasy with no consequences, no past or future, only now.

I whimpered, crouching over Reeve on the leather couch, lost to everything except the desire in the room. Blake slid more fingers into my mouth until it was crammed full. Muffled, helpless noises left me as my damp panties were pulled away from my body. Casually, Reeve caressed the slick heat between my legs, grazing my swollen clit until I was in agony.

When Evan pushed me forward, I was helpless to do anything but ride Reeve's palm. I'd felt powerful when I exposed my breasts, but now I felt like a doll in Evan's grip. A toy.

Dark arousal shot through me. I lifted my hips, trying to get more of Reeve's teasing touch. Evan's fingers dug into my ass, and I shuddered as he rocked me firmly back and forth on Reeve's knowing hand. With infinite patience, Reeve probed the opening to my pussy, his movements hidden from the others by my long black skirt.

"Please, please," I gasped, pulling my mouth free of Blake's fingers.

"What a tease, Daisy. Putting on a show with me in front of my friends." Reeve's voice cloaked me in lust. "Do you really deserve to come tonight? Because I have serious doubts. Maybe you should beg for *all* of our permission."

The front door banged open, echoing through the House.

"Nate's home," Blake said.

I stiffened. "I — I can't."

Reeve reacted immediately. "Enough," he said to Evan and Blake. They stood. I sprang off Reeve's lap, pulling my corset up to cover my breasts.

He took my arm. "Would my room be better? Just you and me?"

I nodded, blood pounding in my ears. Reeve led me swiftly toward the stairs.

A low chuckle came from Evan. "Try to keep him in line, Daisy."

I looked back, my body aching with desire. Blake raised his glass to me. But there was no glimpse of Nathan.

18

Faster

Daisy

Upstairs, the long hall was quiet. Reeve opened the last door on the right, too quickly for me to inspect its carved, snaking designs, and pulled me inside. My heart sped up as he shut the door and backed me against it.

We were in his bedroom.

I had just enough time to take in the dark wood furniture, the gilded walls, the floor-to-ceiling velvet drapes, and the enormous, black-sheeted bed jutting into the center of the room.

As with the living room, the only light came from a few candles.

He pressed his lips to the crook of my neck.

My hands fisted in his hair as he kissed my throat. A hot tongue ran over my collarbone. I felt the sharpness of teeth and gasped.

"Please." I clutched at his collar. "Hurry."

He laughed, the sound strained. "Oh, no. I'm going to take my time with you."

"Do you and your friends — share women?" I breathed out the question, wanting and not wanting to know.

He slipped my shawl over my shoulders, and it fell to the floor.

"No. As I said, you're exceptional." He chuckled. "How did our hands feel on you? All that attention? You like the spotlight, don't you, Star?"

I inhaled sharply when he took the strap of my tight black corset in his teeth and pulled it down my shoulder.

"I do." Heat and cold chased over my skin as he tugged down the other strap, pushing out my confession. "I like being alone with you too."

"I know you do." His mouth hovered over mine.

"Are you going to tell me how much I want a kiss next?"

Swiftly, he peeled the lacy black cups away from my breasts, letting them bunch below the small curves. "Actually, you're wondering if we'll fuck tonight."

My breath was disjointed as he stroked my puckered nipples. "So you're a mind reader? Is that it, Reeve?"

He hissed when my fingers thrust into his hair. "No. I can taste your desire right now, that's all."

"We barely know each other. I met you less than a week ago—"

"Does that really concern you? Or do you only think it should?"

My hands tightened in his hair. I ran my lips over his stubble, kissing his jaw. "I keep dreaming about you."

His lips found mine. I was spinning, off balance, anchored only by his arms.

"I won't fuck you." His words kissed my ear like a hot wind. "And I won't hurt you. But I want to do crazy things with you, Daze. Dirty things."

"You won't fuck me?" I heard myself say, shaking in anticipation. "I really am cursed."

Unexpectedly, Reeve laughed. The sound rolled out from his body, deep and full, and made me laugh too.

"You're not cursed with me." He kissed my earlobe, my jaw, my throat. "Just impatient. I didn't say I never would."

He sounded so possessive. So sure. And in the moment, it was hot as hell.

I arched toward him, my hand going to the back of his neck, and put my mouth on his. His tongue burned mine, searing it, and I fell down the well of his kisses.

When he broke away, it felt like I was being hauled up from the depths by a long, never-ending rope. Dimly, I became aware of my braid in his fist. Pulling. I hadn't imagined it.

"Watch, Daisy." His voice was rough. "Watch me take your clothes off."

"You too," I pleaded.

"Not tonight. You'll have to wait for that. But you want to be naked for me, don't you?"

My chin trembled. "Yes."

"Hands against the wall," he ordered. "You watch. I do."

Gritting my teeth, I pressed my palms against the wall behind me. I was on display, my chest thrust forward as Reeve unfastened the tiny hooks that ran down the front of the corset. The stiff black fabric sprang apart, baring my skin.

When I trembled, he chuckled. "Waiting isn't your strong suit, is it, Star? You want to do, not be done to."

"I'm not answering that."

He pulled the corset open and ran one finger down my belly. Goosebumps followed in its wake.

"It really is hard for you to receive," he mused. "You think you don't deserve it."

"I'm not used to receiving," I protested.

"Get used to it."

My palms clutched the wall. A twinge in my left wrist made me wince, and I shifted my weight to the right.

Reeve's eyes flickered. Kissing my left shoulder, he pushed the corset down. It hung behind me, dangling from my arms. Dark eyes, hot and hungry, drank me in.

"Even more beautiful than I remembered." He cupped my tits,

caressing them until my nipples were tight and rosy with need. Holding my gaze, he pinched down until I yelped, then let go, eyeing the dark pink peaks with satisfaction. His thumbs hooked in the waistband of my skirt. "Don't move."

He tugged my skirt over my hips. Involuntarily, I thrust toward him as he knelt to skim the ruffled black fabric down my legs.

"I said don't move." The order cracked across my skin like a velvet-clad whip. I did my best to keep still, but my thighs shook. "It's very difficult for you to control your desires, isn't it, Daisy? When you want something, you have to have it. Immediately. If you can't have it right away, you're working full speed to get it."

"Are you any different?"

Though he crouched at my feet, looking up at me, I felt defenseless. I rose above him, wearing only my black lace panties, my hands braced against the wall in a mix of vulnerability and power.

"I, sweet girl, know how to wait. I've been waiting for years."

My gaze flashed around the beautiful bedroom, the luxurious furnishings and art, half-lit by the candles that threw long shadows over Reeve's sculpted face. "Looks like you have everything already."

A slow smile quirked his lips. "Not everything, Daze. Not yet."

Gripping my panties, he pulled them down.

I twitched, trying to remain motionless. Rising on his knees, he leaned so close I could feel the heat of his breath. Reeve McClellan was staring at the soft triangle between my legs. The first, the only person to ever see my pussy.

"Reeve, please—" I was aroused, impatient, but also exposed and so fucking bare. I wanted to race past all the discomfort and just feel him.

"Shhh." He slid his hands up my thighs. "Let's not rush this moment, Daisy."

My breath caught. It was like he could see inside me. Read my fears. He rubbed my thighs until they eased apart. When he pressed a kiss to my mound, I let out a whimper. Then there was a second kiss, and a third, and a fourth, as he stroked the damp curls, his fingers sliding between my closed lips.

"I'm not going anywhere," he murmured, looking up at me with those endless dark eyes. "Not when there's such a sweet little pussy to play with. And such a naughty girl in my bedroom who has so much to learn."

When he found my clit and circled the swollen nub, my hands clutched the wall behind me.

"Reeve..." I shuddered. My corset hung by its straps from my wrists, like a binding. I was bound — to him, *with* him, in an invisible spell circle that ensnared us both.

"Let go of the wall, Daisy. Let that pretty corset fall to the floor, but otherwise, don't move."

His hand still cupped my pussy. I obeyed, unable to keep my folds from rubbing against his palm. My nipples were tight and puckered in the fever-heat of his avid gaze.

Suddenly, I was swept off my feet and into Reeve's arms. The abruptness of the floor dropping away made me gasp. I was nearly his height, but he carried me easily.

Then we were on his bed. My hips, my back, my shoulders met the silken black comforter. Instinctively, I pulled my left wrist into my chest to protect it.

He touched my shoulder. "I'll be careful with your hand."

I let it fall to my side.

Kisses rained on my neck, my breasts, the center of my chest and over my belly. I twitched, ticklish, my thighs shaking as juices trickled down my bare pussy. When I reached for him, he stopped me with a look.

Shivering deliciously, I fisted his comforter in my hands. His gentleness, coming on the heels of abruptly stripping and carrying me, was disorienting. I couldn't get enough of it, of the contrasts, of him.

He was playing me.

Expertly.

Like a fucking instrument.

For once, it was enough to be the music instead of creating it.

When he reached my pussy, I tensed in anticipation of his touch. Instead, he reared back on his knees.

"*Fuck*," he muttered. I trembled as he stared at me, naked and exposed, my arms and legs sprawled out. Those glittering eyes traveled to the fluff of hair between my legs, taking me in, devouring me.

He spread my thighs to view me at his leisure. I bucked in his grasp. Holding me down firmly, he studied me so intently that I sucked in my breath.

"You're the most gorgeous woman I've ever seen. You're so bright, you blaze."

I touched the shadowed stubble on his jaw. Reeve sounded completely sincere. As if I actually were a source of light, making his breath come faster and his pupils narrow to pinpoints.

"You're ridiculous," I panted. "It's just — it's just my vagina."

He gave my braid a sharp yank. "Not 'just,' Daisy. Never 'just.' Keep dismissing compliments — or yourself — and we'll have a long, long lesson in receiving tonight."

"Tell me what you see," I whispered.

"I see your rosy clit," he murmured. "The apex of a soft pink shell. You're so wet that you glisten in the candlelight." His thumbs glided downward to spread me fully open. "And here..." He stroked my entrance. "The soft flesh of your cherry, peeking at me from your tight little hole. So eager, so fucking reckless and greedy."

"Reeve." My breath came in short bursts. "Please, can you — are you going to — will you take your clothes off too?"

He lifted his head, his voice gravelly. "Put that question away, Daze. Ask again and there will be consequences."

His threat shouldn't have made me moan. But dammit, I did. Loudly.

I heard his soft laughter as his thumb teased my clit in slow, firm circles, and cried out when two big fingers pressed leisurely against my opening.

"Oh God, oh God—" I buried my face in a pillow, sheathed in black silk.

"Aren't you tight, Star," he crooned. "Mmm, and dripping."

I bucked my hips instinctively as he sank into me. He fingered me deliberately, his thrusts sharply exciting. Every muscle and tendon, every inch of skin, was tuned to him. Taut, about to snap.

But each time I came close, he backed off, pressing his thumb firmly on my clit and squeezing my pussy to hold me still.

"Enough teasing," I panted. "Please, just let me come—"

He chuckled darkly. "Star of the cosmos, I'm only getting started with you. Why settle for a brief flash when you can light up the sky?"

I stared up at him, half-illuminated in the candlelight. He knelt between the vee of my legs, his fingers busy inside me, his snowy shirt open at the collar, his ebony bowtie loosened. His tousled hair hung over his forehead, and the flickering light of the flames licked his stubbled jaw. His eyes, blank and shining as obsidian, roamed over my body.

On and on it went, until I lost track of time. Teasing and backing off, teasing and backing off, creating an exquisite torture that set every nerve ablaze. My pussy was soaked and swollen, gripping his fingers, trying to suck him deeper with every maddening stroke.

"Please," I gasped, as he tickled my clit. My body rose off the bed, following his hand.

He pushed me down firmly. "No."

"Is this a punishment? Do you think I did something wrong?" My mind flitted to the utility closet where I'd touched myself in disobedience. Sweat beaded on my skin, and his smile gleamed in the candlelight.

"Sweet flower, this is only the beginning."

His attentions were delicious. Cruel. Tantalizing. I soaked up every touch like a sponge and trembled for more. His hand made a thousand promises and whisked them away, dangling them out of reach, taunting me to stretch up. To grab. To aim for the stars.

"I can't take it—"

"Of course you can." His velvet voice was full of understanding. "Show me what a good girl you can be, and maybe, just maybe, I'll have mercy on you. But right now, this little pussy doesn't deserve to come. It deserves to be explored and taken and acquainted with my fingers in every hidden, secret place, until you carry me with you... in you... until you're begging to burst into flames... and when you understand, I'll give you the darkest, dirtiest pleasures you've ever craved..."

As he edged me, my vision blurred, narrowing to his left arm. It reached between my legs, moving sinuously to finger and torment my oversensitive cunt. Tears trickled from my eyes as he brought me to the brink of climax again, then slowed his strokes while his murmured endearments mingled with my profanities.

"Such language, Star." His dimple mocked me. "Not what I'd expect from the innocent virgin on my bed, taken and touched like never before—"

With a snarl, I grabbed his biceps, tugging his left arm toward me. My hand closed over the place where I'd seen the serpent writhe on Nathan, on Evan and Blake.

Reeve's eyes squeezed shut. I couldn't tell if his reaction showed pleasure or pain. His sleek shoulders were — God, yes, they were fucking trembling. He breathed in sharply as I stroked him through his shirt.

"I love the way your body feels," I whispered. "I can only imagine how beautiful you are. I'm picturing you, Reeve. You blaze, too."

A curse dropped from his mouth when I caressed his firm chest with my free hand. More words followed — coarse, guttural — when my hand dipped lower, testing the waters, grazing his abs, his heavy belt buckle. His fingers curled inside me, opening my cunt, and his circles on my clit, more and more urgent, brought me so close to exploding...

I couldn't understand what he was saying. His words were too low and hissed for me to detect the meaning, the language. Curious, drunk on his nearness, waiting for a signal to stop that didn't come, my fingers wandered below his belt to dance over the thick, hard bulge in his tuxedo pants.

His eyes went wide, twin windows onto a starless night. He growled, shoving his fingers deep inside me, and I cried out.

"Don't. Touch. Me."

"Reeve!" I let go of his cock. The shape of it was imprinted on my palm, a phantom echo. My left hand dropped from his arm, fingers tingling as if a snake slithered through them.

He shuddered and eased the pressure on my pussy, though he still penetrated me. "I warned you, Daisy."

"I'm sorry," I said quickly.

"I made it very clear what you can and cannot do with me."

"I was caught up in the moment." My chest heaved. "You seemed to like it..."

"That's no excuse." In the leaping flames and shadows, his forehead glistened with sweat. "You think you can get handsy with me like a horny teenager and tempt me into changing my mind?"

I shrugged. "I *am* a horny teenager." His lips twitched, and I could swear I heard a laugh escape. He squared his shoulders.

"You're right," I blurted, gripping his wrist. "You said you don't want me to touch you below the waist, and I should have listened. But I don't understand why. Please, just be honest with me. Whatever it is, I can take it."

He exhaled. "Show me that I can trust you, Daze, and we'll see."

The responsibility weighed between my shoulders, on my chest. Reeve's fingers were still buried inside me. I wanted him to trust me, to open up in turn.

"Can you at least tell me if you've had sex?" I ventured softly.

He studied me. "Yes," he said finally. "When I was younger, I was incautious. Not anymore."

"Do you ever touch yourself?" I couldn't help asking.

"No."

My eyes flicked to the bulge that distended his slacks. "You don't masturbate? At all? Are you saving yourself for something?"

Sparks curled in his eyes, oddly green in the flickering light. "So many questions. Hush, Star. Now, where were we?"

His fingers began moving again as he caressed my clit. He was distracting me. Coaxing me to sink into the dark chasm of pleasure where I hung suspended at his whim, before we could talk any further.

I opened my mouth to retort, but a loud pounding cut us off. The door flew open with a crash, and Nathan burst into the room.

His fists were clenched, his muscles knotted. He still wore his tux, but his hair was damp. When his eyes raked over me, he froze.

My whole body tightened up in shock and excitement.

I knew what he saw. The beads of sweat on my forehead, my damp golden braid, my tight pink nipples. My spread pussy, slick and radiating need.

And Reeve crouched over me, fully dressed, fucking me tenderly, slowly, yet savagely, with his hand.

A deep flush spread down Nathan's neck.

"Reeve," I said urgently. Easing out of me, he sprang off the bed. I snatched at his black silk comforter, my skin burning, and burrowed under it.

"Out," Reeve barked.

Nathan blinked, standing motionless by the open door. Even Reeve looked surprised that he'd just snapped.

Though I was covered now, I felt Nathan's eyes all over me, his stare etched on my body. I'd been so fucking bare — not only nude, but vulnerable in my conversation with Reeve. I squirmed under the silken covers.

Nathan averted his gaze. "I need to talk to you. Now."

"Which one of us?" I sat up, holding the comforter to my chest, and glared at him. "Me or Reeve?"

"Reeve."

Folding his arms, Reeve took a deep breath. "Later."

"Now." Nathan lowered his head like a bull about to charge.

"Go ahead," I said, looking from him to Reeve. "I'll wait."

Reeve shook his head. "In here, you don't wait for anything unless I say so."

Jesus. Was he referring to the games of domination we'd been playing? Or the entire House? Was that how he saw himself — master of his domain? And the other men jumped when he told them to?

I didn't want to stop what we were doing, but I had so many questions. If Reeve left to talk to Nathan, I could look around his room. Investigate. Maybe find some answers.

"Please," I said firmly, giving my voice an edge. I wondered how much he'd push back. "I insist."

Reeve turned toward the window and rubbed his jaw. It almost looked as if he were hiding a smile.

"As our honored guest, I'll respect your wishes, Star. I must say, I'm impressed by your patience."

Walking to the bed, he took my chin in his hand and gave me a lingering kiss. I shivered when his mouth brushed mine. Nathan's eyes remained stubbornly fixed on the windows, but his shoulders tensed.

"Behave yourself in here." Reeve gave my chin a final caress. "I'll be back very soon."

I expected Nathan to stalk out the door with Reeve following. Instead, he stood back, fists tight at his sides, and allowed Reeve to leave first. Only then did he exit, giving me a look over his shoulder through slitted eyes.

Then the door closed, and I was alone in Reeve's room.

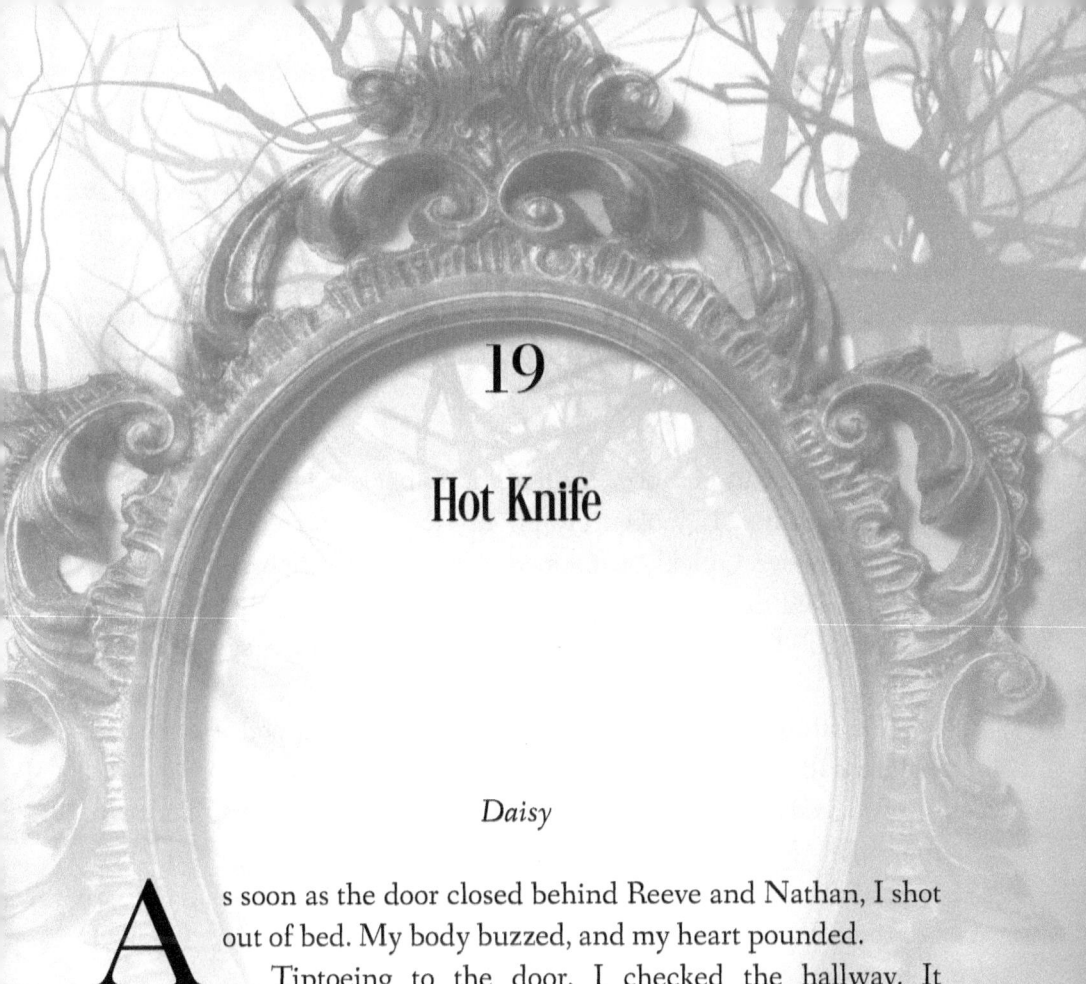

19

Hot Knife

Daisy

As soon as the door closed behind Reeve and Nathan, I shot out of bed. My body buzzed, and my heart pounded.

Tiptoeing to the door, I checked the hallway. It stretched out empty and silent, the grand staircase at one end. I didn't know if the men had gone up or down. This was a house you could easily get lost in.

I closed the door quietly and went to Reeve's carved mahogany dresser.

But as I opened the top drawer, I felt a twinge of guilt. I was about to violate his privacy. He'd respected my boundaries tonight, yet I wasn't respecting his.

When I pictured Nathan's furious face, so different from the sweet boy I'd loved, I forged ahead.

The drawers held silk boxers, fancy socks, and lightweight cashmere sweaters, all smelling of cedar and sandalwood. I slipped my hand under the stacks, feeling along the bottom, careful not to disturb the neat piles.

What was I looking for? I had no idea. Any piece of evidence that tied into the unearthliness of this House and these men, anything to confirm my hunch that something unnatural was going on.

The closet came next, but also yielded no answers. An armoire stood beside it, tall and solid, matching the mahogany dresser. I opened the cupboard doors.

Bingo.

My eyes skittered over leather-bound books, glazed pottery, and marble figurines. I grabbed my phone from my purse, which sat on Reeve's dresser. Quickly, I snapped pictures of the shelves.

I opened one book, bound in emerald green. Unfamiliar words and symbols filled the pages. The next book, bound in navy blue, was similar.

The third had a red leather cover. When I flipped it open, an exquisite illustration met my eyes.

A naked woman, her back arched in ecstasy, was caught between four men. She knelt on her hands and knees, her lips stretched around a cock. Her hair floated in the air, and her hips seemed to rock between the man who lay beneath her and the man who crouched behind her.

Her hand grasped another cock by her face, and her eyes were closed with pleasure.

"Oh my God," I breathed.

They were all fucking her at once.

The actions might be porn-level, but the picture wasn't vulgar. It was beautiful, it was art, it pulled me straight into the center of it.

My thighs quivered, and I licked my lips. A moan escaped me as I felt every sensation that seized the woman.

A distant crash made me jump. I shoved the book back on the shelf and dashed to the door.

The hall was still empty. Taking a chance, I tiptoed naked toward the stairs. My thighs were slick with excitement, and my nipples ached for Reeve's fingers.

God, I wanted both him and Nathan to come back. I wanted

Nathan to crumble at the sight of me and fuck me with all the force in his huge, muscled body. I wanted Reeve to be so jealous that he'd tear off his clothes and give me his cock.

I shook myself. What was going on? Jealousy, anger — I'd never gotten off on those emotions.

The polished stairs spiraled downward. From far away, Nathan's voice rose. I couldn't catch what he said, but he sounded enraged.

Reeve replied, smooth and unruffled. A placating voice chimed in — Blake, followed by Evan's sarcastic drawl. Whatever they were discussing, Nathan was the only one who was upset. The others were trying to reassure him — or win him over.

Reeve's voice grew louder. "I'm not sure yet. But every minute makes me more certain. We'll see when she—"

The conversation subsided to a hum, and I couldn't make out any more.

Pivoting on my heel, I hurried back into Reeve's room.

Time was ticking, and the armoire was full of objects I hadn't explored. I lifted the lid of a copper bowl. It was filled with a reddish dried herb that I didn't recognize. I snapped a photo. Sasha might be able to identify it.

Next to it was a hammered silver bowl, which held dark, curled green leaves. I took a picture of that too.

Beside the two bowls lay a knife.

My heart sped up.

The knife was small and ornamental. Its handle gleamed, wrapped in black leather and studded with clear stones. The steel blade was short, keen, and double-sided — a dagger.

I ran my finger very carefully along the flat of the blade.

Reeve might simply be a collector, and this was a cabinet of curios. He'd made it clear he liked to collect; the art filling his house testified to that, along with the books he'd been so cagey about in his library. Maybe everything in this cabinet was a souvenir, or had senti-mental value.

"Right," I muttered, sniffing the herbs in the first crock. They gave off a sweet, earthy smell. Impulsively, I took a tissue from my purse, shook a pinch of the herb into it, twisted it closed, and tucked it back inside my purse pocket.

On the bottom shelf, a flaxen rope lay coiled. When I bent to examine it, my braid swung forward until the tail brushed the rope. The color matched the ends of my hair, bleached by the sun.

I shivered.

When I touched the rope, it felt impossibly smooth. Sleek. Like the body of a snake.

I took pictures of the rope and the knife. Quickly, I texted the two pictures of the herbs to Sasha: *What are these?* Then I hurried to my purse again and shoved my phone inside.

I should get back in bed before Reeve returned. Avoid pushing my luck. But something else in the armoire caught my eye: the marble figurines.

At first glance, the shapes appeared abstract. There was a cylinder, tapered at the bottom, that rose at an angle and flared into a bulb; a standing semi-circle; and a pointed, curving cone that rose at an opposing angle to the cylinder.

The three shapes appeared in black on the left, echoed by white on the right.

Stepping back, I squinted at them, and the shapes resolved into two recognizable figures.

Snakes.

The figurines showed their heads, their arching middles, and their tails.

"Okay, Reeve," I said. "I like snakes too, but you win the prize for obsession."

My left hand reached for the black snake's head. When I wrapped it around the curving smoothness, it suddenly seized up tight. Instead of a dull throb of pain, I felt sparks.

"What's going on?" I whispered.

Behind me, the door opened. I whirled, still holding the snake. Reeve stood in the doorway.

"Back so soon?" I chirped. Goosebumps dotted my bare skin, and my nipples tightened under his gaze.

His dark brows lifted. He shut the door behind him.

Step by step, he closed the distance between us. I was very aware of his snowy shirt, the fit of his black pants, and my total nakedness.

When he stopped in front of me, he was very close. His eyes moved between my face, my bare body, the marble snake clutched in my hand, and the open armoire.

"What," he said very softly, "are you doing, Daisy?"

I stared straight at him. "Snooping."

"Do you think I have secrets from you?"

"Absolutely."

His lips twisted. "And do you have secrets from me?"

My mind jumped to my love spell, the circle on Greer Hill, my hand down my shorts with the Devil pressed close.

"Tell me about the serpent tattoo," I blurted, going on the offensive.

"You didn't answer my question."

My eyes dropped. I couldn't look away from the thick bulge pushing out the front of his pants.

"Answer me, Daisy DiCosmo Fisher. Or I'll take you home right now to your boring, *ordinary* dorm full of ordinary college students whom you despise."

"I never told you I despised anyone." My head whipped up. "How dare you say that? My roommates are lovely people."

"*Lovely,*" he repeated, rolling the word around in his mouth. "I'm sure they are. But they don't burn, Daisy. You haven't met anyone here who burns, except for us." His gaze fell to the black snake's head in my hand. "This is your last chance. Are you keeping secrets from me?"

"Yes." I stared at him defiantly.

"And?"

"If you open up to me, Reeve, maybe I'll consider opening up to you."

A half-smile twisted his lips. "All right, Daze. I'll permit you one question. And then we'll see how you open up to me."

My mind worked furiously. The question that popped out was, "What is this for?" I held up the black marble snake's head.

"Oh, this." He took it from me and ran it lightly over my shoulder, then my collarbone. I shivered at the smooth, heavy touch. "And this." He swirled the curved marble around my breast. "And this."

He cupped my pussy with a hot hand, spreading it open. I let out a strangled cry, reaching for his shoulders, as the dark head of the snake ran over my swollen lips and flirted with my opening.

"Just as wet as I left you, Star," he said thoughtfully. "Does pawing through my possessions arouse you?"

I gripped his shoulders, unsteady. "You're getting your precious piece of art all messy."

"You're my precious piece of art." The way he smiled at me, he managed to pull it off. "And I do want you all messy."

Overwhelmed, I dug my nails into his powerful shoulders, curling my toes in the thick carpet. When he ordered me to spread my legs, I obeyed. A giggle burst out as he teased my clit more rapidly with the tip of the snake, the intense pleasure verging on pain.

"Please, please, I need..."

"You need what, sweet?"

I pressed my lips together. I wasn't going to give him the satisfaction of begging to come.

"You need what?" he prompted.

I buried my face in his neck, tasting the salt of his skin. As cool and composed as he looked, his pulse fluttered under my mouth. His heart was beating almost as fast as mine.

"I need to know what your game is," I gritted.

He let out a strained laugh. "Turn around and face the wall." He pointed with the snake's head to the gilded wall by the armoire. "Put your hands against it so I can see your beautiful body from behind. It's time for your punishment."

"My *punishment?*"

"You looked through my room without permission, Star. Violated my privacy. Not to mention that I suspect you've gone against my wishes in other ways that you explicitly agreed to."

My throat went dry. "I—"

"Yes?" He squeezed my bare waist, gliding the marble snake over my pussy.

I was nervous. I was excited. I wanted — somehow — to regain his trust. Or to earn it, if I hadn't had it yet.

"I'l do it. But I want a safe word," I said quickly, almost on impulse. "And it's 'Greer Hill.'"

He blinked, and I had a moment's satisfaction in catching him off-guard. "Your *safe* word? Is 'Greer Hill?'"

"And if you don't like it, I'm taking myself back to that boring, ordinary dorm you think I hate."

"Why," he said, teasing my clit with cool marble until I clamped my lips on a moan, "would you choose the one place as your safe word that everyone considers the least safe?"

"Because I'm not like everyone else on campus," I snapped.

A satisfied smirk bent his beautiful lips. "I'm glad to hear you finally admit it. 'Greer Hill' it is. Now go."

The order sent a little thrill through me. My body ached with arousal as I hurried to the golden wall. I put my hands against it and peeked over my shoulder.

Reeve moved swiftly to stand behind me.

"I'd say 'good girl' for obeying me so quickly." His breath was hot on the back of my neck. One hand gripped my waist again, and the other ran the smooth, heavy snake's head down my back. "But you haven't been a good girl, have you, Daisy?"

My pussy twinged at the thought of telling him. "That's a matter of debate."

"You disobeyed me, didn't you? You touched yourself."

A chill ran down my body. Naked in front of Reeve, there was no way to hide. I was spread open for him, aroused and vulnerable.

"Yes," I whispered. "I disobeyed you."

"Not only that, you made damn sure I felt it."

I shuddered. The Devil card... pressed against my pussy in the utility closet... had Reeve really felt that?

"I got carried away. It was a fantasy." My breath came quick and shallow. One hot fingertip traced a taunting path down my throat, snaking around my breast to flick my nipple. "I was thinking about Nathan."

"Is that all, Daze?" A palm covered my breast, scalding the soft skin, and my nipple hardened like a pearl.

"I had to touch myself. I needed him inside me."

Reeve groaned softly. "I'm sure you did. But there's more, isn't there? Tell me, sweet girl. It'll feel so good to confess the truth."

My cheeks burned scarlet. "He was impatient, and — and he took my ass instead."

"And you were impatient too." Reeve's voice was calm and knowing. "You just had to give in... to play with your clit... to feel your soft little cunt convulse. You must have been dripping, naughty girl, because you couldn't deny yourself a moment's pleasure."

I bucked my hips toward him, my body giving me away.

"You were inside me too," I whispered. "In my pussy. You were my first, before Nathan. And Blake and Evan were there, touching me, waiting their turn..."

He jerked behind me, his control fraying.

"Fuck," he muttered. "You're so hungry that I almost hate to punish you for it. I've yet to see you shine this bright." My thighs trembled as he caressed my swollen lips, peeling them apart. "Look at you, spread open for me. You're going to take everything I give you and beg for more."

A tingling sensation rippled through me as he pressed kisses up and down my neck. A rough squeeze on my ass made me tense up. When he spoke again, his voice was admonishing and thick with arousal.

"It saddens me to have to do this, Daisy. To make your pretty ass turn pink."

I rocked against his hand. "You're going to spank me?"

"For a start."

How bad could it be? He was rubbing my ass firmly now, massaging it in circles, and it all felt so good. "Fuck it, Reeve, stop playing. Just do it—"

A swift crack across my ass knocked the air out of me. Reeve wasn't joking around. Tears sprang to my eyes.

"That hurts," I gasped.

"It's meant to." He massaged my swollen clit, and the sudden pleasure, chasing the fire that spread out from my ass, pushed a loud, traitorous moan from my lips.

Another slap rang out, stinging my skin. Swiftly, Reeve's free hand came up to cup my breast. He rolled my nipple between his fingers, soothing me at first, then pinching harder and harder. I groaned, holding back the tears that threatened to wet my cheeks.

"You're fighting your feelings. Let them out, sweet girl."

I bowed my head against the wall as he spanked me. His movements were controlled, the smacks sharp and swift. With each one, it became harder to hold back, until the tears finally spilled out.

"Reeve — Reeve, please —" I didn't even know what I was asking for.

"You're so wet," he crooned as he stroked my slit. "You must really like being at my mercy."

I thrashed, bucking toward him, until a slap on my pussy took my breath away. Heat rushed to my clit. It was the most shocking, arousing thing he could have done.

His voice darkened. "Daisy, Daisy, Daisy. I had so much hope for you. You could be coming right now. All worked up from Evan's concert and getting the happy ending you deserve. Instead, you've got me slapping your naughty, dirty cunt because you can't contain your desires. Little devil girl..."

Heedlessly, wantonly, I lifted my ass for more.

"*Fuck,* yes," he groaned with satisfaction, the profanity a spike of cayenne pepper in the warm syrup of his voice, as more strikes landed on my burning cheeks.

"I need to come," I gasped. "Please, please, Reeve..."

"Oh, Star, I have faith in you. You'll wait as long as I want." I shuddered as he circled the tip of my clit. "Should I torment you all night?" He kissed my shoulder, then smacked my ass hard, leaving me reeling. The next second, he was all kindness, nuzzling my neck. "Will it take you that long to learn your lesson? Or do we need even longer?"

It was only a game. But God, I craved Reeve's touch.

"No!" I cried out. "I'll do it. I'll — I'll save my pussy for you next time. I'll play by your rules for now."

"Good girl," he crooned. "Bend over. I'm going to give you all you can handle."

Quickly, I stepped back, gasping when my bare legs met his body. Leaning forward, I braced my weight on my right hand. I was so dazed with desire, so wet for Reeve, I didn't care what he did, as long as it slaked the fire inside me.

His fingers spread my pussy, sensual and firm. I gripped the wall, steeling myself for whatever was to come.

Hard marble nudged my cunt. I cried out in surprise and excitement as the snake's head pushed inside me.

"What is that?" I moaned, though I knew.

"Something that needs to be there," he said calmly. I arched my back, rubbing against the object. "If you search my room, Daze, expect to be fucked by what you find."

Reeve eased it back and forth, working it in. I panted for breath as the polished stone flared out, stretching my cunt. Finally, it narrowed again, and I let out a sigh of relief. When he let go, it stayed in place.

"It feels big inside you, doesn't it?"

"Oh," I gasped. "God. Yes."

Reeve laughed softly, twisting the carved snake, setting off sparks of need. "You're so fucking wet that it's running down your thighs. You can't stop creaming yourself over a little piece of stone. You wouldn't believe how dirty you look with my marble snake peeking out of your pure pink pussy."

My inner walls clenched on the intruder. It felt so strange and new, yet so good, to be filled like this from behind. When Reeve massaged my clit, I could only moan in response.

"Say something, Daisy. Words are important. I want to hear you."

"I want you to really fuck me."

He cursed, a ragged tear in his smooth surface that made my hopes rise. But instead of taking me, he let go.

"You're eager to be filled, aren't you? Touch yourself." His rough order was sandpaper on silk.

Tense with need, I stroked my swollen clit. My pussy gripped the marble snake, holding it tight while my thighs shook. Sweat slicked my grasp on the gilded wallpaper.

Footsteps retreated. A drawer creaked open. Obediently, I kept my back to Reeve, though I was dying to look. The drawer closed, and I whimpered as he approached.

A sure hand ran down my back and slid between my ass cheeks. I jumped.

"Shhh, now," he murmured. "Relax, sweet flower."

I pressed my forehead to the wall, fingers blurring on my clit, as Reeve explored the cleft of my ass. Every touch made me shiver. Slick with cool gel, his fingers finally found my pucker, massaging that dark, tight place.

"Good girl," he crooned. "Opening for me so nicely. Do you like it when I pet your ass? Mmm, you're taking me so well in both your holes."

It felt incredibly intimate being touched there by him. Naughty and dirty, yet warm and safe. My ass fluttered around Reeve's finger as he worked it deeper.

"So perfect," he growled. "You're glowing, Daisy. Now come for me with your sweet, untouched body. Come hard while I fuck you, little virgin. Think about us both inside you."

I clenched up hard, around his finger and the statue.

"Reeve," I rasped.

"You love it." He bit my neck, his mouth cruel and sensual. "You love that I'm taking your innocence. That you're giving me so many firsts, when you've saved them so long. Surrender to me, Daisy. It's what you're meant for."

His words washed over me in a deluge. I clutched the wall, shaking with need, rubbing my clit in a frenzy.

With a shriek, I convulsed around Reeve and the snake. My body seized flesh and stone, hugging them tight. My climax rippled through my pussy and ass so hard it almost hurt.

Through the haze of lust, Reeve's rough voice urged me on. *Faster, harder, more.* A second crest of pleasure spiked as I rubbed my clit — deeper, more seismic.

For a second, my vision dimmed, then brightened. The whole room was bathed in a brilliant glow. Light flared from every surface, almost too bright to look at.

"Reeve!" I cried out, as I heard his awed curse.

My body arched, my hand flying away from my clit, as my arms and legs splayed out like the points of a star.

When my breathing slowed, I slumped against the wall. Reeve gently eased his finger out of my ass and slid the snake's head from my pussy.

He pressed a kiss between my shoulders. "Wait here, sweet."

I closed my eyes, drifting, my sweaty cheek pressed to the wallpaper. Faintly, I heard water running. Some time later, Reeve came up behind me, his woodsy scent mixed with the citrus aroma of soap.

"Good girl." He caressed my ass. "Very good—"

Pushing away from the wall, I whirled to face him. I wrapped my arms around him and buried my face in his neck.

He inhaled sharply. I was as surprised as he was.

"Is this okay?" I mumbled into his neck.

"Yes." His voice sounded odd as his arms came up to enfold me. His skin was hot, and his heart thudded in time with mine. "Yes, it's okay."

The hug tightened. My breasts pressed against his chest as he held me close. The ridge of his cock, hard as the marble snake, thrust into my belly.

"How can you hold back like this?" I whispered. "I want to make you feel good too."

"I get a lot from your pleasure," he said quietly. "That's all I need right now."

As our heartbeats slowed, a tear leaked from the corner of my eye. I tried to blink it away, and he brushed it with his thumb. "Daze?"

The simple nickname undid me this time. "I can't be numb anymore, Reeve."

"You're not meant to be, sweet Star."

I turned my face into his neck again as he rubbed my back. "If I feel everything, it's going to hurt."

"Is that so bad?" he asked quietly.

"Maybe not."

He stroked my hair rhythmically, running his hand over my braid from my scalp to the tail. A small, insistent part of me wanted to say, *Don't ever stop. Let me feel everything with you.*

In Reeve's opulent bathroom, I floated in a hot bath, watching candlelight flicker on the black tiles and gold fixtures through half-closed eyes. The marble tub was so big, my toes barely touched the opposite end.

Reeve sat on the edge, dressed. His soapy hands moved in circles over my shoulders, my breasts, my belly.

"You're being so nice to me." I lifted my right hand, bubbles sliding down my arm, to smooth his tousled hair.

"If you're going to stay the night, Star, I want you clean before you get in my bed." White teeth gleamed at me. "By the way, you're invited to stay the night."

"I don't understand why you're doing this."

"No one has ever taken care of you?"

"Not this way."

"Well, they've been missing out. Turn over."

Sighing luxuriously, I turned in the steaming water so he could soap up my back. His thumbs dug into my tight muscles, melting the tension.

"You're way too good at this," I laughed.

"And you're as uncomfortable giving compliments as you are receiving them." He kneaded my ass with sure hands.

"Reeve!" I pillowed my face in my arms. He chuckled and squeezed the soft cheeks. "Fine, I'll try again. Your touch feels amazing. It — it overwhelms me. When I'm with you, it feels like..." He spread my ass, fitting his hand between my thighs in the hot, perfumed water, and I gasped. "It feels like there's only the here and now."

"Oh?" He continued the massage on my thighs. I kicked my legs in the water, splashing.

"Like nothing in the world matters except being here, with you, in this moment."

"Mmm. That's nice. I like that much better." He ran his thumbs along my lips, unfurling my pussy.

"Reeve, please..." Wanting washed over me in a sudden wave.

"Come again for me, Daze." One finger teased my clit, and my hips bucked in agreement, angling for more. "I enjoy it so much, and I'm so pleased with you right now."

Two big fingers pushed inside me up to the knuckle. I gasped at the flash of intensity. Reeve rubbed my clit rapidly, and it swelled under his touch.

"Oh God," I gasped.

"Your little pussy's sensitive right now, isn't it, Star? It won't be long before you come."

I bit my forearm to keep from crying out as he fingered me hard and fast.

"This is what it means to receive, sweet girl," he growled. "You like this? I can't tell you how good it feels to overwhelm you."

I peaked in a smothered moan, my pussy rippling on his fingers. A flare flashed through the bathroom, brightening the dim candle glow like a flashbulb. My heart slammed in my chest. I bucked and cried out sharply, thrashing in the water, when he kept going. He pressed into a tender spot on my clit, his fingers sinking deep, pushing me relentlessly to another orgasm.

"Reeve, Reeve, Reeve," I panted in short bursts.

"Oh, Daisy," he whispered as I collapsed in the water. Gently, he eased his fingers out of me, leaning down to kiss my shoulder, and I moaned at the sweet sting. "What am I going to do with you?"

He glanced down at his snowy shirt, which was sopping now. I'd splashed him thoroughly when I kicked in the bath. Rolling over, my limbs heavy with pleasure, I grinned up at him.

"You could take it off."

He shook his head. "I know better than to tempt you." But as he left the bathroom, he unbuttoned his shirt, the wet fabric molding to his chest, and stripped it away.

I only got a quick glimpse of his magnificent bare back, his carved chest with its dusting of dark hair, and the coppery skin with — I drew in a sharp breath — silvery scars swirling over his shoulders and upper back.

But he meant for me to see. I knew it, because he looked over his shoulder to catch my eye as he left. Reeve McClellan might be reticent about revealing his body, but there was a part of him that wanted to show himself off to me. To let me get drunk on his beauty, maybe even to learn who he was.

When he reached for the doorknob, I caught a glimpse of his inner left arm.

A tattoo coiled there, crimson and onyx, identical to Nathan's, Blake's, and Evan's. The serpent's knowing eyes pricked my skin until I clenched my thighs in defense.

And in the steam-filled air, I heard a soft and eager hiss.

20

Syrinx

Daisy

I woke to a crack of light streaming between drawn velvet curtains. Blinking, I shifted against a warm body. Where was I? Reeve's room.

My cheek rested on his chest. His strong arm curved around my back, and his woodsy scent surrounded me.

I was naked. I'd come to bed straight from the bath, barely able to keep my eyes open. But Reeve was wearing the crimson silk pajamas he'd changed into before bed — in privacy.

Turning slightly, I rubbed my body against his, and he murmured something in a deep rumble.

Sleep had never been my friend. Before my accident, I'd fought it, striving to use as many hours of the day as I could. Afterward, the nights were a row of numb hours, interrupted only by dreams of faceless men.

But last night? Last night had been peaceful. I'd fallen asleep in Reeve's arms as soon as he joined me in bed, lulled by his warmth and the crisp, smooth sheets. It was the first full night's sleep I'd had in months.

The covers were mostly kicked off. Reeve burned even hotter in sleep; I'd be worried he had a fever, except for the peaceful smile on his face and his untroubled breathing. Not to mention that his heat warmed my bones in a way that the California sun couldn't do.

"You feel amazing," I whispered. He sighed and pulled me closer. His hand drifted down my chest, palming my breast, as his knee nudged between mine.

How long had we slept? I glanced at the antique clock that stood on his dresser.

"Shit!" I gasped. Reeve's dark eyes opened. I bolted out of bed, racing around the luxurious room to grab my clothes. "Shit, shit, shit!"

He sat up. "What's wrong?"

"I have class in twenty minutes. It's almost two o'clock in the afternoon! I missed my morning class. How did we sleep so late? I never, and I mean *never*, sleep in like that." Yanking on last night's lace panties, I rescued my black corset top from the floor. "Oh God, I can't wear a corset to class. I'm freaking out."

"Daze, relax." Unhurriedly, Reeve climbed out of bed.

"You don't understand. I have to care about something. Otherwise... I won't care about anything. I can't live like I did this summer, when nothing mattered. I just need to be on time for class. I have to."

Reeve put his hands on my shoulders. "Take a deep breath, okay? I'll loan you a shirt. Put your skirt on and I'll drive you to class."

"I don't have my books, my laptop—"

"We'll swing by Lee Tower."

"Thank you," I said fervently.

I grabbed the first shirt I saw in Reeve's closet — a dove-gray button-down that felt like a swan's feather — and pulled it over my head. I tugged on the long skirt and slid my feet into my high-heeled sandals.

As we left the House, Reeve swept the roses he'd given me out of the vase in the living room and put them in my arms. The stems dripped water on his borrowed shirt, but I hugged them close, heedless of the thorns.

In Reeve's car, I called Michelle and asked her to meet me outside the dorm with my class materials. Her mouth fell open when Reeve's car pulled up.

"I want details," she mouthed, as we drove off.

Stares greeted me when I exited the sleek gray car outside the quad. Reeve encouraged the attention by rolling down his window.

"Bye, Daisy." His deep voice carried to the sidewalk. "Be good, okay? I'll text you, sweetheart."

He had the nerve to blow me a kiss. Cheeks burning, I waved and raced inside.

Reeve McClellan didn't do anything by accident. For some reason, he'd chosen to make a public statement that tied the two of us together. Whispers followed me as I rushed down the hall.

"Is she dating him?"

"He doesn't date."

"Who is she?"

Patting down my hair, I stopped outside my English composition class, took a deep breath, and strolled inside just as the professor took the podium.

Afterward, I checked my phone. There were three texts from Sasha, all replying to the photos of Reeve's herbs.

> *The first one's an aphrodisiac. Also used to induce visions. Can be smoked or burnt.*
> *I don't know about the second one.*
>
> *Where'd you get them?*
>
> *And who are you hanging out with???*

She'd sent the messages a couple of hours ago. It was midnight in Marrakech. I texted to see if she was up, but there was no response.

An aphrodisiac? It didn't make sense. Not when Reeve refused to let me touch him or see him naked.

Shaking my head, I went back to Lee Tower to shower and change.

I was pulling on a T-shirt Sasha had given me — printed with the slogan "Witch by birth, bitch by choice" — when the phone rang. I made a grab for it.

"You're awake!" I exclaimed, not bothering with a word of the day. "Talk to me. An *aphrodisiac?* Those are Reeve's herbs, and the man will not let me near his junk. He put all the moves on *me,* but I kid you not, he wore an actual pair of pajamas while I slept naked."

"Slow down. You did what?"

"I went to his mansion." I cupped my hand around the phone to whisper, even though I was alone in my room. "Sasha, he made me come. The curse is sooooo broken. Well, except for the whole not letting me touch him part."

Sasha exhaled. "Okay. I think I follow you. He gave you these herbs, you hooked up, and you slept over."

"No! I snooped in his cupboard when he was out of the room."

"Really? Why?" Her voice held no judgment, only curiosity.

"Because — I have questions about him and his friends. They're up to something that doesn't feel right. But they're also — he's also —" I blew out a breath.

"What?" she prodded.

"He's ridiculously hot. He's silver-tongued and seductive and... ugh. He knows exactly how to push my buttons."

I squeezed my legs together. I was getting wet, thinking about

Reeve's velvet caresses and rough slaps, and I didn't want to have to change my panties again.

"Daisy, listen. I googled Reeve today, and he doesn't feel right to me either." She snorted a laugh. "I mean, Forbes 30 Under 30? Most eligible fuckwad... Come on. So not your type."

"Except that he kind of is." I rubbed my forehead. "It's not about the money and the style. It's more that we understand each other. He knows what it's like to burn."

There was a silence. The dark roses from Reeve, now sitting on my desk in a Mason jar, drew my eye. The whole room smelled like them.

"Do you know anything else about the herbs?" I asked quickly.

"I'll see what I can find. Especially about the second one." Sasha's voice brightened. "So what are you up to? Besides snooping in rich boys' closets."

"I'm upping my practice."

"Of flute?" She sounded so hopeful.

"No, magic. I'm reading everything I can get my hands on. Finding places with good energy on campus. There's this place, Greer Hill, with truly magical woods — that's where I helped with your spell for Farida. I feel like I belong there." I hesitated. "I'm looking for healing spells."

"Daisy, are you trying to heal your hand?"

I paced the length of my room. "Maybe."

"Stick with science. Do your physical therapy, girl."

"Sasha—"

"Listen, magic's fun. And I'm not saying I don't believe in it. We've been casting wish spells, hoping Farida will let me in her kitchen, and she finally has. But I'm worried about you." She blew out a breath. "I'm afraid you're going to go down a rabbit hole of expecting too much from magic."

I stared at the remnants of the love spell on my dresser. The ashes, rose petals, and half-melted red candle were still there. "That's not going to happen. Please, just find out more about those herbs if you can. Okay?"

There was another silence, which was unusual for Sasha. "Daisy, you talk a good game about Reeve, and I know I was the one who was like 'your school's a giant playground, ride all the bouncy toys,' but this is — new for you. Very new. And I'm making assumptions from the internet, but he doesn't seem trustworthy. He looks like the type of guy who will turn every situation to his advantage."

"And you think I don't?" I forced a laugh. "Since when are you the voice of caution?"

"Since I started worrying about you."

I rocked on my heels. Sasha rarely talked openly about her feelings. "You don't need to. I'm the best that I've been in a while."

"How's my big brother?" she asked abruptly. I was used to her changing the subject when a conversation got too intense or exposed, but she'd never resorted to using Nathan as a distraction. "You still think he's on steroids? You have to admit, it would be the most interesting thing he's ever done."

"Sasha..."

"What? He's nice, he's bland, he's totally forgettable."

You mean, he's not like you, so you don't understand him.

"He's on something." I picked up a handful of crystals and scattered them across my dresser. "I don't think it's steroids anymore. Maybe it's those herbs in Reeve's room."

"And you would know because..." Her voice was arch, but a threat lay beneath it.

"Relax. The only interaction I've had with your brother is him telling me to go away."

"Huh." A note of concern crept in, but I could practically see her shake it off.

"I should go," I said quickly. "It's late where you are, and I want to get to Greer Hill while it's still light."

"Fine. But be careful, okay? Promise me." Her voice took on an edge.

I breathed in and out. "I promise."

As before, Greer Hill was dotted with blankets. But it was later in the day, and people were leaving. The movements seemed oddly synchronized, everyone shaking out their blankets and gathering their backpacks, as if swept by a tide that urged them all to go.

Shouldering my bag, I started up the path to the forest.

"Are you sure you want to go that way?" a guy called out as he closed his laptop. "The sun's setting soon."

I halted. "Not for another hour. And I have a flashlight."

The girl with him shook her head. "I wouldn't. It gets really dark, and there are a lot of places someone can hide."

"Have you heard anything about it being haunted?" I asked.

The guy stuffed his laptop in his backpack. "Supposedly, some guys disappeared. Before my time — like three, four years ago. The story goes, they were stuck in the woods for seven days with no food or water, but they came out alive."

"No one could find them before that?"

"No one could get in. The woods closed up." Hurriedly, he zipped up his backpack. "It's just an urban myth."

I looked from the deep green trees to the couple. "Have you tried to go in?"

"Hell no." The girl laughed.

"Who were the guys who got lost?"

"We should get going," the guy said to the girl, ignoring my question. He turned to me. "And you probably should too."

I shrugged. "I'll take my chances."

The girl's whisper followed me as I headed along the path. "She's craaazy, going up there."

The higher I climbed, the fewer people I passed. By the time I neared the woods, there was no one in sight.

A breeze set the branches stirring. I eyed the point where the path entered the woods. It looked clear. Still, I gripped the strap of my tote bag, treading quietly and carefully.

The breeze blew inward as I entered the woods, bending the branches back.

As soon as I crossed the threshold, the wind in the trees seemed to take on pitch. I could almost make out the haunting, hollow notes of *Syrinx,* the piece I'd tried to play the night I kissed Nathan.

The forest was cool and green, as welcoming as before, but I shivered.

According to Greek mythology, Pan pursued the nymph Syrinx until she turned herself into a water reed to hide from him. He cut the reed to make his pipes, accidentally killing her.

I loved the piece, but I hated the story. It hit too close to home. All the years I'd played flute, I'd worried that my passion for music was selfish, that it would cut off my other loves. In fact, I'd stayed awake all night before the day of my fall, tossing and turning, because I had so much doubt.

In the months since, I'd wondered if the sleepless night had been the cause of the fall.

Or if the doubt had.

The trees rustled around me. I focused on the path, the here and now. But as I treaded on pine needles, sending up a sharp, resinous smell, a memory surfaced.

I was holding my first press write-up in my hands, a review of a concerto competition I'd won.

"*Rising star Daisy DiCosmo, only eleven years old, wowed audiences with her astonishingly mature interpretation of Mozart's first flute concerto. Poised in front of the orchestra, she took command of the stage while responding to the nuances of the ensemble...*"

I remembered the giddiness of performing, the excitement of the back-and-forth with the orchestra, the astonishment that the conductor was waiting for my cues.

When I stepped deeper into the forest, another memory hit me.

I was standing onstage at the concert that got the press write-up. My flute was in my hands. My knees were shaking. I had braces. The lights were bright, an orchestra of adults sat behind me, and a middle-aged man stood above me on the podium.

Don't sweat, I thought. *Don't let your hands get slippery. Do not, under any circumstances, throw up.*

Then chords crashed in the brass section. I lifted my flute to my lips, and I forgot everything except the music.

A bird flew low overhead, almost hitting me. With a shock, I slammed back into my body, with fingers that hadn't touched my flute in months. A body that had been suspended in Reeve's hands last night, hovering between pain and pleasure.

I stopped short in front of the clearing. The spell circle sat undisturbed, exactly as I'd left it two days ago. Dropping to my knees, I touched the sticks.

As the sun sent slanting golden rays between the trees, shadows lengthened in the woods. A flash of movement by a rock caught my eye — a fox?

Quickly, I took five votive candles from my bag. Lighting them, I set them out in a circle. I breathed in the greenness of the woods, channeling it to my muscles and bones.

More.

My eyes flew open. "Who said that?"

The votives flickered in their glass jars. *More.*

Cautiously, I gathered a bundle of small twigs. Placing them in the center of the candles, I enclosed them with rocks. I tossed a lit match in the center of the kindling and the flame crackled, catching the dry twigs in a blaze.

A stiff breeze blew through the leaves overhead, and the sudden hiss seemed to say *Yes.*

Chills ran through me. Had the forest really just spoken again?

Jumping to my feet, I looked around. There was no one in sight. But the air pulsed with anticipation.

I hadn't come to cast a spell this time. I'd just wanted to sit in the woods with my candles and gain some clarity. But quickly, I searched my purse for materials. Anything to channel the energy that whispered through the air, warming the ground beneath my feet.

As I rummaged in my bag, my fingers brushed the twist of paper with Reeve's herbs inside. A sharp, sweet scent filled my nostrils when I unwrapped the parcel. I crushed a few of the leaves between my fingers, and a shiver ran through me. The flames seemed to stretch toward my hand.

Emptying the herbs into my palm, I tossed them in the fire.

The blaze leapt up higher than my head, sending out an enormous plume of scarlet smoke. Its scent submerged me — woodsy, intoxicating, the scent of the four men.

I fell to my hands and knees, coughing violently.

"Shit!" I gasped, fighting for breath. I tried to scoot backwards, but the flames curled toward me, almost dragging at me. I dug my fingers into the earth, and my left wrist throbbed in protest.

My vision blurred as smoke filled the forest.

There was something above me. Around me. But I couldn't see — There were flashes of scales, red and gold against the blackness.

What... want... Star...

A gravelly voice. Hissing. Filling me until I shook.

My skin stung. I saw fangs — above me? Something brushed between my legs. A tongue, it felt like. I tried to cry out.

I was in a mouth, a huge mouth. Outside stood a young girl — blond hair falling down her back, her face bent over her flute.

There were the faint sounds of Mozart, distorted. The smell of slightly singed hair, the heat of an iron by my cheek. I glimpsed my mom curling my hair before the concert.

She vanished. Nathan looked up at me from a porch swing, his face sweet and transparent. Actually transparent, because I could see through him...

"You're the reason I'm here." His hollow voice was snatched, blown away. "You've made me what I am today."

"No!" I wanted to shout, but my body was being squeezed. Coils wrapped around me, strong and smooth, and a deep rasp hissed in my ear.

I gasped, suddenly hovering above craggy land, surrounded by mist. I was in the gray place from my dreams after the fall.

Shreds of tissue paper swirled around me — no, those were my clothes, ragged and gone. Then the smooth coils looped all over my naked body, winding between my legs and binding me in a knot.

I was lifted, kicking, and swung high over the gray, misty land. My stomach dropped.

A snake. This was a snake. Holding me, carrying me. It was sleek and massive. Its body passed between my legs, too thick to close my thighs around as it rolled against my core. Its movements were so insistent that I had to seek relief. Instinctively, I rocked my hips.

Desperately, I tried to make sense of the hissing. It almost sounded like words.

Everything... desire... trust...

Abruptly I swung over an open plain, and the earth cracked open beneath me. Terror kicked in. I was staring into darkness, a chasm with no end. I couldn't fall. I refused to.

Dreams... patience... no limits...

The serpent rocked against me, squeezing rhythmically. It could make me come, dangling over this abyss. It was going to. I was help-lessly aroused, my wetness slicking its scales. I tried to squirm in my bindings, but I had only enough room to rub my cunt against its thick smoothness.

"No!" I shouted, my voice finally sounding. "I made Reeve a promise. I won't come without him."

Why did I care? Did I want Reeve's trust? His books? His—

Abruptly, the coils loosened and flew apart. I screamed, sharp and shrill, as I fell...

With a thump, I slammed back to earth and into my body.

I was slumped in front of my spell circle in the woods. My little candles flickered bravely in the center. There was no sign of the fire that had blazed up and overwhelmed me with its fumes.

The woods had grown darker, and the patches of sky between the canopy of branches were streaked with the aftermath of sunset.

Had I fallen asleep and dreamed it all?

Stiffly, I rose, brushing leaves from my jeans. My throat was raw, and my hands were covered with dirt. Picking my way into the circle, I stared down at the cluster of candles. Behind it lay a pile of blackened twigs and ash.

So there had been a fire. And when I checked my purse, the packet with Reeve's herbs was gone. A scrap of tissue lay at my feet, and I stuffed it in my purse.

What did the herbs make Reeve see? What did he use them for? Did the other men use them, too?

Crossing my arms, I hugged myself. As frightening as my vision had been, it hurt to be dropped by the serpent. I wanted its coils, its voice, its tantalizing hints. I wanted my flute; I wanted the men.

Reluctantly, I followed the overgrown path through the forest, remembering the "urban myth" that the couple had told me at the foot of the hill.

Maybe those boys had stayed in the woods for seven days not because they lost their way, but because they couldn't bear to leave.

As I exited the rustling trees, the real world rushed back in. The sun hung low over the horizon, and the hill was empty. Tomorrow night, I'd be meeting Blake here as we'd agreed.

A shiver of nerves tightened my body. Once I saw how Blake behaved on the hill, maybe I'd get some answers. Maybe I'd find out if he was one of those boys, forever changed by the woods.

21

Queen of the Woods

Blake

Shortly after midnight, Evan and I stood at the foot of Greer Hill.

I buttoned up my flannel shirt as the breeze blew back Evan's hair. He slouched against a tree, hands in his pockets, humming a tune while his eyes tracked the dark landscape.

The heat of the day had turned cool, and the wind carried the smoky scent of fall.

"How's it feel to be back here?" I asked. Every so often, a pulse ran through the ground, responding to our presence.

Ev raised an eyebrow. "Did we ever really leave?"

We didn't say much else as we waited for Daisy to arrive. After three years together, we could read each other easily.

Ev knew I was buzzed from a busy night at the restaurant. I knew he was coming off the high of another sold-out concert with the symphony — the third in a run that would go through the weekend. He was aware that I was eager to see Daisy again, and I sensed that his hunger for her went far beyond eagerness.

The waning moon outlined the shape of the woman running toward the hill.

Reeve had insisted I bring Evan as backup tonight. But I couldn't see much threat in the slender figure sprinting over the grass. Her braid bounced behind her, thick and shining. She was covered up with a black sweatshirt and ripped black jeans, but they didn't hide her straight posture and graceful stride.

Those long legs would look gorgeous naked. The serpent on my arm prickled, sending me an image of Daisy bent over in my kitchen, gripping the counter while I tasted every inch of her.

Evan grinned, giving me a knowing wink.

When she reached us, I beamed at her. "Hey, Daisy."

"Oh." Her eyes darted over the two of us, to the hill, and back. "Blake, I thought this was just you and me?"

I gave her a megawatt smile. "I texted you that Ev was joining us. I hope that's okay."

Daisy pressed her lips together, a blush rising on her cheeks. "I guess I didn't check my phone."

Evan eyed her black canvas sneakers. "You look great. You're dressed for running away from all the scary things we'll see."

She raised her eyebrows. "Do tell."

"Ghosts... spirits... oooohhh." He made cheesy, spooky noises. "Don't worry, we'll protect you."

Daisy rolled her eyes. She seemed more skittish than she'd been the night of the concert. Even Reeve had been surprised by how much she'd trusted us, how much she'd welcomed all our hands on her.

"Are you okay?" I brushed my fingers down her arm. Her breath caught, and she leaned into my touch.

"Fine," she said brightly, clearing her throat. I caught her scent as I tweaked the hood of her sweatshirt. She smelled woodsy, enticing, smoky.

She smelled like our magic.

"Good." I leaned in to kiss her cheek. There was an awkward moment when she turned her head. Our noses bumped; our lips brushed. She sprang backward, smoothing her hands over her hair.

"Sorry," she laughed, her cheeks pink. Fire flashed through my groin and the tattooed sign of the serpent. "I, uh— Try that again?"

When Reeve was with us, everything was smooth. Choreographed. Without him, the encounter felt too close to human.

"Hold still," I murmured. She shivered when I slid a hand into her hair, and Evan raised an eyebrow at me. I gently kissed her cheek, forcing myself to step away afterward. "Better?"

"Much."

"Looks like it." Evan played his flashlight over her graceful body, and she blushed harder, grabbing his hand and pushing the beam toward the gravel path.

"Let's go." She walked between us up the path, her strides long and determined. She hadn't been bluffing; this wasn't her first visit to the hill.

"Tell me about the boys who disappeared," she said abruptly. "I hear there's an urban myth floating around?"

I laughed. "People love to tell that story. But all we know is that there's an area on the hill, up in the woods, that people stay away from."

"Why?" She looked at me keenly, sandwiched between me and Evan as our shoes crunched on the path.

"They feel something, and it scares them off. But you don't scare easily, right?"

"Nope." When she smiled, those gray-blue eyes seemed entirely guileless.

Dangerous? Not likely.

I trusted Reeve in all matters, including my life. But there was the teeniest, tiniest possibility that he was overreacting.

This afternoon, before I went to the restaurant, Reeve told me what had happened in his bedroom. Even at his mercy, pressed against the wall, she'd almost undone him. She'd taken the marble snake as if it were made for her, and she glowed when she came, flooding him with power.

But despite the emerging signs of the Star, he wasn't sure about her yet.

There was nothing Reeve liked less than being unsure.

Images streamed before me: Daisy caged in by Reeve, pleasured with an icon of our lord, coming apart for him while he fought to contain himself. I wanted to strip her naked right here on the path. I was hard — well, I was pretty much always hard. I was used to the constant ache of unfulfilled desire. My dreams were coming true, so I endured it.

As we climbed, Evan's flashlight bobbing over the dark bushes and grass, Daisy's body pushed against mine. She grabbed my arm for support.

"What are you doing, Evan?" she groused. "Can't you keep the flashlight on the trail?"

He raised an eyebrow. "You seemed very sure of your footing, pet."

"Enough with the nickname," she retorted, her cheeks stained with pink.

"Would you prefer 'baby girl'?" Evan chuckled. "How about 'plaything?' 'Toy'?"

Daisy crossed her arms. "That's demeaning."

"Then why is your breath coming faster?" he asked softly. "You don't seem to have a problem with Reeve's terms of endearment. 'Sweet flower'... 'Star of the Cosmos'... He's just calling it like he sees it. And so am I. There's more than one side to you, Daisy Fisher."

She huffed out a breath. Ev was right; her chest was rising and falling rapidly. But he was coming on too strong, too soon. Of us all, he was the most susceptible to temptation.

And if Daisy really was the Star, she was temptation itself.

"Evan's just excited to be let out to play," I joked. "He needs the exercise… too much time sitting on a piano bench." I reached over and poked his stomach. "That and drinking. Can't have him getting a beer belly."

Evan laughed and shoved me off the path. We tussled while Daisy waited with a long-suffering look.

"Don't listen to him," Evan said when we separated, patting her on the back. His hand lingered, making her dark lashes flutter. "I barely practice."

Daisy's whole body stiffened. "*What?*"

He leaned close, whispering in her ear. "I don't need to."

Before he could continue, his lips twisted. My shoulders tensed in sympathy, feeling the serpent's restraint.

Daisy was too incensed to notice. Her eyes widened, and she muttered something unintelligible.

"What was that?" Evan cupped his ear, a mocking grin playing over his face.

"I said, 'I hate you,'" she snapped, only half-joking. "How can you be such an incredible player? You need hours and hours each day with your instrument. It has to dominate your life. You make sacrifices for it."

"I'm past all that, baby girl. I made my sacrifices. Now I get to enjoy the benefits."

"So what does that make you?" she demanded. "A beast? Or a god?"

"Why not both?" Evan draped an arm around her shoulders. She flushed, and I shot him a warning look.

"I thought I'd seen egos in the music world," she gritted, though she didn't shrug him off. "Yours is the size of Jupiter. Why aren't you at a conservatory? This school isn't known for its music department."

An answering flush crept over his cheeks. "I didn't get in."

Daisy stopped short on the path. "But you're unbelievable. Truly, you're a genius. Have you, I don't know, magically gotten better since you auditioned?"

Evan coughed. "I don't like to talk about the past, pet."

"At all?"

"Blake and Reeve told you our principles, didn't they?" He caressed Daisy's face, and she sucked in a breath. "Number one — forget your past. Grow up with Rowan Hayes for a father, and you'd want to do the same."

"I believe it," she said quietly. "I played under his baton in an orchestra at my old school."

Evan's lips twisted. "'Under' is the right word. He wants everyone and everything under his heel."

He cupped her cheek. Slowly, she turned her head into his hand, like she couldn't help herself. Her lips brushed his palm, and they both tensed. Daisy shook herself, stepping back a pace.

"You know, it's funny," Evan continued. "I seem to remember him talking about you. The beautiful flutist with the long golden hair..."

Daisy tried to laugh it off. "It must have been someone else. He's conducted a million orchestras."

"No." Evan's eyes were pale and intent. His fingers splayed out, sliding into her loosened braid. "I'm very sure it was you."

"Sshh. Look." I beckoned them to the side of the path, pointing to a couple wandering on the slope above us. I hadn't expected to see anyone here, but every so often, lovers were lured to the hill, unwittingly offering their energy. "Watch what they do."

Daisy eyed the two girls holding hands. Every so often, they'd stop to nuzzle noses.

"I don't see anything unusual," she murmured.

"Wait till they reach the woods up there."

The girls looked smaller as they climbed. We watched in silence. They got closer to the woods than they should have been able to, making me wonder if Daisy was disrupting everything on campus. But as soon as they reached the line of trees, they abruptly turned and walked in the opposite direction. Their body language didn't show surprise, or even awareness.

Daisy's eyes widened. "It's true. The woods turned them away."

She clutched both our hands. Behind her back, Evan winked at me. His smile vanished when she pulled us forward. "Come on! Let's go investigate."

"Daisy, you don't want to rush in there."

"Why not?" She flashed me a teasing smile. "Are *you* afraid?"

"Yeah, are you scared, Blakey?" Evan needled. A lot of help he was.

"Hell no," I protested. "But it's a longer walk than it looks."

"Oh, please. We're here to explore. We can chat on the way." Her voice sweetened. "Blake, tell me about you. My roommates can't stop talking about your creations. How'd you get into food?"

I shrugged. "I loved it from the time I was a kid. When my mom was well, she was always in the kitchen. My dad ran a roadside cafe."

Evan looked over at me, his brows raised in surprise. But Daisy was easy to talk to. There wasn't any reason to keep my basic history a secret from her.

"I liked being around them while they did what they loved best," I continued. She was still holding our hands, and when her fingers linked with mine, I almost groaned at the contact. Was she feeling the pull of the woods? Responding to it, even from this distance? "My dad taught me about seasonings. My mom loved color and presentation."

"What happened to them?" she asked gently.

"My mom's in an institution." At this point, I was detached about my family. I'd made the decision to be, and the serpent had helped. *Renounce your ties. Renounce your past. You will love only me.* "My dad checked her in when I was thirteen, and she's been there ever since." Daisy opened her mouth to respond, but I shook my head. I didn't want to go deeper. "My dad remarried. He sold the roadside diner and took an office job. I didn't get along with his new wife."

She tilted her head. "You seem like you'd get along with anyone."

"Yeah, well, I was a hotheaded teenager, and I didn't want to get along with her. I blamed my dad — thought he'd given up on my mom. Eventually, I ran away. I made a deal with my dad: I'd contact him once a month if he didn't try to bring me home. And he agreed."

"I can't imagine that," Daisy whispered. "My parents freak out if I go a week without calling either of them. Our relationship isn't perfect, but..."

Evan put his arm around her. This time, she didn't tense up.

"A year later, I met Reeve." I smiled as my shoulders relaxed. I hadn't realized they were hunched. "After that, we joined up with Nate and this loser over here." I reached behind Daisy to whack Evan on the back.

"I prefer 'god,'" he said grandly, "but we'll get there."

Daisy laughed, relieved, as the mood lightened. "How'd you meet Reeve?" she asked.

Thinking back to that first meeting, I wondered how much to tell Daisy.

I was seventeen and living on the streets. I had a habit of haunting the back doors of restaurants, drawn to a world I dreamed of. Some of the restaurants gave their leftovers for the night to homeless folks, and they knew me. On more lucid days, I tried to do something in return — clean up the back alley behind the restaurant, take their trash to the dumpster for them.

Late one night, at the restaurant I admired most, I asked about a job. I was high and thought I could make any long shot. I knew their menu intimately and had read every article in discarded newspapers that I could find about them. I offered to wash dishes, bus tables, wipe down the floors — anything to get inside and work up to the kitchen. I promised I'd get clean.

They looked at me with pity. The truth was in their eyes: I could never do it. I was a junkie: skinny, dirty, unreliable, my eyes too bright and my hair twisted and matted.

I turned away, hunger knotting my stomach. Not just for a meal, for a hit, for the now, but for a lifetime of doing what I ached to do.

From the shadows, a man emerged.

In the yellowish light of the alley, he was young, around my age. His collared shirt, neatly combed black hair, and smooth-shaven jaw screamed cleanliness.

And his eyes — I couldn't say I'd ever been captivated by a dude's eyes before, but I wasn't able to look away.

Shit, I *knew* this guy from somewhere. Where?

"Are you hungry?" he asked quietly.

"Always." I sized him up.

"If you had enough to eat, would you still be hungry?"

I stared at this preppy guy who was looking at me with sudden intensity. I knew exactly what he meant. He understood the burning desire for *more*, the ambition to rise.

"Yes," I said. "I would."

But I wasn't just hungry to work in a restaurant. Like a sudden slap, I hungered for him. I'd never experienced that kind of lust for another man. I wanted to kiss his mouth, strip the squeaky-clean clothes off his sleek body.

"You like what they're doing in there."

"Food appeals to me." My stomach growled loudly, and the irony wasn't lost on either of us. "I want to" — I leaned a hand on the wall and laughed, because it was so fucking ridiculous — "I want to be a chef."

He cocked his head. "Can I buy you dinner? I'd like to talk with you."

My laughter turned harsh. "If you're looking for a fuck, look elsewhere."

"I'm not."

"I'm not joining a cult, and I'm not looking for religion."

He held up his hands. "I'm not offering it."

"I don't need to be saved or converted. I'm not going to hop on board with your fill-in-the-blank group."

His dark eyebrows lifted. "I work alone. But I'd rather not." He pointed around the corner of the restaurant. "Why don't we go in through the front?"

I glanced down at my ragged shirt and the jeans that were more holes than denim.

His dimple showed. "I've got more clothes in my car. You're welcome to borrow some. And there's a public restroom over there?" Even then, Reeve knew how to phrase a command as a question, a suggestion that you'd want to follow. "I've got toiletries... Happy to wait while you freshen up. I'm a runaway too."

I was a couple of inches taller than him. Definitely skinnier. But anything clean he had in that car would look better than what I was wearing.

"So what do you want?" I asked. "My soul?"

A slow smile spread across his face. "Dinner first, business second."

Daisy listened quietly, her eyes fixed on my face, as I told her part of the truth.

I told her that Reeve loaned me his clothes, took me to dinner, and asked for my commentary on every aspect of the meal. I told her that he had already graduated high school and was taking a year off before college to work. And I told her that he talked me into getting clean, earning my GED, and applying to the same college that he had.

But I didn't mention anything about souls or business, or how Reeve had helped me get clean, or how easy it had been to earn my GED in just a few months. I didn't tell her that he'd taken me back to the apartment where he was staying, and he'd put his hands on me in the dark and it felt better than anything I'd ever imagined, but he wouldn't let me touch him.

I didn't tell her that he refused to fuck, refused to kiss. And that once we moved deeper into dedicating our bodies to the serpent, all touching among the four of us stopped.

I didn't tell Daisy that eventually, I remembered where I'd first seen Reeve's face — in a dream.

"That's quite a story," she said at last. "You must have really trusted him."

"I owe him my life."

"Awwww." Evan clutched his heart in mock affection, but I knew the truth beneath his mask. He'd fallen at Reeve's feet too, the one god Evan would bow down to.

"Is he your friend?" Daisy peered at me astutely. "Or your savior?"

"My friend," I said firmly.

We topped the crest and paused to take in the view. The lights of Pacific Crest spiked and twinkled below us.

I felt the power of the hill beneath my feet. I knew Evan did as well. His pupils dilated, almost taking over his pale green eyes. From the way Daisy's hand tightened on mine, I guessed she felt it too.

"What about you, Evan?" Her hand moved over his arm. "How'd you meet these guys? Don't tell me you escaped Rowan Hayes to live on the streets too." When he stiffened, she added quickly, "He's very talented, but, um—"

"He's an ogre? A demon? A spawn of hell?" Evan raised an eyebrow. "He'd wear those names with pride."

She touched his shoulder. "What did he do to you?"

Evan was silent. I didn't expect him to open up to Daisy; it had taken months for him to tell us everything. But as we approached the woods, he stopped and faced her.

"What didn't he do?" he said casually, like it was all a joke. "However he was with his orchestras, it was worse at home. I had no talent. I was an embarrassment to him, a constant fucking disappointment. I was lazy and bad and only cared about having a good time.

When I was a kid, he'd lock me in a room with a piano and tell me I couldn't eat until I'd mastered some damn passage."

Daisy gasped. "Are you serious?" Her cheeks reddened with anger. "How could he do that to you? How could he do that to *music?* I hate that he twisted something beautiful into such ugliness. What a monster."

Evan blinked. "Don't worry, pet. He's no monster. He's just a weak bully who pushed me too far one day. At my high school graduation party — picture it, all the stops pulled out — he got drunk and wouldn't stop going on to everyone about what a disappointment I was. It gets old, you know? Your dad telling you on the daily that you're useless, talentless, a waste of air. Wondering if you're even his, when you're the spitting image of him. I'd had enough."

Daisy squeezed his arm, her voice low. "I'm so sorry. That's awful."

Pity was the last thing Evan would ever want, but his voice softened. "I left. I drove until I reached downtown L.A. and walked the streets, so fucking mad. I was never going back. I wanted to hurt someone, I wanted to do damage."

"You were a marshmallow," I said with genuine affection. "Rich boy from the hills... you never would have lasted."

"Don't be so sure." Evan cracked his neck. There was a beast inside him and there always had been, more bitter and gnawing than the rest of us. When he caught Daisy staring at him, he put his arm around her reassuringly. "Trust me, there's a happy ending. I turned a corner and walked right into Reeve. He caught everything I threw at him, calmed me down... let's just say he had a magic touch." He gave Daisy a crooked smile. "Don't you think?"

She eyed him skeptically. "Well, I'm glad you got away from Rowan, at least."

A stiff wind blew over the top of the hill. The night air was noticeably cooler, and Daisy shivered, hugging herself.

"Here." I shrugged off my jacket and draped it around her shoulders. She took it gratefully.

"What about Nathan?" she asked, zipping up my jacket. The wind picked up blonde strands that escaped her braid and blew them around her face in a halo.

Evan grinned. "You'll have to talk to him."

"Then can I ask you a very personal question about Reeve?" she said abruptly, her eyes darting between us. "Why won't he let me touch him?"

Evan and I exchanged looks.

"Did something happen?" she persisted. "Something bad? After last night — I need to know."

She was worried about Reeve. I couldn't believe it. She wasn't searching for a weakness to exploit; she simply cared.

"There's no deep, dark secret in his past," I assured her. With a mind of its own, my hand slid into her wheat-colored hair, and her breath quickened. "Reeve likes to take his time, that's all."

"Could've fooled me. We've gone really fast. But he has so many rules. So many walls up... I don't understand it." Her cheeks were scarlet now.

We were near the woods, close enough to feel the heat rising through the ground and the energy fuzzing the air. Daisy turned toward the rustling trees, her lips parting as if she could taste the magic.

This was what Reeve wanted, what he'd told us to report: how Daisy behaved in the aura of the forest. An ordinary person would be pushed away. Reeve, Evan, Nate, and I could get close, but we couldn't breach the line of trees without supplies and preparation.

But the Star — if the prophecy were true, the Star could visit the serpent's dwelling place whenever she pleased.

We just had to be careful not to lose her in there.

Or to lose our self-control with her.

A flash of auburn behind some bushes caught my attention. An animal, probably. A fox, or a coyote.

My fingers tightened in Daisy's braid, and Evan slipped an arm around her, persuading her closer. The three of us formed a tight triangle, pulsing with heat and anticipation.

"Tell us." Evan's voice was sinuous, coaxing. "Tell us what happened when you went to Reeve's bedroom."

She stared from us to the forest, her breath coming faster as its energy coiled toward her. "He — he stripped me naked and brought me to the edge. He ordered me against the wall..." Her voice trembled as the words tumbled out. "He spanked me, he put his snake statue inside me. I've never —"

"We know, Daisy," I soothed. My body screamed for her. My cock pulsed, angry and insistent to be buried in her soft, tight cunt. "We understand."

"I've only ever experienced that intensity when I'm performing. And only a few perfect times." Her eyes dropped. "I promised I'd wait for him and not touch myself."

"And you're going to this time, aren't you?" Evan traced his thumb over her lower lip. She gazed at him, her reservations forgotten, as the power of the woods curled its tendrils around us. "You're going to be a good girl until Reeve's ready for you to be bad."

Her eyes widened, glazed with desire. "I want *him* to enjoy himself. It's so one-sided right now."

"That's very giving." I stroked her back. "You're a generous girl, Daisy. You'd like to make Reeve feel good, wouldn't you?"

She nodded, breathing shallowly.

Evan nuzzled her ear. "Mm-hm. You'd like to unzip his pants... free his raging manhood..." Daisy laughed, but her breath came in short bursts. "Stroke his cock in both your hands..."

Eyes glazed, she nodded. "God, yes."

He dragged his lips down her cheek, courting danger. "And won't you be surprised when he comes all over you?" Daisy gasped, and he continued mercilessly. "Spurt after spurt... coating your sweet, hungry body... dripping between your legs..."

Jesus. Evan was going much too far. I could smell the animal lust rising off of his body. I gripped the back of his shirt in a warning.

"Surprised?" Daisy pulled back, her voice husky and defiant. "I wouldn't expect anything less."

I chuckled, relieved, though I kept my grasp on Evan's shirt. "I like you, Daisy. You're our kind of girl. You're shameless. You know what you want and you're not afraid to take it."

"Shameless, huh?" Daisy looked from me, with my fingers twisted in her braid, to Evan, deliberately massaging the back of her neck. It would be so easy to close the gap between our faces and kiss her.

"Completely shameless," Evan murmured. "Our kind of girl, Daisy. Our kind of girl."

Slowly, her arms wrapped around us both, and I bit back a groan.

She stroked me gently through my flannel shirt, rubbing my aching muscles. Reeve hadn't said how soft her touch was, or how tender.

I needed to stop this. We were too close to the woods, to temptation. I couldn't count on Evan; his eyes were closed as her hand wandered into his shaggy hair, and he leaned in to mutter filthy words in her ear. His tongue followed, tracing the pink shell, and she shuddered as he sucked her earlobe into his mouth.

When she tilted her face toward his, Evan didn't hesitate. He moved in, hungry to claim a kiss.

Before he could, Daisy's head bounced up.

"Something's here." Her voice was alert. "It's watching us."

Evan's eyes snapped open. "Where?"

"There." She pointed straight at the woods. "We need to go in. We need to see."

Grabbing our hands, she pulled us toward the whispering trees.

Could she really enter like this, unwitting and unprepared? Reeve would want us to observe every reaction as she got close, but we'd have to hold her back at the last minute.

"Hurry!" she exclaimed, breaking into a run and forcing us to keep pace with her.

The power was getting stronger, sizzling the air. She breathed more rapidly, squeezing our hands as a blush heated her face and neck. The trees were almost close enough to touch.

"Ready to turn around?" Evan teased, but he looked less steady on his feet.

"*No,*" she exclaimed. "God, I just want to get closer. Come on."

"Careful," I warned.

"This is where the other people turned away, right? Why would they do that? I don't understand. It feels so *good* to be here."

Putting on a burst of speed, she ran between the trees, leading us straight to the darkness of the woods.

Shit. What was happening? Suddenly, I was very glad I had Evan's ass with me.

"Okay, this was fun, pet. Time to go now." Evan tried to yank her back, but he stumbled, following her as she raced forward. So did I.

Trees closed around us, pulling us in. We had to get out, but between Daisy and the woods, the tug was irresistible.

"Come on, guys!" she giggled, practically skipping down the over-grown path. "I want to be here with you."

A glow flared around her, lighting our way, as moss-covered trees snaked toward us. Our hands caught in hers, she twirled around, and I got a glimpse of what this woman would be like if she were totally happy and carefree.

She dragged us into the center of the clearing. Sticks lay on the ground in a circle around us. Had she been casting spells in these woods?

Evan jerked free. "No," he hissed at Daisy. "Not here, pet. Not tonight."

Laughing, she reached for him, and he backed away. Evan hated showing vulnerability, but his shield was down right now. Fear and lust mingled in his eyes as he tried to evade Daisy's pull.

"Evan," she called coaxingly. "Where are you going? Don't you want me?"

He bolted out of the circle. Veering around a rock, he jumped over a log and wove toward the path we'd taken. But the woods were already swallowing it up, branches lowering and spreading.

Abruptly, Daisy lunged at him. He swerved past a tree. But his size slowed him down, and she was fast, her long legs pushing her forward like a gazelle, powered by the woods.

Racing behind the tree, she caught him and sank her fingers into his shaggy hair. I stood frozen in the clearing, staring at the hell about to go down.

"You're not in charge," he gritted.

"Of course I am." She smiled up at him. Slowly but surely, she pulled his head to hers. "You may be the all-powerful musician, but this is *my* place."

Evan's muscles strained as he gripped Daisy's waist to thrust her away. But it was too late. Emotions warred on his face as his lips parted and his jaw went slack. When scales shimmered on his skin, I knew his self-control was gone.

I prayed I wouldn't lose mine so easily.

The fight went out of his body, roughening into greed, lust, hunger — all the emotions that concentrated in Evan, making me worry he was the weakest of us.

"You're fucking mine," he hissed, and kissed her hard.

When their mouths met, Daisy's eyes flew open. I knew she feared her curse. I wished it would take hold here, but there was no chance of that.

Instead, Evan growled, crushing Daisy to him. He lifted her, grasping her thighs, and she wrapped her legs around his waist. Staggering forward, he slammed her up against a tree. I winced, but the impact turned Daisy into a tigress. She shredded Evan's shirt in a burst of strength, ripping the ragged cloth from his body and raking her nails down his back.

I saw him through her eyes: thick and husky, furred with blond hair, masculine and leonine. Dammit, I ached for him too, for both of them.

251

Backing away from the tree, he pushed her down onto the soft moss and covered her mouth with his.

I tasted their kisses, hot, wet, and needy. I felt Evan shudder as Daisy stroked his back and chest, the first touch on his naked body from a woman in ages. I felt her skin pucker into goosebumps as he swiftly pulled off her sneakers, unbuttoned her jeans, and pulled down her panties to reveal the lush delta between her thighs. She thrust her hands into his hair as he nuzzled her belly.

I dropped to my hands and knees, fighting the pull of the serpent. In the forest, we risked losing everything. Our control would be shattered. Evan and Daisy already seemed to have lost theirs. I had to stop them, but if I got closer, my hunger would blot out all thinking and pull me into their twisted web.

In the clearing's center, Daisy spread her long, smooth legs. Energy sizzled around her, golden and electric. The fact that she could survive in here... with no preparation, no effort... not just survive, but revel in it...

When I saw the soft, velvety triangle between her legs, a hint of pink pussy peeking through, my whole body jerked. I racked my brain for every kind of magic that could stop this. I thought desperately of Reeve and Nate, who would never sense us here.

Evan peeled open her cunt, running his fingers over the glistening lips. She writhed beneath him, and he growled with pleasure, holding her down with his free hand on her belly. She was moaning his name, which surprised me. How could she think clearly enough to speak at this point, to even remember Evan's name?

I saw, I *felt* everything — her clit under his thumb, his big fingers sinking into her, her cries and his growls when he added a third finger.

Dammit, Evan, stop, I thought desperately. *We need to keep her pure for the ritual. She's the Star, no question.*

But more than that — I didn't want her first time to be like this. Tumbled in the dirt, driven by forces so powerful that her mind wasn't her own. This wouldn't be happening if she didn't want it, since these were her own hidden desires being acted out, but—

The earth rippled under me.

She's not yours to care about.

The voice hissed through the pine-scented air, inside my mind, in my dreams. For three years, I'd lived intimately with the serpent. It gave us everything we wanted — for a price. And I'd never argued. I chose this path again and again, during every full moon, when we pledged our devotion.

For the first time, I answered back.

"You can't stop me from caring."

Coils squeezed around my throat, my heart, my cock. The serpent laughed, cruel and heartless.

You're going to come anyway. It may as well be inside her. Go to them.

Evan unzipped his pants to free his erection. I tried to yell for him to stop, but the woods swallowed my voice. Daisy's head was thrown back, so she couldn't see him bared — a small mercy as his hand closed around his thick, veined shaft. His growls sounded more animal than human.

"Aren't you going to stop this?" I hissed to the serpent.

The grip on my cock tightened, and I groaned.

Her energy feeds me, whether you fill her here or in your dwelling. How that affects you is not my concern.

"Blake!" Daisy's voice was soft and strained, but it carried. "Why are you all the way over there? I need you."

How could she talk? Think? Everything about Evan's face and body told me he had sunk into bestial lust. Her thighs shook uncontrollably as he — Jesus fuck — worked a fourth finger into her.

Wouldn't he hurt her? She was so inexperienced. But her cries were all pleasure as his bunched fingers, slick with her juices, plunged into her pussy. His thumb relentlessly worked her clit, and she rocked shamelessly against his hand.

I dug my hands into the mossy undergrowth, but my knees moved inexorably forward. I was crawling to her, like a dog. And when I reached her, I'd lose all control.

I caught her scent, like tart, ripe fruit — mangoes and green apples. Her pale hair had come loose and shimmered on the ground around her.

Seeing Evan crouched over her like a lion with his prey — it aroused me so much I could barely think.

"I'm gonna put my whole hand inside you, baby," Evan grunted. Lust wracked my body, but I tried to focus. He shouldn't be able to speak either. What power was holding the woods at bay? "And then I'm gonna fuck you with my great big cock."

"Yes," Daisy gasped. "Oh — oh God —"

Her back arched, and her pussy thrust into Evan's hand. I stared at the delicate pinkness stretched around his fingers. There was no way he'd be able to get his entire hand inside those rosy furls, but with the effects of the woods...he might.

"Baby girl, you're so tight," Evan groaned. She giggled and spread her thighs wider on the soft moss to allow him access.

Then she saw me.

"Blake, Blake, Blake," she chanted. Each utterance of my name pulled me tighter into her web. "Finally, you've come to me. Let me see you."

I crawled the last few paces to her, breaching the circle. I had to.

Immediately, her hands were on me. She stroked my chest through my flannel shirt, skating over my nipple piercings. I wrapped my hand around the thick rope of her braid, and she gasped when I tugged her head back.

I yanked my shirt off. I was so fucking hard for her, and I didn't care anymore about the consequences.

As she brought my head down to hers, a hand squeezed my cock through my jeans. I knew Evan's touch; I'd know it anywhere. His firm grasp on my shaft sent my blood rushing south.

The first taste of Daisy's lips was heaven. It was everything I'd been wanting and missing for a year. She kissed me softly, and I sucked on her luscious lips until they were swollen. She twined her arms around my neck. Just the sweetest little kisses...nibbles, really... what could be the harm?

When I kissed her hard, she gasped and thrust her tongue into my mouth. Evan unzipped my jeans swiftly, reaching into my boxers to stroke my cock, and it jumped in his grasp. His hand devoured me, gripping my dick, sliding up to smear precum everywhere.

"Fuck me," she breathed, rolling her hips. Evan's fingers were still buried inside her, working back and forth. He really was trying to get his whole hand inside, and Daisy was begging for it with her entire body. Her hunger blazed out, and all I wanted to do was satiate her, screw her, worship and fill her as nature intended. "Evan, oh please —"

From the waist up, she was dressed. With a quick scrape, I unzipped my jacket that she wore, then her sweatshirt, and pulled down her tank top to expose those gorgeous little tits. Her breasts were alluring as hell, small, sexy curves capped with pink nipples that begged to be sucked swollen.

I took one taut nipple into my mouth, encouraged by her cries of pleasure, and sank my hand into her hair.

Daisy shuddered beneath me, making unearthly noises. Lifting my head, I stared at Evan's hand, half-buried in her flowerlike pussy, the most erotic sight I'd ever seen. Until I couldn't take it anymore and drank her moans from her lips.

"So fucking wet," Evan purred. Leaves rustled overhead, and her power flooded us both, lancing through the sign of the serpent with razor-sharp sparks. "You're going to come soon, just from the little games we're playing. The three of us? We've barely gotten started."

I lifted my head from Daisy's mouth, blushed red with my kisses. "Reeve," I managed. "Nate. They should be here."

Daisy's eyes cleared.

"Wait." She grabbed Evan's wrist. "I promised Reeve— And Nathan, I—"

"They'll understand, baby girl." Evan was at his most persuasive. "If they were here, you'd be fucking each other raw already."

She blinked, taking in his words, and pulled back.

"Guys—" she began, looking around the clearing. Shoving away the nearest stick, she broke the spell circle. "Wait. Stop. We can't do this."

Startled, I let go. Evan's mouth opened in surprise, but he eased his fingers out of her pussy.

She struggled to stand, her face pink. "I'm not ready. Let's —" Her muscles tensed.

She was trying to resist the pull. But she wouldn't be able to. I couldn't, Evan couldn't... and we didn't want to. I didn't care about dreams and plans, I just cared about *right now*, the wanting, the fucking and the having and the taking.

Her.

Her.

Exploding inside her, giving her my cum, giving her everything I'd worked for.

Losing it all.

"We shouldn't be here." Her voice strengthened, reverberating off the trees. "Not like this."

With an effort, she grabbed our hands and pushed through the resisting air.

We stumbled after her. Out of the clearing, out of the woods, past the dark, ever-rustling line of trees that silently allowed us to pass.

On the open slope of the hill, our cocks stabbed at the air, which was cooler than in the woods. I forced mine inside my boxers and zipped up my jeans. Evan did the same. Daisy gasped for breath, pulling up her tank top to cover her breasts.

"Are you all right?" I put my hand on her shoulder. Greer Hill careened under me, and I fought for control.

She heaved a breath. "I — I'm okay, I think. You?"

I made my voice gentle. "Don't worry about us."

Buttoning her fly, she peered at me, and I wondered just how much she knew.

I rubbed her back, trying to soothe us both. I wanted desperately to wrestle her to the ground and suck out every last drop of her sweetness. "Let's get you home."

Evan scrubbed his hands over his forehead. His eyes were wide, betraying more vulnerability than I'd ever seen from him. Taking a deep breath, he squared his shoulders and made an obvious attempt to regain his swagger as he approached us.

"Need some help with that?" He pointed to Daisy's sweatshirt dangling open. She nodded like it was an afterthought and let him zip it up.

"Evan, where's your shirt?" she asked, frowning. He exchanged a glance with me. We both knew she'd shredded it to ribbons. The scratches she'd given him crisscrossed his broad back. "Aren't you cold?" Her brows drew together in concern. She put her hand on his back and pulled it away, a smear of blood on her fingers. "Oh my God. What happened to you? You're hurt."

He took her arm possessively.

"Don't worry about it. You sure you're okay?" His voice was low, as if he wouldn't be caught dead showing that he cared.

"Positive." Her cheeks were pink.

"Blake and I will take you home. Don't come back here alone, baby girl. It's dangerous."

I wondered what Evan was playing at. Protectiveness wasn't his style. Daisy tucked her free arm into mine, but said nothing.

Evan glanced over his shoulder to mouth at me, "What the *fuck* just happened?"

And Daisy's blue-gray eyes were... foggy. Puzzled.

Shit.

Were the woods pushing away her memory of what we did?

Reeve was going to have a fit.

Back at the House, Evan sprawled in an armchair in the library. A fire blazed in the grate. Behind him, I drained a gin and tonic. I hadn't bothered to jazz it up; I'd had enough magic for one night.

Reeve paced between the bookshelves, his face creased in a frown. Nate stood by the fireplace with his arms folded.

"She's the Star," I said. "We don't need any more evidence. Daisy is it."

"We haven't determined all the signs," Reeve said, lost in thought.

"Do you need a checklist?" Evan winced as he shifted in the armchair. He'd put on a fresh shirt, and I'd applied salve to his back for the scratches, but they were still red and angry. "Who else would have gotten us in and out of the woods with no preparation or fucking effort?"

Nate's jaw clenched. "Did you hurt her?"

"Brother, she was *begging*," Evan said. "We were her humble puppets, dancing to her tune. No one's asked how we're doing."

Reeve shoved his hands through his hair. "Don't make jokes. The three of you could have died in there."

He was right. If she hadn't pulled us out, Evan and I would still be in the forest, fucking Daisy into the moss. We'd forget the need for food, for water, for sleep. We'd rut until our lust consumed us in a blaze and we went back to the earth.

I rubbed my mouth. I could still feel the softness of her lips, the eagerness of her tongue. Her kisses and nibbles were a brief flash of sunshine amidst the dark, inky coils of lust.

"If we'd died, it would've been a great way to go," Evan said dreamily. "She likes fisting, did you know that? She was about to come with my hand halfway inside her before she decided to haul us out."

A vein pulsed in Nate's forehead as he gripped the back of the couch. Cracks ran through the wood, widening.

"Nate..." Reeve put a restraining hand on his shoulder. With a shudder, Nate released the couch. "It doesn't help anyone to destroy the furniture."

"Evan, do you care about her at all?" Nate growled.

"Yes." I set down my glass with a hard clink. "He does."

Evan's lips thinned, and he gave me a warning look. *Not another word.* It hurt Evan too much to care. When he wasn't at the piano, he protected himself behind a wall of crude jokes and callous remarks.

"And what about you, Blake? Do you give a damn about her?"

I held Nate's gaze uncomfortably long, longer than we'd dared to look at each other in months.

"What do you think, Nate?"

He looked away first. Walking away from the couch, his shoulder brushed mine. After the wildness of the woods, the contact felt like an electric shock. Evan let out a low chuckle, and I thumped the back of his head.

Reeve began pacing again. He wore his analytical expression, measuring and calculating — the place he felt safest. "We have to be sure. The risks are huge. She could damage us all."

"She pulled us out because of you and Nate, brother." I caught Reeve's arm to stop him. When he flinched at my touch, I let go.

Evan stretched lazily in the armchair. "Yep. Our girl remembered her promise to Reeve, and her high school crush on Nate."

Nate turned brick-red. "What promise?"

Reeve's dark eyes met his. "She agreed to save herself for me. It excites her to play with that kind of control."

"I don't fucking believe you," Nate stormed. "Leave her alone."

"Oh, it's far too late for that. Would you turn your back on this kind of power, Nate? She's willingly playing a game. Stop thinking of her as your little sister's friend."

"It's not willing if she doesn't know the stakes," Nate shot back.

"Enough time with us and she'll put the pieces together."

Evan spread his hands. "She won't leave *us* alone, Nate. You could have had her years ago, but you didn't. Why? Was there a voice in your dreams, hissing, *don't touch Daisy? Wait until it's time?"*

"Damn you." Nate's fist closed around a fragile lamp.

Reeve held up a warning hand. "So the serpent spoke to you about Daisy," he said slowly. "You never told us."

"I told you there was a girl who got me aiming higher," Nate muttered, the lamp trembling in his grip. "We had midnight talks and then the serpent started coming."

Back in the early days when we'd lived out our desires, Nate and I had had our late-night talks too. He'd told me about Daisy, but left out her name. Whatever he felt for her, I hadn't been jealous.

Instead, I wanted to include her.

A year ago, when we dedicated our lusts to the serpent, the talking stopped along with everything else. Any contact among the four of us now was brief and charged.

Reeve stopped pacing. "You didn't say that she could be the Star. You've known for years, haven't you? All this time, we've wasted our energy on Tara."

Raising the lamp, Nate hurled it across the room. It smashed on the polished wood floor, scattering shards of colored glass.

Reeve inspected the mess. "Jesus, Nate, I said don't destroy the furniture!"

"Tara for the ritual," Nate gritted. "Not Daisy. I don't care how much power she has."

Evan rose from the armchair with an ironic smile. "Is that really what we should be arguing about?"

"What do you mean?" Reeve asked, his tones slow and measured.

"Come on, Reeve. You haven't been yourself. You lost money this week for the first time in who knows how fucking long. The day after my concert, you were grinning like a fool. I heard you *singing* around the House, for Christ's sake. Please don't ever do that again."

"We don't all have your talents, Evan." Reeve's face was stony, but the twist of his lips gave him away.

Evan pointed at him. "Feelings are a liability. Don't catch them. You shouldn't be able to."

"I'm building trust with Daisy for practical reasons," Reeve said coolly.

"Will those 'practical reasons' involve her sleeping in your bed again?" Evan stretched his arms above his head. "Because last I checked, you hate sharing a bed. You're bad at it, too. You kick and yell out and talk in your sleep. Also, you steal the covers. Yeah, I know — you were always cold as a kid."

Reeve's nostrils flared. "Enough. We'll make absolutely certain that she's the Star, and we'll take the necessary steps. There's nothing more to discuss."

22

Insomnia

Daisy

I lay awake. It was nearly four in the morning.

I couldn't remember what had happened.

I remembered approaching the woods. The pull, the tug, the excitement. Catching Blake and Evan's hands and running forward, wanting nothing more than to be in there. With them.

I remembered the tension in their arms, their muscles contracting in warning as we approached the line of trees.

The next thing I remembered was zipping up my pants, Blake's hand on my shoulder, and the complicated expressions on Evan's face: shock mingling with relief.

Both guys looked stunned and shaken, yet escorted me home like perfect gentlemen. At the entrance to Lee Tower, they both kissed my cheeks — in unison. And the spark that leapt from their lips zigzagged through me in a triangle of fire that kept me awake, wondering why the hell I'd promised Reeve I wouldn't touch myself.

Every time I tried to summon a memory of what happened in the woods, whispering leaves closed over my mind.

What was I supposed to do? Ask Blake and Evan directly? I didn't want their version of the story; I wanted my own.

My only comfort was the feeling of power as I'd pulled up the zipper on my jeans. Whatever had happened, I'd been into it. Consenting. Maybe I'd even taken the lead.

Rolling onto my back, I tugged my panties down, quick and needy. As I imagined Blake's savoring kisses on my core and Evan's greedy tongue on my clit, I moaned. My pussy was soaked and swollen, and I just wanted more...

No, Daisy.

Reeve's voice heated my skin.

"Ugh!" I bolted out of bed and strode across the room in my tank top and panties. Rooting around in my purse, I yanked out my phone and dialed Reeve's number.

"Star." He sounded startled when he picked up, which I didn't think was possible for Reeve.

"Did I wake you?"

He laughed a little. "No. I was already awake."

I sank down on my bed. I was dying to ask him about Greer Hill, but stubbornness prevented me.

"What is it?" His question was sharp, alert.

"I can't sleep," I muttered. "And I'm pretty sure it's your fault."

"Mine?"

"No, don't say it. You're about to claim that nothing is your fault, and you'll thoroughly convince me. Don't put me through that."

When he barked a laugh, he didn't sound like Reeve, the velvet-voiced charmer. "Many things are my fault. I don't know if I can take credit for your insomnia, though."

"Well, you should. Because this whole 'you only come when I say so' thing is driving me up the wall."

"But you're choosing to obey me."

I gritted my teeth. "You're in my head. I didn't ask for you there."

He drew in a long breath. "Who else is in your head, Daze? I doubt I'm alone."

I closed my eyes and leaned back against the pillows. "You're not."

Blake's and Evan's bodies pulsed against mine. I was swinging on the porch swing with Nathan, the ground falling away. And when I landed, I had a sudden ghost memory of holding my flute.

"I always used to have music running through my head," I said abruptly. "It drove me nuts sometimes, but it was reassuring. It was *there*. After the fall, my head went silent. But since Evan's concert, it's like a dam burst. And tonight..."

After Blake and Evan kissed me goodnight — carefully, like I'd detonate in their embrace — I couldn't turn off the sound.

"This one piece keeps looping around. It's the Finale of Beethoven's Third Symphony, the Eroica symphony. It's a huge piece, but I don't just hear the orchestra. Or the flute solo, which I practiced in so many places. In L.A. New York. On tour in Washington D.C., in Vienna. I hear the world, Reeve. The beat of everyone's hearts, their hidden desires. I've got the world in my head, and I can't go to sleep." I paused for breath. "Can you relate to that at all?"

"I can. It happens with stocks."

"Oh my God." I dissolved into ungainly gasps of laughter that turned into snorts. "I'm so... so... sorry."

"Are you laughing at me, Star of the Cosmos?"

"Yes! That sounds horrendously boring."

He chuckled. "No. It's beautiful. It looks chaotic, but you can find patterns if you understand how everything fits together. You think it's dry, Daze, not like your music. But money is full of emotion."

"I guess so," I murmured. "You said 'my music,' but it isn't. Not anymore."

"It is. Don't let anyone tell you otherwise."

I bit my lip. "Reeve, there's something I need to confess."

Silence stretched out. I'd wanted answers from him, but now, I just wanted release.

"I almost touched myself," I blurted. "Tonight, before I called you."

There was a low growl in his throat. "But you didn't."

"No. I just wanted you to know so you can picture me doing it. Maybe then I'll be able to sleep."

He inhaled sharply. "You bad girl. I'll deal with you soon, Daisy. You need to be taken in hand."

Need rushed through me. "Please, can I come now? I'll do it any way you want... however you tell me... I'll follow all your directions."

This was crazy. But I was into it. I wanted his rules, wanted to push against them.

He chuckled, the rasp of claws on velvet. "Aren't you a wanton little flower?"

"Please..."

"I love hearing you beg, Star. It's music to my ears. But you need to wait."

"Then help me get to sleep," I burst out. "Because otherwise, I won't be able to."

For a minute, we listened to each other breathe. Then he said quietly, "Are you comfortable?"

I laughed. "The sheets are all twisted."

"Smooth them out. Tuck yourself in."

I did as he said.

"Snuggle up under the blanket. Close your pretty eyes and I'll tell you a story."

"Jesus, Reeve, I'm not a kid." Frustration rolled over me. "Are you getting back at me for laughing at your investments?"

"No one's ever too old for a bedtime story. We all need stories, Daze."

My eyelids felt heavier. "Fine."

"Once upon a time," he began, "there was a sweet, beautiful girl." His voice pooled around me like melted chocolate. "She was smart, curious, fearless. But in her own way, she was innocent... untouched... and so very wanting."

"*Reeve.*"

"Sshhh," he admonished. "Listen to the nice story."

I burrowed my face into the pillow and squeezed my thighs together.

"Everyone who saw her wanted to touch her. To taste her. To take her sweetness for their very own. But she was too strong for most people. When they got close, her light burned so brightly that they were afraid. They ran away."

My breath quickened.

"She needed strength to match hers. It would require immense power to approach this girl, to capture her lips, take possession of her body, and give her what she so desperately needed."

I whimpered, rubbing my breasts against the sheets.

"And finally, she met her match. She found all the strength she needed and more. She was caught, pinned between big, heavy bodies. She was eager but overwhelmed as hungry mouths kissed and sucked her everywhere, biting her tender nipples, marking her vulnerable neck. She trembled with helpless desire when her clit was licked for the first time, then her soft thighs spread, firm hands holding her in place as she was pierced by a hard cock."

"Reeve, Jesus." I rolled over and bit my pillow.

"But it wasn't enough for her to yield her virginity this way," he continued inexorably. "She needed so much more. When another cock nudged her lips, she sucked it in and moaned as the thickness filled her mouth. And when a third cock pushed against her sweet ass, slick and ready to penetrate her, she yielded blissfully to losing the very last scrap of her innocence. There was a fourth cock to squeeze, and she played with it, hungry for it to fuck her too."

I held the pillow between my teeth, crossing my legs. "Please, I'm on the edge from your words, don't make me..."

"Poor baby." His words flowed over me like molten gold. "Don't think about your naughty little pussy. Think about the beautiful girl, her long hair spread out around her, undone and taken and completely possessed. She's so close to coming on the huge cocks that fill every hole. She can't think, can't speak. She's consumed by the need for those who fuck her and what they can give her. Finally, one takes mercy on her. He gently rubs her clit, and with a few touches, she explodes. The cock in her mouth pulls out and showers her with cum, more than she ever thought could be possible. Coating her perfect body, flowing down over her clit as she's fucked and fucked..."

I let out a cry and came.

A hot flash bloomed out from the center of my body. My heart raced, and my pussy throbbed with a primal rhythm. I clutched the phone tighter with my right hand, my left hand rigid on the sheets. Heat sparked through my wrist.

"Reeve," I panted, coming down from the high.

"I know, Daze."

"I just came." My breath slowed, and I pressed my sweaty cheek against the pillow. "I swear I didn't touch myself."

"I believe you." He sounded amused, but a telltale catch gave him away.

"Are you going to punish me for that too?" My throat was dry.

Reeve laughed softly. "No, sweet girl. Now go to sleep. And the next time we see each other, we'll talk."

My breath caught. Did he mean Greer Hill? What did he know?

"Why don't I pick you up tomorrow night," he continued. "Or should I say, this evening. Eight o'clock? Make sure you dress up."

"Where are we going? Will it just be you and me, or—"

He sighed. "So many questions. Sweet dreams, Star."

23

Keep Digging

Daisy

After a long day of classes ended, I chose my outfit carefully for the evening ahead.

I'd tried to regain my memories, but no amount of thinking, journaling, or experimenting with spells had done the trick. I'd even considered going back to Greer Hill, but had stopped short.

Now, I paged through my closet. What could I wear to drive Reeve crazy? To tempt him into giving me answers?

Slipping on a sheer white blouse with puffed sleeves, I tucked it into a pleated black miniskirt, finishing with a studded belt and chunky black boots.

The look was both innocent and decadent. If I understood Reeve at all, it would seriously do things to him. Slicking back my hair into a fresh braid, I added hoop earrings and armored myself with red lipstick.

Most of these pieces had come from a second-hand store in L.A. where Sasha and I used to go thrifting. I could hear her voice in my head like a commentator:

"A little goth, a little witchy, a little bit slutty schoolgirl — go conquer that playground."

But she hadn't exactly been cheering me on the last time we talked. And for the first time since reaching Morocco, she hadn't texted me a photo of the day.

Our prickly conversation made me uneasy. There was so much I wanted to tell her, but how? Even Sasha would be concerned that I went with Blake and Evan to Greer Hill at night.

Reeve making me come with his voice alone — I wouldn't know where to begin.

Or how to explain that Nathan was behind all this.

When Reeve pulled up to the curb outside Lee Tower, he braked with a jerk. The effect of Slutty Goth Schoolgirl was everything I'd hoped for.

I leaned against the wall, one boot propped up, refreshing my red lipstick and pretending not to notice Reeve until he approached. As he guided me into his gleaming car, I felt a rush of power.

I'd made everything much too easy for him so far. All he had to do was touch me, or whisper pretty, dirty words, and I melted like wax in his hands.

Tonight, things would be different. Settling into the luxurious leather seat, I counted off my goals: get my memories back. Find out what these men were up to. Access Reeve's locked-up magic books. Save Nathan.

But sensations of pleasure intruded, snaking around my limbs.

As Reeve's car purred away from campus, I kept my legs pressed together. The pleated skirt barely covered my thighs.

"You look beautiful." He dropped a hand on my knee.

"So do you, Reeve." Lifting his hand, I placed it firmly on the steering wheel. His mouth opened and closed. "I have a lot of questions for you. What's the deal with Greer Hill? What are Evan and Blake afraid of? They were terrified last night, and they didn't do a good job of hiding it."

He raised an eyebrow. "You don't remember?"

"No," I admitted.

To my surprise, a wry smile broke across his face. "Then Greer Hill's protecting you."

"What do you mean?"

"If you remembered, you might still be there, chasing whatever you felt. You'd be—" His voice sounded oddly choked. "You'd be gone."

"But *why?* How?"

"Don't you know? You skipped into those woods without a care in the world. You stole herbs from my room — I know that was you." His tone became stern, making my cheeks burn. "If you're going to play with fire, you need to understand it."

"Then tell me!" I protested. Reeve stared straight ahead at the road. "Talk to me, goddammit. Are you angry about last night?"

Coming to an abrupt stop at a red light, he leaned toward me. His black eyes smoked.

"The three of you," he growled, "were very incautious. Blake and Evan should have known better. As for you, Star — you obviously can't stay away from the flames."

All these half-hints were driving me mad. How could I get Reeve to talk? Impulsively, I tugged on his tie.

"Can you blame me?" I asked breathily. "Maybe you should teach me how to behave. I *obviously* need your discipline. Your knowledge. Your sage, all-knowing wisdom..."

I expected Reeve to laugh. Instead, he covered my mouth with his.

There was none of his cool calculation. The kiss was devouring, possessive, and painfully arousing. Our tongues fought to claim each other. I ran my hands over his shoulders, pulling him closer by his tie, and he didn't stop me.

A sharp honk sounded behind us. Reeve straightened and stepped on the gas.

"I should take you back to the House right now and teach you a lesson." His voice was low and threatening and made me want to rub against him like a cat.

"Do it," I panted.

"No. That's much too easy for you. You're going to learn exactly what you need: patience."

"Only if you tell me what I want to know. *I've* made things much too easy for you."

Now he did chuckle. "Is that what you think, Daisy?"

His obsidian eyes moved over me until I felt hot and needy and small. I shifted in the seat, rubbing my thighs together, trying to regain control.

"Let's make a deal." Reeve's dimple flashed. "Be a good girl for me. Do as I say. And when the time comes, you'll get answers."

I crossed my arms. "Do Blake and Evan remember what happened in the woods?"

Reeve's smile disappeared. He nodded briefly. "You got them in and out of serious trouble."

"If there's danger, I need to know about it."

"Why?" He squeezed my thigh, crumpling my skirt. "Surely you're not planning to go back?"

The car slowed on a busy city block. Twinkle lights, strung in the trees, lit the street.

I leveled my gaze at Reeve. "I go where I want, when I want. In case you haven't noticed, I don't have much to lose."

"On the contrary, Daze," he said softly. "You have a tremendous amount to lose. You think you've lost what matters to you, but there's a lot more that someone could take."

"What are you saying?" I whispered.

Flames flickered in my vision. Jaws opened around me. Hissing filled my ears. *Everything... .desire... trust...*

"I'm saying, don't put yourself in danger." Reeve eased the car into a valet parking line at the curb and held out his hand calmly. "And give me your panties."

"Excuse me?" I gasped.

"You heard me. You think you have nothing to lose? Let's see how you feel without them tonight."

"This skirt is way too short for that," I sputtered.

His lips quirked. "Isn't that why you wore it? To tempt me? Panties off, Daze. I need to believe you'll obey me if I'm going to give you answers."

We inched forward in the valet parking line.

"No," I said firmly. "I need to believe I can trust you if I'm going to hand over my favorite underwear."

He laughed. "If you insist. But you might feel a little more... *exposed* handing them over to me later."

He was so smug. So sure of his powers to seduce me. A dark thrill flared between my thighs, and I crossed my legs more tightly. "We'll see."

Reeve pulled alongside the valet stand. A uniformed man stepped smoothly up to the car.

"Welcome to Étoile," he said.

I stared at Reeve. "Blake's restaurant?"

"Of course. Get ready for the meal of a lifetime."

The interior flashed with black and gold, a mix of leather, metal, and smooth wood accents. Servers bustled among the packed tables.

Under the low-hanging lights, Reeve greeted the hostess.

"Reeve! So good to see you." She clasped his hand as Reeve flashed his dimple. "We always love it when you come in. I'd say Blake has his hands full in the kitchen, but I swear it's impossible to rattle him. And you're Daisy? Wonderful to meet you."

Our table was set against the wall, facing the center of the room.

It was slightly elevated on a platform, a table to see and be seen.

Gingerly, I settled onto the leather banquette, smoothing down my short skirt. Reeve's knee nudged mine.

"Order whatever you like. But if you want a recommendation, I suggest we put ourselves in Blake's hands."

Quick as lightning, an impression came to me: Blake's hands cupping my breasts, his lips seeking mine. The thrust of his pierced tongue, the scrape of fallen leaves against my back, the earthy scent of the forest floor...

I swallowed. "Sounds good to me."

I could barely focus on the menu. The food was a mix of upscale comfort and exotic ingredients, all with tantalizing descriptions. The dishes brought to the tables around us were perfectly composed works of art.

At the far end of the dining room, the kitchen was open. Chefs moved through the space in a smooth ballet, fast yet unhurried.

My stomach lurched when Blake's lithe figure emerged. He wore chef's whites, and his earrings flashed in the light. Joking with the other chefs, he pulled two knives from a block, his hands moving in a blur over a cutting board.

The diners nearest the kitchen stared, and even the other chefs paused to watch.

Looking up, he caught sight of Reeve and me in the central booth. A complicated expression crossed his face before it lit up in its customary dazzling grin. I nodded back quickly and turned to Reeve, crossing my legs.

A waiter appeared with a carafe of water and a basket of bread. When I lifted the napkin, the essence of fresh-baked bread hit my nose: warm, yeasty, laced with piquant herbs.

The waiter gave Reeve a little bow. "Wonderful to have you back, and with such beautiful company."

"Good to see you, Daniel," Reeve said easily. "Chef's choice for both of us."

"Very good, sir. The sommelier will be by soon."

"Daze, do you like wine?"

I nodded. "Red, white, it's all good."

"Tell him he has free rein," Reeve said. "We trust his pairings."

Daniel whisked the menus away. Apparently, Étoile didn't check IDs for drinking age, at least if Reeve McClellan was footing the bill.

Reeve folded his hands on the table. "Now talk. I'm very interested in learning all about you."

When I opened my mouth to argue, his shoe stroked my calf, making me shiver. *Shit.*

"You were saying?" Reeve raised an eyebrow.

The message was clear: play by his rules. If I gave him what he wanted, he'd offer me answers.

Or maybe he just enjoyed toying with me.

"Where should I start?" I sipped from my water glass to buy time.

"Tell me about your parents."

I drummed my fingers on the table. "You're rubbing your foot on my leg and asking about my family life?"

Reeve shrugged. "I have no problem with those things happening at the same time."

Heat bloomed over my body. Rummaging through the bread, I helped myself to a rosemary roll and offered the basket to Reeve, who shook his head.

"My parents got divorced two years ago," I said abruptly. "It was a long time coming. They still talk. I'd even call them friendly. But sometimes I think they never should have gotten married."

Reeve cocked his head. "Then where would you be?"

"I was the reason they got married. They were still in college."

"I see." He briefly squeezed my hand.

"They were very much in love, don't get me wrong. They might have gotten married anyway. Both of them are artists, a dancer and a filmmaker. But my mom gets so caught up in her work. She dreams it, speaks its language, breathes its air. Sometimes, she forgets about everything else. And my dad — my dad didn't want a wife who did that." I looked away. "He wanted someone who'd put him first."

"Oh?" Reeve turned my hand over and ran his thumb along the base of my palm. "I think being passionate about your work is attractive."

I flushed. "Really? I was the same way with music. I was afraid it would get in the way of a relationship."

"Believe me, I'd enjoy seeing you absorbed in what you love the most." His eyes traveled over me as he stroked my wrist.

Staring at our joined hands, I shifted on the banquette.

"My mom's in New York," I said quickly. "She managed sixteen years out in L.A. for my dad's career, but she hated it. I moved out there with her for my last year of high school because..." I looked down at the table. "She needs me more than my dad does."

"So you feel responsible for your parents' happiness."

"I never said that." Freeing my hand, I fiddled with my rosemary roll. "Jesus. Is this dinner or therapy?"

Reeve shrugged his sleek shoulders. "I'm just saying."

I tore the roll in half. "My dad's dating a very nice woman named Carmen who recently quit acting. She goes to bed early and sends out holiday cards. They'll probably get married and have kids. He always wanted more; my mom didn't."

"You're an only child?"

I nodded. "Star of the cosmos," I muttered. "And you're the oldest of five? What's *that* like?"

The waiter appeared with an appetizer and placed it in front of us. Slices of portobello mushroom fanned out on a bed of cream sauce, with pesto dotting the edge of the bowl in circles of bright, grassy green. The scent made my mouth water.

Reeve held out a forkful of mushroom. "Taste."

I forced myself to focus on him, not the food. "I asked you about your family."

"Try this first."

"I will," I said sweetly. "As soon as you tell me a little about yourself."

Reeve's dark eyes smoked. "Daisy, you're being a brat."

"Oh, really?" I fluttered my eyelashes at him. "I think I'm being completely reasonable. Most conversations are a two-way street."

The fork hovered in the air.

"Or did you have a different plan tonight?" I rested my chin on my folded hands and gave him an innocent look. "Were you going to push all my buttons until I melt at your feet? I think we've done that already. Ooh, you're pressing your lips together. I must be pissing you off."

His nostrils flared. His mouth opened to speak.

"McClellan!" boomed a deep male voice. "Great to see you."

A middle-aged man strode over to our table. Built like a former linebacker, his salt-and-pepper hair was neatly combed. He wore a Pacific Crest pin on his suit lapel.

Chancellor Weston. I'd seen him from a distance when he gave a speech at orientation. Up close, he still seemed to be speaking into a microphone.

He was smiling affably, his eyes trained on Reeve, but I suddenly felt awkward, all arms and legs. Quickly, I took the fork from Reeve.

"Chancellor," Reeve said smoothly, rising and pumping his hand. "Always a pleasure."

"Really something, isn't it?" The Chancellor waved at the bustling restaurant. "Our very own Blake Phillips at the helm. Hasn't even graduated college and his food is the talk of the town."

"Blake's talent is unmatched," Reeve agreed. Was it my imagination, or had his nostrils flared when the Chancellor called Blake 'ours?'

"Well, that's par for the course with you and your friends. I haven't forgotten the concert this week. A talent like Evan Hayes coming out of our university... it's a once-in-a-lifetime situation."

"At the very least." Reeve's tone was pleasant. I waited for him to introduce me to the Chancellor. He didn't.

The Chancellor's eyes moved over me, and he suddenly leaned so close that I could smell the discreet hint of his cologne.

"I'm going to let you in on a secret," he said in a low voice.

"You're a lucky young woman, crossing paths with this one before he graduates. Your friend Reeve practically holds this place together." He turned to Reeve. "Your recent donation couldn't have come at a more crucial time."

I smiled at Chancellor Weston, though my heart thumped. "I believe I've heard him referred to as a 'golden boy.'"

"Have you?" Reeve interjected smoothly. "I just want to bring this academic institution the level of recognition it deserves."

The chancellor clapped him on the back. "Well, you're elevating us all, my friend. Enjoy your meal," he added to me.

Reeve sat down and took a controlled breath.

As the Chancellor walked away, the sommelier appeared, pouring us a crisp white wine and waxing eloquent about the bouquet. I took a big gulp, then stared at the appetizer on the fork I still held.

Finally, I met Reeve's eyes. The lights of the restaurant sent strange, flashing green specks across the irises.

"If you won't tell me about yourself, tell me about the Chancellor."

Smiling pleasantly, Reeve spoke in a barely audible tone. "He's corrupt. Avoid him. That 'donation' probably lined his own pockets."

"Was that the money you paid him for preserving Greer Hill?" I asked. He gave a slight nod. "He had a definite creep factor. I think I've lost my appetite."

Reeve took back the fork and held the untouched mushroom in front of my face. "Daze, if you can count on anything, it's Blake's food. In an uncertain world, this is guaranteed to be delicious."

I glared at him, wanting more of an explanation. But dammit, I was hungry. Opening my mouth, I allowed Reeve to feed me.

"Oh," I whispered. "Oh wow."

The mouthful of portobello was exquisite. The cream sauce was luscious, and the pesto? Happiness, pure and simple. Though the dish was rich, the burst of basil transported me to running on grass under the summer sun and lying on a blanket as the stars came out.

I had to keep myself from grabbing the bowl and dunking my face into it to slurp every last drop. Quickly, I speared a mushroom.

"Reeve, you have to try some." I offered him a bite in return.

Indulgently, he closed his mouth over the fork. "It's tasty."

"Just 'tasty?' It doesn't make you happy to the marrow of your bones?" I demanded. "Are you genuinely getting more from watching me than from eating this yourself?"

"Yes. I'm not complaining." His knee nudged between mine, and my body responded traitorously.

I gripped my fork, then stuffed another bite of mushroom into my mouth. My veins flooded with sweet contentment. It was impossible to be angry with him when the food was so good.

All around us, people ate with expressions of ecstasy.

"More?" Reeve broke off a piece of rosemary roll, dipped it in the cream sauce, and held it out.

Why was Blake's food so unbelievable? The flavors were so intense, they took over my body and mind, beckoning me to another place.

Like magic.

I stared at the cream-soaked roll in Reeve's hand. I should have known better than to trust it.

Magic food? It seemed too crazy to be true. But in the past twenty-four hours, I'd hallucinated a snake and had my memory fogged over by a forest.

As Reeve raised an eyebrow, a group of girls in short dresses and strappy sandals swarmed through the restaurant's entrance. Leading the group, her coppery curls spilling over her freckled shoulders, was Tara.

The hostess led them to the booth next to ours, and my stomach turned a somersault.

I'd been looking for Tara on campus since Evan's concert. If I could get her alone — maybe she'd give me the answers Reeve refused to.

Tara blew me a kiss as she and her friends sat down. "That outfit looks *amazing* on you," she gushed, looking over my Slutty Goth Schoolgirl getup. I gave her a slight smile.

Reeve's jaw clenched. "Ignore her. We're having a very nice dinner, and you're mine for the night."

I sucked in a breath. "Am I?"

His eyes narrowed. "It's not a question, Daze."

My stomach lurched. "Okay. Are you going to feed me that bread now, or what?"

He pushed the bread between my lips. Instinctively, I bit his fingers, and his nostrils flared.

"Someone's really being a brat tonight." He pulled his hand away. "You're trying my patience."

"What are you going to do about it?"

"Push me any further, naughty girl, and you'll find out."

My heart beat fast. When I glanced to the side, Tara was staring at us. She'd probably overheard every word, and judging from their amused expressions, so had her friends.

A smirk crossed her exquisite face. "He's a piece of work, isn't he?" she said to me. Her friends nodded in agreement. Reaching into her purse, she rose gracefully, approached our table, and dropped a folded paper in my lap.

Quickly, I covered it with my napkin.

"Let her be." Reeve's voice, quiet yet forceful, made the flesh crawl on the back of my neck.

I turned to see his eyes leveled on Tara, two flat black discs. As she stared defiantly back, something — *slithered* across his eyes, a flash of yellow-green. A wave of malevolence rolled out from him, sending a shiver over her freckled shoulders. She drew back.

"I'm helping her," she said, with a toss of her hair. "She deserves to have someone looking out for her."

"We've discussed this, Tara," Reeve said pleasantly. "Go back to your nice dinner. And leave my friend alone."

"Your *friend?* You don't give a damn about anyone except those three boys you love so much," Tara snorted. "Daisy needs actual friends. Not you."

As they glared at each other, I peeked at the note in my lap.

I saw you on Greer Hill last night with Evan and Blake.
    I'm sure you have a lot of questions.
    Meet me outside later.
    XOXOX Tara

The note smelled like jasmine. I shoved it in the pocket of my skirt.

Tara leaned toward me conspiratorially. "Remember my advice? Make the most of this thing with Reeve before he gets bored and moves on. It's no reflection on you, Daisy — it's just the way he is. You like this necklace?" She displayed the diamond four-leaf clover hanging at her throat. "It's from him. And it's just a drop in the bucket."

Heat bloomed in my cheeks. Reeve had bought that for Tara, then claimed she meant nothing? I felt like I'd been slapped.

A vein twitched in Reeve's forehead. "You want gifts, Daisy? Just say so. Jewelry? I'll buy you jewelry. A car? I'll spend all the cash on you that you want."

"No! Stop it. I've only known you a week. Don't buy me any gifts. I don't even like cars." Flustered, I took a deep breath. "You know what I want the most. It can't be bought, and you can't give it to me. Even if you want to."

His mouth opened, but nothing came out.

"Something you want to say, Reeve?" Tara tilted her head. Her friends watched us avidly.

Reeve's lips moved, then twisted as if they were blocking his own words. Finally, he spoke. "Get away from us."

"Aren't you adorable," she said sweetly. "You're almost fooling me into thinking you care."

"Not another word." His ice-cold voice narrowed to a hiss. Tara quailed and scurried back to her seat.

"Fine." She lifted her glass of wine. "Have fun while you can — *if* you can."

Relaxing, Reeve took my hand. "Let's enjoy ourselves, Daze."

I linked my fingers through his. "Let's."

We smiled at each other, but my stomach fluttered with a sense of unease.

The note from Tara burned a hole in my pocket. When she caught my eye, she tipped her head toward the back of the restaurant.

"We'll talk," she mouthed.

Whether it was actual magic or culinary wizardry, the food and wine put me at ease. As a parade of dishes appeared from the kitchen, gorgeously arranged on plates in various shapes and colors, I ate dreamily, absorbed in the vibrant flavors and textures. Each bite dissipated the awkwardness in the air, smoothing out the evening.

I did my best to ignore Tara at the next table. Between Blake's food and Reeve's company, I almost forgot about her. But the note still nagged at me.

Did she know about Greer Hill? The ouroboros tattoo? Could I get answers on my own terms?

Reeve drew me out over dinner. I found myself telling him everything from how I fell in love with the flute at age six, when I heard my mom's friend accompany a dance concert, to how Sasha and I had bonded over movie marathons and cooking adventures, to exactly what I liked about riding the subway in New York.

He listened closely, asking occasional questions. But while we talked, he kept touching me, teasing me, stroking my bare legs.

As the meal went on, it was harder to concentrate. The sparkling lights of the restaurant swam in front of my eyes. Just before dessert, he beckoned me to slide forward on the banquette and massaged a path up the inside of my leg, rolling the ball of his thumb along my muscles. My thighs shook under his touch.

A triumphant smile flickered over his lips. "You're being so good for me now." His voice was soft and silky. "As soon as we're done with dessert, I'll take you back to the House. Unless you need me to touch you here? Is your little pussy so hungry that it can't wait?"

I breathed in sharply. When my head tipped back, arching to the side, I glanced toward Tara's table. Her ravenous stare made goosebumps rise on my skin.

"*Now,*" she whispered, her crimson lips shaping the word.

She rose from her chair, swaying to the back of the restaurant. Glancing over her shoulder at me, she disappeared through the back door.

I knew an invitation when I saw one.

And Reeve was much too good at distracting me. If I let him continue, I'd melt into the seat, forgetting every doubt and suspicion I had.

Quickly, I stood up, jostling Reeve's hand. "I need to go to the ladies' room. Be right back."

He looked at me carefully. "Go. Be quick about it. Don't even think of touching yourself."

I bit back a moan at the order. My skin flamed as I walked across the restaurant, feeling the force of Reeve's gaze on my back.

As I passed the kitchen, my eyes met Blake's. I stopped short, unable to look away as he paused his work. The shock of his bright blue gaze sank to the pit of my stomach. His expression was the strangest mix of wariness and longing.

He came to the doorway. "Everything okay, Daisy?" he asked carefully. "Is the food tasting good?"

"It's amazing," I tossed out. "Gotta go." I pointed to the restroom, my cheeks turning warm. Sparks flew through my veins as I hurried down the hall.

At the end of the hallway, past the restrooms, was a door. I pushed it open and walked into a dark alley.

24

Use Me

Daisy

S oft hands grasped my shoulders and pushed me against the wall. Coppery curls fell around my face, and the scent of jasmine filled my nose. Tara was too close, much too close.

We were alone in the alley, bracketed by piled-up crates and dim lights that sent shadows over darkened windows and doors.

"He's really got you worked up, hasn't he?" Tara's pillowy lips brushed my ear. "You weren't lying to me. He does touch you. What I don't understand is why."

My hands tensed on the wall behind me. "Reeve said there's never been anything between you."

She laughed. "You can't ever believe that boy completely. He twists everything around. I'm trying to protect you so he doesn't screw you over the way he did to me."

"Maybe I don't need protection." My voice was throaty. I slipped one hand into my purse to squeeze my tarot cards.

"What do you have in there, Daisy?" She drew one of her jeweled nails down my cheek, and I sucked in a sharp breath.

"What's in your purse that's so special? I bet he doesn't know, but you can tell me."

"Oh, it's just Reeve's soul." I gave a jaunty shrug. "I collect them. He's the latest victim."

A slow smile spread over Tara's crimson lips. "You're joking, huh? But I almost believe you. Why else would he touch you?"

Her fingers trailed down my neck. Reeve had turned me on in the restaurant, but Tara's taunts and touches drove my panicked arousal up a notch. My hands scrabbled for purchase on the rough bricks behind me.

"He touches me because he enjoys it."

"You don't understand, Daisy. He's ice-cold. He doesn't actually enjoy anything, except money and power and those three boys he loves so much."

"Are they — Have they —"

"Fucked each other? You'd like to know, wouldn't you?"

A memory bubbled up, framed by the woods: Evan's hand wrapped around Blake's cock, stroking him expertly, as he filled me with his fingers and Blake sucked my nipple into his mouth. The two men had a fluid ease with each other that made me desperately aroused. They'd touched, if not fucked, before.

"You're wrong," I whispered. "I give Reeve pleasure. He said so."

She laughed derisively, squeezing my shoulders. "Reeve's word means nothing, honey. His tongue was made to lie. You know that, right? If you don't, it's time to learn."

I wanted her to be wrong about Reeve. I wanted Tara to be the liar. But if she was speaking the truth — I needed her help.

"Why'd you follow us on Greer Hill?" I leaned in close, letting my breath brush her ear.

"*Follow?*" She toyed with my braid. "I was taking a walk. I saw you with Evan and Blake and got worried, so I climbed up after you."

"Then why didn't you say anything? Why'd you slip me the note? What do you want?"

"Maybe I just want this." Her fingers played over the hollow of my collarbone, unbuttoning the demure collar of my blouse. "You and me, having some time alone together. I like you, Daisy. You're smart, you're fun, you're hot. I'd hate to see you become nothing more than a plaything for those boys."

I shivered. When she slid her hand to the back of my neck, I was so taut with desire that I moaned.

A sudden sensation flashed between my legs. Rough, hungry, firm. Evan's pale green eyes stared down at me, narrowed with lust. That was his hand on my pussy — his fingers moving inside me, large and forceful, making me impossibly full, as trees chorused overhead in a rush of wind...

I moaned louder as Tara's face came back into focus. At her look of triumph, I thrust my hands into her thick red curls and pulled. She gasped, her pale blue eyes opening wide.

The power of the woods thrummed through me, memories beckoning and darting out of sight, and I couldn't stand the tease anymore.

From anyone.

"Tell me what you know," I ordered.

"Ooh, bossy," she teased.

"I want to hear you talk." Leaning in, I dared to swipe my tongue over her soft, perfumed neck. She let out a gasp, thrusting her body against mine.

It was so heady, so exciting, to feel someone respond. To know I could please them as much as they pleased me. I felt a flash of anger toward Reeve — dammit, and Nathan — for denying me that.

"Do you?" she teased breathily. "You want to hear me talk? Why?"

My mind raced.

"Because you're right. Those boys aren't telling me the truth. They're not giving me what I want. But you? You can. And I think it would be hot to give each other exactly that."

Jesus. What was I saying? The words spilled out, and somehow,

289

they were the right ones. Lips curving in satisfaction, Tara ran the jeweled tips of her nails down my throat.

"Aren't you afraid Reeve will punish you for breaking his little rules? I'm sure he's given you some."

"Let him." I twined my arms around her neck, biting back a gasp when she rubbed her breasts against mine. But when she leaned in for a kiss, I ducked my head away.

She laughed softly. "At least you don't want to curse me."

"Tell me about Greer Hill."

She nuzzled my neck. "I was just out for a midnight walk. It was very trusting of you to go up alone with Blake and Evan. Very reckless, Daisy. You need someone who cares to keep an eye on you."

My stomach lurched. "They didn't do anything I didn't want them to do."

"No? How do you know?"

"I felt it."

"Mmm. Do you feel this?" Her hand slid up my leg and under my short, pleated skirt.

"Oh God," I gasped.

"You're so innocent, baby." Soft fingers teased my thigh. "Did it feel this good when Reeve touched you? Or am I better?"

I let out a sound between a moan and a sob as she brushed the edge of my panties. "God, oh, God…"

"Evan wanted you so bad last night. He's rough, isn't he? It would be pretty scary if he'd actually fucked you."

I gripped her hair. "What makes you think we didn't?"

Her blue eyes narrowed. "Things would be very different if you had." Before I could ask, she licked my neck, making me shudder. "Awww, and Blake looked at you like he'd never seen a woman before. He acts so smooth, but once he got his hands on you in those woods, I bet he lost all control."

I shivered, feeling — *remembering* — Blake's hands on my breasts, his gentle touch, the way he'd rolled my nipples between his skilled fingers until they were puckered pink points. In the space of that memory, his eyes had been wild, but his hands had been careful and reverent.

And I remembered Evan's savage mouth, which wasn't reverent at all. The scrape of his teeth, his ravenous sucks that made the blood rush through me.

I shuddered, pinned between the rough brick wall and the lushness of Tara's body. She eased her knee between mine. I let her, half-drunk on memories of the men, caught between the woods and the alley.

"What's between you and them?" I panted.

"According to your beloved Reeve, nothing."

"And according to you?"

Ignoring the question, she pinched my nipple hard, all gentleness abandoned. Her eyes were flinty. "If you're going to get close to those boys, Daisy, you need me to prepare you for everything they'll do. They have... no... mercy."

In response, I ran my palms over her shoulders. Her skin was unbelievably smooth, and her gasp was everything I wanted.

Images flickered through my mind. Pulling the two men toward the woods, *dragging* them. They were — Jesus, they were trying to fight me. Somehow, I had the strength to yank these two tall, well-built guys along until we reached the line of trees. There, their struggles ceased and the three of us rushed in together.

"What if you'd never come out?" Tara squeezed my breasts, making me gasp. "What if the woods had eaten you up?"

"It drove you crazy, didn't it?" I breathed, the truth flashing through my mind. "That you couldn't go in after us."

Her crimson lips twisted. Breathing hard, she pushed her thigh more firmly between mine. "Come on, Daisy. Hurry up and touch me. Let's get off before Big Bad Reeve comes out to punish you."

"Keep talking," I panted.

"Touch my tits and I will."

Taking a deep breath, I pulled down her dress, along with the cups of her bra.

Her breasts were as exquisite as the rest of her, round, tilted upward, and sprinkled with freckles. Instinctively, I cupped the full curves, rubbing my thumbs over her nipples. The butterflies in my belly went berserk.

"Fuck," she groaned. "You were in there with them for hours, Daisy. When you came out, they were so damn careful with you, acting like gentlemen, but they're no gentlemen. They want to suck out everything you have to give."

I gasped. Her words shouldn't be turning me on, but my panties were soaked, my pussy hot and aching.

"Why are you trying to control yourself?" she breathed, running her lips down my jaw. "Why are you pretending to be a good girl and follow Reeve's silly little rules? You're obviously a slut through and through. Embrace it, Daisy. I can give you so much more than they can. I can make you come all night. I can get you a nice fat dick in a heartbeat. You don't ever need to hold back with me. I know you're dying to be fucked."

"Oh God," I gasped. Tara sucked hard on my neck as she slipped a finger inside the elastic of my panties. When she brushed my soaked lips, I cried out.

"See?" She glided upward to find my clit. I jerked against the wall, my hands tightening on her breasts. "This isn't Reeve's, Daisy. It's yours. *Your* pussy. Don't let him control it. Come out with me tonight and I'll show you how much fun you can really have."

"What makes you think I'm dying to be fucked?" I rasped.

"Because you and me, we're the same." Her breath was sweet. Taking one of my hands, she guided it underneath her dress and pressed it between her thighs. I gasped when my hand touched silky bare flesh. She wasn't wearing panties. "We're both whores. We're chasing fame and fortune by hanging around the ones who've got it."

I was panting now, overwhelmed by the attention and stimulation.

"Mmm, that turns you on, doesn't it?" she teased, sliding the tip of her finger inside me. I let out a strangled moan. "You're tired of having to be special all the time. It's more fun not to be."

Was she one of them, with a ouroboros tattooed on her arm to prove it? Why else would she know so much?

Impulsively, I pulled my hand away and shoved her dress farther down her shoulders. The light was weak in the alley, the shadows deep and dark. If I could just expose her upper arm...

"Come on, honey," she whispered. "Come all over my hand. It's okay to let go. It's all right to be nothing special."

"Nothing — special," I repeated.

"It's okay to be *nothing* for just a little while."

"I'm nothing," I whispered, the words leaving my lips without thought.

A dark abyss opened in my vision. Yawning, whispering *come to me.* I shuddered with arousal.

It would be so easy to yield. A relief, to let go of the desire to strive. To fall instead of rise.

All those years of struggling with the flute, trying to prove myself, the grief at the loss of my future — it would feel so good to let it all go.

To be nothing.

To finally sleep at night, because there was nothing to keep me awake.

Tara thrust into me, putting pressure on my tight opening, making me gasp.

"Let's ruin you for them." Her whisper was excited and sharp. "You and me, Daisy, we can do so much..."

When a strong hand gripped my braid, I cried out in pain and excitement.

A male voice, smoking with anger, spoke in my ear. "Daze, you've been a very bad girl."

I stared into black, shining eyes, an unsmiling mouth framed by precision-cut stubble, and a crisp dress shirt that flared white against the oily darkness of the alley.

"Oh, look," Tara cooed. "Daddy Reeve's here to spank us."

I shivered. "Reeve, please..."

He twisted my hair firmly. "Tara, let go of her. Or the consequences will be severe."

Whatever she saw in his face, it convinced her to slide her fingers out from under my skirt and step back.

When she did, I caught a glimpse of her inner left arm. The skin was blank and free of tattoos.

"You're not the boss of us. We were just having fun." My voice sounded slurred, drunk. Was it the wine? The wine had been very good tonight.

"You made me a promise, Daisy." His voice was cold as ice now. "And Tara is not your friend."

"Who said she was?"

Tara adjusted her dress defiantly to cover her breasts. "Me and Daisy are two peas in a pod. Guess one of us is as good as the other."

"You're nothing alike." His lips thinned. "We're going back to the House, Star. I'm very displeased with you."

"Uh-oh." I cocked my hip. "I must really be in trouble. Don't tell me we're skipping dessert."

Reeve lifted the plastic bag in his hand. "The restaurant packed it up. Blake put together an assortment just for you. We're going now."

"Phew," I said exaggeratedly. "I'd hate to miss dessert."

For a split second, his dimple flickered, and Tara raised her eyebrows. "So you go for brats now, Reeve? I wouldn't have expected you to have the patience."

Reeve studied me, his smile gone. "You're going to learn what happens when you break a promise to me. I don't give second chances."

I stared at that handsome face, those bottomless eyes that seemed to glisten with green-edged gold. I tugged at the hem of my short skirt, painfully aware of my wet pussy begging for more.

"Why should I go with you?" It came out a whisper.

A slight smile flitted across his lips. "Because you want to."

"Don't go with him," Tara sniffed. "You can't trust him."

Reeve ignored her. Slowly, he brushed back a loose strand of hair and tucked it behind my ear.

"I'm very angry with you, Daisy," he said quietly. "I expect an explanation. But with me, you can find absolution."

His touch promised tenderness. I wanted the moments of connection we'd had. His embrace, his understanding.

I wanted the darkness of his punishment.

I wanted an explanation of my own.

"Let's do it." My throat was dry. "Show me what you're made of."

"You're going to fucking regret this." Tara's voice rose behind us as we walked down the alley. "He's going to use you and hurt you. He'll break every promise he makes. He'll offer you the world, then drop you like he dropped me. He's a snake."

25

You Are

Daisy

The drive to the House was silent and charged. I glanced at Reeve's inscrutable profile, then at the dessert in its plastic bag on the back seat.

"Please tell me what's going on with Tara."

"I told you, Daisy, she's nothing to me. What a naughty girl you were, letting her touch you."

I swallowed. "I wanted to know what happened on Greer Hill. She said she saw us. You were right, I got Blake and Evan in and out of the woods."

He pulled into the circular driveway in front of the House and gave me a stare of piercing intensity. "How?"

"I don't know," I muttered, shifting on the butter-smooth leather seat.

"And you needed to pull Tara's dress down to do this? To put your hands on her?"

I folded my arms, feeling every inch the sulky schoolgirl. "I was looking for your sign on her arm. The ouroboros." Reeve stiffened. "Or do you call it something else? You all have it."

"Well, Tara doesn't." His voice was deceptively mild.

"I know that now." I caught his arm, and his gray jacket rustled in my grasp. "You're right, I wanted to touch her too. I wanted to give her pleasure. I've never been able to do that with anyone. The curse, and then... you. You still won't let me, and it's—"

"It's what?"

I blew out a breath. "It's very, very frustrating."

His face softened. "Believe me, I know. Haven't we been talking about patience?"

I nodded reluctantly.

"When the time is right, you'll be able to touch me. As much as we both want. I believe in you, Star, which is why I'm putting in the effort to teach you a lesson tonight."

The dark, hungry look on his face made me shiver.

Inside the House, the heavy front door closed with a sound of finality. It echoed through the foyer, where wall sconces cast warm pools of light over the marble floor.

I grabbed Reeve's hands. "What are you going to do?" My voice shook, and I willed it to be steady. "Fuck me with a stone snake again?"

His predatory stare relaxed into something lazy and patient, and all the more menacing for it. That heavy-lidded gaze implied that the chase was over. I was in his House; I was his now.

"This isn't about me, Daisy." He squeezed my hands, then let go. "No, it's about what *you're* going to do." Tenderly, he tucked my chin in his palm, keeping my eyes leveled on his. "You used to charm people all the time with your flute, didn't you? I've watched you. Even on a screen, you made love to your instrument. Maybe that's why no one got close to you, because they sensed they could never compete."

I suddenly felt naked, and my eyes stung. "Why are you saying this? Are you *trying* to make me feel like shit?"

"No," he said firmly. "Now you can prove yourself to me. Without an instrument, without a tool or a go-between. Just you, Daisy. And me."

I was shaking all over. "That's fucking terrifying."

"I believe in you." Reeve's velvet voice was edged with steel.

"Then take these for a start." My breath caught as I reached under my skirt. Catching my thumbs on my panties, I skimmed them down my legs and tugged them over my boots. "They're all yours."

Reeve blinked, thrown off balance as I'd hoped. He tucked my panties in his jacket pocket.

"I'm very pleased. Now take your braid out," came the rough order.

Hands trembling, I pulled the elastic off the end of my tousled braid. The House was warm, a humid jungle that coaxed a sheen of sweat to my skin. Even in the heat, my nipples tightened to points that pushed against my bra.

Reeve let out a hiss as I unraveled the thick strands of hair. Heavy waves the color of wheat and amber fell to my hips.

"No one has seen my hair down in years," I admitted.

"Good." His nostrils flared. "You're going to be completely undone by the time the night is over. Push that sexy hair back. I want to see your tits through your blouse."

My heart pounded to hear Reeve being so crude. I flung my hair back. The tips of the strands brushed my ass.

"Now crawl to the living room."

"Crawl?"

"You heard me."

"Greer Hill," I blurted. "I'm using my safe word. I am not fucking crawling for you."

"No?" he asked softly, cupping my chin.

Dammit, his dimple flickered, just for a second. Making me think that crawling could be hot. Could even be a good idea.

I hesitated, wetting my lips.

299

"In the alley, you wanted Tara to drag you down. You wondered where the bottom was and if you'd ever hit it, didn't you?"

I stared at him. Finally, I gave him a single nod.

"I felt it, Star. You're terrified and fascinated by the abyss. But you also want to rise. Here, you can have both. *If*" — he rubbed his thumb over the curve of my cheek — "you prove yourself."

He was right. I wanted both, and I was afraid.

I swallowed. "I'll do it."

A narrow, richly colored rug made a path through the marble-tiled entry hall. Reeve and I stood at the head of it. He pointed to the carpet and waited.

"The tile's available too," he commented drily when I hesitated. "But I don't think you want that for your first time, sweet flower."

My knees shook as I dropped to them. When I braced my weight on my right hand, Reeve inhaled sharply. Gingerly, I rested my left hand on the plush carpet beside it.

I stared up at the enormous entrance hall. Mythological scenes frescoed the ceiling. I felt very small crouched on the floor, a single speck below the expanse of the heavens.

Impulsively, I lowered my forehead to the carpet. Reeve wasn't ordering me to grovel, but I felt compelled to contact the ground. To lower myself even farther in this grand hall.

It was strangely freeing.

When I raised myself on all fours and peeked over my shoulder, Reeve loomed behind me. His long-lashed eyes slitted, his sensuous lips set. A large, telltale bulge pushed out the crotch of his charcoal-gray pants.

"Crawl, Star of the Cosmos," he ordered, and the command washed over me in a deluge.

The carpet cushioned me, but the floor was hard and unyielding. Inching toward the living room, I supported myself on my right hand and my knees, careful not to lean weight on my left. My hair spilled over my shoulders, trailing on the floor.

"You look so sweet like that, Daisy," Reeve murmured. "I think this is a good place for you tonight. On my floor, doing my bidding. That short skirt is giving me the cutest peeks at your needy little cunt." My voice betrayed me with a moan, and he chuckled. "How does it feel to crawl for me when you're turned on? Is it uncomfortable, Daisy?"

Jesus. I ached, I buzzed, I fucking throbbed for him.

"Yes," I whispered.

A hot palm ran over my back, making me gasp. "Good."

I could only pant as we got closer to the living room. From my position, I was on eye level with the sumptuous couches and pillows. The broad black slab of the marble table rose on its thick legs. Myriad candles flickered, and I wondered who'd lit them.

"Is anyone else home?" I breathed.

"No. It's just you and me."

I gritted my teeth. My thighs rubbed against each other, smeared with my juices, as the pleated skirt brushed my ass. Perspiration stuck my sheer blouse to my chest, and my boots were heavy as I dragged them forward to crawl.

"Get on the table, Star."

In the center of the room, the marble table towered. I maneuvered to it and pulled myself to a standing position. Though his voice was stern, Reeve moved swiftly to give me a boost as I gripped the table with my right hand to clamber up.

I felt a surge of gratitude that he was being protective, yet not coddling me.

"Move," he ordered. "Now. To the edge of the table. Head on your arms, ass in the air. Spread your knees so I can really see you."

Each command landed with a blunt thud, reverberating through my body.

Trembling, I scooted backwards to where Reeve stood impassively at the head of the table. Lifting my ass, I pillowed my head on my arms. The pleats of my skirt clung to my skin, the hem ending just below my cheeks.

He chuckled. "Look at that blush, Star. Who knew you could

301

blush so hard? No, no, don't try to rub your thighs together. I know exactly what you're trying to do. This sweet little pussy is mine. Just for that, you're going to open your knees even wider."

My heart thumped in my ribcage. I spread my knees as far as I could into a V-shape, tucking my toes underneath. The polished black marble was cold against my skin.

"Now I can really see everything." Reeve's voice was smoky with satisfaction. "You obviously dressed like a naughty little girl tonight because you want to be treated as one. So that's exactly what I'm going to do."

His fingertips traced a burning line up my thighs. I stifled a moan in the crook of my elbow. When he pushed my skirt up to my waist, baring my ass, I drummed my boots on the edge of the table.

"Hush, little slut," he commanded. "Your ass belongs to me."

I moaned more loudly. My knees quaked on smooth, hard marble. I didn't know how much longer I could hold this position.

His hands reached the creases of my thighs, sliding up...

Abruptly, both palms cupped my ass, squeezing and pinching. He urged my thighs wider, spreading my folds. It felt so wanton, so dirty to expose myself while I buried my face in my arms.

"Twice, Daze," he murmured. "Twice you've broken your promise to me. I'm looking directly at the sweet little pussy that you said you'd save."

"I'm sorry," I tried. "I truly am. I didn't mean to hurt you."

His movements stopped abruptly, then began again. "And with Tara, of all people." His thumbs ran casually up my lips, massaging my slickness. I moaned, trying to hump his hands.

A sudden slap made me yelp. Oh my God, he'd just smacked my pussy. Not hard, but it stung.

"Why, Star? Why do you want to sully yourself with someone so visionless, so parasitic? Someone who only wishes you harm? Simply because you're so horny that you'll take any attention that comes your way? Are you really that impatient?"

He stroked my dripping cunt, then slapped it again. I cried out, my voice ringing off the walls and ceiling.

"I wanted information!" I cried out. "You weren't giving it. I thought she would—"

More slaps landed on my ass, quick and stinging. I was breathless, overwhelmed. Just when the buildup was about to make me scream, one hot palm slid between my legs to rub my pussy.

"All I want is your honesty," he insisted.

"I was horny," I whispered. "Like you said. You and I — we haven't made any commitment to each other. I've only kissed one other girl before this, and she ran away. Tara's beautiful, and I was curious..."

"I want the truth," he hissed. "The deepest, darkest truth."

I cried out when he spanked me again. "Greer Hill! Just for a minute."

Reeve lifted his hands instantly and came to my side. "I'm here, Daisy," he said softly. "Take all the time you need. If you want to stop, we'll stop."

I buried my face in my arms, and a tear trickled down my cheek as he stroked my back. "Okay. You were right... I wanted her to drag me down. I wanted to be nothing."

He exhaled, running his hands over my shoulder blades. "Oh, Daze."

My eyes stung. "Don't be nice. Not right now, I don't deserve it."

"You at least deserve my understanding." Was it my imagination, or did his voice sound huskier?

My shoulders shook. "No, I don't."

His fingers dug into my thighs, gripping the soft skin. "Believe me, Daisy. I'm not nice. I just know how it feels to be nothing." His voice hardened. "But you're something to me."

Heat flooded my veins. God, I wanted this. I wanted Reeve to dominate me and punish me and prove that I mattered to him.

I pushed my ass higher. "Then show me. I want to go on."

He growled, moving behind me again. A slap landed on my pussy, open and pulsing for him.

"You told me I could trust you, Star. Yet you disobey me and make one reckless, dangerous decision after another." More smacks peppered my ass. "Don't you know about Greer Hill? Don't you know the woods can swallow you up if you're unprepared?"

"No! How would I know? You never told me. Blake and Evan didn't say a word."

"But you know things, Daisy. You were able to get in. You've caused disturbances since you came here."

What disturbances did he mean? The love spell? The fight with Nathan?

"I don't know anything about Greer Hill," I groaned, praying he'd tell me more. "What is it? What's there?"

More slaps rained down on my ass. I sank down toward the table, my knees spreading farther. I was so wet that my juices were running over my clit. A hot hand pushed down on my waist, pinning me to the table, as Reeve spanked me firmly.

A sob broke from my mouth, and two tears rolled down my cheeks. It was hot and overwhelming and frustrating and fucking disorienting to be submitting to Reeve so wholly. On a deep, strange level, it was bliss.

"You call me a star." My voice trembled. "But you insist on keeping me in the dark. Don't you want me to be safe?"

The spanking ceased. Reeve rubbed my ass in circles, soothing the hot skin,

"More than anything," he said, his voice low and charged. "Daisy, listen to me."

Footsteps sounded behind us. "Are we interrupting something?"

The low drawl made my body seize up. I twisted to look over my shoulder, around Reeve's side.

Evan stood in the doorway, his huge body outlined by the light, his face flickering in the shadows cast by the candles. Behind him loomed Blake, his hair loose and earrings gleaming.

Reeve stood between the two men and me, blocking their view. Still, nervous excitement jolted my body.

"I thought Blake was at the restaurant," I managed, my throat dry.

"Kitchen's closed now and they let me go early." Blake's voice was light and cheerful, but edged with lust. "I saw you go out after Tara. Something told me I might be needed here."

"And Evan has a concert. Shouldn't you be—?"

"I'm done for tonight, baby girl." He flexed his fingers.

I shivered. As I craned my neck, images flashed through my vision like a tail disappearing beneath a rock: kisses, touches, thrusts.

If they joined us, I might get the rest of my memories back. I might find out what happened on Greer Hill.

"Well, Daisy?" Reeve stroked my ass, adjusting my skirt to cover the burning cheeks. "Are they interrupting?"

Three hungry pairs of eyes glinted golden in the candlelight as the men studied me like I was a particularly tasty morsel. Drawing in a shuddering breath, I hesitated.

Reeve's voice was low and confiding. "I know you want to remember. Would you like us to help with that?"

I searched his eyes. Like a starless night, they sucked me in. His smile, lifting one corner of his mouth, was so knowing.

I arched my back, thrusting out my ass, though Blake and Evan couldn't see it. "Yes," I breathed.

Reeve's fingers pressed into my back, heavy and insistent, driving the drumbeat of my heart. Slowly, he moved to the side, exposing me inch by inch to his friends. One hand stayed on my ass, gripping the soft flesh through my skirt. His fathomless eyes locked on mine, gauging my reaction.

When I was fully revealed, submitting to Reeve on my hands and knees, the air in the room crackled. My skin popped into goosebumps at the famished eyes staring at me from the doorway and Reeve's hand casually, possessively running over my ass.

"Do you want them so far away, sweetheart?" Reeve massaged

my thighs, leaving a trail of fire on my skin. "Or should they come closer?"

I breathed rapidly and shallowly, on the edge of giving in. But a question pulled at me.

Something told Blake he might be needed here. What?

A flash of scales flicked across my mind. My skin felt the sinuous caress of an enormous serpent. Whimpering, I bowed my head.

"Closer." The word dropped like a stone into a pool. "I want them to come to me."

"Good girl." Reeve squeezed my ass, running an approving hand between my legs.

I bucked toward him, trying to increase the contact between my pussy and his fingers. He laughed and gave me a swat as Blake and Evan crowded close. The Devil stood behind me, the Ace and the Beast on either side.

"Mmm, what's this? Let's see what you have for us." Slowly, lasciviously, Reeve pulled my cheeks apart, displaying every inch of me to his friends: my hot, throbbing pussy, my juices running down my thighs, my obvious desire.

As if I were his to show off.

My hair was falling over my face, but I looked from one side to the other, my hands fisting on the table.

Blake's teeth bared in a fierce grin. "Beautiful," he murmured. "So fucking perfect."

Evan let out a low, strangled growl. For once, he didn't say anything, but his huge hands opened and closed. I shuddered, imagining those hands holding me captive to his desires. Squeezing my throat, filling my pussy.

"That's how you deserve to be looked at, Daze," Reeve rasped. "Like a shining, glorious star. Not the way Tara looked at you, like she wanted to fuck you to bits and crush you under the sole of her shoe."

I moaned, bucking my hips toward his hand.

"Tara, huh?" A smirk twisted Evan's mouth. "Was someone a bad little pet tonight?"

"Very," Reeve tsked. "Our Star tried to give herself to someone who could never, ever appreciate her."

"Oh no," Blake murmured. "We can't have that. Not when we appreciate her so very much."

"You guys..." I pleaded as Reeve caressed my hair. When Blake and Evan stroked my back, I truly felt like a pet. Pampered, on display, kneeling on the table for the men's enjoyment. I couldn't resist rubbing my head against Reeve's hand.

"Evan. Blake." Reeve's caramel voice swirled over us all. "Daisy put you in grave danger, dragging you into the woods. Seems like you should teach her a lesson."

Then it was a blur. Each touch, each slap, sparked the conflagration of my body. I was spanked and stroked and pinched through my clothes, dressed in some mockery of modesty, while my pussy and ass were on display. Six hands roamed over me, stealing touches of my naked skin beneath my skirt's short, fluttery hem, and I rubbed helplessly against polished marble, gasping when it heated beneath me.

As the table warmed, bits of memories flashed in the spaces between the men's knowing, hungry touches. Trees, dark and rustling, flickered around us. We were in the woods — no, the House. One minute, Evan was unzipping my jeans while Blake tried to resist. The next, they were palming my breasts, stroking my thighs, smacking my ass, driving me to the brink in the dancing flames of the candles, as Reeve held me down and urged them on with words so dirty, I couldn't believe they came from his velvet voice.

"Stop," I burst out suddenly. "Please stop."

The men froze. Blake and Evan stepped back. Perspiration stood out on Evan's forehead, and Blake's face was flushed, his tattoos coiling over his taut muscles.

Reeve moved his hands to my waist. "Too much?"

"I can't keep receiving like this. I need to touch you."

"No, Daze. Not tonight. You haven't earned that."

This was crazy.

"Please." I looked from Evan to Blake, feeling Reeve's heat behind me. "Don't you want me to — to just kiss you? At least that? I know we kissed in the woods, and you didn't run away."

Blake's hands fisted at his sides, the veins in his lithe arms standing out. Evan braced his palms on the table with a low growl. His glinting eyes roved over my body as he licked his lips.

"You pulled them into danger," Reeve said softly. "I said no. Show us you can handle it, Daze. Show us you deserve it."

My breath came quick and fast. "Oh, I will," I whispered.

Then hands and mouths were everywhere again. I trembled at the effort of keeping my ass in the air. My arms and face pressed against hard marble. I smelled the scents of smoke and melted wax, mingled with Reeve's expensive woodsy cologne, bread and wine from Blake, the indefinable dusty velvet smell of a concert hall from Evan.

My hair fell over my face, veiling it. An appreciative hand stroked the long tresses. Another twisted them in a fist and pulled. When I cried out, the sound was met with male groans of arousal.

Those same hands moved down to my breasts, stroking them with myriad touches: crude, delicate, punishing, tender. Cool air met my cunt as it was peeled open.

Someone was sliding a finger into my pussy and, oh God, a teasing touch tickled my ass. Candlelight danced on the table, and I gasped when I realized that the soft, hot, probing flutter between my cheeks was a tongue. Someone was *licking* my tight back hole. My face burned with humiliation, but the attention felt incredibly good. When I wriggled, the slaps on my ass became harsher, which only made me gush over the fingers that filled my pussy and rubbed my clit.

"Hold still, baby girl," Evan hissed, and I felt hot breath over my cheeks. "Let me into your cute little ass."

His big hand stung again as it descended, and I tightened around the tongue that tried to enter my dark, sensitive pucker.

"Don't be too rough tonight, Evan," Reeve warned smoothly. "Our Daisy might be a very naughty girl, but she's an inexperienced one."

"Fuck, she is loving this," Blake groaned. "She's dripping all over my hand."

I inhaled sharply. So Blake was fingering my pussy, stroking the swollen flesh, while Evan licked my ass. It was dirty, it was shocking, it was everything I'd dreamed about.

"I'm going to come," I sobbed.

Between my knees, someone slid a long, flat, narrow object onto the table.

A mirror.

"Look at yourself, baby girl," Evan hissed. "Tell us what you see."

I glowed.

Light shone from my face, my chest, and my pussy, rosy and slick with need. Stunned, I focused on my tender opening stretched around Blake's fingers. My clit stood out in a little bud, his thumb circling it. He pumped his fingers slowly in and out.

"Tell us what you see, Daisy." Blake's voice was so encouraging, but, God, so commanding. Evan landed a rough smack on my ass.

As I stared at my reflection, my long locks creating a fuzzy halo, a dark shadow coiled around me.

You want to be dragged down? I'll give that to you. But in the end, you'll rise.

"I see desire," I panted.

"Do you want us?"

"Yes!"

Reeve vaulted onto the table in front of me, quick and graceful, his sculpted body taut. He'd shed his jacket and rolled up his sleeves. Kneeling in front of me, he took my face in his hands.

"This is where you turn, Daisy. If you feel like a little slut who's helpless to handle her desires, you come here. To us."

I sobbed openly, tears running down my cheeks, as Blake's long fingers curled inside my pussy.

Evan squeezed my ass, working a finger inside me, and my tight back hole clenched around him. "Fuck, yeah," he grunted, when I arched into Blake's hand. I rocked between them, eager and excited. "Ride us, baby girl."

"I'd rather you learn patience," Reeve continued mercilessly. "But this is far better than offering yourself to those who want your destruction. We will always take care of you, Daze. We'll fulfill every need your naughty body desires. Here. In this House. With us. Do you understand?"

God, this was crazy. I was *glowing*. I'd known these men for a week, and they were utterly possessing my body.

Was this why Nathan warned me away?

"Nathan," I whispered, so close to peaking.

My hair fell over my face. Reeve brushed it away tenderly. He gripped my chin, smearing my tears over my cheeks.

"Do you understand, sweetheart?" he repeated. "Tell us yes or no."

"I think so," I breathed. "Yes." In the moment, I did. It felt too good to stop.

"Good girl," Blake crooned, fingering me forcefully. His thumb blurred on my clit, stroking the most sensitive spot. "Good, good girl."

"Come on, pet," Evan whispered. "Come for us. Give us a huge fucking orgasm."

The floodgates opened. As the men urged me to the edge, everything that had happened in the woods rushed in. I relived each touch with Evan and Blake, each soft kiss and rough caress, superimposed on the thick fingers buried inside me and their hot, tugging hunger.

Light flared in the mirror, so bright that the room went white. Blake and Evan swore, and Reeve uttered an awed whisper.

I came, spasming again and again. The light was too intense to keep my eyes open, so I buried my face in Reeve's lap, bucking helplessly against Evan and Blake's hands, rippling around them both, until the storm subsided and they eased out of me.

The mirror slid away. The men cradled me as I slumped onto the sweat-slicked marble. Hands caressed my skin, soothing me after the cascade of intensity.

"You're incredible, Daze." Reeve petted my hair, and I purred in contentment. "You really are."

Questions still swirled in my head, but fatigue weighed me down. Reeve had promised to give me answers, right? Now that I'd cooperated, he had to make good.

I curled up sleepily as Blake rubbed my back from my shoulders to my waist. Evan's hand rested possessively on the nape of my neck, and Reeve gently smoothed my braid out of the way.

But when I reached out to pull them closer, they evaded me.

"Let's get you to bed, sweet Star." Reeve coaxed me off the table, supporting my waist. "Leave us," he said to Evan and Blake.

They each kissed my cheek, as they had outside Lee Tower last night.

I blinked awake, watching Blake's graceful exit beside Evan's husky prowl. Both confident and powerful, both obeying Reeve's orders.

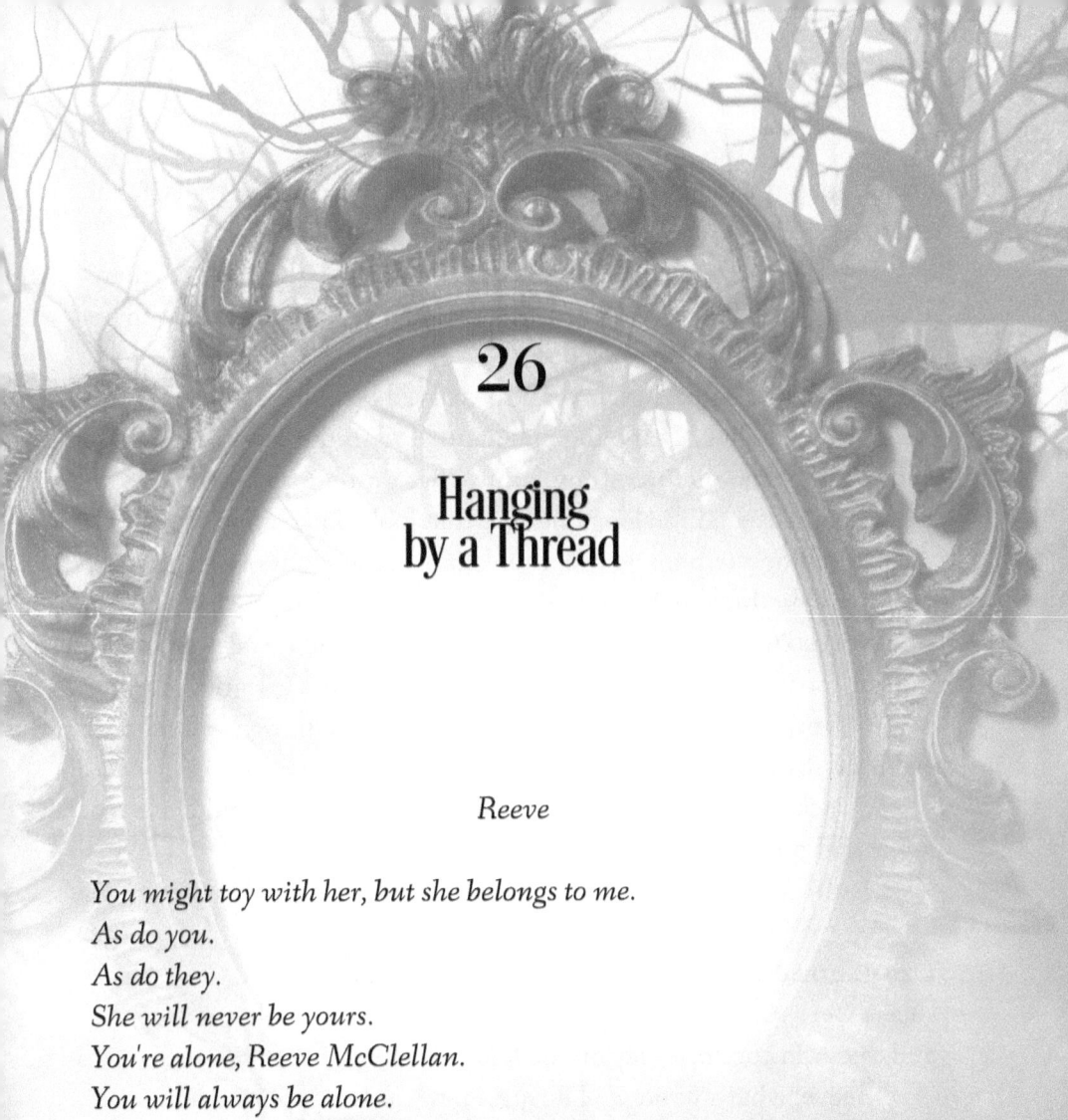

26

Hanging by a Thread

Reeve

You might toy with her, but she belongs to me.
As do you.
As do they.
She will never be yours.
You're alone, Reeve McClellan.
You will always be alone.
I'm all you have.

Breaking through the surface of an endless chasm, I bolted out of the dream, taking shuddering breaths. Coils wrapped around my throat, squeezing my heart.

"Down," I croaked. "Get down."

The pressure eased a fraction. I rolled over to reassure myself that Daisy was still here, sleeping soundly beside me. Though I'd thrashed, she hadn't stirred.

We'd worn her out on the marble altar. I touched her warm

313

cheek, taking a moment's comfort in the slow rise and fall of her chest.

Then, shoving myself out of bed, I staggered to the cabinet where I kept my supplies. I uncorked the decanter of liqueur I kept there and drank directly from the bottle.

After a few gulps, I groped for the carved box I kept hidden in the back of the cabinet. Fumbling one-handed with the lock, I opened it and took out the picture of my family that sat on top. I stared at the faces I hadn't seen in so long, the eyes that looked like mine.

Clutching the photograph, I took another draught of the liqueur. It burned my throat going down.

I was sixteen when the serpent first came to me in a dream, and I prayed for its return the next night. When it didn't, I grieved. The death of my father was still fresh, and another loss right afterward, even of a dream, was too much.

A week later, the serpent came back, and I swore I would give it a home and proper worship if it stayed.

I hadn't counted on a nightly battle by the time I was twenty-two.

As I wiped sweat from my forehead with the back of my arm, Daisy turned over, looking at me dreamily from the bed. The black sheets were rumpled. I'd scattered the pillows as I fought the serpent, and the satin comforter lay on the floor.

"Reeve, what's wrong?" The question was heavy with sleep.

"Bad dream," I forced out.

"Ohhh." Her voice warmed with concern. The sheets rustled as she sat up. "You're afraid?"

"I'm fine."

I stepped into the slice of moonlight that showed through the gap in the curtains, and her eyes widened.

I was naked. I must have torn my clothes off during the dream.

The tattoo on my arm writhed, and silvery scars crisscrossed my chest and shoulders — offerings to the serpent. It didn't ask for blood anymore; we'd proven our loyalty. Now it only wanted to feed on our desires.

Instead of moving back into the darkness, I stared at Daisy, then down at my cock, soft and hanging between my thighs. For once, everything in me rebelled at the serpent's possession. I wanted to share myself with another.

With her.

The bed creaked as Daisy climbed out.

Wisps of hair stuck out around her face. She was naked as well — she'd fallen asleep that way, in my arms.

Gently, she took the bottle from my hand and set it on a table. I dropped the photo of my family next to it. Along with the herbs we took that controlled its presence, alcohol dulled our awareness of the serpent. When Evan drank, it was to get drunk, plain and simple, but the rare times I picked up a bottle, it was to find a moment's peace.

"Reeve." She stopped short. "I — you're — God, you're beautiful." Her eyes flicked up and down my naked body, unsure where to land. They fluttered over my shoulders and chest, darting around my cock, bouncing back up to my face. "I mean — do you want me to see you like this?"

Fuck, yes, I wanted her to see me. I wanted to catch her in my arms and hold her close, feel her pressed against the length of my body, every inch of our skin touching. I wanted to drive into her and spend myself.

"I'll be right back." Striding into the bathroom, I retrieved a robe from a hook and wrapped it around myself.

"Can I hug you?" She lifted her arms and paused when I stiffened.

No. No hugs. I didn't need her kindness. I should stop this idiocy right now.

But I nodded, and she put her arms around me. When I sagged against her, I expected her to recoil. Instead, her embrace tightened, and her fingers curled in my hair.

"It's okay," she soothed. "No matter how awful it was, dreams aren't real."

"They are, Daze," I said hoarsely.

315

"Do you want to talk about it?"

"No. Except that my body wasn't my own." Coils forced the air out of my lungs, and I closed my eyes until I could breathe freely.

"Oh, Reeve. That's the worst feeling." Her voice held understanding.

"You must have felt terrible when you broke your wrist," I muttered. "So out of control."

Now it was her turn to sag against me. "That's exactly how I felt."

For the first time, I wanted to tell her the truth. We didn't have all the signs yet that she was the Star, but who else could she be? She deserved to know.

But the four of us couldn't speak of the serpent, or the rituals, or the magic that infused our bodies. The blood oath we'd taken prevented us from doing so. If a confession managed to slip past the barrier, our tongues would fork and our skin would scale. Permanently.

"Reeve," she said suddenly. "I remember everything from the woods now. And it scares me, because I wasn't in control then either."

"Don't go back," I said, more harshly than I meant to.

"But I belong there." Her eyes were luminous in the hint of moonlight. "I don't know how to explain it, but when I go alone, it feels right." She let go of me, smoothing down her hair with quick, self-conscious motions. "It's something that's my own."

I knew she was referring to my dream, to the little I'd told her — that my body wasn't my own.

"Daze, the nightmare wasn't just that," I said abruptly. "It was about being totally alone. No friends. No family. No love. No possessions, no accomplishments. Nothing."

She crossed her arms over her bare chest, her eyes skittering to the photograph on the end table. "Is that your family?"

I watched her in silence, until she hurried to fill it.

"I looked you up. I read about your life on the farm—" She broke off when I made a low noise. "It sounded sweet. I've always had a farm fantasy."

"That's because you're a city girl," I said, shaking my head. On an impulse, I went to the armoire, dug for the carved box, and brought it to Daisy. "Yes, it's my family. You can meet them."

Her eyes widened. "'Meet them,' as in go visit?"

I laughed, but it came out bitter. "That won't be happening any time soon. Not because of you — strictly because of me. But I'll show them to you."

I motioned for her to sit on the leather couch by the tall windows. She gave me a quick glance, then complied. Sitting beside her, I handed her the photograph and opened the clasp on the box.

Why was I doing this? It was reckless, unplanned, foolish.

"This is the McClellan gaggle," I announced. "All of us kids have 'R' names. Robbie, Rachael, Russell, Ruthie..."

Her gaze followed my pointing finger. "You're all beautiful. Those big dark eyes... your mom has them too."

She didn't comment on my brothers' too-short pants, or the family's homemade haircuts. The picture was taken ten years ago, when I was twelve and scheming endless ways to get rich. My parents were already careworn, looking at least a decade older than their years.

I remembered, but didn't speak of, the long, cold nights when I kept myself and my siblings afloat by spinning castles in the air.

I'd fed us words in the dark when there was little else for comfort. But there'd always come the moment when someone would say, *Aw, Reeve, that's not real.*

You mean it's not real yet, I'd say patiently. *The first step is believing. Do you believe me?*

No, they'd grumble.

I know we don't have much right now. But someday, I'm going to build us these castles.

You're full of it. Now stop stealing the blanket.

I'd built my castle. I'd made more than enough to build theirs too, but my hands were tied.

Daisy reached for the box as I put the photograph aside. "You've got a copy of *The Great Gatsby* in there? It looks like it's been through a lot."

I handed her the ragged paperback, and she turned the dogeared, underlined pages. I'd read the book in high school English class — a strange assignment for my rural school, where half the class didn't graduate, most never left town, and social-climbing aspirations were never realized.

"So this is your playbook?" She raised her eyebrows. "A guide of what to do when you're newly rich?"

"No, Daze. It's my guide of what not to do."

"You throw huge parties, though."

"Mine are better than his," I said, and a smile tugged her lips.

"How do you feel about me being named Daisy?"

"I think you're nothing like the Daisy in the book. These are my mother's," I added, placing the open box on her lap.

Silently, she leafed through the worn tarot cards, faded astrology charts, melted-down candles, and herbs that had lost their scent.

"She practiced witchcraft?" Daisy asked finally.

"If she did, she kept it a secret. I found her supplies in the attic when I was fifteen. She told me to burn them. As you can see, I didn't."

She looked at me curiously. "Have you ever used them?"

I opened and closed my mouth. "They're keepsakes. Strictly sentimental."

"That's sweet." She eyed me warily, then shuffled the tarot cards. "Want me to do a reading for you?"

I put my hand over hers and the deck. "I don't want to know what would turn up."

"Reeve!" she chided indignantly, turning her fingers up to link with mine. The touch was sweet and tender, and I had to force myself to hold still, to keep from kissing her sleep-swollen lips. "There are no bad cards in tarot! The messages are always complex. That's why I love the cards. I've been using them for years. The interpretation depends on the person who's doing the reading — like a piece of music. The notes are the same, but the nuances are different." Pink crept over her cheeks, and she laughed self-consciously. "Why are you looking at me like that?"

Because I can't take my eyes off you. Can't stop listening to your voice.

I shook my head. "No reason."

"The cards told me you're the Devil," she said quickly. "But here I am spending the night with you, so you can't be that bad." Tentatively, she brushed her lips over my cheek, swirling over my earlobe, and I gripped the couch. "I don't think you're bad at all, Reeve," she whispered. "I don't think the Devil's so bad, either."

Every word she said pulled me in deeper. I stroked the curve of her cheek, and her flush deepened. "Why don't you keep them?"

"The cards?" She shook her head, her mouth forming an O. "I couldn't. They're your mom's. You said they're a keepsake."

"That's why I want you to have them." I gave a casual shrug. "You won't let me buy you gifts, Daze. At least accept a pack of old tarot cards."

She looked down at the time-softened deck, shuffling it slowly. "Thank you. This means a lot to me."

"More than a car?" I couldn't resist asking.

She sniffed. "What would I do with a big hunk of metal at this point in my life? From someone who I" — she glanced up at me — "barely know." Her lashes fluttered, and she looked away again. "Can you please tell me why you bought Tara a diamond necklace? If there's history between you, I understand. What I don't understand is why you're denying it."

My jaw set. I chose my words carefully, dancing along a knife's edge.

"There's history, but not the kind you think. There was a time when I thought she might be of value to the four of us. I told her things I shouldn't have. She threatened to spread them unless I bought her confidence."

"She *blackmailed* you?"

"She's been extorting me for years. So, yes, indirectly, I paid for that necklace. Between you and me, I wouldn't have chosen that particular style."

"God, that's awful." She touched my arm and pulled back. "Is it going to end? Or will you keep paying her forever?"

I covered her hand with mine. "It's going to end very soon."

"And that thing you shouldn't have told her..."

I laughed. "I'm not telling you. Not yet."

"Thanks, Reeve," she said dryly. "Glad you have so much faith in me."

"I don't expect you to blackmail me, Star. But as I said, I do need to trust you."

She raked a hand through her tangled hair, hugging the pack of tarot cards to her breasts. Goosebumps puckered her arms.

She was cold.

I took a pair of pajamas from my dresser and held them out to her. She put them on with a wry smile.

"I won't lie, Reeve. I'm impressed that you own purple silk pajamas."

I shrugged. "They make my life complete."

"Do you want to go downstairs?" she said softly. "Sometimes it helps to get away from your bedroom. When I was a little girl and had a nightmare, my dad would make me hot chocolate in the middle of the night. Scary things hate chocolate."

I couldn't help smiling. "Is that so?"

"Absolutely. I'll make you some."

I let her take my hand and lead me down my own staircase. The purple silk pajamas shimmered around her long, slender body. Her hair was disheveled, and she held my hand tightly, as if she were afraid I'd disappear if she let go.

In Blake's kitchen, she rummaged around, opening and closing cabinets and marveling at the setup.

"Sasha would *die* over this," she muttered. "But is there a single packaged item here? All I see are fancy ingredients to cook from scratch. Don't you guys ever want to grab a snack? What does a girl have to do to find some Nesquik?"

Slouched at the long kitchen table, I watched her flit about, bemused. "I'm sure there's a bag of chips around here somewhere."

Her hand closed triumphantly on a sack of chocolate discs. Filling two glass mugs with milk, she popped them in the microwave.

"When I was little," she said with a sudden smile, "there was a patisserie in L.A. that I loved. They made hot chocolate like this, with real chocolate whisked into cream. Sasha and I would copy it for sleepovers in high school. She even let me take charge, which is saying something. I'm not much of a cook, but I've always liked making hot chocolate this way."

The microwave beeped. She took out the mugs, dropping a handful of chocolate discs into each and whisking the chocolate into the hot milk.

Food wasn't a comfort to me the way it clearly was to Daisy. But seeing her bustle around the kitchen, listening to her talk, was more steadying than anything she could whip up.

She set a steaming mug in front of me. "Goodbye nightmares, hello hot chocolate."

I took a sip to be polite. If Blake had concocted it, the hot chocolate would be flawless. The milk would be the ideal temperature, foamed to perfection. The melted chocolate would be smooth and luscious, and one drink would evoke the recipient's most cherished associations.

Daisy's hot chocolate tasted homemade. The milk was a touch too hot, and bits of not-quite-melted chocolate floated on top.

Yet I didn't want to drink anything else.

It tasted like a version of home I'd always longed for, and had only just found.

"You're being too nice," I said quietly.

"Now you understand how I feel." She dropped into the seat beside me. "If you won't let me touch you, at least let me comfort you. Try receiving for once, Reeve."

I sipped the hot chocolate. "I don't like receiving. I like being in charge."

"Believe me, I know." She wrinkled her nose playfully. "I've seen you boss the other boys around. It's not just me." She cocked an eyebrow. "Makes me wonder if *they've* ever had to crawl on your marble table for a spanking."

"Would that surprise you?" I teased.

"Honestly? Not so much. At this point, nothing would surprise me." She raised her cup to her mouth and sipped her drink, leaving a smear of melted chocolate on her upper lip that I wanted to lick off. "Friends punishing friends... spanking friends... getting them off..."

She met my eyes and laughed, waiting for me to join her in the joke. I held her gaze.

"Have you gotten your friends off?" Her laugh died on her lips when I didn't respond. Her eyes widened, shocked and electrified. *"Have* you? Holy shit, Reeve, you have. I see it on your face. Blake and Evan — Nathan — all of you? Have you all been together?"

There was nothing I could say. My tongue was tied. All I could do was snatch up a napkin to wipe that damn chocolate off her upper lip before I lost control. She stared at me as I dabbed her mouth.

"I thought you don't let yourself come," she persisted. "You don't even want to be touched. You said none of you are together, not like that."

"It's complicated. In the past." I managed to force those few words out, dropping into my chair and gripping the mug.

It had been fucking overwhelming in the beginning, being connected by the serpent — the living embodiment of desire. As novices, we hadn't reached the level of initiation where we dedicated our lusts solely to the serpent's appetites. For the next two years, we would have to prove ourselves through rituals and devotion. We weren't even at Pacific Crest yet, where the land would feed and anchor us.

We were in a constant state of horniness that only we under-stood: four guys in our late teens, opening our bodies to powerful magic, sharing a small, crowded apartment in L.A. during a sweltering summer while we plotted our glorious future.

As the leader, I'd struggled to maintain a measure of control. But Evan, Blake, and Nate — if they hadn't fucked, the lust could have literally driven them mad.

Daisy's brow furrowed. She was silent for a long time. I tensed, worrying that I'd scared her off. But she was still here, in my kitchen, her ankle twined around mine.

"And... Nathan?" she asked hesitantly. "You've touched him? You've — made him come?"

I jerked a nod, though it pained me to do that much.

Her cheeks colored, and she stared down at my chest. Absurdly, an apology wanted to push its way out. Even though all of this, including Daisy in my home, was for one purpose only.

"Why does he keep warning me away from you?" she asked quietly. "Is he jealous of me? He wants to keep things to the four of you, and I'm the intruder?"

No. Nate wanted Daisy, but he also wanted to protect her. He was better at resisting her than I was. Until tonight, I'd focused on investigating and understanding her.

Now, I just wanted her. A delicious armful to hold at night, her face the first thing I woke up to in the morning. Her body and soul all mine, to taste at will.

And that would be the most selfish indulgence of all.

My words came out with an effort. "Nate thinks he doesn't want you here, but he'll come around. That's all I can say." She looked like she wanted to reply, but pressed her lips together instead. I buried my hands in her hair, pulling her close. "We all want you here, Daisy."

She rested her head on my shoulder, daring to put her arms around me. I didn't stop her.

"If you guys are ever together again, can I watch? Or even join in?" she asked hesitantly. "You've watched me... touched me..."

My cock stirred, and I held back a laugh of disbelief. She was perfect for us — eager, unfazed, and curious. Every glimpse I revealed of our ways only attracted her more.

"When the time is right, Daze." I stroked her back, knowing my touch was more possessive than it had a right to be.

I wanted to tell her the truth. I wanted to share her with my friends. I wanted to spirit her away and have her all to myself.

You can have everything you want, the serpent had hissed when I first dreamed of it. *Everything, in return for devotion.*

The serpent had lied.

27

Fame

Daisy

The Pacific Crest stadium was packed. Banners waved, horns blew, and the school colors rippled over the stands in a sea of red and gold. As I entered with Michelle and Amy, I put my sunglasses on, trying to block the sensory overload.

After a night in the velvet darkness of the House — and Reeve's arms — my first college football game felt like a shock.

"Where's your Titan spirit?" some guy roared at me as my roommates and I made our way up through the crowded bleachers.

I glanced down at my black tank top and gray jeans. Michelle and Amy were both kitted out in full school colors, down to the ribbons on Amy's pigtails.

"I've got spirit on the inside," I tried.

The guy gave us a strange look. "Trust me, by the time this game's done, you'll be red and gold all over. You'll be a Nate Davis fan for life."

Climbing the stairs, we settled into seats near the top of the bleachers. The sun beat down, and everyone around us was yelling.

Far below, football players were stretching on the field, which spread out in a perfectly mowed green carpet.

"Who are they playing?" I shouted over the beat of the pep band.

"You mean, who are *we* playing?" Michelle said, leaning over Amy in the middle. "The school that's always kicked our asses up until last year. With your friend Nate on the team, it's a different story."

"You can think about that while we wonder why you're ghosting Reeve McClellan," Amy added.

I pressed my palms to my burning cheeks. "I'm not *ghosting*. I left the House a few hours ago, and he was still asleep. That's all. It was almost twelve o'clock! I had things to do."

"And you're not returning his texts?" Michelle raised an eyebrow. "We saw you silencing your phone. I don't know what they call it in New York, but around here, that's the definition of ghosting."

I shook my head. "I'll get back to him. I just need a minute."

Of course I would. I'd thought about Reeve — and Blake, Evan, and Nathan — all afternoon. I wasn't holding off because I didn't want them, but because I wanted them so much.

In the dark, everything had made sense with Reeve, night terrors and all. I wanted to hold him, to comfort him, to take away his pain. But in the brilliant light of day, all the questions resurfaced. My heart was tender, and so was my body.

On the way out of the House, I'd stopped in the majestic library and pressed my hands against the glass that protected Reeve's collection of magic books. The ornate lock taunted me. Why did he refuse to share his knowledge? Why did he insist they were simply collector's items when that seemed less and less likely?

The security guard patrolling the lawn had given me a side-eye as I left the property, adding to the surreality.

Now, I felt exposed, full of all the men, squinting in the sunlight like some nocturnal creature. The crowds were too loud, the band too raucous, the colors too bright. I'd come to see Nathan in action, but what could I learn from being here?

I squeezed Reeve's mother's tarot cards, which were tucked inside my purse.

The football team was jogging across the field. It was easy to pick Nathan out; he loomed in the center, and the crowd shouted his name, cheering and whistling every time he looked toward the stands. They'd probably congratulate him for sneezing.

Across the stadium, three pairs of eyes locked on me. One pair electric blue, one pair jade green, and one pair so dark they made me shiver.

Blake, Evan, and Reeve.

They sat much lower in the bleachers than we did, close to the field, yet they stood out in the crowd. People clustered around them, and I wondered if they were party guests from the night of The Crush. But a subtle space surrounded them like an invisible electric field.

I forced myself to stare back.

Evan grinned broadly, and Blake gave me a cheerful wave. The teams were getting into position; the game was about to start. But Reeve's gaze burned holes in my shirt.

I ran my hands over the ribbed black cotton, feeling suddenly naked.

Had I hurt his feelings by ghosting?

Or was it anger? Wounded pride?

This time, I was the one to look away.

On the field, the referee tossed a coin on the ground.

As the game began, Reeve was still looking at me. From across the field, I saw the purplish shadows under his eyes. His fingers laced tightly around one knee, tension outlining his sleek shoulders. Though Evan and Blake both wore Pacific Crest tees, Reeve was dressed in an immaculate button-down shirt.

Did he ever relax?

The crowd roared, surging to their feet. "Davis! Go, go, go!"

Michelle and Amy leapt up, cheering, and my cheeks went hot. Whatever Nathan had done, I'd missed it, because I'd been playing a staring game with Reeve. Had the other men blotted Nathan out completely? How could I forget him?

I focused on Nathan's hulking figure as he high-fived all his teammates and accepted pats on the back.

"Isn't he incredible?" Amy whispered.

I had to agree. Nathan or no Nathan, I would never be into football. But there was a brutal beauty to his next charge across the field.

He was obviously the star. All the action rippled out around him. Yet I had a sinking sensation as I watched him play.

"Something's wrong," I yelled above the cheering. "He's holding back."

Amy held up her hands. "Nate Davis? I'd say he's giving it his fucking all."

Michelle squinted at Nathan speeding across the grass. "How can you tell?"

"It's only a feeling. Something about the way he holds his body." I propped my chin on my hands, zeroing in on Nathan's flexing muscles. "He's being too careful, like he's keeping himself on a leash."

"Are you sure?" Michelle wrinkled her nose, and Amy also looked skeptical.

"Forget it. I'm just thinking out loud."

Michelle reached for her purse. "I could go for a smoothie. It's hot as hell today."

I stood up quickly. "I'll get it. I want one too."

Like a magnet, my eyes were pulled across the field once again. Cheering teammates surrounded Nathan. Blake raised his arms in triumph, while Evan watched with an amused expression.

Reeve's seat was empty.

"Strawberry?" I said to Michelle. "Amy, you want anything?"

"Cherry slushy."

As I edged out of our row, a lag in Nathan's movement caught my eye. He was arrowing across the field, ball tucked under his arm, but at the center of the grass, he slowed down. Stumbled.

It happened in half a second. He recovered and picked up speed so quickly, I wondered whether I'd really seen it.

Inside the stadium, arches held rows of concession stands. I followed the curving path, tracing the circular interior until I reached the smoothie stand.

Once I picked up two strawberry smoothies and a cherry slushy, I walked a little farther to look around. I'd never been in a stadium before, except for the one time I'd sneaked out to a game at Nathan's high school.

Sasha wasn't there; she never went to Nathan's games. But he was a senior, and this was his last game before the season ended. At least, that's what he'd told me during our late-night porch swing talks.

I'd come alone, without telling him. Beneath the dark November sky, the stadium lights had been bright and cold. People shouted and cheered, but Nathan didn't play once.

I thought he must be sick. Or something had happened, a flat tire, and he couldn't get to the game. But when it was over, he walked out, his shoulders slumped.

I ran over to him, and a strange expression crossed his face.

"Sorry you wasted your time, Daisy. I could have told you I probably wouldn't play."

"That's not fair," I burst out.

"It's completely fair. I'm not good. I barely made it on the team. Not sure why Coach even allowed me on."

"But you love football," I protested.

His face twisted. "That counts for nothing. If you don't have what it takes, all the love in the world doesn't make up for it. You think you can make a career out of loving the flute?"

Stunned, I reached for him and dropped my arms. I'd never seen Nathan lose his temper.

As quickly as his outburst came on, it evaporated. He smiled tiredly, stretching a hand toward my face. Before we could touch, he pulled back.

331

"Thanks for coming, Daisy. It really means a lot to me. I'll see you around."

Feeling hollow, I'd walked alone to my parents' car, which I'd borrowed on the pretext of going to a concert. I'd hoped Nathan and I would do something together after the game, though we'd never hung out beyond our midnight talks. But it seemed like he would have been happier if I hadn't come.

A familiar deep voice brought me out of the memory.

"You've bled enough from me." The words were low and bitter, drifting from around the corner.

"You don't even have blood in those veins," came the shrill response.

I stepped back, flattening my body against the wall. I couldn't see the speakers — they must be down a hallway around the corner. But I knew exactly who they belonged to.

"We don't need you anymore," Reeve said quietly. "We're done, Tara."

"We're not done," Tara snapped, her voice quivering with anger. "We'll never be done."

"You've gotten more out of our success than you ever should have. Consider it a win."

The smoothies and the slushy were sweating condensation on my hands. Cautiously, I edged closer.

"You're going to pay for this," Tara stormed.

"Like I've been doing on a monthly schedule for the past six years? There's a word for that, Tara. A word for what you've made yourself."

Six years. How did Reeve and Tara know each other? I'd assumed they met at college.

"You're the whore, Reeve," she sneered. "How would your precious Daisy feel if she knew the truth? I'm going to wreck you all."

"Oh, no." Reeve actually sounded amused now. "You can't."

Tara's voice sharpened. "Maybe you shouldn't trust so easily."

High heels clicked on the linoleum. I whirled, ready to dash, when a noise halted me.

A collective gasp came from the bleachers, followed by an urgent shout of "Davis!"

Taking to my heels, I rushed out of the concessions area and into the stands.

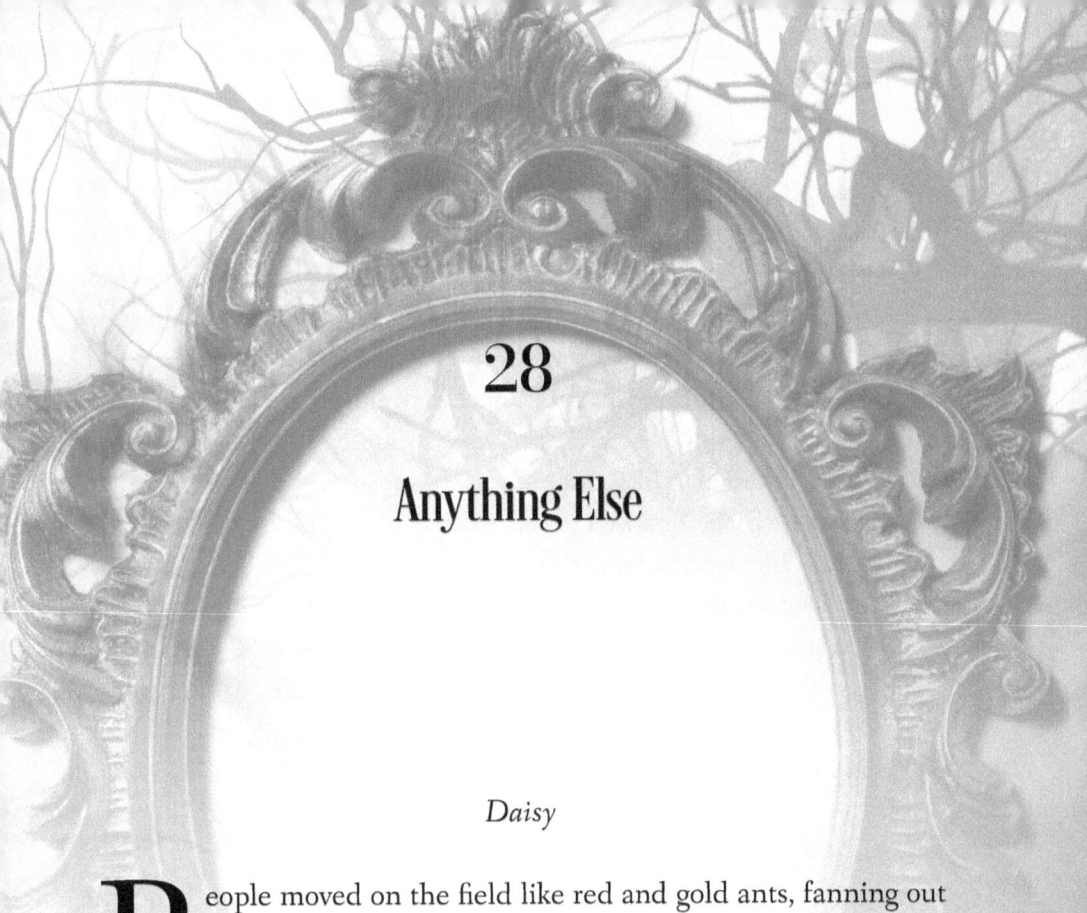

28

Anything Else

Daisy

People moved on the field like red and gold ants, fanning out around a fallen figure.

I tried to race for the grass, but everything moved so slowly. The air was molasses; the sounds distorted. At the bottom of the stands, a railing blocked my path. Setting down the drinks I carried, I gripped the railing and scrambled over. It was a big drop, yet I barely felt the impact. Even the pain from my left wrist was muted.

"Nathan," I whispered, wavering.

A man rose up in front of me. He was saying something about clearing the field. A medical emergency. *Go away.*

Someone caught my right arm — Blake, his face stricken. Reeve stepped between me and the security guard. He pressed something into his hand, and I saw the flash of a hundred-dollar bill.

The guard hesitated. Reeve cocked his head, looking at him intently.

"You stay right here on the edge of the field," the guard said finally. "Don't get any closer."

Though Nathan was far from us, both Blake and Reeve looked relieved. They dropped to the grass, Reeve heedless of his sharply creased khaki slacks, and beckoned me to do the same.

Confused, I knelt down. From here, I could see that Nathan was still wearing his helmet, and that he lay motionless in a way that you don't want someone to be motionless, ever.

I clutched Blake's hand. He squeezed back even harder.

"Nate." The word dropped from his lips.

He loved Nathan. And I didn't care. No, I did care. I wanted Blake to love him, because Nathan deserved love. He needed it. But all the love in the world wouldn't help him lift his head right now.

"What happened?" I thought I asked, but I wasn't sure if I spoke.

"He collapsed," Reeve answered quietly. "Crumpled like a paper bag. No one touched him."

Evan sank down on my left, all swagger gone. He put his hand on my shoulder. His eyes met mine, pale and urgent. "Help us."

"I can't." I had no medical knowledge beyond basic first aid. No healing spells at my fingertips.

Nathan lay still and unresponsive as people huddled over him. The commentators were speaking solemnly about doing CPR. A gurney stood at his side, the straps open and waiting.

Anger suddenly gripped me. This couldn't be happening. This was wrong. I'd fallen, but Nathan shouldn't.

Reeve's lips moved soundlessly, shaping words I didn't recognize. His golden skin looked sallow, his dark eyes even more hooded and shadowed than before. Blake was pale. Evan's head was bowed, and perspiration dampened his blond hair.

They'd all been hale and healthy. Now none of them looked well.

What afflicted them? Had it caused Nathan to fall? Or had the ailment affected Nathan first, and it reached the other men because they were somehow connected?

Reeve's lips ceased moving. Almost imperceptibly, he shook his head at Blake and Evan.

Evan squeezed my shoulder. "Help us," he hissed again.

"How?" My voice was thick in my throat.

"Think. Think about how you got us out of the woods. Then... stop thinking."

My mind raced. If only I were on Greer Hill. If only I had more supplies, more knowledge, Reeve's books...

Evan's grip on my shoulder loosened, and his arm fell away. His head dropped to his chest. Sweat bloomed outward, soaking his shirt. When I met Reeve's sunken eyes, he mouthed, *"Do something, Daze."*

I closed my eyes. The forest opened in my mind, spreading green branches.

Holding Evan's limp hand in my left and Blake's in my right, I remembered pulling. Wrenching. Dragging them both out of the woods in a burst of pure voltage that shot upward from the ground, penetrating my body, infusing my veins. My left hand ached from the pressure, but I didn't let go.

Fire crackled in my field of vision. Jaws opened, unhinging around me. I was caught in the serpent's mouth; blackness below, brightness above. Fear flashed through me at the yawning, endless expanse.

Trust.

Beneath me, the earth grew warmer until it blazed hot. Trembling with the effort, I held the heat within me, containing it until I thought I would shimmer and explode.

A jolt surged through my body. It raced down my left arm and sparked where my palm met Evan's, buzzing insistently like an angry fly.

I wanted to drop my hand. Fighting my instincts, I squeezed as hard as I could. It hurt. I gritted my teeth. The sparks increased until they burst into a shower of electricity and fell away.

As I panted for air, Blake's fingers tightened, suddenly strong and vital. Evan lifted his head, gulping in a long breath. Reeve's eyes cleared, and I swear I saw that dimple lurking.

"His eyelids just moved," the commentator said. "Davis is lifting his head..."

A sigh of relief ran through the stands. The last spark cooled and vanished, and Nathan sat up.

He pulled off his helmet and turned toward me. Across the field, our eyes met. Even at this distance, I could see — could sense — the sweetest, purest smile on his face, making my heart quiver. For one wild moment, I prayed that recovering from the fall would restore Nathan's original personality, like a factory reset.

Then he scowled and got to his feet, turning away.

I'd be lying if I said my heart didn't sink to the ground.

Nathan was spirited away to some kind of tent, where the commentators assured us that he was being examined by doctors. Minutes later, he stalked out, helmet in hand. There was no sign of weakness or stumbling.

After a brief consultation with his coach, he turned around and stretched his massive arms to the crowd. A cocky grin flashed across his face. On the swell of his left biceps, the serpent sank its fangs into its tail.

An enormous cheer rose from the stands. People stamped their feet and banged on the bleachers until the noise was deafening. School colors rippled over the crowd.

Nathan waved to the stands as his teammates spilled into the field, mobbing him.

"Behold the champion," Evan drawled, his sarcastic half-smile back in place. Reeve pushed his damp black hair off his forehead and applauded.

Blake held out a hand to help me up, tattooed and silver-ringed. "You were amazing, Daisy. Just incredible."

Grasping Blake's hand, I hesitated. Nathan was being pulled this way and that by his teammates. The hugs and back-pounding reminded me of Evan's audience after his concert, everyone trying to rub him for luck and get a piece of him. Nathan's fierce, triumphant grin looked like a grimace.

"Are you guys jealous of that?" I pointed to the hugging, yelling mass on the field.

After Reeve's revelation that all the men had been sexually involved once upon a time, I couldn't get it out of my head. Even if they were celibate now, they were intertwined. Locked into each other. I hadn't seen Reeve, Evan, or Blake show genuine interest in anyone outside their brotherhood — except for me.

Evan laughed. *"Jealous?* Not for a minute, baby girl. We're Nate's true friends. He has fun out there, but his loyalties lie with us."

I let Blake help me to my feet, but whatever energy I'd pulled from the earth had left my body, leaving me unsteady and nauseated. As I struggled to walk, Reeve quickly took my right arm. Evan moved to my left, supporting my waist. The security guard Reeve had bribed eyed us nervously, motioning us off the field.

We filed through the closest stadium entrance. Blake turned toward the seats, clearly eager to watch the game, but I touched his shoulder and caught Reeve and Evan's eyes.

"We need to talk."

"Of course." Reeve took the lead, ushering us inside the stadium. Guiding us down one hallway, then another, he turned a doorknob and motioned us into an empty office. I didn't know how he guessed the door would be unlocked, and I didn't ask.

Once the four of us were inside, Reeve locked the door and closed the blinds.

"What just happened?" I croaked.

All three men were staring at me, their gaze narrowed, as if I were almost too bright to look at.

"Let's sit you down, Daze," Reeve said quietly. Together, he and Evan eased me into a folding chair. Blake shrugged off his flannel shirt, leaving him in a loose tank top, and draped the flannel over me like a blanket. I was shivering violently.

"Hey, now, baby girl." Evan came behind me to rub my shoulders. His hands were as hot as ever, but his touch was surprisingly protective. "You did good."

"What, exactly, did I 'do good' at? What the *hell* was going on?" My voice rose, echoing around the small office.

"Nate had a fall." Blake perched on the desk in front of us. He tried to give me a cheerful smile, but his eyebrows were pinched. "That's all."

"The earth got so hot." My voice was cracked. "It filled me..."

The men were quiet. Blake picked up a pen from the desk, twirling it nervously. It flashed between his fingers like a chef's knife, moving with unnatural speed. Reeve turned toward a ficus plant in the corner, picking up a dry, curled leaf in an abstracted way, but tension gripped his back. Evan stroked my shoulders, easing his hands beneath the straps of my tank top. I shivered at his touch.

"It's okay now, pet," he said softly. "You're safe and so are we."

I jerked to face him. "You knew what was going on! Evan, you told me to do — whatever I did. You knew it would help Nathan." With a jolt, I realized that it had only been a week and a half since Nathan and I had kissed. Only eight days since Reeve took me into his tower the night of The Crush. Time had expanded, so full of strange new experiences that it felt like a year had been packed into a week. "His collapse — has that happened before? What's wrong with him? Aren't you worried?"

Reeve, who had been pacing the office while I spoke, pressed his fingers to his temples. His eyes were endless, black and glittering. "Everything's going to be all right, Star. We know that now for sure."

When I looked at Blake sitting on the desk, then behind me where Evan loomed, they both scrutinized me with the same eerie intensity. The same absolute *certainty*. Then the moment broke.

"What about Tara?" I asked.

Reeve blinked. Blake shook his head, smiling, and Evan let out a snort. "What about her?"

I pulled Blake's flannel around my lap as Evan dug deeper into my muscles, kneading out the knots. I had to admit, he had magic hands, and his talent wasn't limited to a keyboard.

"I overheard Reeve talking with her earlier," I admitted. I expected him to be upset, but his dimple flickered in his cheek. "It sounded like she was threatening you. Threatening — us."

"We have nothing to fear from Tara," Blake said easily.

"You really think so?" I persisted. Evan's fingers moved up my neck, making my head droop forward because his strokes felt so good.

Blake chuckled. "For better or worse, we've known her a long time. She can cause minor problems, but not major ones."

"I wouldn't underestimate her. And what *did* happen to Nathan?"

"A moment of weakness," Evan offered. "Doubt. Fighting—" He broke off abruptly. Reeve and Blake were both giving him warning looks. When I twisted around to peer at Evan, his lips were pressed together. As if the words were trying to bubble out, but he couldn't allow them to.

Frustrated by the secret-keeping, I shook off Evan's hands and rose to my feet, handing Blake's flannel back to him.

Reeve caught my waist. "You're shaking, Daze."

I shrugged, but my shoulders twitched, then shuddered beyond my control. "I'm just glad Nathan's okay."

Blake wrapped an arm around my shoulders. "What about you?"

"I've been through worse."

"You're strong no matter what," Reeve said softly. "It's very human to react, Daze."

Were *they* human?

The thought jumped into my mind, and I tried to dismiss it. Of course they were. We weren't in a fucking fairy story. There was the magic that worked in this world, the craft of herbs and spells and crystals, but not magic that altered reality.

If there were, though — it would explain so much.

"She's strong, all right." Evan's grin split his face, broad and open for once. "She's our shining Star."

"Yeah, right," I groaned, just before my legs gave out.

Fifteen minutes later, I was propped up in the bleachers with Reeve, Evan, and Blake, wrapped in a blanket someone had found, sipping a paper cup of sugary coffee even though the temperature was close to ninety.

"Better?" Reeve inquired.

"Still a little shaky, but much better." My stomach jumped at the curl of greenish-gold that licked the edges of his dark eyes.

Are you human, Reeve McClellan?

Why does it excite me so much that you might not be?

My phone buzzed in my purse.

"Oh — oh *shit*." I realized who it was half a second before I saw the texts. "I got rid of Michelle and Amy's drinks."

"Daisy—"

"They have no idea where I am. They probably saw what happened on the field, but—" Frantically I scrolled through the texts, which progressed from *where is strawberry smooooothie* to *Jesus Christ, Daisy, WHERE ARE YOU???!!!!*

Blake stood up. His bright blue eyes, back to their full wattage, beamed at me. "I'll bring them new drinks. Where are they sitting?"

"That's so sweet of you," I began. "But—" Reeve squeezed my arm and gave me a significant look. I let out a breath. "Thanks. They're sitting up in that section. Second-to-last row on the far left." I pointed. "They'll die of happiness to see you. They'll probably beg you for more sweets."

Blake kissed my forehead. "Always happy to provide."

I shivered as I watched his lithe body stride up the aisle. His tattoos disappeared into his shirt, licking his neck. His curls bounced on his shoulders, and his ass, beneath baggy, faded jeans, was taut and narrow.

Reeve chuckled, and the sound was rich, dark velvet. "Evan was right," he said softly, following my gaze to Blake. "You're our shining Star. But you're no angel, Daze. You've got as much devil in you as we do."

I shuddered. "Reeve, what are you doing to me?"

His eyes glinted like black diamonds in the sun. "Let us take you home. You belong with us, Star. Seeing you save Nate — there's no question."

Belong.

The word was so powerful, it sent a wave of warmth over me.

I wanted so badly to belong. To have a place and a purpose. A hope, a vision — a future.

Down below us, Nathan bounded across the field. As the crowd went wild, I let the blanket slide off my legs to puddle at my feet. "You think so?"

Reeve's finger grazed my knee through the hole in my jeans. "I know it."

I sucked in a breath. "It's not enough, Reeve. I need answers."

His dark eyes turned hooded. "It's easier for me to show than tell."

29

Here and Heaven

Daisy

Back at the House, Reeve and Evan led me swiftly through
the gardens, the cool, dim front hall, and the high-ceilinged
living room.

Graceful statues and richly colored paintings seemed to follow us
with their eyes. The last of the evening sunlight poured onto the
ebony piano.

After the noise and color of the game, the House was peaceful
and quiet. I was shepherded into the library, where a fire crackled as
the setting sun sent shadows through the room. Despite the heat of
the day, the fire was welcome.

In the back corner, Reeve's collection of magic books whispered
to me.

Reeve and Evan dropped into the leather wing chairs. Reeve
patted his lap. "Come sit, Daze."

I still held the fleece blanket I'd been given at the game. Climbing
into Reeve's lap, I tried to arrange my long legs across his and ended

345

up draping them over the arm of the chair. He tucked the blanket around me with a proprietary pat.

You belong with us, Star.

Did I?

Nathan was upstairs, resting at Reeve's insistence. The two of them had had a brief, intense argument when I stepped out of Reeve's car at the House. Nathan had pointed at me, then stormed inside, followed by Blake, who was probably upstairs fussing over him.

I opened my mouth to ask about their relationship, but at that moment, Blake appeared in the doorway, holding a tray with four steaming mugs.

"Drink up." He walked around, handing each of us a mug. "You'll feel better."

We clinked our mugs.

"To survival," said Evan grandly, leaning back in his armchair and taking a deep draught.

I sipped the herbal brew, which was sweet and floral, a crimson tisane that warmed me from the inside. Each swallow made me more relaxed, until I sprawled against Reeve's hard body, resting my head on his shoulder.

"Daze, you deserve a reward," Reeve said, lifting his mug to me. "Something very special, since you risked yourself for us."

I straightened in his lap, my heart beating faster, and pointed casually to the locked cabinet of books. "How about access to those?"

The three men exchanged glances.

"Reeve doesn't let anyone get their paws on his beloved first editions," Evan drawled.

"I'm not just anyone."

"Choose something else." Reeve stroked my braid, but his firm tone left no doubt about his intentions.

I sprang up from his lap, too agitated to sweet-talk him. "They're only books. I'll wash my hands first, I swear. I'll wear gloves if you want me to. I won't breathe on them."

"Why are you so curious, Star? Why those dusty old books, out of all that we can offer you?"

Stubbornly, I held back my answer. *Because they're the key to what I want most.*

Sasha was probably right. There was no way I could heal my hand with spells. But seeing how the men were linked, the strange, snakelike flickers in their eyes, the serpent who rose in the flames, the woods that opened and closed... Everything I'd believed about magic was thrown into question.

"Okay, forget the reward for now." I paced the library. "Nathan's not well—"

Rising, Reeve took my chin in his hand. "Nate took a little stumble, that's all."

I jerked away. "You call that *little*? Reeve, there is so much you're not telling me."

Reeve pressed his lips together. Blake raked a hand through his loose curls, and Evan drummed his fingers on the arm of his chair. Unclenching my fingers from my empty mug, I set it on the polished desk.

"I saw the three of you suffering with Nathan," I said more quietly. "You're all connected. How can I help you if you don't talk to me?"

"You really want to help us?" It was Blake who spoke.

"Yes," I said impulsively. "When Tara said she'd wreck you — all I wanted to do was help."

Blake moved in front of me. His hands cupped my cheeks, gentle and intent. I marveled at how his touch differed from that of the other men.

"You can," he said softly. "Reeve's right, you belong here. At our side. *Ours.* Stay with us in the House, because we need you, Daisy."

My mind whirled. "You don't *all* need me. Nathan hates me."

"Nate doesn't hate you, I promise," Blake soothed, his smile dazzling. "But we're talking about you, Daisy. What do you want right now?"

My eyes darted to Reeve, who stood by the desk with an unreadable expression.

"Don't think," Evan urged from behind me. "Just answer."

I stared up into Blake's bright blue eyes as his curls fell around his face.

"I want to kiss you," I whispered.

This time it was Blake who glanced at Reeve. After a pause, he received a slight nod.

His lips came closer. I remembered their softness from the woods, but I wanted to kiss him here and now, with my mind clear.

"The curse," I said quickly. "What if the woods were an exception?"

"Never cursed," Blake whispered. "Not with us."

His lips met mine.

It was the sweetest kiss, like a poignant melody on a lone cliff. I wrapped my arms around his neck and gave in to his adoring touch.

He took my mouth in quick nibbles. His curls were so thick and soft that I couldn't stop running my fingers through them. His beard tickled me, but it was smoother than Reeve's carefully groomed stubble.

I shivered when Blake cupped my breasts, coaxing my nipples to tight peaks through my thin tank top. When noises left my mouth, whimpers and gasps, he slipped his hands underneath to caress my bare tits.

As we kissed more deeply, his pierced tongue rubbed mine, driving me to reach under his shirt in return. I found the metal hoops in his tiny hard nipples, stroking them experimentally until he groaned.

A husky body pressed into mine from behind.

"I'm hungry, pet." Evan gave my braid a firm tug, jolting my pleasure higher. "Give me a taste too."

Heart pounding, I turned my head from Blake's lips to Evan's.

"That's enough." Reeve's voice was quiet. He stood by the desk, watching us with those bottomless eyes. Reluctantly, Evan let go of my hair. Blake pulled his hands out of my shirt. "Daisy, you want to learn our ways? Let us show you."

"I have to kiss Evan first," I panted. Blake let out a strained chuckle.

Reeve shook his head. "Patience."

I twisted to stare up at Evan, wondering if he'd override Reeve. His nostrils flared, but he shook his head at me and stepped back.

Reeve led the way out of the library and down a labyrinthine hallway. Blake and Evan swept me along, my arms linked in theirs. Blake smiled reassuringly, but Evan seemed half-animal, barely contained, as his hand gripped my right arm. When I dared to look at him, he let out a low hiss, his fingers digging into my flesh.

At the end of the hall, Reeve opened a door.

I blinked at the bright, hazy light. Swirling steam thickened the air. The men ushered me inside, where the fragrance of herbs filled the room, along with the continuous sound of bubbling water.

As my eyes adjusted, I took in a circular wooden hot tub, black and gold mosaics tiling the floor and walls, and a wood-lined sauna.

Was there no end to the House? It had everything.

Reeve pressed a kiss to my lips. "Strip."

"Right here?" I squinted at Evan and Blake through the mist, both watching me eagerly.

"Right here." The calm statement made my stomach lurch. "No shame, Daisy. I want you completely uninhibited. Now peel that clingy outfit off your luscious body so we can see you naked. Blake and Evan have waited very patiently for this."

My heart pounded. "I thought *you* were going to show *me* what you're all about."

"We will."

"I'll only take my clothes off if you all do, too."

"Look who's so feisty." Evan raised a blond eyebrow.

Blake grinned, but Reeve held up a hand. "One thing at a time, Star. Patience."

"Then help me get naked." I meant to sound bold, sultry, but it came out in a whisper.

Reeve's smile gleamed. "What do you say?"

"Please."

My heart pounded as Reeve pulled the elastic from my braid and unraveled it. My hair fell down my back in heavy waves. Blake cursed under his breath, and Evan's pale green eyes flared with appetite.

Reeve moved behind me. Slowly, he lifted the hem of my tank top. Blake's and Evan's eyes were glued to my body.

"You know that if I'm undressing you, I'm going to take my time." Reeve kissed my neck, then sucked on it. My head went light.

"Reeve..." I gasped as he played with my nipples through the bunched-up tank top. "Enough teasing. It's not funny."

"Sweet flower, I'm deadly serious about teasing you."

Mutely, I appealed to Evan and Blake, who were burning holes through my clothes with their gaze.

"I'll test your patience, Star. But I promise, it will all be worth it." Reeve raised my tank top inch by inch. With a tug, it came over my head. He tossed the shirt on a bench.

I cried out as my breasts were bared. The moist air condensed on my skin, beading over my tight pink nipples. Evan let out a low growl.

"It's different out of the woods, isn't it?" Reeve whispered. "All Evan and Blake can do right now is watch. And believe me, they will."

Another tug, this time on my zipper, and my jeans slid down my hips. To my surprise, Reeve knelt in front of me to pull them off. I was barefoot, my flip-flops abandoned in the library. With agonizing slowness, he peeled my panties down my thighs, revealing the soft fluff of curls.

My face blazed as I stood naked in front of the three men.

"Perfect," Blake muttered. "So gorgeous."

Evan let out a low growl, baring his teeth.

"Gorgeous and *wet*," Reeve said approvingly. I gasped when he pressed his face to my panties, licking the crotch. I'd never felt jealous of a pair of underwear, but I did now.

"Reeve, I need your tongue," I pleaded.

"Hush." He held my gaze as he lapped up my juices, making me squirm, then turned to his friends. "Look at her, glowing and powerful. Our Star."

Stepping behind me again, he pulled me close, my skin bare against his dress shirt and crisp slacks. I shuddered at his cock pressing against my ass, his fingers deftly opening my thighs.

"I can smell you." His voice was just loud enough for Blake and Evan to hear. "I *taste* you every fucking hour of the day. Do you know that, Daisy? Do you know what you've done to me?"

He squeezed my cunt, and I cried out. Peeling apart my soaked lips, he stroked my clit. When he clapped his free hand over my mouth, stifling my whimpers, my arousal spiked.

Blake groaned, and Evan's fists clenched at his sides.

"Spread your legs," Reeve ordered, his voice hypnotic. "Let them see." Shaking, I obeyed. "You love this, don't you? You're opening like a flower for us."

I thrashed in his arms, letting out a muffled moan when one big finger penetrated me. It was tighter, standing up in this position. I felt incredibly exposed, pinned in Reeve's embrace.

"Tell us, Daisy. Confess to how much you enjoy being put on display." He lifted his hand from my mouth so I could speak.

"Yes!" I burst out. "I — I love it. Oh God —"

"That's our good girl. Look at this sweet little cunt," he murmured to Evan and Blake, filling me with a second finger. "Don't you think it needs our attention?"

Evan stared at my pussy, his gaze searing. "It needs to be fucked," he said softly. "It needs to be thoroughly used."

"Evan," I gasped.

"He's right, Daisy." Blake's eyes were fixed on my face, bright and intent. "You need us."

Overwhelmed, I turned my head to kiss Reeve. Evan and Blake's attention set my body ablaze, while Reeve's fingers kept moving, stretching me open as he stroked my clit. Sharpness mingled with pleasure. When my mouth met Reeve's, it was all animal need: teeth nipping, lips sucking, tongues devouring in a burst of fire.

I was tumbling down a waterfall, only to be incinerated at the bottom. Reaching behind me with both arms to clasp his neck, I yielded my body to Reeve's hands. To Evan's slitted gaze, to Blake's parted lips.

"I'm going to come," I sobbed.

Evan chuckled. "Are you?"

As if he had a sixth sense, just as I was about to tip over into climax, Reeve pulled his hand away.

Empty, furious, and achingly turned on, I spun around to face him.

"Get in the tub," he ordered, his eyes dark and smoking.

"I'm so close. Please..." I grabbed his wrists.

"I said get in the tub. I want you wet all over. Do as I say if you want to come at my hands."

I dropped his wrists, caught between warring impulses to touch myself, to rip his clothes off, to surrender to him. "Why are you tormenting me?"

"Because it's so much fun." Evan gave me his sardonic smile. "Better follow Reeve's orders, or we'll be here for hours, seeing how long he can edge you."

"Blake?" I asked, hoping he'd convince Reeve to relent. His blue eyes were wide, and his chest rose and fell beneath his loose tank top. His erection tented his faded jeans.

"Evan's right," he responded tightly. "Listen to Reeve."

Reeve stroked my cheek, his eyes black and fathomless. "You're mine, Star. You're ours." The Devil card flashed in front of my eyes, with its naked figures chained for the Devil's pleasure. That was us. Me, Evan, Blake, all playing to Reeve's whims. I shuddered with nerves and need. "We're going to push you onto the precipice of desire. You're going to taste what we deny ourselves every day."

Throbbing, I went to the hot tub and lowered myself into the steaming water. The three men clustered close. I felt like the deer in the woods that Tara had called me — defenseless, excited.

God, I wanted to surrender. To be taken over by them. It was heaven, but my body cried out for deliverance.

"Why do you deny yourselves?" I gritted.

Evan dropped into a feral crouch beside me. "Think, pet." He pressed his forehead to mine, his shaggy hair brushing my skin. "Think about why we bottle it up. Think about what and who we might be saving it for."

"You know why, sweet girl," Reeve murmured. "We want to control desire."

My mind whirled. This was the heart of it; the crux of the mysteries in the House and on the hill. But I didn't have all the pieces yet.

"Show me," I panted, my lips almost touching Evan's. "Help me understand."

Reeve nodded at Evan and Blake. "Take your clothes off."

Evan's brows shot up. But he leapt to his feet and immediately ripped at his clothes, shedding his polo shirt, then yanking the buckle open on his belt.

"Reeve?" Blake frowned. "Are you sure?"

"This is why we're here. Show Daisy what we can endure."

Cautiously, Blake lifted his tank top, exposing his lean abs and a peek of his beautiful chest.

Evan's belt, shoes, and jeans hit the gold-tiled floor. He held my gaze as he skimmed off his boxers.

"Oh my God," I whispered.

Evan's body was husky and broad, the muscles covered with an inviting layer of softness, dusted with sandy hair that glittered in the light. And his cock—

God, he was huge. His shaft was thick and veined, the head swelling plump and dark red in a crown of flesh, jutting from his groin in seeming defiance of gravity.

I let out a gasp, and Evan grinned.

I'd never seen a naked man up close before, not in full light. Reeve, waking from his nightmare, had seemed like a dream, brief and shadowed. I couldn't tear my eyes away from Evan, wondering how that warm thickness would feel in my hands. Whether his balls would be as soft and velvety as they looked. How his face might twist when he came.

"I can't tell you how long I've waited for you to see me, pet," he rasped.

Blake was shirtless now, his intricate sleeve of tattoos swirling up his arm and across his chest. We locked gazes as he slowly undid his pants. The room held its breath.

All eyes converged on me. The tops of my breasts swelled above the water, my nipples peeking through the foam, and the jets in the tub pulsed against my body.

"Fuck it," Blake muttered. He shoved his jeans and boxers down together, kicking them away.

I stared at his long, ropy muscles and the patch of golden-brown hair on his chest that formed an arrow-shaped trail to his groin. His cock stood out proudly: darker, more curved, and a much more manageable size than Evan's. My breath came faster when I saw the silver barbell that pierced the underside of his tapered head, shining in the clouds of steam. His balls looked ripe and full.

A moan escaped as I licked my lips. I swear his cock rose under my gaze.

"You like Blake's pierced dick, Daisy?" Evan smirked. "You have no idea how full of cum his balls are for you. If you behave, maybe you'll find out someday."

My face blazed, and Blake let out a strained chuckle. Reeve's dark eyes narrowed, lust soaking his sharp-cut features.

"What are you showing me?" My voice was breathy. "That you're both hot? That you'll do anything Reeve says?"

Reeve knelt next to me, still fully dressed.

"Self-control." He gripped my wet hair in a hard twist, pulling

354

my head back until I felt the tug in my bones. "That's what we're showing you. They're going to watch me bring you to the brink. They'll see your beautiful body shudder with pleasure as I torment you. They'll ache for you just like I will. And none of us will do anything about it. We'll burn, but we won't seek relief. We'll endure."

"Why?" My body was strung as tightly as an over-tuned instrument.

"Watch and learn."

"Only if you strip too."

His Adam's apple bobbed, and his long dark lashes flickered. Then he smiled, the picture of calm.

He didn't fool me.

"Come on, Reeve," I rasped. "If you're so good at enduring and holding off and controlling your desires, show me your body. Would you really ask Blake and Evan to do something you couldn't do yourself?"

The men traded glances. Leaning closer, Reeve's fathomless eyes half-closed. "Undress me, Daze."

Evan growled, his cock pulsing in the steam-filled air. But Blake looked alarmed.

"Reeve, listen," he began.

Reeve held up a hand and shook his head.

I leapt out of the tub before he could change his mind. Hot water sluiced from my body. Fumbling and eager, heedless of the strands of hair that clung to my back and breasts, my hands went to his tie, frantically unknotting it. I tossed the length of silk on a bench, followed by his beautifully cut shirt.

His muscles flexed. On his biceps writhed the serpent, scarlet and obsidian and gold, its jaws wide in eternal appetite.

I barely had time to take in the coppery swells of his shoulders, his toned chest with its dark shadow of hair, before I unbuckled his belt.

I tensed up. Reeve was going to allow me to expose him. And what the hell would I see when he did?

Both Evan and Blake looked like men in every respect. But once the idea had crept into my head that this quartet wasn't wholly human, it stayed there. Taking up residence, curling around my thoughts.

Making me nervous.

And very, very wet.

I unzipped Reeve's slacks. His erection tented his black silk boxers. He held my gaze as I pulled them down.

His cock sprang free, and my mouth watered. As far as I could tell, it was human, except that it was more beautiful than any penis had a right to be. Exquisitely proportioned, it seemed to be sculpted from rosy marble. Only the dark thatch of carefully trimmed hair made it real. A bead of clear liquid hung from the flared tip.

"You're perfect," I whispered.

Greenish sparks curled across his eyes. "I'm far from perfect, Daze."

"To me, you are." I grabbed his hand. "Let's get wet together."

Blake stepped forward, a warning written on his face. Evan's hands fisted at his sides as Reeve stood motionless.

I tilted my head at him. "Don't you want to feel the water? You can show me all about self-control. You can even teach me up close... I need you to teach me so many things, Reeve..."

Reeve's lips pressed together, and a shudder ran through his body. Then he laughed, flashing white teeth. Catching me around the waist, he led me into the hot tub.

"Where were we?" He gripped my head in his hands. "Oh, yeah. Desire."

He kissed me forcefully. His tongue was so alive, licking mine, sucking on my lips. I tried to take control of the kiss, but he wouldn't let me. The water swirled and foamed as I wrapped my arms and legs around him, the thick stalk of his cock pressing into my belly.

"I want you." My fingers clutched his tousled black hair. "I want you to be crazy and dirty with me."

"Sweet Daisy, you have no idea." His voice tuned my body tighter. I was shaking, soaked, wound around him.

He cupped my breasts, lifting them in the water, and I gasped when he pressed his face to them. His stubble scratched my sensitive skin as he took one tender swell completely into his mouth. He sucked my breast roughly, pinching my other nipple, until my moans filled the room.

"That's it. Let them hear you. No shame, sweet girl."

When I dared to look up, Evan's pale jade eyes met mine. He tipped his head, gripping his hands together behind his back. Blake's lean body was clenched, his pierced cock thrusting toward me, his hands fisted at his sides.

"See? They're good boys," Reeve assured me. "They're the masters of their desire. They'd love to fuck you out of your mind, but they won't lay a hand on you. Not tonight. No matter how much you beg, Star."

I let my head fall back, clutching Reeve's shoulders as he sucked and bit my other breast.

"Look at her," he ordered Evan and Blake. "Absolutely gorgeous."

I stared at my breasts, covered with dark pink marks. Reeve's marks. My nipples stood out, puckered and desperate for more.

"Climb out." The order was delivered with total confidence that it would be obeyed. "Sit on the edge, sweet girl."

With my right hand, I positioned myself carefully on the ledge of the tub, grateful when Reeve caught my waist.

Below me, he spread my legs, bracing his forearms firmly on my thighs so I wouldn't have to rest too much weight on my wrists.

I felt utterly exposed to these men in the swirling steam.

Beautiful. Wanted.

"Daze, you're a fucking dream come true." Reeve dropped kisses on my thighs, burning the delicate flesh.

I bucked shamelessly toward his mouth. "Please lick me..."

"Don't you want to save some firsts for later?"

"No," I gritted.

"I do." He stroked my slickness, radiating hunger. When his fingers closed over my clit, I arched sharply, throwing my head back, and met Blake and Evan's eyes. Open wide, staring directly at me.

Motionless or no, they were not good boys. Their erections strained, and their gazes roved over my water-beaded breasts, the tight buds of my nipples, my sensitive clit that their friend was lavishing with attention, and back to my pleading face.

Slowly, Evan spread his fingers and curled them around his cock.

He didn't move his hand. He simply squeezed, the huge, flushed crown protruding from his fist, his body taut, mastering every ounce of need.

I want to control desire.

Blake's eyes slitted as our gazes locked. When Reeve's fingers sank into my pussy, moving faster as he massaged my clit, his mouth opened as if he were in pain.

I cried out, need shocking my body.

"Our good, good girl," Reeve crooned. "You're our shining star. Don't ever try to hide your glory."

I tightened sharply around Reeve's fingers as he forced my thighs hard against the tiled edge of the tub. His touch was a blur, merciless and determined.

Blake and Evan's eyes roamed all over my naked flesh, sucking at me. Every inch of my skin felt pulled and rubbed and stroked and licked.

When I came, I screamed. I was floating, shaking, hot water rushing around my legs, juices dripping down my pussy as Reeve fucked me with his fingers.

He didn't stop. He just kept going, pressing into my clit, wringing fresh peaks from me.

Behind him, Blake gripped his dick, agonized need written on his face. I imagined his curved cock opening my pussy as Reeve caressed my clit, his silver piercing rubbing against the softness inside me, Evan's dick sliding into my mouth to fill my throat, and cried out as another wave of pleasure crashed through my body.

"I need you," I gasped. "I need your cocks..."

"*Fuck*," Evan groaned. "You're killing us, baby girl."

Finally, Reeve eased up. Kissing my thighs, he rose from the foam. The serpent writhed on his inner biceps, crimson and jet black and gold, twisting endlessly.

"You've been very good for us, Star." His voice was the rough scrape of gravel, without a trace of velvet. "Come with me for your true reward."

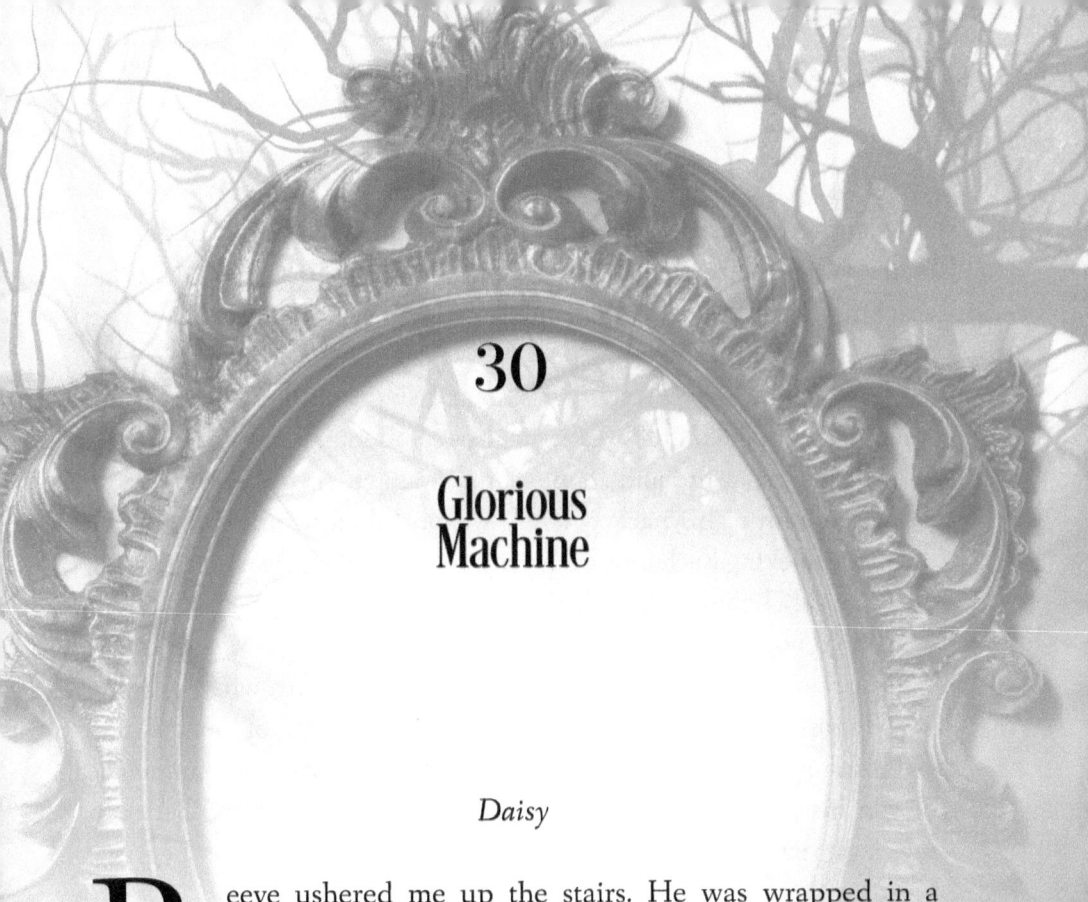

30

Glorious Machine

Daisy

Reeve ushered me up the stairs. He was wrapped in a towel, his hair wet and disorderly, but I was naked. Every part of my body felt alive and awake. If Nathan came out of his room and saw me like this —

Worry chased the thrill of excitement. But Nathan had seemed completely recovered from his stumble. Surely it would be fine to let my concern go and focus on Reeve, on the reward he'd promised me.

In his bedroom, he shut the carved door. The velvet curtains were drawn, showing only a trickle of orange light, the last flaming ember of sunset.

Without warning, he kissed me hard. His lips were urgent. Taking. I slid my hands up his back to clutch his sleek shoulders.

"Don't leave my bed again without telling me, Daze," he said huskily.

"I won't. I promise." I sucked on his neck, and he didn't stop me. When I bit the coppery skin, he grunted, rough and animalistic, cracking his polished surface.

"Harder."

I sucked as hard as I could, his neck hot and smooth under my teeth. When he squeezed my ass, pulling me against the hard ridge that strained at his towel, I moaned.

"Harder," he growled.

Tugging his hair, I tasted his skin and sweat until my head swam. Finally, I stopped, out of breath, my lips swollen.

His eyes spat fire and shone as black as jet. A bruise marred the strong column of his neck where my mouth had been. Abruptly, he lifted me, locking his hands under my ass.

"Reeve!" I clung to him with my arms and legs.

"Hold your wrist to your chest," he ordered.

I tucked my injured wrist close to my chest. "Why, what—"

He tossed me on his bed, knocking the breath out of me. Pushing me onto my back, he cupped and stroked my breasts. I whimpered as he ran his palms down my belly. When his hand arrowed between my legs, parting my cunt, words tumbled out of me: begging, pleading.

"Look, little slut. Just look at this naughty pussy." Shaking, I propped myself up on my elbows, staring at Reeve's hand as it possessed every inch of my flesh. Fingers, burning and insistent, roved over my slickness, stroking my clit, sliding inside me. "It's getting my hand so fucking wet."

"It's for you." I grabbed his hand, holding it in place.

"This pussy, Daisy? It's for me?"

"Yes!"

He let out a strangled groan, relief and fierce joy mingling on his beautiful face. "Finally, we agree on that. Don't move."

Rolling off the bed, he went swiftly to his cabinet of curios. The towel fell from his waist, and he made no attempt to reclaim it. His naked body was so beautiful that it hurt to look at him, like gazing at the sun during an eclipse. Every muscle stood out, sleek, carved, and tensed, and when he turned back to me, his hands full, his cock jutted proudly.

Inviting. Beckoning. Calling.

In a heartbeat, he was back at the bed. The flaxen rope was looped over his arm, and he held a marble snake's head in each hand. Reverently, he set them on the nightstand, along with a small crystal jar.

Trembling with anticipation, I stared at the snake figurines. Reeve had fucked me with the black one, the night of Evan's concert. But I'd never felt the white one, which was smaller. Both heads were bulbous and tapered, flaring out in the middle and narrowing at the bottom.

With a sinuous movement, Reeve climbed up to crouch over me on the bed. As he caged me in, he stroked my hair off my forehead. The movement was measured. Careful. But his hand shook and seized up halfway through, thrusting into my hair and making me cry out with the sharp pull.

"Reeve, oh God—"

He collected himself with a shudder.

"Turn over." His voice was low and dangerous. "You're such a good girl, Daisy, giving me your body. Entrusting your pussy to my care and safekeeping. In return, I'm going to give you everything you've dreamed of. The pure and the profane, the glittering heights and the darkest fucking urges. I'm going to give you everything you need."

Deeply aroused and a little nervous, I turned over so I lay on my stomach. Hot hands spread my ass open. One sure finger stroked the dark pucker between my cheeks.

"Oh..." I groaned.

"Sshhh." His finger was back, slick with lube. He caressed my tight hole as he kissed the back of my neck. He'd spoken the truth: Reeve's touch on my asshole was so dirty, yet intimate and pure. When I arched my back, he worked the tip of his finger inside, cursing as I clenched and fluttered around him.

"That's good, my sweet girl. You're opening so well for me. Your beautiful ass is going to be ready for more very soon."

"Are you going to fuck me there?" I whispered, a tremble in my voice.

"You'd like that, wouldn't you? Naughty slut. Hoping I'll fuck your ass before I've even taken your pussy."

The rough dirty talk made my heart race. I pushed my ass toward him. "I just need you inside me."

"You don't even care how? Or where?" Fangs caught in his velvet voice, flooding it with sweet venom.

My ass rippled eagerly as his finger sank deeper. His thumb teased my wet pussy, and his free hand roamed over my back and hips, spreading heat.

"I'll take you any way I can," I whispered. "I trust you, Reeve."

Behind me, he growled, and for the briefest moment, his hands went rigid on me. Then he eased his finger out of my ass.

"On your back, dirty girl," he said, his tone tight and leashed. I obeyed, leaving a trail of pussy juice on his silk sheets. "Arms above your head."

A little hesitantly, I lifted my arms. He laughed and pushed my right arm firmly against the pillow.

"Faster when I tell you what to do, little slut."

My own laughter died on my lips at the dark arousal of being talked to that way. I followed suit with my left arm.

"Hold on to the headboard," he commanded.

I grasped the polished slats of his heavy wooden headboard. Kneeling over me, his skin bronze against the dimness of the room, Reeve lifted the flaxen coil from the nightstand.

It was the most beautiful rope I'd ever seen, slim, silken, and gleaming. The pattern mimicked the snake knocker on the front door, the undulating spirals on the hallway wallpaper. In Reeve's hands, the rope looked alive.

His dark eyes showed shades of amber and green. I could swear his pupils flickered from circles to slits.

Then he covered my mouth with his — warm, male, hungry.

As we devoured each other, he looped the rope around my right wrist, tying it to the headboard.

"I won't tie your left hand," he murmured into my mouth. "Keep it next to your right, and if you need to change position, keep it still."

I nodded quickly. Two lengths of rope tickled my arms. I squirmed, pulling on the knot at my wrist, but it held fast.

"Spread your legs, innocent girl."

Heat flamed over my chest, my belly. "I thought I was a 'little slut.'"

"Oh, you are." He stroked my thighs, running his thumbs along my throbbing cleft. "You're an innocent virgin and a total slut and everything in between. I love it, Daisy."

Champagne bubbles chased the burning excitement.

Love.

We were talking about sex, but just hearing him use the word made me giddy.

"I love it too," I breathed. "I mean, I love — I love being all these things with you. I love being with you, Reeve."

His eyes darkened. "So do I."

He kissed me one last time and picked up the smaller marble figurine, the white one. Kneeling between my legs, his cock thick and gleaming in the candlelight, he squeezed lube all over the snake's head.

"Oh God," I moaned, as he rubbed the tapered end over my asshole. "Oh God, oh God..."

At his touch on my clit, I arched off the bed and snarled. Rubbing the swollen bud, he patiently worked the figurine into the tightness of my ass.

Finally, it filled me. He let go, and it stayed in place.

Heat rushed over my skin as my thighs shook. "Reeve, it feels so big."

"Of course it does. What a sight you are. It needs to be there, Daisy. You know that, don't you? That pure white marble, peeking out of your perfect ass..." He twirled the snake inside me, and I thrashed against my bonds, my ass seizing up on the intruder. "Very good. Now your pussy."

My toes curled on the silk sheets. Dammit, I wanted *him* — his warmth, his flesh, his cock. But when the larger figurine teased my wetness with cold, smooth stone, I moaned.

"Reeve, please..."

"Open for me, sweet flower." He pressed the figurine against my entrance. "Let me into your pretty pink cunt."

"They can't both fit," I whispered.

"They will," he said, with absolute certainty. "I promise, Daze, you can do this."

Taking a deep breath, I nodded. "All right."

It seemed impossible, but my pussy yielded to his steady pressure. I shuddered as he slowly penetrated me.

"Does that feel good?" he crooned, twirling the statuette with tiny motions.

"*Yes.* I'm so full." I tugged on the silken rope, tightening on hard marble in my pussy and ass. "But I want more... I want your cock..."

"No."

I sobbed in protest, but when warm palms closed over my breasts, I shuddered with pleasure.

"This is my desire, Daisy." Reeve's voice was hypnotic. "This is what's inside me. If you're good, you'll get much more."

I shivered. "I'll be good for you."

Springing over me, Reeve pressed his lips to my neck, hissing strange words that I couldn't make out. I arched against him, molding my bound body to his, as the figurines began moving inside me.

Moving.

Inside me.

They were *moving*.

Writhing like snakes.

Reeve wasn't touching them. One hand was cupping my cheek, the other flung out to the side.

"Reeve," I gasped.

"Relax, baby," he soothed. "Stay open."

"They won't hurt me?"

"I would never allow anything to hurt you."

I was being opened, explored in my most private places by slithering stone, and the invasion balanced on the exquisite edge of pleasure and intensity.

Why, I didn't ask. *What,* I didn't say. *How...* No, I didn't give a damn about how right now. All I cared about was Reeve, sliding one hand down to lift my breasts in the hot, close air.

I gasped when the golden ropes suddenly crept down my arms, caressing the tender inner skin.

They were alive.

The tips curled over my armpits and down the slopes of my breasts. Reeve pushed my tits together firmly in his hand, allowing the cords to explore. His steady grip grounded me as I jerked and cried out.

The ropes twined eagerly around my nipples. I stared down at the rosy buds that turned dark with excitement as the golden cords pinched them again and again.

Reeve kissed my throat. "Are you frightened, sweetheart?"

I was hot and dizzy, my breath coming fast. "Yes and no."

He let my breasts go and caressed my clit, unbearably aroused and sensitive as the figurines thrust deeper. "Mmmm. Let your fear become your desire."

The air was thick and crackling and smoky sweet. I was bound, anchored, and screwed by snakes, sparking at Reeve's touch.

"Is this my reward?" I gasped out.

His chuckle rolled over me. "This is only the beginning. Give me all your hunger, and you'll find out how rich your reward can be."

"I need you," I pleaded.

"Kiss me," came the soft, confident order. He leaned close, his woodsy scent a drug that opened a chasm at my feet.

Our tongues twined together in concert with all the movement in and on me. Golden ropes pulled at my nipples, crushing the tender buds. When the intensity made me cry out, Reeve massaged my clit more firmly. The stone snakes writhed in response, thrusting faster, until I came.

The room exploded as I gripped everything tight. My pussy and ass spasmed around hard marble. My shrieks mixed with Reeve's deep growls, my body shaking helplessly as he and whatever the hell was inside me brought me to peak after peak.

"You want cock?" he hissed. "You want cocks inside you instead of toys?"

Lust-filled images flashed through my head. Reeve and Nathan taking me together, giving me my first time. Blake and Evan having their way with me in the woods, coming deep inside me as I sprawled on the earth. The five of us kissing and stroking and touching and fucking.

"*Yes.* Yes..."

"You really are a little slut. How many times do we need to make you come before you're satisfied, Star? Will we ever satisfy you?"

We.

I bit the pillow as a fresh wave washed over me. The golden rope twined fully around my arms, coiling over my breasts, pinching my nipples hard enough to take my breath away.

"Reeve... Reeve..."

"What is it, sweet girl? You need to come some more?"

"You!" I cried out. "I need *you.*"

He reared back, crouching over me. His cock pointed at my face, dark and stiff.

"You're so beautiful," I husked. "I can't stand it."

His dimple flickered, yet his smile was strained. "It's a good thing you're bound and at my mercy."

"Please, Reeve. You have needs too. Who takes care of you? Anyone? I know you're dying for me to touch you."

Everything in the room went still. The marble snakes inside me, the golden ropes, my own breath.

Reeve lifted his hand from between my legs, glistening with my juices. Slowly, he curled it around his shaft, and his eyes closed in a grimace.

"Just for a minute," he muttered. "Sweet Daisy."

Straddling me, he lowered his cock to hover over my face.

I strained at the golden cords, but they held me firmly, pressing into my flesh. They'd formed a lattice of diamonds over my entire upper body.

"Closer, Reeve."

He hesitated, but hunger pulsed in his glowing eyes, fuzzing his sleek outline, darkening the air around him.

With a groan, he thrust forward. His cock came within an inch of my lips.

Impulsively, I arched my neck and managed to kiss it.

"Fuck," he gasped.

I flicked my tongue over the head, and his cock jerked. His skin was satin-smooth and fire-hot. A clear bead of liquid hung suspended from the tip.

"Don't take it inside," he gritted. "Play with it. Taste me, baby."

I gazed up at him as I ran kisses over his broad, flared head. His eyes — oh God, his eyes weren't shining and dark now. They fizzed and sparked with shades of grass and gold, the pupils narrowing and lengthening so quickly I could only suck in my breath.

Finally, the dazzling array settled, and two brilliant green eyes stared down at me. Black diamonds marked the centers, and the whites were completely absent.

They were unblinking. Hungry.

The eyes of a serpent.

Fear flashed through me. But I was also soaking wet and desperately excited.

"Like this?" I managed, planting smooches on Reeve's impossibly soft skin, caressing the length of his cock with my lips. "Is this how you want me to taste you?"

"Yesssss," he hissed. "Like that, Star of the Cosmos."

I shuddered, caught in the embrace of the golden ropes. The

marble snakes still filled me, thrusting deep. My nipples were two dark points, aching and constricted.

I was going to come again.

I wanted — I needed — to take Reeve with me. To share the pleasure he gave me so much of.

"Fuck my mouth," I rasped. "You've already got your snakes inside me. Fill me everywhere."

Reeve's powerful shoulders quivered. "Not — yet." The words came out with difficulty. Another pearl of liquid oozed from his cock, smearing my lips.

"You're in pain." I yearned to touch him. With my hands, my arms, my whole body. "Let me help you."

Running my tongue over my lips, I flicked it out to swirl over the tip of his cock. He groaned, thrusting forward. Eagerly, I licked along the beautiful veins on his shaft. I breathed in his musky scent, speeding up my pace, sucking on the flared underside, unsure of what to do but knowing that I was pleasing him.

As soon as my lips closed over the satin head, he exploded. A stream of hot, salty cream lashed my tongue.

"Daisy!" He jerked back. His beautiful face was a mix of agony and pleasure. He gripped his cock, trying to control it, but his body wrenched as his desires took over.

Cum splashed onto my breasts, spattering the golden cords until they writhed in a frenzy. It dripped down my pussy and ass, slicking the marble snakes that filled me. The pale drops burned, making me gasp with each new spray.

"Sweet Star," Reeve panted.

God, there was so much of it. How could there be so much? Reeve's cum lashed my entire upper body, spilling onto the silk sheets, coating me from throat to thighs, as I lay bound to the bed. He groaned, his fist locked on his spurting cock, spasming helplessly. And the serpent on his arm — it coiled and clenched, swallowing its tail with a hunger that I felt in my bones.

The intensity set off my own climax. I came so hard it hurt, rippling in the embrace of the snakes and Reeve's essence. As my breathing subsided, his hand dropped from his cock.

"My God," he stammered. "Daisy, I—I—"

He stared at the magnificent mess he'd made of me. His eyes flickered, darkening and warming. For once, they looked ordinary. Just a pair of brown boy eyes framed with long, pretty lashes. He rubbed his hand over his stubbled jaw, then stroked my cheek.

I gazed up at him, captive to his toys, splashed with his fluids, yet feeling—

Powerful.

"You're so good, baby," I said. "You're no devil."

His mouth snapped shut. Panic flashed across his face. Twisting, he peered at the inside of his left biceps.

"Still there," he whispered. "Fuck, it's still there."

"Your tattoo?" The twining coils were as vivid as ever against his skin. "Did you expect it to disappear?"

The door flew open.

Blake and Evan charged in, fully dressed, stopping short when they saw me on the bed.

"Holy fuck," Evan breathed. His pale eyes moved shamelessly over my cum-soaked nakedness, the golden cords that had gone quiet, and the marble snakes peeking motionless from my pussy and ass.

All I wanted was for him to run his big hands over my body, rubbing in Reeve's cum while he called me filthy names. And Blake, staring in shock beside him — I wanted his lips on mine, then traveling downward, soothing my tender cunt stretched around the snake.

"Do you still have it?" Reeve asked quietly. Both men ripped their shirts open to stare at their left arms.

"Still there." Blake sounded shaky.

Evan nodded, a strange smile stretching his lips. "Did you ever doubt it?"

Reeve pressed his fingers to the inked coils. Simultaneously, his friends flinched, and his shoulders relaxed.

"Is everything okay? Was something" — I laughed a little — "was something terrible supposed to happen when you came?"

Reeve stroked damp tendrils of hair off my face, his voice filled with wonder. "Everything's fine, Daze. Completely fine. I'll untie you."

He exchanged glances with Blake and Evan, who reluctantly left the room.

When Reeve bent over me, the cords and snakes began moving feebly again, as if they were responding to his presence. I arched off the bed, overstimulated.

"I — I — Enough."

He kissed me tenderly, murmuring into my neck. The figurines quivered and stilled. The golden ropes released my throbbing nipples and fell slack to my sides. Reeve undid my right wrist, then gently eased the figurines out of my pussy and ass.

We rolled to the other side of the bed where the sheets were dry, exchanging smiles at the sticky puddle we'd left behind. I lay sprawled beneath him, blanketed by a blissful, exhausted haze. Everywhere his snakes had touched me was deliciously sore.

"Are your arms okay, sweet?" He looked at me with such concern, massaging my right arm.

"They're fine." When he stroked my chest, the drops of cum sizzled on my breasts and belly. "But, um, a towel, please?"

He chuckled. Bringing a thick black towel to the bed, he wiped the milky streaks from my skin.

I curled up against him, my head pillowed on his chest. He dragged his fingertips through the sticky residue he'd left behind, sweeping from my belly button to my collarbone.

"Bath, Daze?" he teased. "I know how much you love my tub."

"Mmmmm, in a minute," I said sleepily. "I want to keep some of you on me for now."

He let out a deep sound of contentment, halfway between a sigh and a hiss, and ruffled my hair. For long minutes, we lay together. Then he stirred.

"I'll be right back." He picked up the marble figurines and disappeared through the bathroom door, shutting it quietly behind him.

Downstairs, Evan was playing the piano — slow, deep, poignant chords. The heaviness of the air in Reeve's room rippled and diffused.

A little part of my mind asked, *What the fuck just happened?* My blissed-out body answered, *don't question it.*

Some time later, Reeve opened the bathroom door and beckoned me to join him. He'd drawn a bath. I sank into his opulent tub, hoping he'd climb in with me. But he sat on the edge, covered in a fresh pair of silk boxers.

As he splashed me with hot water, washing away the last traces of his cum, his gaze was intent. I'd told him that I trusted him. And dammit, I did. Surely, he'd feel the same way.

"Reeve, I don't want to push, but can I ask you one more time about your rare books?" I asked tentatively. "You said you really have to trust someone to loan them out. Do you finally trust me now?"

He raised his eyebrows. "I do. But there's nothing of interest in there."

"They're of interest to me," I said quickly.

"Why?"

I tucked my left wrist against my chest. "For reasons."

"Then maybe someday, sweet Star."

The message was clear: if he was going to trust me completely, I needed to be open with him. I needed to tell him why I wanted his locked-up books.

But I couldn't.

31

The Spy

Daisy

On Monday morning, I caught up with my geology professor after class.

"Could you tell me more about Greer Hill?" I asked. "You mentioned at the first lecture that the composition is different from the rest of the land, and I was wondering how, exactly."

He turned to face me, one eyebrow raised. "Indeed. Better not to ask too many questions, uh—"

"Daisy," I supplied.

"Yes. Well, I believe the chancellor has plans to demolish the hill, so it's a moot point."

"No," I said quickly. "He moved the plans for the parking garage. There's no reason to blast through the hill."

The professor squinted at me. "How do you know this?"

"Why is it better not to ask too many questions?" I countered.

"Look," he said, checking his watch, "I have a meeting to get to. But if you're interested in the area, I'm sure the library has resources on the history of Pacific Crest. Best of luck."

He hurried off.

Right. The library. Which had been no help at all.

Sighing, I headed toward it anyway, trying to clear my head. I couldn't stop thinking about the men.

About Reeve, in particular.

His touch burning, his voice pouring over me. And the drops of his cum... the golden cords that crisscrossed my body in a lattice of writhing snakes... My pussy and ass throbbed as if the figurines were still inside me.

I hadn't given the men an answer yet. About whether I'd join them in the House, be at their side — be *theirs*, whatever that meant.

I'd spent Saturday night in Reeve's bed, in a fever dream, and when he drove me back to Lee Tower on Sunday, the rest of the day was a haze. I'd tried to do more research on Greer Hill and the ouroboros, which led nowhere, as well as my class assignments, but I hadn't had the time or the focus for magic.

As I turned off the main path toward the library, a hand closed on my arm.

"I told you to stay away from us."

I looked up at Nathan. Heat flushed his skin, like he'd just finished a run. His short hair was damp, appearing almost black in the sunlight, and a trickle of sweat traced his forehead. His tight blue T-shirt looked ready to burst.

"I saved your life on Saturday," I said quietly. "Maybe you could start with 'thank you?'"

"Thank you," he muttered, like it pained him to say it. "Now let's talk."

He jerked his head toward the nearest building. I followed him around one corner, then another, until we stopped in the shadow of a tall wall. He backed me against the warm, baked stucco.

"The whole school is gossiping about the girl at the football game who was with Blake Phillips, Evan Hayes, and Reeve McClellan," he snarled. "People think you're sleeping with all of them."

I rolled my eyes. "So?"

"You'll ruin your reputation."

"My *reputation?* That is the most antiquated thing I've ever heard. I don't care, okay? I don't give a damn what anyone here thinks about me."

He looked to one side, then the other. "I care."

"So you're trying to shame me through some twisted sense of honor? I see why you're the Knight, but reversed," I snapped. "You've got all the worst traits of chivalry and none of the best ones. You won't even speak to me like a decent person. Do you remember when you used to do that? We used to be friends, Nathan."

"They just want sex," he burst out. "Blake, Evan — Reeve. They want your body."

"Is that so terrible? It's nice to finally be wanted. And you're wrong, because I don't think Reeve just wants sex."

"Daisy," he began.

"Yes?" I raised my eyebrows.

"You need to know..."

"Know what?"

"All of us, we—we're—" He struggled to speak.

"It's okay. I won't judge you." My voice softened. "Whatever you need to say, you can tell me."

His lips moved soundlessly, as though two voices inside him battled for control. Strange patches shimmered on his arms like scales.

"Tell me what you've done with him." The words burst out abruptly.

"With Reeve? We've gone on dates, we've—"

"Sexually."

Shock sparked through me at the wrongness, the dirtiness of it.

Standing on my tiptoes, I leaned close enough for my lips to brush Nathan's ear. Oh, how I'd longed to touch him this way in high school.

"We've kissed," I whispered. "Many times. Because that's what happens when someone doesn't run away."

His face flushed. "How does it feel?"

"Like I'm falling and soaring at the same time." I dared to run my lips along his jaw. "Like the world is tilting. I'm on a merry-go-round in the dark and I want to be as close to him as possible."

His fists clenched on the wall, veins standing out on the massive arms that surrounded me.

"And then he gives me orders." Gathering courage, I stroked Nathan's damp hair off his forehead. He let out a strangled noise. "He tells me to get naked. He tells me to crawl for him, and I do, because it feels so good."

His face contorted. "Go on."

"He's touched my breasts." Nathan closed his eyes and groaned. "He's sucked on my nipples."

"Don't play games, Daisy," he muttered. "I know you've gone further than that."

"He's — he's touched me everywhere. He's put his fingers inside me." The confessions spilled out like a runaway train. I needed to talk, to tell the truth. "God, I get so wet when I'm with him."

"How does that feel?" His voice was rough, his breathing faster.

Nervous excitement fluttered in my belly. "Amazing."

He bent his head until our foreheads touched. He was so close that my breath mingled with his. "You're tight, aren't you?" he ground out. "No one had ever been inside you before. But now they all have."

God, how I'd wanted Nathan to be the first. I strained forward, but he wouldn't let me close the gap.

"Nathan, I don't know what to do," I whispered. "They're keeping secrets. They want something from me, and I know it's not just sex. I can't stop thinking about him — about them —"

Perspiration rolled down Nathan's forehead. A vein stood out, throbbing, as his lips hovered inches from mine. The face of the boy I'd loved for years was unrecognizable.

"I'll tell you what to do," he growled. "Walk away. Now. While you can."

"Never."

Nathan's face twisted. "I've seen you, Daisy. I know what the others have touched and tasted. You showed me on purpose, didn't you? When you were sleeping over last summer, you left the bathroom door open because you wanted me to see. I know how beautiful you look naked, how pink your skin was when you came out of the shower because you'd turned the water up so hot. What would you have done if I'd come in?"

My heartbeat rocketed. "Why didn't you?" I'd hoped, but I hadn't known he was there. I thought it was just me and my fantasy.

"Because you're a naïve, inexperienced girl. When you play with fire, you don't even notice that it burns."

"Is that why, Nathan?" I asked softly, daring to push for more. "Or were you afraid? Is there a reason why you never touched me during all our midnight talks? Why you always left space between us on the swing, more than we needed for the ice cream? Because I see now that you want me. I don't know how I ever could have wondered."

A growl left his lips. Biceps flexing, he pressed his hands more firmly into the wall. A crimson mark caught my eye.

"Your tattoo," I said. "Show me."

His nostrils flared. Slowly, he pushed up his sleeve. The knots resolved into an endlessly clenching serpent.

"This is what I live with, Daisy. Don't go here."

But my hand didn't listen. Rising, it traced the serpent's body.

"*Fuck.*" Nathan closed his eyes.

As if possessed, I dragged my fingers over each sinuous coil. His skin was so smooth, so hot, and something was... *moving* underneath.

"Do you like that?" I whispered. A groan was the only response. His erection pointed toward me, tenting his athletic shorts. "Do you want me to stop?"

"Don't stop," he breathed.

I was drunk on the power of controlling his excitement, the pleasure of vicariously experiencing every sensation. I understood

Reeve's enjoyment in seduction now. Touching Nathan's arm was getting me desperately aroused.

I pressed lightly on the snake's head and was rewarded with a gasp. Nathan's eyes were fogged over with lust, his long lashes brushing his cheeks, his shoulders contracting.

When I caught sight of the damp spot on his shorts, I couldn't take it any longer. Reaching down, I grazed the tip of his erection. He jerked, uttering a strangled curse, and thrust into my palm.

Oh God. Nathan's cock. Eagerly, I stroked the thick ridge, daring to rub the head as it pushed against the soft fabric.

"Will something bad happen if I touch you here?" I teased. "I did it for Reeve this weekend, and he came all over me. And Nathan, he liked it. He had nothing to worry about. Will you come all over me too? Pretty please? I promise—"

"Daisy. Stop. Now." The order was sudden and sharp.

I longed to keep touching him, to ride every peak together. But I dropped my hands.

"Holy shit." He squeezed his eyes shut, breathing through his nose.

My heart was thumping in my chest, and my loose dress stuck to my back with sweat. Had I really just uttered those words to Nathan? I'd meant them, of course, but saying them out loud was a different story.

I looked around quickly, but we were alone.

"Are you okay?" I whispered.

"You almost made me come in my pants," he said bluntly.

A hot blush swept my cheeks. "Aside from needing to wash your pants, that's a bad thing because...?"

His hand closed over my arm, then opened with a jerk. "Find some other friends. Real ones."

"I'm not going to stop seeing Reeve. Or Blake, or Evan."

"They'll destroy all your innocence."

His words were meant as a warning, but they dangled before me, the most delectable treat imaginable.

"I want you," I said softly. "And I want them."

He turned deep red, gripping his biceps where the tattoo writhed. His words came out in a hiss.

"Is that all you want? Is that how your wonderful ambitions turned out, the ones you talked about so much in high school? All you want now is sex?"

"No!" I gasped. "I want my music. I want my life back. I want Reeve's books."

"Reeve's books?" Nathan blinked in surprise.

"He has a whole collection of books on magic. Healing spells, amulets, you name it. I don't care what he says, those books have power. Nathan—" I shivered in the warm air, and the trees of Greer Hill whispered in my mind. "There's magic here. I need those books."

"Then I'll help you."

"What?"

He pulled his sweat-soaked T-shirt away from his chest, fanning himself, and ran a hand over his hair. His honey-colored eyes locked on mine. "I'll help you get the books. Guaranteed."

"You would do that for me?"

"On one condition."

"Name it."

"Quit fuckin' around with my friends. Forever."

My lips parted, but no sound came out.

"No more 'dates,'" he sneered, doing air quotes. "No more hookups, no more heart-to-hearts. Don't let Reeve put his hands or his anything else on you ever again. Don't chat with Evan, don't go for a stroll with Blake in the woods. And don't come looking for me. Stay the hell away from all of us. And especially Reeve."

"No," I blurted.

"Yes."

"I don't want to stop."

"Then no deal. Take it or leave it."

I stared over Nathan's shoulder at the lush bougainvillea spilling over a white stucco archway.

A lump rose in my throat. For the first time in my life, I'd felt desired. Celebrated in a way that had nothing to do with my flute.

The touch, the sex, the games were all intoxicating. But just as addictive was the sense of belonging. The excitement of being with men who were so good at what they did. They burned, and I'd known what it was to burn.

My eyes stung and filled. I made the mistake of looking down at Nathan's chalk-white athletic shoe, planted between my black sandals, and a hot tear clung to my lashes. I shook my head, and the tear splashed onto Nathan's shoe.

"Jesus, Daisy, don't—" He reached out to me, then pulled his hand back, his voice hardening. "Don't think that'll work on me."

"When did you become such a jerk?" I whispered.

"Do we have a deal or no? The others are leaving the House in fifteen minutes. They're rarely all gone at once. It's now or never."

"I need more time to think."

"No time. Now."

"But Reeve needs me," I blurted.

"What?" Nathan's head lifted. He stared at me incredulously.

"He had a nightmare on Friday night. I held him, we talked, I—I made him hot chocolate. Something's wrong inside of him. He's terrified. He's never told you about it, has he?" I asked, realization dawning. Nathan shook his head. "And you — you were off balance at the game on Saturday. What if that happens again? Who's going to save you?"

"Don't worry about us," he said harshly. "Worry about yourself, Daisy. Don't put our well-being ahead of yours."

"I want to. Someone needs to care about you."

"I won't let you do that." His face was hard.

Looking away, I turned my left wrist over. My arms felt like a scale, weighing the possibilities. On one side, there were the men, promising dark pleasures, belonging and connection. Hidden mysteries and strange, unexplored magic. Feelings beyond anything I'd known or might experience again. And on the other, my music.

My flute in my hands once more. The deepest expression of my soul, the future I'd always hoped for.

When I spoke, my throat was dry. "Only if the spells work. We only have a deal then."

Nathan shook his head. "Deal now, or no deal."

I closed my eyes, seeking an answer, a flash of intuition, anything. A star burst behind my eyelids, and the leaves in the woods rustled in a frenzy.

The Devil rose before me, along with the Ace, the Beast — and the Knight, right-side-up. All reaching out in an embrace.

The cards didn't lie. I had a purpose with these men, no matter what kind of agreement I made with Nathan Davis.

"Books," I whispered. "We have a deal."

Profound relief flashed across Nathan's face. "And that," he said quietly, "is why I will always understand you the best. I knew you'd make that choice."

My hand opened and closed by his chest. "Don't say things like that right before I'm never supposed to speak to you again."

He flinched. For a moment, I thought he'd take it back. But he just jerked his head toward the main entrance to campus.

"Nathan—"

"Don't argue, Daisy. Follow my lead. We're short on time."

We left campus for the gracious neighborhood that lay to the south. I was a fast walker, but I had to hurry to keep up. When we reached the hedges that hid the House, Nathan held out a warning hand.

"Stay here. Don't let anyone see you. Keep an eye out until I come back."

As he headed down the driveway, he glanced over his shoulder.

"Not moving," I said through clenched teeth.

His face softened, and his eyes skated over my body. He turned and hurried away, so swiftly that he was a blur.

Creeping toward the driveway, I watched the path.

The door to the House opened and Reeve strolled out, rolling up his sleeves over tanned forearms. He put on a pair of mirrored sunglasses and smoothed his tousled hair. As usual, he looked perfectly groomed, but a grin broke across his face when he saw Nate, and there seemed to be an extra spring in his step.

At the sight of him so happy, a weight crushed my chest.

What did I feel for him? Was I really going to walk away?

Blake had made an offer to join all the men, to be theirs. What would they do when I left?

Nathan clapped Reeve on the shoulder, and they conversed in low tones. Reeve's dimple flashed, while Nathan was actually smiling.

It hurt to watch Reeve climb gracefully into his car. He'd been more open and relaxed this weekend than I'd ever seen him. We'd talked, we'd laughed. Nathan was wrong; it wasn't just sex.

The car purred to life. Quickly, I darted into a gap in the hedge.

You're so bright, you blaze, Star, Reeve had said. If he really saw me that way, my ridiculous hiding spot didn't stand a chance. I edged farther into the dense branches, ignoring the scratches on my skin.

At my feet, there was a faint hiss. I looked down to see a California kingsnake curving on the ground. For a moment, we stared at each other.

"I don't mean any harm," I whispered, moving back an inch to give it space. "I'm a friend."

The snake lifted its head. Reeve's car exited the driveway and turned away from my hiding spot. When I looked down, the snake was gone.

Carefully, I eased out of the hedge, and a minute later, Nathan appeared. His lips thinned when he saw my scratched arms and messy hair, but he said nothing. He simply took my hand.

My heart rose into my throat. After five years of longing, I was holding hands with Nathan Davis.

We walked in silence to the House, through the cool marble entrance hall, the shadowed living room tiled with squares of light from the windows, and into Reeve's library.

Nathan let my hand go and swept his arm at the rows of books. "Have at it."

I wanted to see them all, but I went to the shelves in the very back of the library, locked behind glass doors. "They're in here."

Coming to my side, Nathan grasped the ornate lock in his fist and muttered a few hissed words. Green sparks shot out between his fingers, and the lock fell open.

"How—"

"No questions."

As he palmed the lock and stepped back, I examined the books. There were so many, and I only had room for two or three in my bag. But they glimmered at me from the shelves — the leather bindings, the gold letters, the promise of arcane knowledge. The tempting array almost distracted me from the pain of Nathan waiting behind me.

My hand stopped at the spine of *Healing Spells* and hovered over it. As I paused, doubts crept through me.

My hand was injured, end of story. I couldn't expect magic to fix it. I needed to accept reality, move on with my life, and leave Reeve's books alone.

"Do it now," Nathan hissed. "Time is ticking."

I hesitated, remembering everything that had happened since I arrived at Pacific Crest. I'd made myself vulnerable to all the men, while their secrets piled up and Reeve calmly deflected me from exploring the treasure trove of information in this library.

I felt a twinge of guilt about my own secrets, but I buried it in righteous indignation.

"Knowledge is meant to be shared," I said firmly.

"You think so?" Nathan asked.

"Yes, I do."

His honey-brown eyes narrowed. "Come here."

My heart sped up. I crossed the library to stand in front of him. It seemed to take an eternity.

"Daisy, I want to kiss you," he whispered.

I stared at his contorted face. "I want you to."

His hand curved around the back of my head and pulled me in.

Those were his lips. On mine. Hot, soft, and demanding. I wrapped my arms around his neck and clung to him. My mouth opened to his tongue. His hands ran over my body, urgent and hungry. I shuddered as he stroked my neck, my breasts, my hips, my ass. His back was massive under my palms, the unyielding face of a cliff, and I was tumbling with him into the abyss.

When his hand slid between my thighs, I rocked in an agony of need, reaching for him. His cock was thick and hard, burning me through the mesh of his shorts, and the heat shocked me, but I never wanted to let go...

He gripped my shoulders and held me firmly away.

"Get out," he said gruffly. "Get out while you can."

"Nathan, there doesn't have to be a deal," I breathed. "We can have it all. You, me, Reeve, Evan, Blake—"

He shook his head. "That's not possible. There's always a trade-off, Daisy. You can never have it all."

"No," I protested.

"Yes. In life — in *my* fucking life — you give something to get something. A win means a loss. Now get your fucking books and don't speak to me again."

He let my shoulders go.

I stared at him, my eyes bright with tears. "That was selfish. Kissing me like that, when you knew you'd push me away."

"I'm completely selfish, Daisy. All four of us are. It's one of the many reasons why you need to stay away from us."

Holding his gaze, I walked to the bookshelf. "Just do one thing for me, okay? Call Sasha and be her big brother, even if you think she doesn't want that. You need each other."

He pressed his lips together and said nothing.

I pulled out *Healing Spells*, a thick, heavy brick of a book, and recoiled as an electric shock bit my fingers.

Quickly, I dropped it in my tote bag. I'd used my right hand, which tingled. But my left hand smarted, pain lancing through my tendons and wrist.

Scanning the shelves, I chose a second book, *Wards and Amulets*. This time, I was prepared for the shock. Someone must have spelled these books so they wouldn't be stolen — or they contained so much power that they sparked like live wires.

"Daisy, you okay?" Nathan's brows pulled together.

"I'm fine." I turned away so I wouldn't see his concern, his caring. Those honey-colored eyes, gentle for once. This was all so much easier when he was angry and mean. "Can you help me return these? Even though we won't be on speaking terms? That better be part of the deal."

"You're planning to *return* them?"

"Of course. They're Reeve's. I'm not a thief, just a—a borrower."

"We'll figure that out later." He motioned to me, and my heart gave a treacherous leap at that *we*. "Go."

Shouldering my tote bag, I took a deep breath and put my hand on the doorknob. "Goodbye, Nathan."

On Greer Hill, the woods reached out to welcome me.

It was my first visit since the night with Evan and Blake. The trees parted as I approached the forest. The path to the clearing stood open.

My eyes blurred with tears, and I dashed them away. The loss of the men made every part of my body ache.

But in the woods, sinking to my knees in front of the remnants of my spell circle, I felt more at ease. I felt like myself.

Home, the trees whispered. *You belong here.*

I tweaked my bag open. Cautiously, I took out *Healing Spells* and opened the thick, green-bound book. It didn't try to shock or bite me.

It was very old. The paper was creamy and thin with uneven

edges. A breeze stirred the top page, blowing it over. I squinted in the dim light of the forest to make out the close-set, archaic words.

The book seemed to cover every medical issue imaginable, plus a whole bunch I'd never imagined. After an hour of searching, my back stiff and my legs nearly asleep, I found a spell that could fit: "Setting joints right."

It called for herbs I'd never heard of. A twenty-four-hour fast before performing the spell. And the assumption that you'd cast it on behalf of someone else — not yourself.

But what did I have to lose?

A lot, Star, came Reeve's silky whisper.

Pulling out my phone, I found a shop downtown that specialized in herbs and magic supplies.

"Call first to see if we're open," said the purple cursive at the bottom of the screen.

I called.

"We're just closing," said the girl who answered the phone. "But we have everything you need. Come in tomorrow, okay? What did you say your name was?"

"Daisy."

"Perfect. We'll make sure to be open for you."

Now came the harder call. I switched my phone from hand to hand, dreading it. In the end, I lost my nerve and wrote a text to Reeve.

And I begged the woods to help me forget them.

32

Self-Made Man

Nate

When I let myself into the House, the front hall was empty. The pretentious frescoes Reeve had commissioned looked down as I stalked across the marble floor. Melancholy chords came from the living room.

A huge new painting was on display by the curtained archway — Reeve's latest acquisition. An abstract swirl of colors, with no frame. I wondered whether the art spoke to him, or just the price tag.

It was almost midnight. Since sneaking Daisy into the House this morning, I'd stayed on campus all day — going to class, working out, attending practice, studying in the library. I told myself I wasn't avoiding the others.

But when I walked into the living room and saw Evan at the piano with a bottle of vodka close by, Blake working in the open kitchen, and no Reeve, I breathed a little easier.

I flapped my T-shirt, transparent with sweat. I overheated quickly these days. Just another glitch that made me itchy and restless. I'd wanted to take it off on the way home, but girls followed me with greedy eyes on campus, staring openly at my body. Once, I would have relished the attention.

Not now.

From the kitchen, Blake rattled a bag of chocolate chunks. "Half of these are gone. Who's been getting into my supplies?"

"You know I don't touch what's in the kitchen until you put your magic hands on it." Evan smirked. "What's wrong? Worried you won't have enough to make cookies for your mommy?"

Knife strokes hit a cutting board, swift and precise. I stopped by the marble table, watching Blake chop the chocolate. He was so fast with the knives that they blurred.

"You can't cure her, you know." Evan knocked back a swallow of vodka.

Blake paused. "If I can make my mom happy by mailing her a box of treats each week, it's a small thing."

"Remember, Blakey? Forget your past."

"Yeah, well, the past doesn't always forget you."

"And you think that after the Joining, you'll be powerful enough to make her happy forever. I have faith in you, Blakey, but even you can't do that."

Blake raised an eyebrow. "I can try. Just like you're trying to make the world love you with your music."

Unexpectedly, Evan grinned. "With our Star, we've got a shot."

A pile of books sat on the table — Reeve's. All about gaining more knowledge, more money, more things. More, more, more.

I swept the books off the table. They landed on the floor with a crash.

My friends' heads swiveled toward me. "What happened, Nate?" Blake asked.

His gaze was too keen, too penetrating. I turned away.

"What happened?" The question was gentler this time.

"Nothing." I refused to look in his direction.

"You're upset. You feel off."

"Blake, leave me the fuck alone," I snarled.

Like a coward, I couldn't face him. I still dreamed about him at night, and I didn't want the complications. It took all my energy to push Daisy away, to keep my head in the game, because every time I got on the field, I fought an inner battle. The serpent urged me to take all the glory. It wanted me to forget that the other players were people, that they mattered at all.

Holding back drained me. And apparently, it was making me black out.

"I'm worried about you," Blake insisted.

"Stop hovering. You're not my goddamn mother."

Behind me, the knives paused. "No," Blake said, in the measured voice that made it clear he was containing himself. He was always so *nice,* so controlled. For once, I wanted to see him lose his shit. "Your mom never hovered."

"She was never even fucking there." I tore off my shirt and tossed it on the couch. "Where's Reeve?"

"You don't feel him?"

Blake and Evan blazed near me, two points of green light. Far away in the House, above us, a much fainter light pulsed. Reeve was usually the brightest of us, but I almost didn't recognize him.

"He's off being a drama queen." Evan jerked his thumb toward the stairs. "As usual. Brooding and angsting that he doesn't have total control of the world yet. I don't know what his deal is, but he went up to the tower hours ago and hasn't come out."

"I'm going to him." I made for the staircase.

"At your own risk, brother." Blake scraped the chocolate chunks into a bowl.

"Relax, Nate. Sit down and drink with me." Evan lifted his bottle. He stretched nonchalantly on the piano bench, but his eyes were watchful.

"Evan, when are you going to lay off the booze?" I stalked past him to the stairs.

"When I get what's coming to me." His voice echoed as I climbed.

Turning off at the landing, I went to my bedroom to clear my head. Dealing with Reeve would take all my focus. Otherwise, he'd sway me.

I fed the array of tropical fish in the central tank, pretending to be normal for three minutes. I made my bed, tucking the dark blue covers over the thick, cushy mattress. Every night, I kicked them off, along with the pillows, and the sheets were soaked with sweat as I hissed and grappled with my dreams.

It was a gilded cage. This room, this House, this campus. My body. We couldn't leave. Not yet.

But fuck, I craved more than just freedom. Every night, I dreamed of falling asleep in Blake's arms with my head on his chest. I dreamed that Daisy would look at me with her clear gray-blue eyes and never stop kissing me. And I never knew if those desires were mine, or the serpent's.

I'd dreamed about being sandwiched between the two of them. About her between us. Blake between me and Daisy. Every possible combination. I'd fantasized about watching all the sensual torments Reeve devised for her, keeping her on the edge until she almost lost her mind. And when Evan boasted about nearly fisting her in the woods on Greer Hill, I'd pictured that too. In detail.

I shoved a pillow into place. I'd made my own bed; now I had to lie in it. I couldn't ever talk to or touch Daisy again.

It was worse than holding back during the years when we talked in my family's backyard at night. At first, I'd been shy and unsure. From the start, she seemed too good for me, out of my league, even though she was younger. Her confidence and sense of purpose were intimidating. But the more she talked about her ambitions, the more they kindled mine.

Then the serpent began invading my dreams.

It showed me her image, whispering in my ear, promising greatness if I pledged it my heart and joined with its disciples. It ordered me to look but not touch. I'd wake up in a thick, dark cloud, smoking with desire, cum streaking my thighs and sheets. I became resentful.

Angry. Secretive. I had been for years, but it all surfaced now, bubbling from under my skin. I knew I was meant to be great, just like Daisy. And I'd fucking do whatever it took to get there.

After each talk on the swing, when she'd lean toward me, eyes shining, and confide things she told no one else, I'd go to my room and furiously jerk off. Over and over and over. At first, I felt shame. For making her into an object, lusting after her with animal need. Then the shame coiled through my body and twined around my heart, my limbs, my cock, until it was part of the desire.

All I had to do was think of her — her laugh, her whispered confessions, her long legs tucked under her — to get painfully hard.

I swore to protect her from my friends, from the serpent that wanted her so badly, but most of all, from myself.

I walked to my desk, where a hammered silver bowl sat in one corner. Taking a pinch of the dark-green dried leaves it held, I crumbled them into a glass of water.

We weren't supposed to use the herbs more than once a day — or to skip a day. We needed to control the serpent's possession of us, but if we took the herbs too often, they'd lessen its presence. We'd lose our magic touch.

Taking a deep breath, I knocked back the glass of water. The herbs might weaken me temporarily, but right now, weakness was pretty damn attractive.

On campus, everyone wanted me. My strength. Everyone knew my name.

Nate! Hey, Nate! Nate, talk to me. Nate, look at me. Touch me. Let me touch you.

My head was about to crack.

Growing up, I'd dreamed of this. I'd felt invisible all my life. Nice, harmless, forgettable. I'd longed to be seen.

Known.

I'd told Blake, that first summer in the crappy apartment Reeve found for us, during the long hours that we talked between sweaty fucking. *All I want is to be seen.*

I see you, Nate. His arms had tightened around me, and he rested his forehead against mine. For the first time, I'd felt loved.

I shook off the memories. If Reeve was to be believed, we'd have everything we wanted in a few weeks. But I knew that wasn't possible.

And if he'd shut himself in the tower, chances were, he knew it now too.

Leaving my room, I climbed the stairs three at a time, turning left into one hallway and right down another. Pressing on the hidden door, I squeezed up the narrow staircase to the tower.

The circular room was dark. Overhead, the stars shone through the glass ceiling. Reeve's beloved telescope stood motionless.

A figure slumped in one of the armchairs. A bottle sat on the small table beside it — Reeve's crystal decanter, filled with the most expensive liqueur he could get his hands on. Now it was less than half-full.

I went to him quickly. Reeve wasn't one to overindulge, but his jaw hung slack, and his arm dangled from the side of his chair.

When he saw me, he lurched to his feet with difficulty. Stumbling, he grabbed my arm and pointed to the decanter.

"How much is it going to take?" he slurred.

"A lot," I said. Cruel, but honest.

Reeve fumbled in his pocket. Finally, he managed to get his phone out. Pawing at the screen, he held it up. "Look at this."

The screen showed a text, in a chat named "Star of the Cosmos."

I'm sorry, Reeve. I can't see you anymore. I don't want anything to do with you, Blake, Evan, or Nathan.
Don't contact me.
If you do, I won't reply.

I hid a smile.

"What did I do wrong?" he whispered. "Everything was going so well. Was it the nightmare? It must have been the nightmare. I shouldn't have been so weak."

My heart hardened. "So you lost your prize. And now you're drinking yourself into a stupor."

He shoved the phone in his pocket and gripped my shoulders with sudden, vicious strength. "We need her, Nate. We *need* her to get out of this prison. We need every goddamn way the Star fits with us. I —" He stared at me, his eyes wide and blank, rocking on his heels. "I need her. I *need* her."

"Reeve," I began.

"I don't understand it. I fucking hate not understanding."

I eased him back. "Did you contact her?"

He looked at me like I was crazy. "She said not to."

My stomach roiled. This wasn't the Reeve I knew — the ruthless seducer, caring only for his ambitions. Why the fuck did Daisy show up at Pacific Crest? Why did she have to be the goddamn Star?

"That doesn't sound like you, brother." I forced cheerfulness into my voice.

Reeve's hands dropped from my shoulders. He walked slowly to the curving wall of glass.

"Nate, do you remember the Binding? For seven days, we felt everyone's desires on this campus. It almost drowned us."

"It was hell," I acknowledged.

He swayed toward the nearest window. "And the worst? The worst was the people who couldn't take no for an answer. Calling, clinging, pushing, pulling. Forcing. It made me physically sick!" He spat the words, lips curled in disgust. "I won't sink to that level. And I will never do that to Daisy."

"You don't think someone put her up to it?" I heard myself say. "Tara, for instance."

Reeve smiled faintly. "No. Daisy wouldn't let anyone blackmail her. She's smarter than I am."

"You idealize her," I muttered.

He staggered to the table. Grabbing the decanter, he drank from the bottle. "Damn right I do."

"Forget about Daisy," I said. "Tara's willing. She always has been."

Reeve set down the decanter with a crash. "I'm not touching Tara."

"Listen. She's a tool, just like we are to her. It's simple, it's clear, it's cut-and-dried."

He lurched into the armchair, head lolling between his knees. "I don't want cut-and-dried." His voice was muffled. "I want Daisy."

Cautiously, I put my hand on his back.

"Look at me," he whispered. "Talk about pathetic people who can't let go. I'm the worst of all."

"You barely knew her."

"And you knew her so well, huh?" His shoulders shook.

His misery pulled at me. It twisted around my guts, filling my own throat with a lump. I couldn't stand it any longer.

"It was me."

"What?" His head lifted.

"Daisy dropped you because of me."

Reeve straightened. His eyes cleared, eerily calm. His laser focus unnerved me. "What did you say to her, Nate?"

"We made an agreement. She wanted you, but she wanted your books more."

"My books," he said slowly. "I told her no."

"And I told her yes. She wants a chance to heal her hand. You'd deny her that chance?"

"*We* can give her that chance." He got to his feet, his voice rising. "We can give it to her better than any spell in those books. You know that, Nate. You fucking know that!"

"You're drunk."

"Not anymore." He crossed swiftly to me. "How'd she get the books?"

"She took them out of the library."

"*Herself?* She survived? She got them out of the House?"

"Yes."

He paced the tower, energy smoking off of him. "You couldn't have done it. I couldn't have done it either."

I stared at him. "The books are spelled?"

"Nate... I trust you, but you have no idea what you're messing with here." He put a hand on my arm, his voice soft and gentle and deadly. "You're afraid, aren't you? Afraid of the Star."

"Don't do this, man." I shook him off. "Don't turn it around on me."

"She's more powerful than us both. It frightens you."

"Fuck that! I'm giving her a shot at a normal life."

"Who says she wants that? Has Daisy *ever* told you she wants a normal life?"

"She's a vulnerable girl whose dreams are wrecked. She doesn't know what she wants."

"No, Nate. She knows exactly what she wants. That's part of her appeal."

I folded my arms. "It's done. We made a deal, and she won't renege on it."

He laughed quietly, shaking his head. "This is about you, brother. Not her."

"This is about her, goddammit! I want to save her from what we've become."

"You're not gunning for her, Nate. You're trying to protect yourself. You're afraid of how much you want her. *What* you want from her."

"And you just want to use her."

Fury flooded me. At Reeve, at myself, at the fucking serpent.

Rearing back, I threw a punch at his perfect face. He caught my arm in an iron grip.

"Nate, Nate, Nate," he chided. "You know you can't hurt me."

I did know. But anger made spots of light and dark behind my eyes.

I launched myself at Reeve, aiming to tackle him. I crushed him against the wall, but he flipped me around and shoved me away. I staggered backward.

"You're wasting your energy—" he began.

I lunged again, taking him down. He struggled when I tried to pin him. For once, I had an opponent who matched me. For once, I knew I wouldn't win.

As we wrestled, I broke myself against him. I didn't think. Didn't feel. I crushed his thigh between mine and pushed his face into the carpet. He retaliated, whipping me around and catching me in a bear hug. Finally, he rolled me off of him.

I lay on the floor and glared at him, breathing hard.

"Nate." He knelt over me, his face full of concern. "Take it easy. I know you're hungry, but you won't get what you want from me. You don't have to wait much longer."

"Tara," I gritted, getting to my feet. "Not Daisy."

Reeve raked a hand through his hair. He looked completely sober, the alcohol willed out of his system.

He grasped my shoulders. "It frightens me too, you know. How much power our Star has. She's barely scratched the surface."

"It's over. Forget her."

"How can I, if you can't?"

Damn him for being right, always. For knowing my deepest wishes and desires. For knowing that Daisy was in my mind, my blood, my bones. And that after wrestling with Reeve, I was rock-hard for her.

He clapped me on the back. "I meant it, Nate. Take it easy the rest of the night. You're overwrought. You should relax."

"I haven't relaxed in a year. I don't know the meaning of the word anymore."

"Let Blake make you something—"

"No," I ground out.

"But he wants to." Reeve's voice softened to the persuasive tones I knew all too well. "He wants so badly to take care of you."

I stared at the midnight-blue carpet. "I'm going to lose my fucking mind. I can't make it until—"

"You will. We all will. Together." Moving his hand to my neck, Reeve kneaded the muscles firmly. I was so keyed up with magic and thwarted lust that his touch made me shudder. "You're thinking about her," he said softly.

Fuck, yes. Her, and Blake, and the things the four of us could do to her helpless, naked, willing body.

Her laughter, her ambitions, her dreams.

The inked serpent sent spikes of painful pleasure up my arm. I'd gotten used to blue balls, but I needed to unleash a year of pent-up passion.

On her.

"She deserves honesty," I heard myself say.

Reeve rubbed the back of my neck, getting his fingers into the knot of tension that lived there. "Go soak in the hot tub, brother. Use the sauna and sweat this out. We'll eat a late dinner, and you'll feel better."

"What about you?"

"I need to think."

"Don't go after her. You said you wouldn't."

He tapped his chin meditatively. "I won't. The question is, how soon will she come back to us?"

"Never. She honors her promises."

"Does she?" A knowing smile flickered across his face. "She'll create her own path to paradise, and it'll be paved with desire."

"There's a fucking chasm between paradise and hell."

"Not for us, Nate. Never for us."

Exiting the tower, I hunched my shoulders to squeeze down the narrow steps.

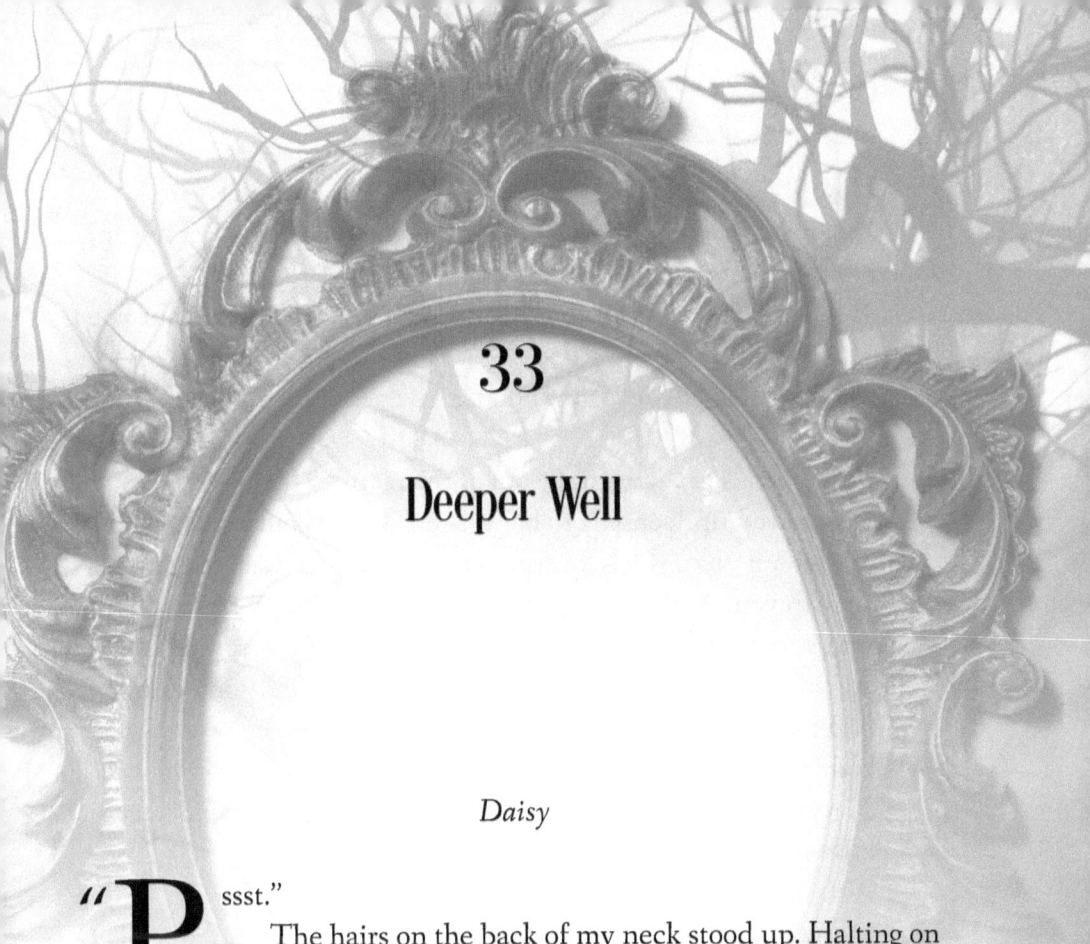

33

Deeper Well

Daisy

"Pssst."

The hairs on the back of my neck stood up. Halting on the path to the quad, I turned to see Evan leaning against the side of a building. The wall cast a shadow over his shaggy blond hair and intent green eyes, his husky shoulders and knowing smirk.

He flashed a dangerous smile. "I was hoping we'd run into each other."

"I can't talk." I turned away as my stomach growled. It was lunchtime, and I was halfway through the twenty-four-hour fast in preparation for the healing spell.

"We know what happened, Daisy. How are those books working out for you?"

I stubbornly faced away from him. "I made Nathan a promise. I want to be honorable."

"Yeah, well, I don't. He's not trying to help you, pet. He just wants you out of the picture. Reeve's precious magic books won't do shit for your hand."

403

"How do— He told—"

"He didn't need to," Evan said affably. "You're a witch, yeah? Good for you. No surprise there."

My face flamed, and I whirled to face him. "Did Reeve put you up to this?"

Evan laughed. "Believe it or not, Reeve doesn't control everything I do."

"Why does Nathan want me out of the picture?"

"A screwed-up sense of honor, maybe? Would you know anything about that? He's overprotective. Doesn't like his friends playing with you. As if you're just a toy he can take away from us. But you and I know better."

I stared into Evan's sea-colored eyes, trying to find something in their depths, but they were clear as glass.

"Your point?"

"The books are not the way, Daisy." His voice was unexpectedly sympathetic.

"What's the way, then?"

He put his hand on his chest. "Us. Days and nights of sweet pleasures..."

I flushed. "I'm done talking to you."

"I know what you need more than anyone else." His face turned serious. For once, Evan wasn't hiding behind a wall of sarcasm. "You and me, we're musicians. Performers. You're dying to be seen and heard. You feel like you lost yourself, don't you? I hear you, and believe me, I definitely see you. You were on your way to greatness once. With us — with me — you can be even greater."

"I can be great on my own," I said stubbornly.

"We're both hungry," he said softly, and my empty stomach growled in agreement. "Hungrier than the others. Beneath your sweet shell, you're as much of a beast as I am, Daisy. You want glory, and I'll give you exactly what you crave until you see stars. It's not just about pleasure. It's about power. Purpose."

He opened his mouth to go on, then shut it quickly. The dappled sunlight shimmered on his forearms like scales.

I shook my head. "Evan, please don't make this harder for me."

"I'm trying to make it easier." He stepped closer. When he curled his finger under my chin, I stifled a cry at the spark that flew between us. I was rooted to the spot, my skin hot and my head light. "I understand you, pet. And I say, do what you want for once. Forget about pleasing your parents and teachers and friends and being the good little flute player who wins all the awards. Do something that's just for you."

"I never told you about my parents," I whispered. "Did Reeve— Or Nathan—"

"I just know," Evan said softly. "Poor baby, you even spent all those years dancing to your best friend's wishes and hiding your feelings for Nate. Have you thought about being fucking selfish for once?"

"Too many times."

He caressed my jaw, sending shivers down my neck. "And you feel guilty. Whose life is it? Yours, or someone else's? So what if you did kiss Nate? Would it be so bad if I kissed you right here?"

"Evan—" I sucked in a sharp breath as he sank his fingers into my hair.

"No guilt, Daisy. Put yourself first for one goddamn second. Not your music, not the people you think you love, not your promises that give you the short end of the stick. Just yourself."

Was he right or wrong? Impulsively, I reached up and stroked his hair, thick and soft in my hands. His lips came closer.

At the last moment, I turned away. Our cheeks brushed. His skin was searing hot, and he smelled faintly of the woods.

I put my hand on his chest. "Evan, no. Not now."

His green eyes glowed, eerie in the afternoon light. "Then when, baby girl?"

As if it were inevitable. As if it would happen, no matter what anyone said or did to prevent it.

"I have to go." Evading him, I backed away, then ducked around the building. When I looked over my shoulder, he was gone.

Tote bag over my shoulder, list of supplies at the ready, I took the campus shuttle downtown to the herbal shop. I tried to forget Evan's words and focus on the magic ahead. Today was a scorcher, one of those hot September days that Southern California loved to bestow before fall set in. The pre-spell fast was taking its toll; my throat was parched, and I felt dizzy.

"This spell better work," I muttered.

The shop was a small purple cottage at the end of a quiet side street. Vines grew over the porch, and a bell tinkled as I walked in.

"Daisy?" the girl behind the counter greeted me. "I've got every-thing you need right here."

"Thank you," I said fervently. She bustled around behind the counter, gathering up herbs and tying them into parcels.

The shop was cute. Crystals and decks of tarot and oracle cards sat alongside wind chimes, beaded jewelry, and handmade pottery. Incense sent up curls of pungent smoke from a small dish on the counter. My senses were sharpened by the fast, and the heady scents of patchouli and neroli made my head swim.

In one corner hung a selection of goth-fabulous necklaces that looked like ornate collars. As the salesgirl bundled my herbs, I wandered over for a closer look.

The necklaces were beautiful, black leather inlaid with intricate silver. They'd be heavy to wear but stunning, commanding attention, declaring the wearer both a goddess and a slave. A star who fell to earth and might need to crawl.

I imagined Reeve putting one on me. Whispering, *You're mine now, Star. You're ours,* as the leather wrapped snugly around my neck. He'd buckle it and kiss me gently on the lips as he tugged me toward him with the loop at the front. I'd come willingly, I'd do whatever filthy things he wanted...

Shuddering, I turned away from the display.

"You like those necklaces?" exclaimed the salesgirl. "We just got them in yesterday. They're supposed to be imbued with special properties."

"Like what?"

She laughed. "I don't know, extreme hotness? I'm saving up for one. They're not cheap, even with my discount. But if you want to get one, you can use mine. Thirty percent off?"

I smiled at her. "That's okay. The herbs are enough for today."

When she told me the total, I had a moment of vertigo. It would eat up a significant chunk of my savings, the money I'd put away for the long term from flute gigs and teaching. I'd need to get a job as soon as possible to cover my expenses.

All worth it, I told myself. *If it works, it'll more than pay off.*

Shortly before midnight, I arrived at Greer Hill.

The waning moon was a narrow scimitar, hanging precariously in the sky. Reddish clouds scudded across the inky darkness. The Santa Ana winds were sweeping the region, and the gusts whistled and sighed as I climbed, cutting through my thin sweatshirt.

I hugged myself as my tote bag, heavy with supplies, swung at my side. Though the hill was deserted, I kept checking my surroundings, my gaze skittering over grassy slopes and dry bushes. The scuff of my sneakers on the dirt became increasingly louder.

When I reached the woods, the wind sent the trees into a frenzy. I hoped to be welcomed, but the branches crossed, obscuring the path.

Halting at the edge of the shivering trees, I whispered a single word: "Please."

The branches shuddered and cracked, twigs snapping. A tremor ran through the ground, and I braced myself.

An earthquake.

Thankfully, it was a small one. But when the shaking stopped, wind still whipped the hill, and leaves rustled in the gale like a flock of birds taking flight. My nerves were stretched, my senses tuned to hyperawareness.

Please let me in.

I held my breath, walking cautiously to the boundary of the forest.

The trees allowed me to pass through, and I exhaled in relief. But instead of spreading open, the branches thickened immediately, shutting out the wind. The forest's canopy lowered, shifting and whispering. Darkness quickly shrouded the beam of my flashlight.

Stubbornly, I forged ahead. A log lay in my path. When I clambered over it, a crack in the distance made me jump.

"Who's there?"

An animal. It must have been. I shivered as I approached my clearing. My teeth chattered from cold, from anxiety, from the twenty-four-hour fast that was about to end.

I wanted to feel strong as I set up the healing spell. But I was afraid, my intentions fragmented and split. I was performing magic that I didn't feel the mistress of, using a book that I stole. I'd cut ties with the men who haunted my dreams.

Laying out kindling in a latticed pile, I struck a match and tended the fire until it roared high, crackling and snapping.

One at a time, I tossed herbs into the flames, reserving a single handful for the end of the spell. The last three, I'd prepared as a draught. Opening my water bottle, I forced the bitter potion down my throat. My body rebelled at the astringent flavor, and I pinched my nose to finish it.

Walking unsteadily around the fire, I chanted the words in Reeve's book seven times. My voice was raw and cracking. The herbs sent up puffs of fragrant smoke.

Now came the hardest part: a sacrifice, something from my body to give to the fire.

Sucking in a deep breath, I took a pair of shears from my bag, grasped my braid, and pressed the blades against it.

I couldn't give it all. My stomach roiled at the thought of chopping my hair at the nape. So I sawed at my braid just above where the tail was tied off. Six inches should be enough. It had to be.

My hair was thick, resisting the scissors. I worked the blades in and out, wincing as the braid split and frayed. Finally, a chunk of sun-bleached hair came away in my hand, pale as Reeve's ropes. I threw it on the fire and coughed as the scent of scorched hair filled the forest.

As I recited the final part of the spell, I visualized my nerves healing, my hand and wrist regaining sensation and flexibility. When I finished the incantation, I tossed the last herb on the fire.

It sent up a thick black cloud that almost choked me. My head went light, and I could barely breathe with the herbal fumes. But I knelt before the fire and held out my left hand like an offering.

"Heal me now!"

The fire shifted and coalesced. The heart blazed scarlet, twisting and lengthening into a coiling spiral.

The serpent looked at me with flat green eyes, opened its mouth, and swallowed me.

Hissing filled my head. A forked tongue licked my legs until I shuddered. Words swirled, more distinct than before.

My woods, Star...

Fulfill your purpose...

Lacking in trust...

And finally, spoken clearly:

You are not yet worthy.

The serpent vanished. The fire went out, leaving only a pile of burnt hair and ash.

"What the fuck!" I gasped. "How is this your business? I did everything right!" I threw back my head and shrieked to the forest.

"Dammit! I gave up so much for this! How much more do I need to give?"

My voice was hoarse from lack of water and the foul brew I'd swallowed. I tried to summon the serpent by thinking about it, but the fire remained a heap of embers that gave off just enough light to see the forest floor. Regret crept in for screaming at the trees.

"Are these your woods, oh — oh, great serpent?" I tried. "Do I need to seek permission from you?"

No response.

"Was I too vain?" I gripped the choppy end of my braid. "Should I have sacrificed more?"

Silence.

"What do you want from me? How can I be worthy?"

Nothing.

A chill crept through my clothes. My sweatshirt didn't provide enough protection against the late-night drop in temperature. My shoulders shook, and a ragged sob escaped me before I clamped my lips together.

Scooping up the water bottle and the book of healing spells, I shoved them into my bag and stomped out the embers of the fire. I backed away from the circle of my failure. All around me, the leaves whispered.

Go to them.

"Go to who?" I kept backing away. "The men? What are they? Is there even a name for what they are?"

Go to them.

"I'm coming back," I said defiantly. "I'm coming back every night until I get the spell right. Dammit, I will be worthy."

The leaves didn't see fit to answer. I turned and ran out of the woods.

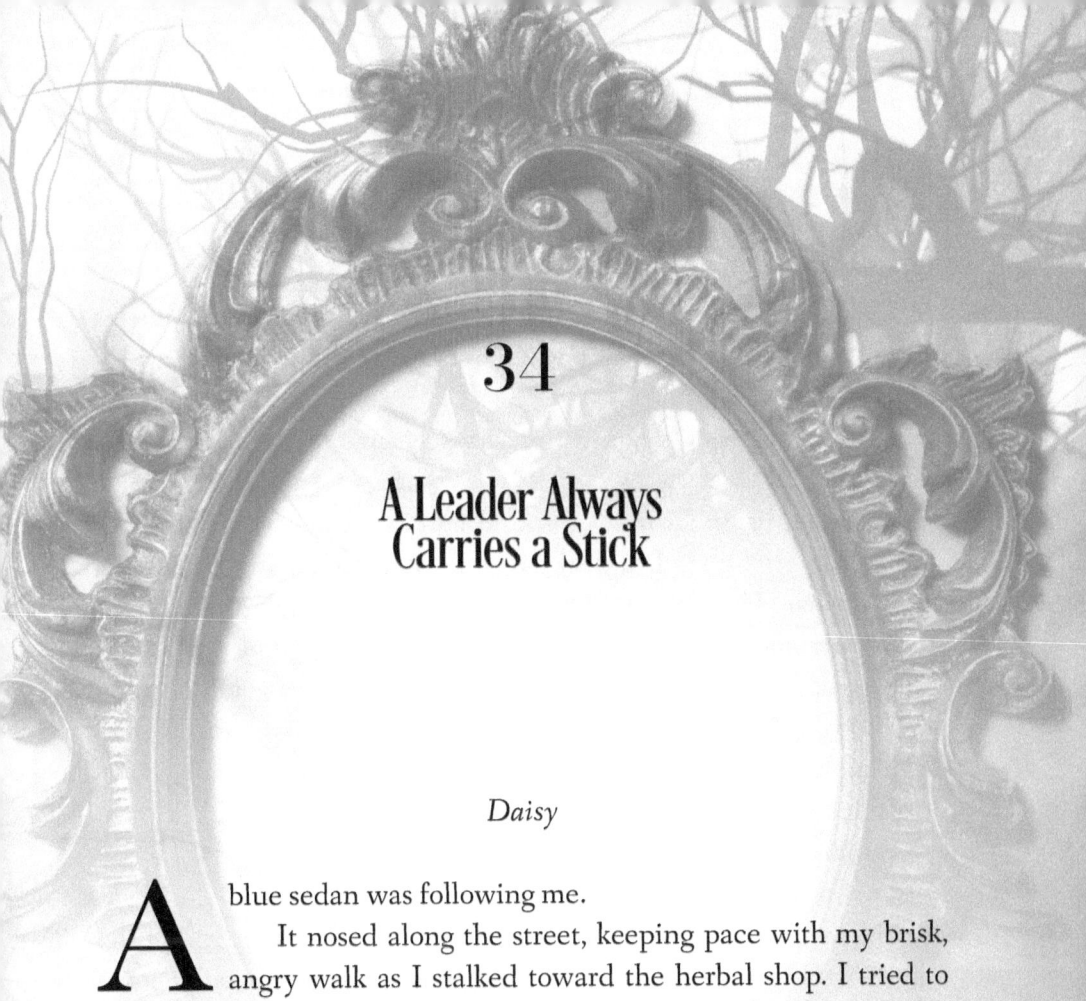

34

A Leader Always
Carries a Stick

Daisy

A blue sedan was following me.

It nosed along the street, keeping pace with my brisk, angry walk as I stalked toward the herbal shop. I tried to dismiss it as coincidence, but every turn I made, it took too.

I stopped abruptly on the corner. The car stopped as well. When I turned, sunlight blasted the windshield, and I couldn't see who was at the wheel.

Ducking into an alley, I tried to catch my breath. All I needed to do was get to the herbal shop and explain that there must have been a mistake in the herbs they gave me. That had to be the reason the spell had failed. I'd spent hundreds of dollars, and it turned my stomach to think of losing it.

But when I peeked out of the alley, the blue sedan was parked at the curb.

Pulling back, I grabbed my phone from my purse, jabbing at the screen. I didn't have Nathan's number, but I had Blake's. And that was easier than calling Reeve.

Blake picked up on the first ring.

"Daisy!" His normally calm, jovial voice was agitated. It hurt my heart. "We missed you—"

"Blake, is Nathan there?" I asked frantically, pacing circles around a planter. "Please, just— Tell him it's an emergency."

"I'll get him."

After a long wait, a tight, clipped voice came through the phone. "This is Nate."

"Nathan, listen." I tried to sound fierce, but my voice came out shaky. "I know we made a deal, but I need to talk to you. Someone's following me. This voice told me in the woods last night that I'm not worthy yet, and I don't understand it. Weird shit is going down, and I'm *scared,* and I have a right to know exactly what's going on with you and your friends—"

My phone beeped. He'd hung up on me.

"Fuck you, Nathan Davis."

I slumped against the wall, burying my face in my hands. Then a burst of anger drove me to my feet. I'd do this on my own.

Shoving my phone in my purse, I hurried to the other end of the alley, planning to shake whoever was following me off my tail. People stared as I passed, and I realized I must look a little crazed. I hadn't showered, hadn't changed my clothes since I started the fast. Hadn't slept or eaten more than a granola bar this morning.

But when I reached the sidewalk and crossed the street, the blue car was trailing me again.

Turning, I glared straight at it. This time, I thought I could make out a mane of red curls and a pair of dark sunglasses inside.

Tara.

Well, she wouldn't get anything if she followed me. I was immune to her charms now. All I cared about was the success of my spell, because it was all I had to hang on to.

Rounding one last corner, I hurried down the street. When I reached the herbal shop's cottage, I slammed the door open. The bell tinkled crazily.

The same salesgirl stood behind the counter. She looked familiar, but I couldn't place where I'd seen her outside the shop. Barging forward, I explained the situation.

"I'm *so* sorry," said the girl, smiling blandly. "But we can't guarantee the results of our herbs. And if you've used it already, we can't offer a refund."

"What about that employee discount you offered me yesterday?" I asked, trying to backtrack and be nice. "That was so sweet of you, and—"

"Nope, sorry. That only counts for the collars."

She pointed to the display, and suddenly I realized why I recognized her. She was one of the girls who'd come to Blake's restaurant with Tara.

"There's no way those could have been the right herbs," I shouted. I was making a scene, and I didn't care. "They're supposed to —"

The bell chimed over the door. Startled, I took a step back, bumped into someone, and whirled around.

"Are you okay? ... Oh."

"Hi, Daisy." Tara smiled at me. "What are *you* doing here?"

"Shopping." I crossed quickly to a display on the opposite wall — the silver-encrusted collar-style necklaces I'd admired yesterday. "How about you? Oh wait, you followed me."

I was shaking. I needed to solve the herb problem before I got out of here, but right now all I wanted was to put as much distance between me and Tara as possible. I'd been wrong; I wasn't immune to her.

She blocked my way. The heat of her body beat against mine, and her jasmine perfume filled the air. "How are our favorite boys?"

I folded my arms. "I'm not seeing them anymore."

"So they dumped you too?" She arched an eyebrow. "That was quick."

"Other way around. I dumped them." We stood next to the

display of chokers, and I couldn't resist picking one up. The intricate metalwork flashed in the light.

"I don't believe you," Tara said scornfully. Hooking a finger into the collar I held, she twirled it, making the silver filigree twinkle. I stared, mesmerized by the etched symbols. "I would have heard from them. Reeve loves to have his bases covered."

Abruptly, I took a step toward her. She stood too close, her hair curling around her exquisite face. "What are you talking about?"

"You don't know?" She covered her mouth in exaggerated surprise.

"Know what?" I barked, my patience wearing thin.

She laughed. "Honey, it's a moot point now. Don't be sad. Let me get you a break-up gift. This one's even nicer. Why don't you try it on?"

She held up another collar, one that I hadn't noticed in the display yesterday. It was stunning. Finely wrought silver snakes chased each other over the soft black leather, hinged so they appeared to writhe.

I glanced over my shoulder at the counter, but the salesgirl wasn't there. She'd probably gone to the storeroom.

"I don't need gifts," I muttered.

"Just try it on, Daisy. Live a little." Tara unbuckled the collar, and her lips curled in a challenge.

I decided to accept.

Facing the mirror, I let her buckle the collar around my neck. It fit snugly, sending a dark thrill through me. When she gave it a tug, warmth trickled downward, collecting in an ache between my legs as the leather ring heated my throat.

What was happening? A minute ago, I'd been angry, sleep-deprived, and revving up for a fight.

Now I was melting.

"Oh," I breathed when Tara tugged on the collar again.

"You like that? It looks hot on you." When her nails tickled my neck, my breath came faster. "Love the hair. I see you chopped it."

"Really?" My voice sounded small. "You think it looks good?" Hazily, I ran my fingers over the ragged ends above my waist. I hadn't been able to look at my hair since last night.

"It's adorable. Let's do something different with it."

She undid my braid with swift fingers, pulled a second hair band from her wrist, and gathered my hair into two high pigtails.

"Put on that lipstick," she murmured. "You know the one. The dark shade you wore at Evan's concert."

Damn, I was turned on. This scenario was surreal, and the counter area was still empty. Fishing the lipstick out of my purse, leaning forward farther than necessary, I pushed my lips into a pout and took my time tracing them in a coat of deep plum. My pigtails swung, the ends spiky and trailing. The collar was stark black against my neck, and my loose shirt hung low, showing the curves of my breasts.

Tara's crystal-blue eyes devoured them, and I shuddered.

When I straightened, she put her hands on my shoulders. "Transformation to wayward jailbait complete."

My dark lips parted. "What do you want, exactly? Because I — I want to do whatever you want."

What was I saying?

"I want *you*," she whispered.

"Me? Not the boys?"

Her lips brushed my ear. "I go for whoever's strongest. And right now, honey, that's you. They're afraid of you; don't you see it?"

"But..."

"Whatever kinky games they played with you to try to establish their dominance, you've always held the reins. You just didn't know."

I shivered at her warm breath on my cheek, her soft hands on my shoulders. "Tell me what to do," I pleaded, the desire to serve running through my core and pooling like liquid wax. The collar pulsed around my neck.

"Give me your obedience. Your power. I don't have any, and you're just this *freak* running around squandering yours without any

417

clue what you're doing. The boys want you desperately, and you can't even see the benefits. We'll be the perfect team. I'll do the thinking; you'll do the work. We'll have Pacific Crest under our heels in no time, my sweet slave. And those arrogant, selfish boys — we'll make them pay."

"The boys," I repeated.

"They humiliated me, Daisy. They made promises to me and broke them. I waited, and they cast me aside. You'll help me punish them, won't you?"

I stared at her in the mirror, my chest rising and falling. A lick on my earlobe made me tense up. "Anything for you."

"Come with me," she whispered. "Come with me now."

I let her twine her fingers in mine and pull me away from the mirror.

"Forget whatever you were doing with those herbs," she coaxed. "From now on, you serve me. Vow your allegiance to me, slave."

"I'm your slave," I sighed. "I'll do whatever you say."

The words left my mouth so quickly that I was stunned.

Awareness shot through me, a stab of ice in the warmth of the collar. I wanted to free my hand from hers, but as soon as the thought crossed my mind, the collar flared with heat, turning me into a molten puddle.

I had to obey Tara. Had to. Of course I wouldn't let go of her hand. How could I have considered such a thing?

I followed her obediently out of the shop, my pigtails swinging, admiring the way her coppery curls bounced on her shoulders. My tote bag bumped my hip.

"You're so pretty," I giggled.

She squeezed my hand. "You like my face? Someday, if you're a good girl, I'll tell you how I got it."

Down the street, she unlocked the unremarkable blue sedan and gave me a push toward the passenger seat.

"In you go. It's not like sitting in Reeve's car, is it? Don't worry,

Daisy. With your help, I'll buy a ride that puts his car to shame. You're going to get me everything I want."

I sighed happily. I just wanted to be near her. Hadn't I always felt that way?

"I will, I promise, I will," I babbled.

"If you're very good, maybe I'll let you enjoy some of the benefits." Her hand wandered up my thigh, toying with the seam of my jeans. "What did Evan call you? 'Pet?' I'll be a much better owner."

As I arched toward her, I remembered Reeve's hand between my legs. Blake's. Evan's... Nathan's. For a moment, I froze. Then Tara filled my mind, and I bucked my hips hungrily.

"So eager," she laughed, stopping just short of my pussy. "It's almost boring now." I whimpered in protest, but the collar warmed again, blowing the frustration away. "You'll wait, my pet, until you've done what I want."

The streets were a blur, my thoughts a haze, until we pulled up at the base of a tall green slope.

Greer Hill.

Clarity pierced my mind. "What exactly do you want?" I breathed.

Her lips twisted. "I want to win at life. I started as low as Reeve, with a family who treated me like shit. Did he ever tell you that?"

Wide-eyed, I shook my head.

"Of course not. He doesn't care. I lived on fucking daydreams, Daisy. I escaped into my head. And now I want those dreams to come true, just like the boys'. Reeve *promised* me. All of it. Beauty. Fame. Money. Influence. He promised me everyone would know my name." She blinked hard, angrily dashing away the tears that squeezed from her eyes. I whimpered, rubbing my head against her shoulder, like a dog trying to comfort its master. "But I want even more now, because you can give it to me. And the first thing you're going to do is take me into those woods."

She pointed to the crest of Greer Hill, where the trees stirred in the breeze.

419

"It's dangerous," I said quickly. "You could get hurt. I don't want you getting hurt."

"Awww, so naïve." She patted my cheek. "With you at my side, it's perfectly safe. You're believing everything those boys told you. The woods are so deadly... be careful... No, no, no! They just wanted to control you, Daisy. They never gave two shits about your safety."

"You're wrong," I forced out. The collar blazed insistently: *don't argue.* Its heat melted my protests until I cast my eyes downward and mumbled an apology.

"I'll forgive you this once." Smiling, Tara stroked my cheek and opened the door. "Come along, slave. You're my ticket to success and the downfall of those boys."

She tugged me up the hill. Her touch was the sweetest seduction, and the collar pulsed around my neck, binding me closer to her. I wanted more of her hands. Her mouth, if she deigned to give it to me. Her creamy skin and beautiful body. I whimpered softly, because it hurt to want so much, and she gave me a smile that didn't reach her crystal-blue eyes.

But as we got closer to the woods, the ground stirred. A throb ran through the earth in a dissonant counterpoint to the collar. My mind began to turn, to wonder.

"What are you going to do to the boys?"

Tara dipped her finger inside the collar. "Slow torture." She drew out the words. "They treated me unforgivably, like garbage. You don't mess with me like that."

"Torture?" The ground trembled slightly. Sparks ricocheted through my body. Tara didn't seem to notice. "You mean, *actual* torture?"

"I want to see them suffer," she said simply. "Just like they did to me. I'm going to take away their hopes, their dreams, their future. One piece at a time, until they're nothing. And you're going to help me do it."

I stumbled, because the earth seemed to crack beneath my feet.

But when I looked down, the grass was unbroken, the path solid. Tara's grip tightened on my hand.

"Careful," she warned. "We don't want you getting hurt before you can get me into those woods. Do you know how much it's *killed* me that I can't go in? While you just prance in and out whenever you want? I've been watching you, Daisy. I've watched every move you've made since you became the boys' new darling."

Her words sent a shudder through me. The crack in the earth, real or imagined, had opened a matching crack in my mind.

I could think now. I could fear.

"What do you need in the woods?" I whispered.

Tara frowned. "Why are you asking me questions?"

She grabbed the collar, tugging it back and forth, as though checking a faulty piece of machinery. With each push and pull, my body changed. In one direction, the need to serve filled me with a blissful haze. With the next yank, reality snapped into focus like a gritty film. I was shaking, anger buried beneath the rosy submission.

The cruel scrape of Tara's nails against my neck left me throbbing and confused. The collar sputtered and flamed, trying to bring me into the soft cloak of total obeisance, but there was a tear in that cloak now.

"I just want to know how best to serve you," I managed, hoping to pacify her.

Tara relaxed. "You know what I want, slave. Access to the serpent. It adores you, doesn't it? You'll ask for what I need, and you'll pass everything on to me."

"It said I'm not worthy." Pain shot through me at the memory of that hissing voice, those merciless green eyes.

Tara grasped my pigtail harshly. "Then you'll *get* worthy. You'll give that snake whatever it wants. Your body, your soul, your desire... if I need to fuck you into oblivion, never to leave the woods, I'll do it."

The ground rumbled again. My fingers flew to the collar. I could unbuckle it, fight Tara, run...

Then her hands ran down my body, and thoughts of fighting or fleeing melted into a forgotten realm.

We were very close to the woods. The pull of the rustling trees became stronger with each step we took.

Welcome, they said. *You're home.*

"That's it," Tara wheedled. "Just bring me in. That's a good girl..."

Confidently, I walked down the path between the arching branches. I was leading Tara now, swinging her hand like we were kids going on a picnic. Her freckled cheeks flushed as the woods closed around us.

"Oh God," she breathed. "Do you feel it?"

I turned to face her, need buzzing through my body. "I do."

Her hands closed on my hips. "Come on, Daisy. Let's light the fire. As soon as the serpent shows up, I'm going to fuck you no matter what."

She hurried to the clearing. *My* clearing. Anger flashed through me at the violation, and my hands went again to the collar. I got as far as fumbling with the buckle before the leather circle dissolved my fury into need.

I ran to join Tara in the clearing, where she kindled a fire in the center. Grabbing the collar, she forced me to kneel at her side. The ground quaked as twin impulses clashed within me: desire, panic.

Tara reached into her purse and held out a handful of reddish-brown herbs.

"You might be wondering where I got these." She jerked the collar, and I moaned. "I saw you with Reeve the night of that orgy at his house. And I knew, Daisy. I knew you were trouble. The way he looked at you, like everyone else could fucking die, and he wouldn't notice or care... I had to make a plan."

"Wait—" I began, but she threw the herbs on the flames. A smoky-sweet scent, familiar and hypnotic, rose into the air.

The fire roared up, throwing out billows of crimson smoke. I gasped, raw and unprotected, as jaws snapped around me. I was caught once again in the serpent's enormous mouth. Sleek coils squeezed me, trying to penetrate. My clothes fluttered, on the verge of tearing.

Tara's hand was knocked from the collar. She staggered back. Swallowed by the serpent, I saw her clearly. Her unloved childhood, her anger at being trapped, her obsessive desire for bigger, better, more. I saw a younger Reeve, smooth-faced and shirtless, kneeling under scrubby live oaks as he drew the tip of a knife across his palm and let a drop of blood fall to the earth. A red-haired girl, visible only from behind, ran up to him, and his face twisted with anger.

Hisses spilled out like falling rocks, but the words were as clear as a mountain stream.

What do you want, Star?

"Not her," Tara wheezed, coughing in the plume of smoke. Determined, she lurched forward. "Me. Me!"

"Help," I whispered soundlessly.

The notes of *Syrinx* filled my mind. I saw Pan with his pipes, and the fleeing nymph who'd died for his music. I saw Reeve's black eyes turning human, the color of the earth. And behind them, Nathan's sweet, shy smile, the lanky limbs he'd once had.

"I'm coming," I breathed. "I'll return..."

The pressure constricting me eased. The serpent's jaws unhinged. Wheeling into the air, I landed on a hard surface with a thud.

I lay on the marble table in the House, the smooth stone slick with my sweat, surrounded by the four men. Their handprints seeped through my skin, their mouths marked my flesh, their cocks filled me as I encompassed them all.

Then I woke with a start, jerked back into my body. I scrabbled at the collar, and Tara gripped my hands in a fury.

"Do it!" she growled. "Tell that snake what I want. Start with the fame. Everyone will know me."

The trembling of the ground increased, and I swallowed. "I don't think it works that way. I can't give orders. I don't even know what it wants from me."

The serpent's huge head suddenly lunged at Tara, jostling me, and she jumped back.

Worship me properly.

"What did it say?" she demanded.

I repeated the words for her, and her eyes widened. "Okay," she sneered, "We'll do that. Sex feeds that thing, doesn't it? Lech."

"I don't think it's just sex," I protested. "It's more complicated than that—"

Hauling me to my feet, Tara gripped my shoulders.

"Go ahead. Deny it. But you've wanted this all along, haven't you, Daisy? You're pure slut. Someone gives you one little smile, one stupid compliment, and you're panting for more. You're horny, but more than that, you're a fucking attention whore. How'd you stay a virgin all this time? Don't tell me... it's that 'curse.'" She laughed harshly. "Just one more way to think you're special. But you're not."

I wanted to argue, but the collar overrode me. Fear chased desire in disorienting waves.

"You know," Tara went on, "if it had to be you with them, I would have loved to see Reeve be your first. Picture it: you, naked and pinned down... crying out, overwhelmed by his size... finally seeing what's beneath that pretty face... fuck, I'd pay to watch that. I've gotten off thinking about it so many times."

"Why?"

Her hands dropped to my hips. She cocked her head. "Oh... because. But he'll never have you. Instead, you'll get to watch what I'll do to him. And he won't enjoy it nearly as much."

Her angelic face came closer. The scent of jasmine enveloped me. She hooked a finger through the loop on the collar.

When her lips touched mine, the ground shook.

You're not hers, Star.

The gravelly hiss coiled through me. As Tara pulled at my

clothes, I broke free. She tugged sharply on the collar, reeling me back in.

Never hers.

Tara came in for a second kiss. When I pushed her hand away from my breasts, she caught my wrist — my left one — and twisted it. I cried out in pain, and she swallowed the cry with her mouth.

Claim your power.

The dam broke. Anger overrode lust. The collar pulsed with heat, but I shoved Tara away as hard as I could.

I was prepared to fight. But I never had the chance. Tara flew away from me, arching high into the air.

She soared through the trees, branches crashing, like a meteorite in reverse. Her scream rang out above the woods. A thump rocked the earth.

"Tara!" I yelled. But the woods were dark and dense. Even if she were alive, conscious, I doubted she could hear me.

And then — oh God — an answering voice, a man's. I could barely make it out, but I prayed those were Reeve's velvet tones.

Except that Tara wanted to hurt him. And he couldn't reach me in the woods, not easily. I'd gleaned that much from the men. I just needed to get to him... but I'd stolen his books, betrayed his trust, cut him off... why would he want me?

The fire went out, leaving only a pile of ashes.

The ground rumbled again, and I scrabbled with the collar around my neck. The leather was stiff and cold now, and my fingers were shaking. Finally, I managed to undo the buckle and yank it off. My head swam as the earth tilted beneath my feet.

With the next quake, I dropped to my knees, clutching the collar. I couldn't leave it lying in the woods. I needed to destroy it.

But a wave of exhaustion washed over me, and I fell to the ground.

Struggling to raise my head, I put one hand in front of the other. The pain in my left wrist was almost unbearable, but I crawled doggedly forward. Rocks and sticks scraped my palms. Trees turned to fuzzy shapes as my vision blurred. Darkness hovered, moving in from the edge of the woods.

Was this even real? Would I make it out before the encroaching blackness closed on me?

The men's faces were all that spurred me on. They showed through in flashes, like a tapestry of light and smoke. Blake, a bright flame, flickering with worry. Evan's cold hunger, turned hot and urgent. Nathan, the restless knight, broken and needy. But it was Reeve's eyes that locked on mine, shimmering between human, abyss, and snake.

"I'm coming." Tears streaked my face as I fell again from fatigue, the forest dimming. "I won't let Tara hurt you. I won't steal from you. I won't tell you anything but the truth. I swear, if I just see your face — all your faces — it'll be all right. I'm coming out of the woods for you."

To be continued

***Deliver the Devil*: Book 2 in the Serpentine Duet**

Coming May 24th

When hearts twist and a serpent lurks in each of us, waiting to devour...

Available Now for Preorder

Acknowledgments

Big thanks and love to:

Jan, for always inspiring me as a critique partner, reading pages (over *many* drafts) since this story's inception, sharing your tarot knowledge with me, and giving frank, forthright, and whip-smart feedback.

Mackenzie of Nice Girl, Naughty Edits, for your thoughtful insights, cheerleading, patience, and commas. You truly believed in these characters. Thank you also for creating beautiful graphics that capture the dark, magical vibe of this story.

L.J. of Mayhem Cover Creations, for bringing your artistic vision to the vague symbols and vibes I sent your way and crafting the most unbelievably perfect pair of covers.

Darci, Marina, and Sarah, for beta reading and offering your hilarious commentary, honest opinions, and helpful feedback.

Annette and Michelle of Book Nerd Services, for your dedication, kindness, and support.

My husband, for always being there while I wander in and out of fictional realms, and for reading my drafts, cracking jokes to keep me sane, and being my rock in the emotional jungle of writing.

The wonderful readers and fellow authors who illuminate the indie publishing world and make this journey worthwhile.

And thanks to you for picking up this book and taking a chance on Daisy, Reeve, Nate, Evan, and Blake's journey. It means more to me than I can say.

About the Author

As a writer of new adult and erotic romance, Miranda Silver lives for exploring complicated characters and steamy love stories. She has degrees in English and music, and has always loved creating with both sounds and words. Miranda lives in California with her family, where she enjoys the perennially beautiful weather when she's not hunched over a screen, putting characters through their paces.

You can find Miranda here:

Instagram: @mirandasilverbooks
Twitter: @silvermusings
Facebook: @mirandasilverbooks
Goodreads: Miranda Silver

MirandaSilver.com

Join Miranda's Reader Group, Miranda's Muses, for exclusive sneak peeks and news about upcoming releases.

Also By Miranda Silver